D1565696

76
HOURS

BOOKS BY
LARRY ALEXANDER

76 HOURS

A NOVEL OF TARAWA

LARRY ALEXANDER

BLACK STONE
PUBLISHING

Printed in the United States of America

ISBN 979-8-200-81600-2
Fiction / Historical / World War II

Version 2

Blackstone Publishing
31 Mistletoe Rd.
Ashland, OR 97520

www.BlackstonePublishing.com

This book is dedicated to the thousands of men,
American and Japanese, who fought and sacrificed
amid the brutal, 76-hour struggle for Betio's 381 acres
of blood-soaked sand and coral.

PART I

SATURDAY, NOVEMBER 20, 1943

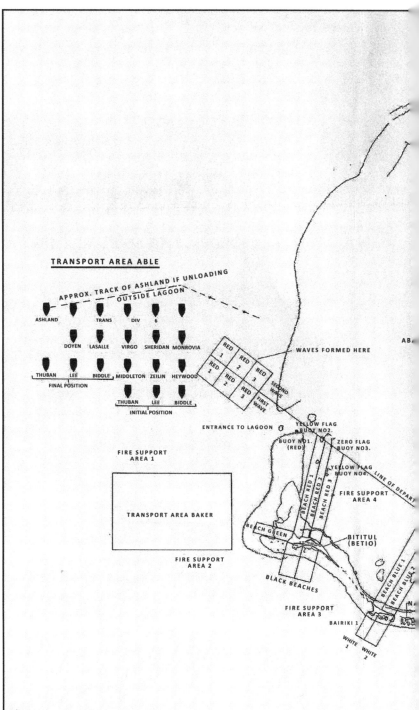

TRANSPORT AREA ABLE

APPROX. TRACK OF ASHLAND IF UNLOADING OUTSIDE LAGOON

ASHLAND   TRANS   DIV   6

DOYEN   LASALLE   VIRGO   SHERIDAN   MONROVIA

THUBAN   LEE   BIDDLE   MIDDLETON   ZEILIN   HEYWOOD
FINAL POSITION

THUBAN   LEE   BIDDLE
INITIAL POSITION

RED 1   RED 2   RED 3
RED 1   RED 2   RED 3
RED 1   RED 2   RED 3

WAVES FORMED HERE

AB

SECOND WAVE

FIRST WAVE

ENTRANCE TO LAGOON

YELLOW FLAG BUOY NO2.

BUOY NO1. (RED)

ZERO FLAG BUOY NO3.

YELLOW FLAG BUOY NO4.

LINE OF DEPART

FIRE SUPPORT AREA 1

FIRE SUPPORT AREA 4

BEACH RED 1   BEACH RED 2   BEACH RED 3

TRANSPORT AREA BAKER

BEACH GREEN

BITITUL (BETIO)

FIRE SUPPORT AREA 2

BLACK BEACHES

BEACH BLUE 1   BEACH BLUE 2

FIRE SUPPORT AREA 3

BAIRIKI 1

N

WHITE 1   WHITE 2

RD5896

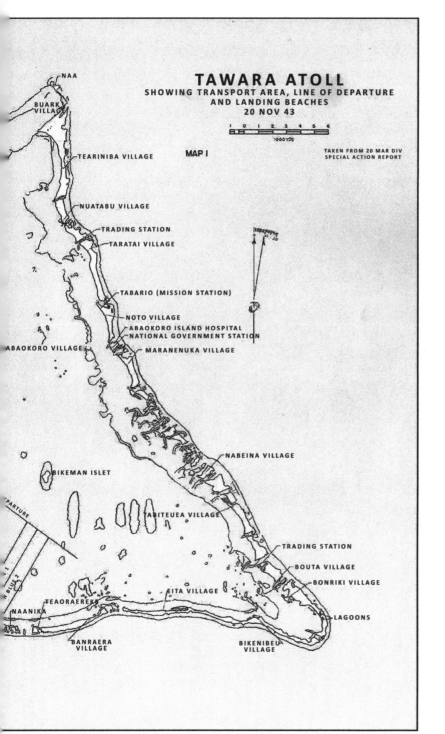

TAWARA ATOLL

SHOWING TRANSPORT AREA, LINE OF DEPARTURE
AND LANDING BEACHES
20 NOV 43

MAP I

TAKEN FROM 20 MAR DIV
SPECIAL ACTION REPORT

NAA

BUARK
VILLAGE

TEARINIBA VILLAGE

NUATABU VILLAGE

TRADING STATION

TARATAI VILLAGE

TABARIO (MISSION STATION)

NOTO VILLAGE

ABAOKORO ISLAND HOSPITAL

NATIONAL GOVERNMENT STATION

ABAOKORO VILLAGE

MARANENUKA VILLAGE

NABEINA VILLAGE

BIKEMAN ISLET

TABITEUEA VILLAGE

TRADING STATION

BOUTA VILLAGE

BONRIKI VILLAGE

EITA VILLAGE

TEAORAEREKE

NAANIKA

LAGOONS

BANRAERA
VILLAGE

BIKENIBEU
VILLAGE

CHAPTER 1

Tarawa burned.

Lying low on the water fifteen hundred yards away, tiny Betio, the main island in the Japanese-occupied Tarawa Atoll, glowed end-to-end like a hot coal as long, squat lines of landing craft ground their way toward the smoke-shrouded shore.

Hunkered down shoulder-to-shoulder with his comrades inside one of the many Higgins boats, Private Peter Winston Talbot nervously clutched his rifle as he watched the boat's coxswain signal to Lt. Edward Pfeffer.

"We're at the line of departure, men!" Dog Company's young shavetail executive officer bellowed over the roar of the diesel. "Lock and load!"

Pete set the safety on his M1 Garand, pulled open the bolt, and took an ammo clip from a pouch on his bandolier. He shoved the clip into the weapon's gaping receiver and gingerly slapped the operating rod forward, closing the bolt. A painful case of "M1 Thumb" and a loud, red-faced drill instructor at Parris Island had taught him the right way to load his weapon.

"You stupid, stupid sonofabitch!" Staff Sgt. Edward "Bull Moose" Blakely bellowed after Pete had pinched his abused thumb for the fourth time. "You're gonna learn how to properly load this piece even if you lose that fuckin' thumb and have to slam the breech shut with your goddamned dick. Christ on a crutch, where does the Corps find fuck-ups like you?"

He glowered at Pete who silently cursed the man. It was Blakely, fully aware of Talbot's loathing of being told what to do, who tagged the hardheaded youth with the nickname "Hardball."

"Heads down!" Gunnery Sgt. Earl Nicholson hollered.

Like the others, Pete ducked, but not before glancing ahead toward "Helen," the island's codename. Spread out before him were waves of landing boats, all LVTs, struggling toward the shore as the roar of the gunfire from Betio's defenders grew louder. The first wave was well beyond the island's protective coral reef and into the lagoon. Some had even unloaded their Marines. Close behind, the rest churned forward, enemy bullets clanging off their steel-reinforced prows while their passengers, soaked by near artillery misses that sent geysers of seawater cascading over them, prayed fervently. Before lowering his head, Pete watched three amtracs explode almost simultaneously, killing all on board.

Pete slid down along the gunwale, staring fish-like at "Professor" Steve Aldrich, the squad's college boy whose face mirrored the horror Pete felt. Hunched down to Pete's left, Robert Sherrod's face was pale as the two exchanged worried looks. In his eagerness to cover the battle, the *Time* magazine war correspondent had hitched a ride in the first Higgins boat with room to spare.

Speaking loudly to be heard above the clatter of battle and the drumming of the boat's diesel engine, Pete admitted to Sherrod, "Sweet Jesus but I'm scared."

Normally one who guarded his privacy as voraciously as a young bride-to-be guards her virtue, Pete suddenly felt compelled to admit his fears to this man he'd just met on the troopship eighteen hours earlier.

"Hang in there, kid. I'm scared, too," the veteran journalist admitted.

"But you've been through landings before, haven't you?" Pete inquired.

"Yeah, but our landing at Attu was a cakewalk," Sherrod said. "The Japs were dug in on high ground waiting for us to root them out. They didn't defend the beach."

Grinding toward Helen's flaming shore, the Higgins boat thumped and jolted as it crossed the low swells, casting up waves that washed over the prow and onto the men inside. The bobbing and jouncing, mingled with the stench of burning fuel and roasting flesh wafting on the morning breeze, was too much for many of the frightened young Marines, and some began heaving their guts. The lucky ones puked over the side while others simply threw up on the deck, splattering their boots and those of their comrades, creating a putrid stew of seawater and semi-digested steak and eggs.

As the roar of battle swelled, Pete wondered if the three-hour pre-invasion bombardment, for all its clamor and fury, had killed even one of the Jap bastards.

Sherrod lifted his head until he could just barely see above the gunwale. He then slid back down, his face pale, fear embedded in his eyes.

"I can't see a single landing craft on the beach," he shouted over the racket, looking at Pete. "Three waves of alligators went in ahead of us. A hundred boats at least. And I can't see a damned one on the beach."

Having to see for himself, Pete raised his head slightly. Sherrod was not exaggerating. The lagoon seemed to be boiling under the impact of artillery and small arms rounds. Smoky clouds billowed, both from the shore and from the shattered alligators. On the island, geysers of dirt, sand, and flame leapt into the air as the carrier planes dropped their bombs. And above it all, Pete could hear men yelling in anger or screaming in agony above the unbroken clatter.

"Talbot!" Nicholson bellowed. "Get your goddamn head down before some Nip shoots it off your shoulders."

Pete did as ordered.

Fuck you, Pete's brain silently cursed.

Sherrod turned Pete's way, a sympathetic smile creasing across his heavily tanned face.

"You know the difference between you and me, Talbot?" Sherrod said, a sad smile creasing his face. "You're in this boat because you have to be. I'm here because I volunteered for this assignment." He paused. "Volunteered. Can you believe that shit?"

Sherrod fell silent, not looking for an answer.

Ted Giovanni squatted beside Pete, his right shoulder against Pete's left. Pete could feel his best friend shaking in fear.

"It wasn't supposed to be this way," he stammered, his mouth inches from Pete's ear.

"Jesus Christ, Ted," Pete told the short but sturdy Italian, "before we left the ship you were complaining about the naval bombardment, saying how you wanted the swabbies to save you some Japs to shoot at."

"Yeah," Ted replied, his dark eyes set deep below two bushy brown eyebrows now open wide with fear. "I wanted *some* left, but not all of 'em."

Pete turned and shrugged.

Something pinged off the steel ramp of the Higgins boat with a sharp metallic ring. Then there came a second clang, followed in rapid succession by three more.

"What was that?" Pvt. Stanley "Pots" Potter gasped.

"Son of a bitch," Pete's squad leader, Sgt. Toby Banks, said. "The bastards found our range."

Two more bullets ricocheted off the ramp. Behind Pete, Ted Giovanni jumped at each hit.

"Oh, God," he muttered.

Pete turned and saw Ted reach inside his blouse, his fingers nervously searching for his rosary.

Rub those beads all you want, Pete thought, *God isn't gonna help you here. He's covering his own ass right now.*

Next to Ted, Private Walter Hullihen saw his friend rubbing the beads in silent prayer and said, "My daddy was a firm believer in the power of prayer. I'll pray for you, Feather Merchant."

"Thanks," Ted whispered.

The North Carolinian glanced at Pete.

"I'll pray for you too, Hardball," he said.

"Pray for your own ass, Honeybun," he replied.

Sherrod tapped Hullihen on the shoulder.

"Honeybun?" he asked.

The fair-haired young man grinned sheepishly. He told the war correspondent about how his great-uncle, also named Walter Hullihen, had been a lieutenant on General JEB Stuart's staff during what the boy called the War of the Rebellion and how Stuart, in a play on the name Hullihen, had dubbed him Honeybun. During the cruise from San Diego to Australia, Hullihen had shared the story with his buddies in the platoon.

"Up until then he had no nickname," Pete injected. "So . . ."

The other men of the squad within earshot laughed, both because the story was funny and as a short relief from tension.

"Don't worry about it son," Sherrod told Hullihen. "I'm a Southern boy too and I think your great-uncle would be proud of you. It comes to you from a fine heritage."

Honeybun smiled.

The men fell silent.

Pete now found that his hands had begun trembling. To calm himself, he removed his helmet and gazed at the black-and-white photo secured between his hard-plastic liner and the webbing. The round, pudgy-cheeked face of Agatha Barnoffski smiled at him.

Sherrod nudged Pete's arm, extending a hand clutching a pack of Chesterfields.

"Cigarette?" he inquired.

"No thanks," he replied. "I'm a Camel smoker myself. I've smoked them since I was a kid." Fearing he might've insulted the journalist, he lamely added, "But I did enjoy listening to the Chesterfield Hour on the radio back home."

Great, Pete cursed to himself immediately after the words left his lips, *now he thinks you're an idiot.*

"Cute girl," Sherrod said, indicating the photo. Pete nodded his thanks and put the steel pot back on his head.

"So where's home, Talbot?" Sherrod asked, emitting cigarette smoke as he spoke.

"Chester, Pennsylvania," he replied.

"Near Philly," Sherrod mused. "I'm from Georgia," he added slowly as if to emphasize his soft Southern accent.

"I got a buddy in my platoon from Georgia," Pete said. "We call him Reb."

Sherrod nodded as Pete again mentally kicked himself.

Think before you talk, goddammit, he told himself. *You sound like a goofy kid.*

A shell from a Japanese shore battery burst like a thunderclap just ahead of the boat, sending up a tall, watery plume that drenched everyone and left many to spit salt water. "Jesus, I shit in my pants," one man moaned. Jarred by the blast, the boat's engine sputtered, then caught and continued churning shoreward.

Another blast, this one closer, sent a jagged shard of shrapnel ripping through the plywood bulkhead just ahead of Pete, burrowing itself inside "Pots" Potter. The skinny, tousle-haired youth from Atlantic City, New Jersey, let out a wail and collapsed to the deck. Blood oozed from a gash in the right side of his blouse just above the waist, mingling with the piss and vomit on deck. Someone cried, "Corpsman!"

"Clear a path!" Pharmacist Mate First Class Ryan Magruder shouted as he pushed his way forward.

Pete watched in horrified fascination as Magruder unflinchingly tore open Pots' blouse. The chunk of steel protruding from his wound was still hot to the touch. Wrapping his hand in a piece of cloth from the torn shirt, Magruder yanked the offending metal free and tossed it overboard. Removing the shrapnel drew a loud moan from Pots who had been muttering, "Oh God, oh God," over and over since he'd been hit.

"Easy, Potsy," Magruder told the injured young man. "You're fine."

"Am I goin' home, Doc?" the boy asked through clenched teeth.

"You'll be strollin' along the boardwalk long before we get stateside," the corpsman replied.

Magruder began treating the mangled flesh, coating the wound with sulfa powder to help prevent infection and coagulate the blood, then applying a layer of gauze before tightly wrapping the area with a bandage. He followed up with a jab from a morphine syrette. Dipping a finger in Potter's blood, Magruder wrote "1 M" on the wounded man's forehead so that the hospital ship would know he'd been given one dose of the pain-killing panacea.

Pete turned away, trying to shut it all out.

"I don't want that to happen to me," Pvt. Charles "Bucket" Harnish half sobbed. "Dear God, I don't want that to happen to me."

"It won't happen to you," the Professor said, trying to keep his friend from panicking. "Just get a grip."

"How y'all know that?" Bucket's buddy, Pvt. William "Reb" Marshall, insisted. "They're killin' us in theah, boy."

"Reb's right," Ted chimed in. "What are we gonna do?"

"You're gonna get out of this boat, get your ass onshore, and do your goddamned jobs," Lance Cpl. Bob Willoughby snarled. "Stick to your training."

The stern words from the veteran of the New Georgia jungles stifled the young men's chatter but not their inner terror.

Then the nightmare got worse.

As bullets continued to flatten themselves on the Higgins boat's steel ramp, the landing craft's engine suddenly throttled back.

"Jesus Christ," the coxswain spat. "It's that goddamned barrier reef. They told us we could cross it without any trouble."

"You can't clear it?" Lt. Pfeffer asked, poking his head up for a look.

"Hell, no," the coxswain said, stopping the craft several feet from the jagged protrusion of the coral barrier. "It's stickin' up a foot outta the fuckin' water. The amtracs could drive over but we're screwed."

Around them, other boats also began to stop. A few struck the reef and got hung up on the gnarled spires.

"Guess we walk," Pfeffer said resignedly.

At that moment another engine sound was heard and a voice called out, "Hold up there! I'll take some of you in."

The voice was from the pilot of an alligator that had off-loaded its first batch of Marines and was now returning to the reef to bring in more. The tracked vehicle ground up and over the coral barrier and stopped beside the Higgins boat.

"I can take half of you in partway then try to come back for the rest," the LVT's coxswain called over.

Pfeffer did not hesitate.

"Lt. Cornwall!" the company XO barked. "Take part of your platoon and a mortar team and go. The rest of us will walk. We'll join up on the beach."

Cornwall nodded then barked, "Nicholson!"

"Aye, aye Skipper," Nicholson returned. Then, "Second Squad, over the side. Baker, bring your mortar crew. Colby, bring that radio."

Wordlessly, Pete and the rest of the men shouldered their weapons and began scaling the slippery bulkhead of the landing boat.

"I'm going, too," Sherrod said and hoisted himself over the side and into the alligator before anyone could object.

Pete was right behind Nicholson. As he climbed the Higgins boat's side and was just about to lower himself into the LVT he froze. Lying on the deck of the alligator was a dead Marine sprawled in a pool of his own blood, a jagged hole through the front of his helmet. The bullet left his young face dark and misshapen, and had the dead man been Pete's best friend, he might not have recognized him. One of the alligator's crewmen saw Pete's horrified face.

"We didn't have the heart to heave him overboard," he explained.

Swiftly, Nicholson knelt at the dead boy's side. Ripping apart the slain youth's pack, he withdrew the camouflaged poncho and covered the body. He glared at the boat's skipper.

"Goddammit, my boys don't need to see this," he snarled.

Pete dropped into the LVT and other men followed, including Magruder. The wounded Potter remained on the Higgins boat.

Barrel-chested Pvt. John "Bull" Marino was having difficulty transferring over while burdened down with the cumbersome Browning Automatic Rifle.

"Bull," Ted Giovanni called. "Hand me the BAR."

Marino did. Freed from the bulky weapon, Marino hustled over the side just before enemy machine-gun rounds stitched the bulkhead.

Dropping into the relative safety of the LVT's armored shell, he turned to Giovanni and sighed, "Thanks, paisano."

"Hey," Ted said with a weak smile, "we wops gotta stick together."

The transfer went rapidly, but not smoothly. Machine gun rounds from shore struck both the Higgins boat and the LVT. Pfc. Lance Tuthill, the squad's quiet Oklahoman whose nickname "Gabby" was bestowed, tongue-in-cheek, because he seldom spoke, had just lifted himself to the top of the Higgins boat's side when a bullet struck him square in the chest. Pete heard the slug strike Tuthill with a sound like someone slapping a ripe watermelon.

"Uh," the young man grunted as he toppled, slow-motion-like, back into the Higgins boat.

"Oh dear God," Ted moaned in horror as he saw Gabby fall.

The LVT's engine roared and its treads bit into the coral reef, lifting the boat up and over. Clear of the reef and into the lagoon.

If the men in the alligator had thought the Japanese fire was heavy when they reached the reef, it paled with what they now began to experience. Machine gun rounds clanged off the amtrac's steel prow and flanks as if someone was pelting it with handfuls of marbles. Just above their heads, the craft's two forward machine gunners poured covering fire at the unseen enemy, their spent brass cartridges jingling down onto the metal deck.

A shell burst in the lagoon sent another water geyser washing over the Marines. As the wave poured on his head, something struck Pete's chest hard before dropping to the deck. Peering down he saw the silvery body of a fish. About nine inches in length, it had been killed by the shell's concussion and tossed into the sky along with the water it had called home. Lying at his feet, the fish stared hard at Pete. He angrily kicked it away. *Don't blame me, goddammit, I didn't kill you.*

Pete poked his head above the LVT's bulkhead and immediately wished he hadn't. Burning, sinking amtracs sat scattered in all directions, creating a flaming panorama. Those LVTs not hit kept moving, some outward bound to retrieve men from the stranded Higgins boats while others ferried fresh loads into the fight. Between and around these madly dashing boats, men on foot were wading through armpit-deep water as rounds from Japanese batteries struck the lagoon around them, exploding and casting walls of greenish water skyward. Bullets from machine guns sang a deadly tune as they zinged by, mostly invisible except for intermittent tracer rounds which marked their passage with streaks of fire. Red for American, bluish-white for Japanese.

An LVT just ahead of Pete's tractor took a direct hit and erupted in a pillar of smoke and flames, sending a shower of severed arms and legs cartwheeling into the air. As he watched in wide-eyed disbelief, Pete saw a Marine, clothes blazing, rise up from the stricken craft and jump screaming into the lagoon. He hit the water with a puff of steam and disappeared. He did not resurface. Another Marine, wounded and dazed, stood, only to be nearly cut in two with an accurate, sustained machine gun burst. He collapsed back into the burning LVT. Pete slumped down, breathing hard, his hands again trembling.

A tough, street-smart kid who grew up on the streets of Chester, Pennsylvania, a grimy little city outside of Philadelphia, Pete had developed a feeling of youthful indestructibility. Now that had abandoned him, and he was gripped by fear. He'd never experienced such terror before, not even during his alcoholic father's most terrible drunken rages. Then, in the midst of this fear, his thoughts flashed to his younger brother, Charlie, killed in action just over eight months ago, and the panic he must've felt as his submarine slipped into the depths. For the first time since that dreadful telegram, despair welled up inside Pete.

Crouched beside Pete, Sherrod drew a silver flask from a pocket, unscrewed the cap, and took a long pull. He offered it to Pete who gratefully accepted. At that moment, the hot feel of the whiskey sliding down his throat was more relaxing than an orgasm.

"Damned odd to be downing shots this early in the morning," Sherrod said.

Pete nodded gratefully and handed the flask back.

"You know," Sherrod said, "I had the option of covering the Makin operation further up north but chose Tarawa because I thought I might see more action. Well, I'm seeing more action all right, and damned if I don't wonder if I made a mistake."

The amtrac's skipper, looking wild-eyed, called to Lt. Cornwall, "This is as far as I can take you. I need to go back for another load. You still have a helluva walk but it's the best I can do. Red 2 is directly ahead. The long pier is to your left." Cornwall peeked over the side, saw total chaos, then hunched back down and nodded. "Once ashore, you'll have some cover by the seawall."

The men in the amtrac braced themselves for what was coming. The craft slowed then stopped. The coxswain gave Cornwall a thumbs-up.

"Over the side!" Cornwall yelled and was the first man into the water.

The rest, seventeen men in all including Sherrod, followed just as rapidly while the LVT's two machine gunners provided cover. The water into which the men plunged was chest deep but pleasantly warm. Pete feared that he might land on razor-sharp coral and heaved a sigh of relief when he felt only soft sand under his boondockers. As soon as the last Marine was off, the amtrac's engine revved as it turned and headed back for another batch.

Pete and the others had no sooner hit the water than Japanese fire from at least three machine guns converged on them. The lagoon was dimpled by waterspouts as if a rainstorm were passing overhead. Hot rounds sizzled into the surf with an audible *hissssss*. Two men were struck immediately, followed by a third just seconds later, and then a fourth and fifth. All disappeared under the water and did not resurface, leaving only a bloody cloud to mark the spot where they had vanished. Pete hoped they had died instantly, for to be wounded and fall meant certain drowning under the weight of their gear.

"Fan out!" Nicholson shouted. "Don't bunch up."

Talbot, Ted, and Pfc. Jim Deaver, a gnarly Guadalcanal veteran and member of Ed Baker's mortar crew, drifted right while the enemy fire forced the rest to the left.

Glancing around nervously, Pete saw men, individually and in clumps, their weapons held above the wave tops, struggling through the surf toward the shore some five hundred yards away. In the deep water, all movement seemed to be in slow-motion, intensifying the horror as the helpless men were gunned down in rows, unable to run and without any chance to defend themselves.

Overhead carrier planes continued to streak inland at wave-top level, while below, LVTs maneuvered around their burning or disabled brethren. Some hung up on barbed wire strung between partially submerged concrete obstacles, while others sat charred and lifeless where the Japanese shore guns had caught up to them.

Surrounded by death, Pete's nostrils flared in disgust as the air he drew into his lungs became heavy with the vile smell of spent gunpowder, gasoline exhaust, blood, scorched flesh, and hair. It stank even worse than the vomit and breakfast cesspool on board the Higgins boat. Everywhere the dull, khaki-colored forms of dead men and the silvery corpses of fish floated serenely together on the gentle waves, oblivious to the violence.

Every inch of the lagoon seemed to be covered by enemy fire. Spouts kicked up by the Japanese machine guns stitched crisscross patterns across the water. About twenty yards in front of Pete a man took a round from a larger caliber projectile. Pete saw the man's head, right arm, and shoulder explode from his torso in a plume of red. The ragged remains plunged into the sea, leaving a slick of bloody gore on the surface. Despite his best efforts not to, Pete vomited his breakfast. With that bitter taste lingering in his mouth, instinct told Pete that he needed to seek out the best way to safely get ashore and out of the crosshairs of the Jap gunners. At least on land he'd have a chance to fight. Here, he was nothing more than a duck in a carnival shooting gallery.

Terrified, Pete Talbot now began the longest walk of his life.

CHAPTER 2

My Dearest Kenji, the letter began.

Leading Seaman Kenji Sakai leaned his head back against the coconut-log wall behind him as he sat on the floor of a reinforced gun emplacement. He didn't have to read the letter. He already knew it by heart. It had arrived three weeks earlier, the last mail the Betio garrison had received before the Americans began regular air strikes on the island. The three-page letter was written in the meticulous handwriting of his mother, Kyoko, with each character neatly etched in black ink. The letter passed along the latest news concerning his family and their small fishing village located in Ishikawa Prefecture. She also included what little news she had from his older brother Ichiro, a corporal with the Imperial Army and a veteran of the fighting that brought about the fall of Singapore, and who was now stationed in the Philippines. Reading always clouded Kenji's eyes with tears, especially now as he listened to American naval shells bursting outside announcing to all that death had arrived.

For the nearly four-thousand-man Betio garrison, the desperate fight for Tarawa had actually begun the previous day. It had been around midday. Beneath a nearly cloudless blue sky, Kenji and three of his comrades of

First Platoon, Second Company, and Seventh Special Naval Landing Force had been seated cross-legged on the sand by the trunk of a fallen tree, one of many that had been toppled during the recent American air raids.

Leisurely munching rice cakes, they were joking among themselves when someone yelled that American ships were offshore. Kenji popped to his feet and gazed out to sea. Swallowing hard, he felt his stomach clench as he noted the dark, ominous shapes of what appeared to be three cruisers steaming slowly toward the island. The men watched, mesmerized, as the approaching ships, dull gray against an azure backdrop, took up position six miles offshore. Within moments, cottony white puffs of smoke appeared, followed by the dull booming of 8-inch guns.

Men dropped what they were doing and scattered as the first rounds burst in the crystalline lagoon. The next volley crashed into the island. With the range now fixed, there followed a tremendous bombardment.

Feeling naked and exposed, Kenji dropped his packet of food and joined his comrades as they scurried across the open ground toward their bombproof bunker. A shell burst close in front of Kenji, shrapnel slicing off one man's head as neatly as from a sword made of the finest *tama-hagane* steel. His torso fell heavily to the ground, while his head, still strapped inside his helmet, rolled to a stop a few feet away, mouth and eyes wide open as if in disbelief. Kenji hurried past the headless corpse.

Pushing his way into the bunker, Kenji found an open spot among a crowd of men and dropped flat. Through the stout walls of steel reinforced concrete and coconut logs, Kenji felt the earth shiver as shells rained down around them. Men whimpered in fear as the ceiling timbers convulsed and a fine coating of sand from overhead dusted them.

A large explosion behind the shelter drew unabashed whimpers from several terrified men. From the doorway at the rear of the bunker, high-pitched voices chattered in shock and outrage. Several soldiers crouching closest to the doorway had been struck by shrapnel. One man had been disemboweled, his guts spilling out as he collapsed onto the sand.

Kenji's ears rang from the loud blast and his body quivered from the concussion. To his immediate right Seaman Noriaki Akiyama had dropped to the ground, burrowing into the sandy floor. Now he slowly arose, his sweaty cheeks and forehead lightly sugared with sand. He gazed stupidly at Kenji.

"You're not afraid, *Jotosuihei*?" he asked, addressing Kenji by his rank.

"Of course I'm afraid," Kenji replied. "But if I'm to die, I want it to be while I'm sitting up, and not digging into the sand like a turtle."

Finally, the shelling stopped and the ships, satisfied with their work, sailed away. Kenji quickly left the bunker, both because he felt trapped inside, and to be rid of the smell of fear and urine emanating from the frightened men.

Outside, the landscape had been ravaged. As Kenji moved almost trance-like amid blasted trees and smashed huts of shattered bamboo with twisted metal roofs, he passed three dead men, their bodies tossed onto a bloody heap. Only one was identifiable, a young seaman named Nagata, who had been in Kenji's company.

Kenji walked toward the beach on the lagoon side of the island. Looking rearward, he saw the island commander, Rear Admiral Keiji Shibazaki, walking along the top of his heavily scarred command structure, surveying the damage from his towering fortress.

Kenji recalled the day Shibazaki arrived on Betio. It was July 20, a hot, breezeless Tuesday. Kenji's squad was helping to dig fire and communication trenches near the airfield's western taxiway when a Mitsubishi bomber, its large red rising sun emblems emblazoned on its wings and fuselage, touched down on the hard-packed, crushed coral runway.

"That might be the new island commander," whispered Seaman Shido Watanabe, who was toiling beside Kenji.

Kenji nodded. He had heard rumors that Admiral Saichiro, the garrison's commander, was being replaced by a new officer.

"I wonder why the change in commanders," Seaman Sachi Tanaka mused.

"That's not our concern," Kenji replied.

"They say it's because Shibazaki has combat experience in China and Saichiro has none," Seaman Harumi Takashima injected. "They say he's younger and more aggressive."

"And maybe they talk too much, *Ittosuihei*," Kenji said, pulling rank on Takashima. He was not comfortable with his friend's idle gossip.

"*Hai, Jotosuihei,*" he said, properly reproached. "*Sumimasen.*"

Takashima was a good man, but he had a tinge of defeatism inside him which tried to emerge now and then. That was not good for the men's morale.

Kenji had done well with the company since joining, and his commanding officer, Lt. (jg) Tamekichi Taniguchi, had seen fit to promote him above many of the comrades with whom he had trained, elevating him to the rank of Leading Seaman shortly after he reached Betio. He took his promotion seriously.

Kenji watched the Mitsubishi roll to a halt. A door on the fuselage opened and a small ladder was hastily pushed against the airplane. A naval officer appeared in the doorway resplendent in his white dress uniform, rows of decorations adorning his tunic.

"He looks like he's no older than us," Watanabe observed in hushed tones, knowing that speaking in such a way of a superior officer would earn him a severe beating.

"Silence," Kenji hissed, not wanting to be beaten along with him.

But Watanabe, who was Kenji's best friend in the squad, was correct. Shibazaki was forty-nine years old, but his round, clean-shaven, boyish face and close-cropped hair gave him a much younger appearance. Kenji watched as Shibazaki descended the ladder. He was greeted by Admiral Saichiro and his staff. The two officers bowed formally but perfunctorily to each other, then set out on a tour of the defenses.

"As you can see, we've not been idle," Kenji could overhear Saichiro telling his replacement as the two strolled by. "We've worked hard to convert this lump of sand and coral into a fortress and a death trap for the enemy."

"That's good," Shibazaki replied. "But they must work harder. This island is part of the Empire's outer defensive ring, so we'll be getting no more reinforcements. We must hold the enemy here, keeping his troops pinned down and forcing his ships to remain offshore until the Imperial Fleet arrives to deliver the death blow. That could be anywhere from three days to a week."

"And if the fleet fails to arrive?" Saichiro probed.

"Then we will continue to fight on until we fall like cherry blossoms before the wind," Shibazaki answered. "Every man must be resolved to fight to the end. Remember *Dai Nippon Teikoku* has not lost a war in 350 years."

The officers moved on.

Kenji hated to see the fifty-six-year-old Saichiro leave. An engineer by training, the *Kaigun Shosho* had frequently walked the island, studying it in-depth in order to devise an intricate design that he was convinced would spell death for the invaders. He hoped that this new commander was up to the job.

Two of the sailors in Kenji's squad, Takashima and Tanaka, had also overheard the admiral. They stopped digging after the officers departed and nervously looked at each other.

"You heard that, *Jotosuihei*?" Tanaka said. "Do you think the Americans will actually come here?"

"I don't know," Kenji replied, looking around. "It's such a small, insignificant little island. A flyspeck in the Pacific. Maybe they'll overlook it."

"It's a flyspeck with an airfield," said Takashima, ever the realist. "That'll make the difference. It'll attract them like bees to a flower."

Takashima's words put a touch of fear into Tanaka's eyes. Tanaka was a nervous fellow, but very artistic, a trait he inherited from his father who created delicately hand-painted kimonos.

Suddenly Kenji felt the sting of a bamboo switch across his shoulders.

"Dig!" Petty Officer First Class Kunihiko Funakoshi snarled as he laid his switch on Kenji's comrades as well. "Dig, you worthless sons of toads. I used better men than you for bayonet practice in Nanking. Dig!"

He glared at the men and then stormed off as Kenji and his friends, properly cowed, continued their work.

"You must learn to stay out of that man's way," a voice said from behind the work gang.

Kenji knew the voice before he turned. It was Chief Petty Officer Tadao Onuki of the No. 3 Yokosuka Special Base Unit and commander of one of the island's seventeen Type 95 *"Ha-Go"* light tanks. Kenji's company, among its other duties, had been tasked with protecting Onu-ki's three-tank platoon assigned to guard the nearby headquarters bunker.

"He does have a way of making his point," Kenji said to his friend with a smile, his shoulders still smarting.

Onuki chuckled and nodded.

"Just be careful," he admonished. "I don't want to see my infantry support injured before we even see one American. Otherwise, how can you protect me?"

He laughed heartily and slapped Kenji on his still tingling back. Onuki continued chuckling as he walked away. Kenji watched Onuki depart. He liked the man and whatever fate may have in store for them, he hoped that both would survive the war and remain friends after their return to Japan.

A tremendous explosion just outside jarred Kenji back to the now.

How odd it is, he thought. *So different from the tranquility of the evening before.*

He and Watanabe had been sitting on the shrapnel-scarred trunk of a fallen coconut tree. How long they sat there he did not know, but darkness began to embrace them as the sun sank below the water. Kenji wondered if he would see it set tomorrow night.

So immersed was he in the beauty of the gathering dusk that he nearly failed to hear Onuki approach.

"A lovely sunset is truly a gift from the gods," Onuki observed as he seated himself on the log beside Kenji. Onuki glanced at Kenji's round, pleasant face and deep-set eyes that flanked a wide, flat nose.

Kenji nodded to his friend.

"I can't imagine war touching this place," Onuki continued. "When do you think they'll be back?"

"Tomorrow," Kenji replied.

Onuki reached into a pocket of his tunic and took out a jade green pack of Golden Bat cigarettes. Removing one for himself and for Wata-nabe, he offered Kenji another, knowing his comrade didn't smoke. As expected, Kenji politely declined. Living in a small fishing hamlet, smok-ing was not a habit he had picked up.

"Yes," Onuki agreed as he struck a match and lit up the cigarette.

"The American fleet will most likely arrive off our shore tomorrow. But I wonder how long it will be until they try to invade?"

"Tomorrow," Kenji said again. "They'll be among us tomorrow. Right here where we're sitting."

"Our leaders say they'll attack the ocean side," Watanabe said, exhaling a cloud of smoke.

"No," Kenji insisted. "The Americans will come ashore here. I know what our commanders think. But I feel they are wrong."

"But it'd be madness," Onuki said. "Especially tomorrow. The tide is too low. The reef will be exposed."

"There is no reason the Americans will know that," Kenji answered. "That will work to our advantage. This beautiful lagoon will be their cemetery. I don't believe any of them will reach shore."

The three men lapsed into silence as the impact of Kenji's words and the images conjured up in their minds took root. The Yankee devils were coming.

His prophecy proved correct.

———————

Unlike the young Marines in ships offshore who awoke just after midnight to a bugle call, reveille for the island's garrison was at 0200 and came in the form of being kicked and roughly jostled by non-commissioned officers.

"Up! Up!" the NCOs commanded. "The Americans are here."

Kenji sat bolt upright, startled from his slumber by a none-too-gentle nudge from his squad leader, Petty Officer Second Class Kazunari Ihara.

"Where are they, *Nitoheiso*?" Kenji asked.

"Out there," he replied, pointing toward the beach. "Just beyond the reef."

Ihara moved on to rouse other men.

"You were right, *Jotosuihei*," whispered Watanabe who sat next to Kenji in the dark bunker.

His best friend's words burned into Kenji's brain. He had been correct both about the time and place of the Americans' arrival. Now he wished he hadn't. With the knowledge that death was knocking at the front gate, he fumbled with the gold coin around his neck and thought of his family.

The coin had belonged to Kenji's father, Goro, who had served with the *Nippon Kaigun*, or Navy of the Greater Japanese Empire, during the Russo-Japanese War. Just eighteen at the time, Goro had been a torpedo man aboard the battleship IJN *Mikasa*, flagship of Admiral Heihachirō Togo, during the decisive May 27–28, 1905, Battle of Tsushima.

The result had been a spectacular victory for *Nippon*. No less than twenty-one enemy ships, including seven battleships, had been destroyed, and 4,300 Russian sailors had perished. Another five thousand were taken prisoner. From one of these men, an officer no less, Goro had obtained the only war trophy he had ever taken: a gold, five-ruble coin dated 1899 and bearing the likeness of Czar Nicholas II. Enthralled by the glittering bauble with the incoherent lettering, Goro had drilled a hole through the coin in the ship's engineering room and wore it on a chain around his neck. Now his son wore that coin and chain, a parting gift from his father. Whenever Kenji felt especially lonely, he would bring the coin out from beneath his shirt and watch its gold gleam in the sunlight. That small gesture, the sunlight symbolic of his home in the Land of the Rising Sun, brought peace to his mind and spirit.

Now the bunker was alive with activity. Kenji fished into his knapsack for his ration kit and removed a container of dried plums. Nearby some men of the squad began brewing green tea over a small kerosene burner. They shared the beverage. Kenji sipped the weak liquid and ate in silence. He listened as men talked among themselves, some muttering fears for the coming fight, others reaffirming their willingness to sacrifice themselves for the emperor. Kenji preferred to go on living but knew that decision was out of his hands.

Beside him, Takashima rooted through his backpack and brought out his thousand-stitch sash. For a few moments he held it in his hands, gazing at it almost sadly, before wrapping the *senninbari* around his waist and fastening it. After he finished, he looked at Kenji and smiled.

"My mother made this," he explained.

"It appears to be very well made and has lovely stitching," Kenji replied politely. "May it guard over you."

"My mother is a member of the National Defense Women's Organization," Takashima said with pride in his voice. "She is a district leader."

Kenji now removed his own *senninbari* from his backpack and unrolled it. It was made by his mother who had gone door-to-door in their village to collect stitches, each one representing a prayer. As he wrapped it around his body, the words of the Imperial Rescript echoed in his head, "Be resolved that honor is heavier than the mountains, and death lighter than a feather."

His thoughts turned to Ichiro, four years older than Kenji, and a combat veteran. What was he thinking as he prepared for combat?

As the men inside the bunker readied themselves for the day's work, Kenji decided he wanted to see the American invasion force. Slinging his Arisaka rifle over his shoulder and pushing past his comrades, he stepped outside into the darkness.

Actually, it was not as dark as he had expected. The moon, just short of full, bathed the landscape with a soft, white glow. Kenji shuffled silently across the sand toward the lagoon. Far out to sea, he could observe ominous shapes, shadowy against the moonlit horizon. He couldn't tell if the shapes were warships or troop transports, but it didn't matter. They were the enemy and they were here.

Then he saw Onuki standing by the same tree they'd sat upon the evening before. Kenji joined him.

"It's like watching death come at you and you're unable to avoid it," Onuki said. "You were correct about their invasion plans."

"Did you spend the night here?" Kenji joked.

"No. In my tank," Onuki replied matter-of-factly, pointing toward the massive concrete headquarters bunker.

"You slept there?" Kenji asked.

"Of course I did," he said as if the answer were obvious. "Where else should a tanker sleep on the eve of battle?"

Onuki pointed to the ships far out at sea.

"You're thinking about them, aren't you?" he asked.

Kenji nodded.

"I wonder what they're doing right at this moment," Kenji mused. "Especially the soldiers who are going to be dying right here in this lovely lagoon."

"Most likely they are sharpening their bayonets and bragging about how many of us they are going to kill," Onuki said.

"Some perhaps," Kenji acknowledged, "but not all. Some may be doing the same thing we are right now, staring at our island and thinking how war makes no sense. How they're being sent to kill men they don't even know only because they look different and wear a different uniform and fight under a different flag, but other than that, are just the same. Young. A lifetime ahead of them."

"You must guard against growing too sentimental, Kenji," his friend warned. "That will do you no good in the battle to come. You might hesitate, and if you hesitate, you die. You must remember what our leaders have told us, that the round eyes have been slowly surrounding Nippon for years, and attempting to make us an inferior power. They wish to stifle our growth rather than allow Japan to fulfill its destiny in Asia."

Kenji nodded. Their enemy's greatest fault, the men were told, was that the American lifestyle was one of excess which had made the people soft and effeminate, and thus poor soldiers and devoid of honor.

Still, Kenji was troubled.

"I have never met an American," Kenji said. "I never even saw one. You did when you drove taxi in Tokyo, Tadao. What were they like?"

"Arrogant is a good word," he replied. "They look down their noses at us."

"Even the young ones?"

"I never met a young one," he said. "Only older men, probably businessmen or politicians. The type of men who create wars, not fight them." He put a hand on Kenji's shoulder. "In the end, it doesn't matter what they're like, if they're good men or bad. We either kill them or they overrun our island, kill us, and eventually conquer our homeland and families. Now we'd best get back to our stations before the Americans start their bombardment and catch us in the open."

Kenji nodded and they headed away from the beach. As he did so, Kenji glanced around one last time. For all its battle scars, Betio would never look this tranquil again.

———————

As the naval bombardment continued outside his bunker, Kenji absently folded his mother's letter and tucked it gently into the inside pocket of his tunic. The day of battle had come.

Kenji knew that the next few hours would decide if he was to live or die.

CHAPTER 3

Amid the crash of shells the soldiers somberly lined up at the small make-shift *Kamidana* or Shinto shrine they'd erected at the rear of the bunker to say a final prayer. Kenji joined the queue. When his turn came, Kenji clapped his hands together sharply three times as he bowed his head humbly before the shrine, its streaming paper *ofuda* inscribed to praise the gods. He prayed to *Yawata no kami*, the god of war and a soldier's protection, to grant them success and that he would perform his duty as a man and a soldier of Nippon. He did not pray that he would survive the coming fight. That was not the Bushido way.

Suddenly the American barrage ended and an ominous silence coated the island. Lt. (jg) Yoshitaki Chuma, the company's stern executive officer, bellowed, "Second Company, outside!" Chuma, a China veteran, sported a short moustache that Kenji and others thought resembled the one worn by American actor Charlie Chaplin. This, along with a high-pitched voice, lent him a comical air, but no one dared laugh, for the harsh disciplinarian carried a riding crop which he used freely on the men.

Once outside the 7th SNLF's CO, the short but stocky Commander Takeo Sugai stood facing his men. By his side was his adjutant, Lt. Masahi Okada, and Lt. Tamekichi Taniguchi, Second Company's leader.

"The Americans will soon try to force a landing on our shores," Sugai said in a loud, raspy voice. "Remember that you are soldiers of Nippon,

Land of the Gods, and trust that each of you will do your duty to the death. The coming battle holds grave consequences, not just for us, but for our families, our emperor, and for Japan. Let us exhibit our samurai spirit. Fight hard. Kill the enemy." He stopped momentarily then threw up his arms, shouting "Banzai!"

The soldiers followed suit, thrice thrusting their arms and their voices into the night air.

Before Kenji's company broke ranks, Taniguchi turned to Kenji's platoon leader, Lt.(jg) Michio Mukai.

"Mukai," he barked. "Send one of your squads to the supply dump to bring back some more machine gun ammunition for the main bunker and the support positions. Bring as much as your men can carry."

"Hai," Mukai replied with a crisp salute.

The run to the supply dump was given to Ihara, Kenji's squad leader, who now led his small group of fourteen men in the direction of the airfield about 175 yards from the bunker. Located between the airstrip and the easternmost taxiway, the underground supply depot bulged with ammunition, food, medical supplies, spare clothing, and equipment. The bunker itself, one of the last built, was not as sturdy as earlier ones due to a shortage of concrete and steel reinforcing bars, now entombed in transports sunk by American submarines and planes. Its protection relied on alternating layers of coconut logs and crushed coral. Inside, some of the men assigned to the supply bunker, mostly Koreans under Japanese supervision, loaded up Kenji and his comrades with ammunition boxes.

"Ugh!" Seaman Tadashi Araki grunted as he lifted a heavy box of the banana-shaped 7.65mm ammunition clips for the machine guns. "I feel like a pack mule."

"You *are* a pack mule, *Ittosuihei*," the ever-gloomy Takashima complained. "You're an enlisted man. That's your lot in life."

Watanabe laughed.

"Next he'll expect comfort women to be sent here to serve him," he said, referring to the women, generally Korean or Chinese, whose purpose it was to entertain men in far-flung outposts.

"You can talk, Watanabe," Akiyama puffed. "Your arms are empty. Wait until they hand you one of these beasts. Then make wisecracks."

"Shut up, all of you," hissed assistant squad leader Petty Officer Third Class Junichiro Kiritachi. "We'll have no defeatist complaining."

"Sorry, *Santoheiso*," Akiyama meekly replied.

The men continued loading up with ammunition, although progress seemed slow.

Irritated by the delay, Ihara glanced at his watch. It was about 0430. Even from this spot well inland from the beach, he could easily discern the shapes of American ships offshore in the growing dawn. The sight was unnerving.

"We need to get going," he said worriedly to Kiritachi. "I'll head back with the men who are ready. You stay here, get the last four men loaded up, and follow as soon as you can."

"Hai," Kiritachi replied.

"Follow me," Ihara said to those men lugging ammo boxes.

Kenji and the other men of the ammunition detail were about a third of the way back to the bunker when there was a loud popping sound and a cluster of red flares arced up into the dark sky to burn brightly high above the lagoon. Moments later one of the island's Vickers guns off to the west barked loudly and an 8-inch shell split the air as it screamed seaward at an American battleship. It missed, exploding into the water beyond its target. Almost instantly, far out at sea, a sudden flash appeared, followed seconds later by the deep rumble of naval guns as an American ship replied. Kenji heard the deep-throated shriek distinctive of a battleship's two thousand-pound shells as they knifed through the sky overhead. Every man plopped down on the sand as the explosives plowed into the island with an unearthly roar. More flashes at sea and more shells began exploding on Betio's shore. Japanese coastal guns replied, joining the terrible racket.

"Quickly! Quickly!" Ihara shouted. "To the bunker! We must get under cover."

Grabbing their heavy loads, the ammo detail raced toward the shelter. The men had covered just a few dozen yards when Kenji jerked his head upward. A large-caliber shell screamed just above his head followed by a terrible explosion. The earth heaved and the ammo detail was bathed in a harsh light. A heartbeat later a concussion wave like the fierce hot breath of *Raijin*, the *kami* of thunder and lightning, bowled over Kenji and his comrades. Debris rained down on them: shards of coconut logs, scraps of sandbags, and small chunks of concrete. Something thudded heavily on the sand near Kenji's head. It was a man's leg, bloodied and severed at mid-thigh.

"The ammunition dump," Kenji heard Ihara gasp. "They hit the ammunition dump."

Looking back, Kenji saw a five-hundred-foot pillar of flame boiling skyward. Heavy black smoke began drifting across the island, pushed by a slight morning breeze. Everything around the dump was a twisted mass of ruin. Kenji thought of Petty Officer Kiritachi, the wise-cracking Watanabe, Araki, and the two others who'd been left behind to pick up supplies. Kenji praised the gods for Ihara. Had he not led those men already laden with boxes back when he did, the entire squad would've been annihilated.

Back in the reinforced bunker, Kenji dropped his load, plopped down onto the sandy floor, and heaved a sigh. He leaned back against the coconut-log wall to catch his breath.

"Poor Watanabe," Akiyama said.

"I thought you didn't like him," Kenji replied.

"Of course I liked him," Akiyama replied as if his feelings had been injured. "I liked firing back at him when he made his wisecracks. It was sort of a game between us."

Akiyama continued, "Did you know he was from Shikoku?"

"Yes," Kenji replied, thinking about his friend. "His father is a fruit farmer. Watanabe would tell me in great detail about the trees hanging heavy with ripe peaches and persimmons, and of the vines loaded down with plump grapes. It made my mouth water. He wanted to take over the farm after the war and continue the family tradition." Another silence. "What was he doing in a place like this?"

"He actually thought he'd leave this island alive?" Takashima injected.

"Yes," Akiyama replied, leaping to the defense of the dead man. "He did. I do, too. I have to."

Takashima grunted at such unwarlike talk and did not reply.

Kenji heard that last comment quite clearly for the shelling outside again ceased. An uneasy quiet followed. In the gloom of the bunker he saw Ihara approach. He knelt beside Kenji.

"With Kiritachi gone, you're the ranking enlisted man next to me," he said. "I'm making you my assistant squad leader." He bitterly added, "I've lost almost half my men and the Americans haven't even landed yet."

Since all was still quiet, Kenji risked a brief walk outside to see what he could of the enemy fleet. Picking his way cautiously toward the shore just east of the long pier, what he saw made his jaw drop. The ocean as far as he could see in the early dawn light was dotted with ships of all sizes. He saw battleships, cruisers, and smaller vessels, possibly destroyers. Although he could not see them, he was certain that, beyond the horizon, there were also carriers loaded with planes that were, even now, being armed and readied.

Ahead he saw Onuki, who turned at Kenji's approach.

"That's some sight, isn't it?" Onuki said.

Kenji could only nod in agreement.

"You know," he continued, "the Americans I carried in my taxi had an expression I sometimes heard that I think they would use right now if they were in our place. It goes, 'I'll be goddamned and go to hell.'"

Kenji glanced at Onuki who just shrugged.

"I'm not sure of the exact meaning, either," he said with a grin. "But I gathered that it was not a phrase used during worship."

Behind the two friends, the supply dump burned furiously and heavy clouds of black smoke continued to drift across the island.

"Quite a show, huh?" he said. "So much of our vital supplies gone as quickly as a butterfly's breath."

Kenji nodded and told him how his squad had been picking up ammunition just before the explosion.

"We lost four men including Watanabe and Kiritachi," Kenji concluded.

"Kiritachi," Onuki said somberly. "That's sad. Kiri-san, I called him. I got to know him quite well in the time we've been here. He lived in Tokyo like me."

"I didn't know that," Kenji replied.

"Yes," Onuki said. "He was a journalist. He worked for the *Asahi Shimbun*. I read that newspaper all the time. I probably read some of his articles." He was silent for a few moments. "He was a very smart man. He should have been an officer." Onuki glanced around furtively. "He'd have done a better job than some of the officers we do have to obey."

This talk made Kenji nervous, and he wanted to change the subject.

"You've wandered pretty far from your trusty tank in case the Americans start their bombardment again," Kenji said.

Onuki grunted.

"They're making the crews of my platoon take shelter inside that concrete monstrosity," he said, indicating the command bunker. "I'd rather take my chances inside my tank."

"What if a big naval shell lands right on your precious tank?" Kenji goaded.

"Then it and I die together. What difference does it make?" he replied. Pointing at the sea full of ships, he added, "Look at that. Do you think any of us are going to walk off this island?"

"In a few days the Combined Fleet will be here," Kenji answered. "Then the round-eyes won't look so imposing."

"I hope you're right," Onuki responded. Then he brightened up. "Meanwhile, if the round-eyes, as you call them, start shelling us now, I can dash inside your bunker with you. I'm sure there's room for one skinny tanker."

The two friends settled into silence. Kenji realized there was much truth in what Onuki had said about their chances. They had been slim at best, but with the destruction of the island's largest supply depot, the odds dropped even more. Kenji thought about being home in his fishing village and about his family, and a sickening feeling of doom settled in his gut. He said a quiet prayer to *Yawata no kami*, to spare them from destruction.

The sun was not yet up, but the eastern horizon was painted in shades of red and purple. Slapping Kenji's back for luck, Onuki began walking toward the command bunker. As Kenji watched his friend, he said a silent prayer that they'd meet again, if not here, then with the many other soldiers' spirits at Yasukuni Shrine. Kenji returned to his own bunker.

The structure Kenji's company occupied was built to protect over one hundred men. From the outside, it looked like a harmless mound of sand about ten feet above sea level, betrayed only by two low T-shaped ventilation pipes protruding from the southern slope.

The bunker measured seventy feet end-to-end and boasted thick walls constructed of alternating layers of coconut logs and steel-reinforced concrete. The interior was a series of sandbag partitions, some in double rows, to protect against grenades or a squirt from a flamethrower. For armament, the bunker featured a 75mm gun aimed at the lagoon, and a 37mm piece to be used both on landing craft and enemy tanks. The defenders also had one heavy and two light machine guns sighted in such a way that they could protect their own and neighboring positions through interlocking fields of fire. There were also several smaller oblong gun slits for use by the supporting infantrymen like Kenji.

This bunker, dubbed *shujin*, or husband, was one of two identical strong points in the defensive arc protecting the island's command center. The second bunker, *kanai*, or wife, was located about thirty yards northwest. The husband and wife were positioned to supply mutual fire support to one another and were linked by a network of camouflaged trenches and tunnels, the latter made by burying empty fifty-five-gallon metal drums end-to-end.

Kenji was back in the safe embrace of *shujin* no more than five minutes when the deep rumble of naval guns resumed and a brace of shells shrieked overhead.

It begins, Kenji thought.

It did indeed, for an instant after the first volley crashed ashore, more shells tore up the island as the pounding became incessant. Betio seemed to be physically writhing beneath the powerful man-made storm of steel.

Kenji and the others cowered inside the bunker, fingers in their ears and mouths open to prevent having their eardrums broken. *Shujin's* 75mm gun was quiet. Lacking range to fire back at the ships offshore, it lay in wait for the more vulnerable landing boats.

With each detonation, sand from the ceiling filtered down on the huddled men. To Kenji's right was Akiyama. On the left, his friend

Takashima. The scent of ammonia was detectable amid the smoke and dust. One of the nearby men had pissed in his pants.

Raising his head slightly, Kenji spotted Ihara hunched up a short distance away, and beside him, weeping in terror, the nervous Tanaka, probably wishing he were at home in Nagasaki making kimonos with his father. Then again, at that moment Kenji would give anything to be home with his father pulling in nets.

The incessant pounding became maddening. A huge roar sounded off to the west, followed by many smaller detonations. Each man knew that another ammunition dump had been hit, this one beyond the airfield in the direction of the cove. Kenji wondered how much more of this they could take before they'd have no spare bullets or food.

The deadly drum roll continued for well over an hour as shell after shell blew the island apart. Each one added another scorched crater to the already lunar-like landscape. Then it stopped and an eerie silence descended over the island. Men raised their heads and looked around the bunker. Why did the Americans cease fire?

"Are the landing boats coming?" Kenji heard one man ask.

Lt. Taniguchi dashed outside. He soon returned.

"No," he reported. "They are not landing. There are two destroyers in the lagoon, but that's all."

Five minutes passed. Ten. Fifteen. And still no more firing came from the Americans. *What devilish trick was this?*

The silence lasted almost thirty blessed minutes, during which many of the men regained control of their rattled nerves. Orders arrived that men not assigned to the bunker were to report immediately to their fighting positions. Kenji bade Akiyama good luck as he moved off to take his place in his spider's web rifle pit a few yards east of the bunker.

Kenji had grown quite fond of Akiyama over the past few weeks, but as he watched him depart, and after being told about the pre-war lives of Watanabe and Kiritachi, Kenji realized he knew almost nothing about his friend. All he knew was that Akiyama was from Nagoya. A short man, maybe five feet, three inches, Kenji didn't even know how Akiyama came to be a member of the Special Naval Landing Force. Generally, the *Kaigun*

Tokubetsu Rikusentai preferred taller men like Kenji, who stood five feet, eleven inches. Perhaps Akiyama's stockiness and strength made the difference, since he was certainly the strongest man in the squad.

Kenji dug into his knapsack and pulled out his *hachimaki*, a clean, white cloth headband with a brilliant red rising sun emblazoned on it. A symbol of the wearer's perseverance, Kenji tied the *hachimaki* around his head, over his helmet. He was ready for battle.

Onuki also made good use of this lull. Crawling out of his tank where he had taken shelter after leaving Kenji, he hurried over to the second of the three light tanks he commanded, this crew led by Toyojiro Hamada.

"Everyone all right in there?" he called into the driver's observation slit.

Hamada popped his head from the top hatch and waved. Onuki nodded and went on to the third of his three tanks, its crew under Nagao Shirasaki. When he called out, he received no reply. Climbing onto the tank, Onuki looked through the observation slit and saw the three crewmen sprawled inside, moaning in pain. All had suffered burns from an artillery explosion flash that had entered through the slit which had carelessly been left open in violation of standard procedure.

"Hamada!" Onuki called out. "Bring your men."

Hamada and his two crewmen, along with Onuki's own crew members, Endo Mitsuru and Motoki Shugo, gathered around the tank containing the stricken crew. Two men crawled down into the cramped interior and began lifting the burned men up. Groaning in agony, the suffering men were helped into a hospital bunker located behind the command structure, which itself was starting to fill with the wounded.

"The Americans will be landing soon," Onuki said to Hamada after Shirasaki and his crew had been taken care of. "I want to move my tank closer to the beach so I can help repel the Yankee invaders. Find three men to take over, Hamada. Even if they can't drive the tank, they can man the weapons."

"*Hai*," Hamada said, and Onuki returned to his tank.

Back inside, Onuki was dismayed to find that he could not turn over the *Ha-Go*'s Mitsubishi engine no matter how many times he and Mitsuru, the tank's driver, worked the ignition.

Popping up from the turret Onuki hollered, "Hamada! Give us a push."

Hamada lowered himself back into his tank. Moments later his tank slowly began clanking in Onuki's direction. Onuki, standing up in his hatch, gave Hamada a thumbs-up as the latter's tank began to push. Slowly the two seven-ton vehicles rolled, picking up speed as Mitsuru expertly worked the ignition and clutch. After about twenty yards, the reluctant power plant caught, emitting a cloud of thick, black smoke.

Onuki smiled from ear to ear—that is, until the American shells began to fall. They were 5-inch rounds lobbed ashore from one of the destroyers in the lagoon where a sharp-eyed lookout had spotted the black exhaust smoke. Onuki slammed his hatch cover closed. Hamada ordered his tank back to the command bunker while Onuki turned left toward the airfield, crossed its pock-marked expanse rapidly, and rolled west, not stopping until he reached the eastern edge of the cove just inland from the beach. He parked the tank near some aircraft revetments, his guns pointing toward the lagoon.

"Now, come and get me, you black-eyed Yankees," Onuki mumbled to himself.

———————

Shortly after Onuki's tank took up its position, the naval shelling resumed in earnest. But after barely five minutes, it ceased a second time. Inside *shujin* Kenji and the others looked at each other in disbelief. Kenji rose up tentatively and gazed out of a firing slit.

"Are the landing boats coming?" Tanaka wanted to know.

"No," Kenji replied. "I think I can see some, but they appear to be circling well out to sea."

Then a new sound reached his ears, a faint buzzing.

"Planes!" he barked, then quickly dropped to the floor and covered his ears in expectation of the impending aerial assault.

The air raid that now arrived was the worst the garrison had been subjected to since the first raids began several weeks earlier. Between the bursting bombs, the chatter of heavy machine guns could be heard as the fighters strafed whatever their pilots could see. The air assault continued for about thirty minutes before the thrumming of the aircraft engines faded away. The respite was brief, for moments later the naval shells again began to fall like raindrops.

Perhaps it was Kenji's imagination, or maybe it was just fatigue from the constant strain of being under such heavy fire, but this time the bombardment seemed more ferocious than anything they had experienced earlier. As the shells crashed and boomed, the garrison waited in air-raid trenches and bunkers, in pillboxes and in rifle pits, huddled together like sheep in a fold.

A tremendous explosion occurred behind Kenji's bunker as a large-caliber shell struck the wreckage of what had been a barracks, scattering debris. Next to him, the always nervous Tanaka moaned pitifully. Kenji put a hand on his friend's trembling shoulder and his mouth to the man's ear so he could be heard above the din of battle.

"Quiet, Tanaka-san," Kenji said softly, using the friendly and respectful "san" even though he did not have to when addressing a man of lower rank. "We must bear up. We must honor our families."

For about eighty minutes the bombardment continued, its ferocity never letting up. It was as if *Raijin*, the kami of thunder and lightning, had taken up residence on the garrison's island home.

A few minutes past 0800, the shelling stopped again. This time no one asked if the American landing boats were coming. Instinctively, they knew the answer.

CHAPTER 4

For more than an hour Pete's squad slowly advanced landward. Pete estimated that they were still three hundred long, deadly yards from shore when he heard a voice shout.

"Head for the pier!"

It was Gunny Nicholson echoing Lt. Cornwall's orders. The gunny was pointing left toward the long pier that spanned the lagoon from the shore to the coral reef. On the pier, and under it, Marines using rifles and machine guns cleared the wooden structure and its supporting pylons of snipers. Especially stubborn defenders were incinerated by the merciless orange flash of a flamethrower.

Deaver signaled to Nicholson that he understood.

"This way," he ordered.

About twenty-five yards separated the three of them from the rest of the squad, but as they angled toward their comrades the water roiled viciously under the impact of Japanese machine gun rounds. Pete stared in wide-eyed terror as a line of waterspouts from machine gun bullets stitched a path straight toward him. Frozen by fear his feet refused to move. Miraculously, at the last second, the line of impact geysers veered right as the enemy gunner, unaware that he had Pete dead in his sights, shifted his aim. Pete pissed his pants but was too wet to give a damn.

"Back! Back!" Deaver cried.

This sustained, heavy volume of fire drove the three men further to the right, away from the pier and the rest of the squad. Gravitating toward any sort of protection, they waded through the waist-deep water near a burned-out, partially upended LVT. Behind the craft's steel corpse five like-minded Marines huddled for cover. The newcomers took a breather despite the unnerving spectacle just overhead of the amtrac's starboard bow gunner, his charred remains still manning his .50-caliber. Comforted by the twang of hostile bullets bouncing harmlessly off the craft's hull, Pete, Ted, and Deaver were greeted by one of the five Marines, a lance corporal.

"This is a bitch, ain't it?" the man snarled.

"We got separated from our platoon," Deaver explained.

"No shit," the lance corporal snarled, sarcasm in his strained voice. "As far as I know, we're all that's left of the eighteen guys who were in our alligator when we left the ship this morning. Goddamned Navy botched it again just like at the fuckin' 'Canal."

He turned to his men. "Come on, you heroes," he growled. "You won't get any medals here."

He turned to the three newcomers. "Good luck, fellas," he said, and they were gone.

After the lance corporal and his men departed, Ted restated his earlier fear. "What are we gonna do?" he asked plaintively.

"We can't stay here, that's for sure," Deaver answered. "Sooner or later the Japs are gonna realize that Marines are using this hulk for cover and they're gonna put another arty round into it and we'll end up like that guy." He jerked a thumb toward the dead gunner.

Deaver fished a hand into a pocket and drew out a waterproof pouch. From it he withdrew a nearly empty pack of Lucky Strikes and his lighter. He fired up a butt. His actions made Pete remember that he had foolishly put his own scrags in the unprotected pocket of his now very wet shirt. He removed the pack from his pocket and, as expected, the cigarettes were soggy.

"Fuck," Pete cursed and hurled the useless pack away. Deaver offered one of his, which Pete gratefully accepted even though they were not his usual Camels. He grimly wondered what Sherrod would think.

Deaver offered Ted a coffin nail but the boy shook his head no. It was a bad habit he hadn't acquired, much to the satisfaction of his squad mates who would divvy up the cigarettes in Ted's K-ration boxes. The three remained behind the protective steel of the ruined amtrac until Deaver and Pete had smoked their scrags down to the point where they burned their fingertips. They then tossed the nubs into the water, and the veteran signaled the advance.

They emerged from behind the half-sunken LVT and were greeted by another gut-wrenching sight. On the reverse side of the alligator floated half a dozen dead Marines. Killed closer to shore, their bodies had been carried out by the tide and now peacefully lapped against the side of the landing craft, bobbing on the waves like driftwood. Around the corpses spread a misty red fog of bloody water. Pete saw one man floating face down trailing a three-foot strand of intestine. The entrails seemed to be alive and twitching until Pete realized they were being nibbled on by small fish. The sour sensation of vomit again rose in Pete's throat but he kept it down.

Sloshing on slowly through what was now thigh-deep water, the three men advanced another hundred yards to a line of concrete pylons topped by barbed concertina wire. Putting the concrete between themselves and the Japanese gunners, Deaver took a peek at the shore, much of which was obscured by pulverized coral dust and heavy battle smoke.

"Shit, we drifted wide," he observed. "We're damned near on Red 1. We need to guide left."

"Let's just get ashore and then find our guys later," Ted stammered.

As they prepared to push on, Pete spotted an LVT about sixty yards to his left churning toward shore until it got hung up on one of the pylons. The pilot shifted into reverse and tried to back up, but his craft was stuck solid as barbed wire choked its bogey wheels. With the amtrac unable to free itself, the Marines on board went over the side. One of the men, a big fellow with a bushy moustache, was none other than their battalion commander, Lt. Col. Herbert Amey. Pete recognized him, having seen Amey on the troopship during the voyage.

"Hey," Pete said. "It's the colonel."

The others turned and followed his gaze.

"Huh!" Deaver spat. "Brass Hat. Doesn't he know a fellow could get hurt out here?"

"Look at that crazy asshole," Pete said as he watched Amey rally his party and start wading inland. "He's wavin' his pistol over his head like Teddy Roosevelt leading the Rough Riders up San Juan Hill."

"Let's take that beach," Pete and his comrades clearly heard Amey shout, his loud, resilient voice carrying above the cacophony of the battle. "Those bastards can't stop us."

Amey had taken just another step or two when he was struck by a burst of machine gun fire that hit him and three other men. The impact sent Amey staggering backward. As he began to sag one of the colonel's aides caught him. Concerned men clustered about their commander but were urged on by another officer.

"No! No!" the officer shouted. "Keep going! Keep moving!"

They did. Then another cry went up from Amey's staff.

"Corpsman! Corpsman!"

Pete was more horrified by this sight than by any other he had seen so far this day. The colonel got hit.

"Fuckin' A," was all he could mutter.

"Goddammit," was Deaver's reaction. Then, "Let's go. We can't do anything here."

With Deaver in the lead they left the shelter of the concrete pyramid, ducking carefully under the bottom strand of barbed wire. Then Deaver got it. A machine gun bullet passed through his left shoulder, ripping and tearing as it went. Deaver stumbled and fell into the lagoon. Pete grabbed him and got him to his feet. Deaver's face was screwed up in pain as he spat seawater.

"Sonofabitch," he snarled, a hand clutching the bloody wound. "God damn it to hell."

Ted and Pete helped Deaver back to the concrete pylon and once again got it between them and the Japanese. Pete began to yell, "Corpsman! Corpsman!" as he looked around for help. "Corpsman! Sweet Jesus, we need a corpsman!"

Amid a nearby group of men who were heading in the direction of Red 1, Pete saw one detach himself and wade their way, his B4 medical supply bag aloft to keep its precious contents dry. Pete waved so the man could zero in on him.

"A corpsman's coming," Pete told Deaver. "Just hang on here."

Deaver fumbled with his mangled shoulder.

"I made it through the fuckin' 'Canal without a scratch," he said hoarsely, his face pinched in pain. "I was one of the few guys who didn't even get fuckin' malaria."

"Quit bitchin', ya ungrateful bastard," Pete joked, trying to draw a smile from the wounded man. "This could be a ticket home."

Deaver gave a grimacing smile. "Yeah," he said, then winced. "Damn it hurts."

Painfully, Deaver removed his ammo bandolier from around his neck and handed it to Pete. It was bulging with M1 magazines.

"Take this," he said. "I won't need it no more. Take my grenades, too." They nodded and did as told. "Here, Feather Merchant, I've also got a bandolier of BAR ammo for your wop buddy Marino and three mortar rounds in my haversack for the 60s. Take all this shit and get goin'. Kill some Japs for me, boys. Semper Fi."

Pete and Ted nodded, then lugging their newly increased loads, again began picking their way under the barbed wire.

The grisly walk to shore seemed endless. It had been more than two hours since they'd transferred from the Higgins boat to the alligator, and they were still two football fields from the beach. To make matters worse, the water grew shallower with every yard. It was just above Pete's knees now, which allowed them to move faster, but also left them more exposed. Like nearly all of the other Marines sloshing in from the bloody lagoon, the two friends instinctively began to walk leaning forward as if advancing into the teeth of a raging storm. The humming and whining of passing rounds was maddening, and all around men continued dropping, more now than in the deeper water. Some fell in silence while others screamed in shock and pain.

Reaching another line of barbed wire, the invading Marines picked

their way through it. Not all made it successfully. Pete saw more than
a dozen dead men either draped across the wire or dangling from the
jagged barbs that had snagged their clothes or limbs. Pete recognized the
nearest one as the lance corporal they had met a short while earlier by
the mangled alligator. He had been shot between the eyes, the familiar
snarl frozen on the dead face.

Unnerved by the sight, Ted began to mutter, "Hail Mary, full of
grace," over and over. Oddly, Pete also found himself praying, but in
silence. He hadn't prayed since he was a boy in Sunday school under a
crotchety old lady teacher the kids called Mrs. Old Bat. Grown now,
he had not darkened the doorway of a church in more than ten years,
yet now here he was, kneeling figuratively before a God upon whom
he had turned his back, asking to be watched over and protected from
what seemed like certain death. Somewhere, Pete thought, God must
be having a good laugh.

Laughing or not, there amid the flames and death, God seemed to
have heard Pete's petition. One moment he was walking forward, the
next a stinging jolt knocked him back on his ass, sending his rifle flying
from his grip. The boy plunged into the water, nearly going under. Instinctively, he pushed himself up to a kneeling position. Ted, who'd been
a few yards behind, was quickly by his side.

"Pete! Pete!" he cried. "Jesus. Are you okay?"

Frantically, Pete felt around his body, especially around his gut where
the jolt had hammered him the hardest. Fully expecting to find a gaping,
bloody hole, he was relieved to discover nothing.

Ted quickly checked Pete out as well.

"I don't see anything," he said. "No blood or wound or anything.
But Jesus. I heard you get hit."

With his initial panic subsiding, Pete began fishing around in the
water with his hands.

"My rifle," he said. "Where the fuck's my rifle?"

Ted fished as well.

"Here it is," Ted beamed, scooping up the weapon. Then he said,
"Sweet Mother Mary."

Holding up the Garand, which Pete had been carrying diagonally at the port arms position, both men saw that the enemy bullet had struck it directly, smashing the receiver, carrying away the rear sight, and splintering the wooden stock by the hand grip. Ted handed the useless weapon to his friend and grinned, relief flooding his face. Pete clutched it protectively.

"It never fired a round at the enemy," he said, laughing foolishly as the initial terror of getting hit gave way to the relief of being in one piece. "Goddamned thing died a virgin."

"So will we if we don't get going," Ted said.

Nodding, Pete rose shakily but held on to the ruined rifle. There was no reason to keep it, but the importance of his weapon had been drilled into him at Parris Island, and carrying it gave him a sense of not being totally defenseless.

Ted now taking the lead, the two continued toward the beach. From the corner of his eye, Pete spotted a Marine wading some fifteen yards to his left. Moments later, he found himself splattered with gore as the Marine took a direct hit from a coastal gun and vanished in a crimson plume of water. His face and clothes streaked with the man's blood, Pete sloshed water on his cheek as he hurried on. A few yards farther along another Marine knelt in the water, wailing and moaning, a ragged stump where his right arm had been. Pete instinctively stopped and lifted the injured man to his feet.

"Come on, Mac," he urged, throwing his right arm about the man's waist. "I'll get you to shore."

Crazed in pain and fear the man staggered along, his good left arm around Pete's neck.

"My arm! My arm!" the Marine cried. "Find my arm! Don't leave it! I gotta have it!"

Pete ignored the frantic man's ravings.

"Jesus Christ, Pete, come on," Ted yelled back at his friend.

"We're coming," Pete shouted back. "We're coming."

They'd barely gone a dozen steps when the wounded Marine was jolted under the impact of several machine gun slugs and collapsed into the surf. Pete stared in horror, his supporting right arm suddenly empty.

"Keep moving!" Ted urged.

Continuing to slosh through the shallow surf, Pete and Ted closed their hearts to the appalling scenes around them. Ahead Pete could see they were still drifting toward the cove. Concave in shape, the cove had become a death trap for Marines who were exposed to enemy fire from three sides. Nine or ten disabled LVTs stood immobile in the surf and a hundred or more men were lying on the sand. None seemed to be moving.

"This way," Ted cried loudly, and angled left to avoid that killing ground.

A hail of machine gun bullets from a Japanese tank onshore near the eastern edge of the cove kicked up the water around the two friends. Then the slugs found Ted, striking him in the chest. The boy from Brooklyn stumbled forward a few steps before sinking to his knees and plunging facedown into the surf.

In a panic, Pete gasped and then quickly knelt by Ted. Lifting his friend from the water and turning him over, Pete gazed down into the ashen face. Ted stared up at him, his eyes wide with fear. Ted's body quivered and he worked his mouth to say something.

"I . . . I," he whispered, a bloody foam oozing over his lips. Then a look of finality seemed to take over, and he said weakly but with clarity, "See my mom."

Pete could just nod. Then eighteen-year-old Theodore Francis Giovanni heaved a sigh and the quivering stopped. Pete stared down at the sightless brown eyes.

Stunned to immobility, Pete continued gazing down at his friend until suddenly it was no longer Ted's dark brown eyes and dead face strapped inside the camouflaged helmet but Charlie's, his lustrous blue eyes now stone gray in death. Horrified, Pete violently shook the body shrieking "No! No!" until the face was once again that of Ted Giovanni. Closing the lids over the sightless eyes, Pete gently cradled his friend in his arms. Overcome by an enormous feeling of hopelessness and futility amid so much death, Pete began to weep.

How long he knelt there holding his dead friend and sobbing Pete did not know. If any Japanese bullets struck the water near him, he was unaware. For a few agonizing moments, he'd shut out the whole damned war. What finally jarred him back to the here and now was a passing sergeant who shook him by the shoulder.

"Snap out of it, Marine," he barked harshly. "Your buddy's dead and you will be too if you don't pull your shit together."

Pete looked up at the grizzled NCO and nodded.

"Okay," he stammered. "Okay."

"Best thing you can do for your buddy is get ashore and kill the Nip bastards," he growled.

"I'm all right, Sarge," Pete said.

Embarrassed at being caught crying, Pete wiped the tears away with his sleeve. The sergeant nodded then was gone. Peering down again at his friend, two things suddenly became clear. First, he knew if he left Ted lying where he was, his body might float out into the lagoon on the tide like so many others he'd seen and maybe disappear at sea. He might not have been able to save Charlie from a watery grave, but he could damn well spare Ted that same fate.

He also realized that he was no longer afraid. The terror that had almost consumed him had left his body much the same as Ted's spirit had departed from his. Laying his useless rifle in the surf, Pete slung Ted's Garand over his shoulder. Taking a firm grip on the straps of Ted's knapsack, he heaved a deep, determined sigh, and began hauling the body forward. Dragging the dead weight was a tortuous task, but the two friends had come halfway around the world together to get to this goddamned island, and now Pete would make damn sure that they would land together.

With less than a hundred yards to go, and with the water now just shin deep, many men made smaller targets of themselves. Some lay in the surf and crawled on their bellies while others duckwalked. Pete was one of the few still on his feet and was the only one pulling a dead man along behind him. Some of the prone Marines shouted, "Get down, you crazy bastard!" while others, no doubt assuming Ted was wounded, cheered him on.

Seventy-five yards.

Bullets whizzed by so close that Pete could feel the air rustle as they passed. Then came a tug on the left side of his blouse by his shoulder. A shell from a Japanese mortar exploded in the surf and a shard of steel ripped through Pete's right pant leg, leaving a jagged tear but without touching his flesh. Another chunk of flying steel gashed his helmet's camouflage cover, causing him to flinch and stumble. But he regained his balance.

Fifty yards.

Bullets kicked up waterspouts all around him and one buzzed by just a hair's breadth away from Pete's right ear. A Marine ahead of Pete staggered and fell, dead before he hit the surf. Pete dropped behind the corpse to take a breather, using the dead man for cover. As enemy rounds thudded sickeningly into the corpse, Pete took several deep gulps of air. Then he grabbed Ted's knapsack straps and continued forward.

Twenty-five yards to go.

Ahead Pete again saw the Japanese tank which had possibly killed Ted. A sudden hatred arose inside him for this iron beast. He saw a Japanese soldier climb up onto the turret. The man paused as he seemed to look directly at Pete. For a brief moment their eyes locked. Then in a solemn gesture the young man briefly raised his right hand to his brow. Pete got a clear look at the round, clean-shaven boyish face with its broad, flat nose and deep-set eyes.

Pete was astonished, uncertain of what he saw.

"Is he mocking me? Or is he saluting me?" he wondered.

Then the young soldier broke eye contact, said something to the tank commander, and climbed inside the vehicle. The iron beast pulled back from the beach. In making its escape, the tank burst through a defensive perimeter set up by some Marines from an earlier wave who had worked their way a few yards inland. Even as Pete ran pulling Ted behind him, he saw Marines swarm around and onto the tank. Silently, Pete cheered them on.

Kill the bastard, he thought.

But the Marines had no heavy weapons with which to fight the steel monster, even though the tank inexplicably paused mid-turn. As a result, they could do little more than annoy the tank and its crew before it managed to break free and clank away, machine guns blazing.

Dragging his dead friend, Pete raced on, his pulse pounding in his ears. Then he was there: Red Beach 2.

He threw himself down by the seawall, breathing heavily as he hugged the safety of its logs while bullets twittering overhead chipped off jagged splinters of wood. Marines lay all around him, three and four deep by the base of the wall. Some were unhurt, some were dead, but many others were wounded. The uninjured Marines and some of those lesser wounded gazed at Pete in wonder. The dead ignored him. A corpsman worked his way along the seawall, stepping over bodies, and dropped by Pete's side.

"Saw you bringing your buddy in," he said hurriedly. "That was a courageous thing to do." He took a quick glance at Ted then quizzically looked back at Pete. "This man's dead."

"I know," Pete gasped, trying to catch his breath after the exertion.

"Then why . . ." the corpsman began. Then he stopped and nodded in understanding.

The corpsman removed one of the two round identity discs from the chain around Ted's neck and handed it to Pete.

"You wanna take this back to your company CO?" he asked.

Pete nodded somberly as he took the disc, gripping it hard in his clenched fist.

"Can I have his rosary?" Pete asked. "Before he died, I promised him I'd see his mom."

The corpsman removed the beaded necklace from Ted's lifeless body. There was blood on it, so the corpsman wiped it off on his wet pants before handing it to Pete. Then he moved on. He had no shortage of living men in need of his care.

Pete now resolved that if Ted could no longer fight the battle he'd come eight thousand miles to fight then he, Pete, would fight on for him. He began by taking Ted's rifle to replace his own shattered Garand. Ted's M1 would seek retribution. Pete then removed three hand grenades from Ted's web belt, along with his ammo bandoliers. Next came the belt of BAR ammo and 60mm mortar rounds Deaver had given him.

Before departing there was one last thing Pete had to do. He knew his friend carried letters from home wrapped in an oilskin pouch inside his haversack. Undoing the haversack straps, Pete fished inside, located the pouch, and tucked it inside his own blouse along with the rosary.

"I'll see your mom," Pete vowed, gazing down on the dead face that now looked so serene. "I promise."

After saying his goodbyes Pete looked around. He stared briefly at a decapitated Marine lying a few feet away on the beach. Nearby the man's head, still strapped inside his helmet, lolled gently in the surf.

"What the fuck have I gotten myself into?" he asked.

CHAPTER 5

All along Betio's northern coast, the men of the island's garrison watched the enemy's approach. Kenji, forty yards from the water's edge, was at his rifle slit from which he could see the small dots of landing boats as they approached.

A runner arrived at *shujin* with orders for Lt. Taniguchi telling him that radio communications were down.

"Initiate Plan Yogaki," the runner directed.

Taniguchi knew what that meant; all men were to operate independently with the sole purpose of stopping the Americans on the beach.

"Prepare to fire the main gun," he barked at the 75mm gun crew.

The men sited their piece toward the American landing boats which had closed to within two miles offshore, placing them well within the gun's four-mile range.

"Fire!" Taniguchi called.

The blast rocked the men inside the bunker as the gun spat a round toward the enemy ships. More batteries elsewhere around the island began firing as the orders were passed along.

Kenji and the other men, aware of the atoll's tricky tide and exposed reef, watched in anticipation as the first landing boats approached.

"Come on, you Yankee devils," Kenji heard Chuma mutter as he peeked through a nearby gun slit. "Your death awaits you."

Chuma grinned, sure of his prophecy. Kenji grinned as well, but their smiles of anticipation twisted into grimaces of horror as the men watched one, then a second and a third of the landing boats climb up and over the reef.

"Incredible," Kenji muttered aloud. He prayed that the entire American invasion force was not composed of these accursed landing craft.

As he watched the incoming boats lumber over the reef, a machine gunner, Kisaburo Hanaki, standing near Kenji said, "The God of Death has come."

Silently, Kenji could only agree.

With the barrier reef now behind them, the American landing craft drew closer despite coming under a withering fire. The gun in Kenji's bunker barked again, its crew blurting out a loud cheer as their round struck a landing boat. From Kenji's position, he saw the landing boat leap from the water in a ball of flame and fly to pieces, sending torn bodies in all directions. Then he saw another boat struck, pouring out thick black smoke. Small figures of men, some with their clothes in flames, jumped over the side into the water. Japanese machine guns found some of them and they toppled into the lagoon. As far as he could see in each direction, Kenji watched seemingly inexhaustible waves of boats approaching. Sometimes a boat would be hit and begin burning. Quite often a man wading slowly through the water would suddenly vanish. It was a horrible spectacle to watch, but they were the enemy, Kenji told himself, and he knew these men were bent on killing him and his comrades. Yet he also acknowledged that they were soldiers like him, doing what they had been ordered to do, and a part of his warrior spirit wept for them. But as they drew closer, his duty was clear and he raised his Arisaka rifle to fire.

Kenji's aim fell on a soldier who was struggling toward the beach, his rifle at port arms, a heavy pack upon his back. Kenji gently squeezed the trigger and saw the man's body jerk, then slowly fall backward into the roiling surf. He had just killed one of the enemy. It was what he was trained to do. What duty demanded that he do. He knew that.

So why was he so sad?

It became obvious pretty quickly to Kenji that the battle was not unfolding as anticipated. Over and over it had been drilled into the men that their concentrated fire would stop the Americans cold; that their well-placed machine guns with interlocking fields of fire, combined with the pre-sighted artillery and mortars, would turn the lagoon into a slaughterhouse. The few Americans who did manage to stumble ashore, the garrison was told, would be bewildered and demoralized.

Their officers told them that the American soldier was soft, coming as he did from a decadent Western lifestyle. To the Western mind, death meant the end of life while to the Japanese soldier, death was a renewal. And even if an appreciable number of Americans did manage to cling to the shore, they were not to be allowed to obtain any sort of toehold or make any headway into Betio's interior.

Or so the plan went. Yet they were making headway and Kenji knew the well-laid Japanese plan was starting to unravel.

It began with an advanced element of Marines swiftly gaining a hold on the long government pier. Moving along its length, the attackers began killing Japanese defenders as they went. Kenji saw a number of his comrades fall from the pier or the support pylons from which they had been flushed. His face reddened with anger.

As the assault grew, Kenji could see hundreds of Americans approaching the shore, many riding aboard those devil boats that had made a mockery of the coral reef. But Kenji also noticed that more and more boats were piling up at the reef and many more men were wading through the surf. The gods of war were kind to the defenders. The Americans did not have enough devil boats for their entire force.

Inside his bunker, machine guns and riflemen unleashed a storm of lead. Outside, the men manning the trenches and spider nests added to the weight of fire. For his part, Kenji guessed that he had shot down no less than six of the enemy and there were still bountiful targets in the lagoon.

Yet in the heat of the fight, he had to give the wading Americans his grudging admiration. They withstood killing much better than he had been led to believe. For each man who fell there were two or three others struggling onward. Once ashore many returned fire, while the more stouthearted began to creep ever so slowly inland.

Some Americans came all the way to the water's edge in the landing boats, and as they reached the beach, Kenji could see why the coral reef did not stop them. These boats were equipped with tank treads. Since there was no seawall along the shore east of the long pier, several of these craft began grinding their way inland to disgorge the invaders ten or twenty yards from the surf line. One or two even reached the northernmost tip of the airstrip to the left of Kenji's bunker before unloading their troops.

The nonstop din of the battle was almost beyond endurance. Kenji's fingers trembled from the strain as he rapidly reloaded his rifle. The noise around him was such that when he squeezed the trigger, he could not hear his own weapon discharging. But the enemy returned an equally appalling volume of fire. Kenji's large bunker began to draw the Americans' attention. Countless rounds struck outside of Kenji's position, making the sand buck and jump as if it were being subjected to a miniature sandstorm. But not all of the Americans' bullets buried themselves in sand or coconut logs. Some lucky, or unlucky rounds entered through the firing slits, where they were apt to strike flesh among the tightly packed defenders. Two of the 75mm's gun crew, both shot through the head, lay sprawled on the floor amid their spent, still sizzling, shell casings.

A gunner's assistant on the light machine gun whose job it was to feed the thirty-round ammunition strips into the weapon, took a horrible wound to the chest. He lay bleeding on the floor pleading, "Kill me. Someone please kill me." Finally, Kenji's platoon leader, Hidemasa Yuasa, took out his revolver, an old Type 26 hammerless weapon, and handed it to the man.

"*Dozo*," the soldier gasped, thanking the junior grade lieutenant profusely through a haze of pain. "*Dozo, Kaigun Chui.*"

Without hesitation, he put the barrel of the weapon into his own mouth and sent a 9mm bullet crashing into his brain. Yuasa retrieved the handgun, wiped the bloody barrel off on the dead man's tunic, and re-holstered the piece.

Shortly after that incident, the loader on the 75mm gun was hit. His name was Kiyami Shimada. Kenji had gotten to know him well since the company had moved into the bunker after their barracks buildings had been leveled by the American air raids. Like Kenji, Shimada came from a family of fishermen and hoped to get back to his nets after the war. The two men had spent many peaceful hours discussing fishing and life in their villages, Kenji's in the Chubu Region and Shimada's in the Tohoku Region, near the east coast city of Natori in the Miyagi Prefecture. Now here they both were, and at this moment, fishing was the furthest thing from their minds.

Kenji had just emptied a magazine from his rifle when he heard Shimada yell something. Shimada, who had removed his helmet in the heat of the fight, was wearing a *hachimaki* around his head. Standing about five feet from Kenji, Shimada had just helped to shove a round into the gun's smoking breech. Amid the cacophony of the battle, Kenji could not hear what Shimada was saying, but the bullet that entered the bunker through the gun slit went into his friend's opened mouth, angled upward, and exited somewhere between Shimada's ears, blowing out the back of his head. Blood, bone, and brain matter plumed outward from the wound, showering several men, Kenji included. For a brief moment, Shimada stood on his feet, dead but seemingly unwilling to acknowledge the fact by falling. Then he collapsed in a heap. Another man took over as loader and the fight went on as if nothing had happened.

As the fray continued, Ihara tapped Kenji on the shoulder. With his mouth close to Kenji's ear so he could be heard, Ihara shouted, "Lt. Chuma is pulling our squad out to reinforce the command bunker. Come with me."

Without a word, Kenji grabbed his haversack and ammunition belt and followed Ihara. At the rear of the bunker, Kenji and his squad, the seven men remaining out of the original fourteen, joined a larger group of about twenty men led by Chuma and Lt. (jg) Yuasa. Crouching low, the men ran toward the massive concrete bunker. Projectiles of all sizes split the air around them. Four of the men were struck down. Whether they were killed or not Kenji did not know because no one took the time to stop and check. After covering the sixty yards to the HQ, Chuma deployed his remaining men into fighting positions.

Before Kenji could be assigned to one, Chuma said, "Not you. The command bunker has no tank protection. The one that's here has no crew, and the other two have gone off to join the fight. Your friend Onuki took his tank to the west. HQ can't raise him on the radio, so you need to go find him and tell him to return to the bunker."

"*Hai*," Kenji replied.

Kenji crouched by the command bunker looking westward and deciding on the safest path to cross the island in one piece. The hardest part, Kenji believed, would be traversing the wide-open airstrip taxiways, which he would have to do not once, but twice. The Americans who'd been carried inland by the devil boats had already seized the juncture of the two taxiways just behind the beach. That meant he might be exposed while crossing.

The cove was located just over eight hundred yards due west of where Kenji sat pondering his best move to cross the deadly space. It would be a trek fraught with danger, for even though the bulk of the battle was still focused on the shore area, enemy destroyers were dropping rounds all around the airfield while fighters prowled overhead licking their lips for targets.

Almost directly across the taxiway from Kenji sat the shattered skeleton of an aircraft maintenance building, in front of which squatted the wreckage of a Nakajima C6N *Saiun*, or Iridescent Cloud. The Navy reconnaissance plane, launched from the carrier *Zuikaku*, had flown in two months earlier after it developed engine trouble while on a scouting mission. It was damaged by American bombs before it could take off and return to its ship. Kenji decided to make this the first stop on his dangerous journey.

Taking a deep breath to steady himself Kenji dashed forward, racing across the open expanse of taxiway. Out in the open on the flat ground he felt as exposed as an ant on a tabletop. He expected enemy fire to churn up the crushed coral surface around him, but none came and he soon found himself taking cover beneath the plane's torn wing.

After a short breather, Kenji crawled around the side of the revetment

in order to get a look at the ground ahead. He was now inside the triangle formed by the runway and two taxiways. Before the American
bombs began to fall, this area had boasted a tropical, postcard-like appearance featuring soft, open sand shielded in many places from the hot
sun by groves of stately palm trees. The tranquil scene was marred only
by a few wooden maintenance buildings and several smaller structures
including accommodations for aircraft pilots. Now all of the buildings
had been reduced to rubble and nearly half of the trees felled or decapitated, standing tall, but with no fronds to wave majestically in the
island breeze. The neat, open ground was now strewn with charred and
twisted debris including blasted coconut-tree logs, twisted corrugated
iron from roofs, scattered equipment and personal property, and hundreds upon hundreds of palm fronds. Amid this wreckage the ground
was a moonscape of bomb and shell craters. Because of Betio's high water
table, many of these ragged holes contained pools of brackish water.

As he studied the terrain ahead, Kenji noticed several low mounds
that he knew housed machine guns. Among and between the mounds, the
earth was scarred where trenches had been carved out. Due to his months
of living on the island, Kenji knew he had four hundred yards to cross in
order to reach the opposite taxi strip. Some of that distance, thanks to the
denuded trees, was now all but devoid of protection from the enemy aircraft
whose engines he could hear droning overhead. Looking up, he spotted
several American fighters circling like birds of prey, watching the ground
for any sign of movement. Kenji decided to head for the nearest trench.

———————

Some six hundred yards ahead of Kenji, the tank commanded by Tadao
Onuki stood just inland from the beach, shielded in part from American naval gunfire by the soft mound of sand that concealed a hidden
bunker. While the bunker obscured some of his view, Onuki could still
see American Marines wading toward the shore. While his goal was to
reach the island's cove farther to the west, he could not pass up the easy
targets that presented themselves at this place.

Ordering the hatches closed and secured, Onuki pitched his tank and crew into the desperate fight. With his driver, Mitsuru, blasting away with the forward machine gun, and with crewman Shugo loading and firing the 37mm gun, Onuki himself manned the machine gun that protruded from the right side of the tank's turret. All guns were firing, and the rattle echoing inside the steel vehicle was earsplitting but still somehow exhilarating, Onuki thought.

Through his aperture, Onuki watched as one of Shugo's shots struck a landing boat, sending up smoke and fire.

"Good shooting, Shugo-san!" Onuki shouted above the roar. "Keep shooting!"

He didn't know if Shugo heard him or not, since the man was also wearing headphones and trying to monitor any radio messages that might come in even though, so far, none had.

Onuki paused in the battle to load a fresh twenty-round magazine into his gun. Out in the lagoon he watched Americans fall in rows, yet more boats and more men kept coming.

"What madness," he muttered to himself, awed by what he saw.

"Sir?" Shugo inquired, having also paused to reload the tank's main gun.

"Nothing," Onuki replied. "Have we had any radio communication?"

"Not between headquarters and us," Shugo replied nervously. "But I did just pick up a message from Admiral Shibazaki to Rabaul. He said that the enemy is approaching the northern shore in strength. He told Rabaul that our forces are in high morale and that we have decided . . ." Shugo hesitated. "And that we have decided to fight to the death."

There was silence inside the tank as even Mitsuru had paused to listen. The battle has just begun and things are already going badly, Onuki thought. He prayed that the Imperial Fleet was hoisting anchor and getting up steam at Rabaul, but he had his doubts.

Hiding his fears from his crew, Onuki said, "Let us hope the Imperial fleet arrives before that happens. Now get us moving, Endo-san. I want to get to the cove."

Tadao Onuki was elated. He and his men were now officially in the fight.

CHAPTER 6

The first hundred and fifty yards of Kenji's trek were made without incident. Keenly aware of the danger from overhead aircraft, he heard raised voices calling, "Keep your head down" and "Take cover, *bonkura*," inferring that Kenji was a dumbass for crossing the open ground.

Reaching a zigzagged air-raid trench, Kenji jumped inside. Taking a short break to steady his nerves, he was about to continue when he heard the whine of a diving enemy plane and the harsh rat-tat-tat of heavy machine guns. Kenji dropped to the ground thinking that the plane had spotted him but then realized the stream of bullets was not directed his way. Raising his head slightly, he saw twenty men running toward him from the direction of the landing strip. American planes had pounced upon them like buzzards on a carcass. Grimly, Kenji watched as the slugs caught up to one man, then another and another, slamming them to the ground. Only eight reached the air-raid trench and dove in, cowering close to the walls as the enemy planes swooped in at treetop level. Kenji hurried to the shaken survivors.

"Are you men all right?" he asked.

One man, breathing heavily, nodded.

"*Hai*," he gasped.

"Who is in command?" Kenji inquired, seeing no man with any sort of rank insignia.

The self-appointed spokesman shook his head.

"We were dug in on the southern beach," he said, his breath return-ing. "A warrant officer came around to us gathering up men to help repel the invaders."

"The warrant officer?" Kenji asked.

"He never made it across the runway," the man replied with an absent wave of his hand. "We don't know where we are to go or where we're to report."

As the only man of rank, Kenji felt a responsibility for these men.

"Space yourselves out at intervals and dig in along this trench," he ordered. "If the Americans break through our lines, we will need to defend the island's interior. You will be needed here." He turned to the man he had been speaking with. "I am on a mission and must go on, so I put you in command."

The fellow puffed up at being so honored. He saluted as Kenji turned and pushed on.

Tadao Onuki was at the same moment guiding his tank through the blasted remnants of what had once been a cluster of barracks buildings. Onuki was eager to take his tank into battle where he felt he could do the most good. The cove, he knew, would make a perfect death trap for the Americans and he wanted to be in on the enemy's destruction.

Overhead, the American planes, their ammo trays empty, turned back to their carriers. Onuki threw open the *Ha-Go*'s Dutch-door-style top hatch and stood in the opening. It was risky and possibly foolhardy, he knew, but he had wanted to see action and was determined to bravely charge into battle like the ancient samurai.

As the seven-ton tank rolled among the remains of the barracks, Onuki was shaken by what he saw. Once consisting of ten elongated buildings that held both enlisted men and officers, the camp was now a desolate landscape of shattered walls, scorched iron, and broken gear. Before the invasion Onuki and his fellow tankers had lived in one of these barracks buildings. But so thoroughly had these living quarters been pulverized that Onuki could no longer recognize his own hut.

What power the Americans possess, he thought to himself.

While the debris crunched and splintered under the tank treads, Onuki ducked inside the turret to give directions to Mitsuru. Onuki's commands were not vocal. The Type 95's 6-cylinder Mitsubishi engine rang so loudly in their ears that Onuki found it best to direct Mitsuru through a series of buttons. These operated a panel of twelve lights and a buzzer located by the driver's side. Each light had a meaning and the buzzer alerted the driver of a change. Satisfied that Mitsuru understood, Onuki stood back up.

Reaching a spot he liked near the northern end of the barracks area, Onuki brought the tank to a stop. From his perch in the *Ha-Go's* turret, his eyes widened in amazement as he took in the full panorama of the invasion. Waves of men were wading toward shore in the face of brutal fire. Wrecked and smoldering landing boats littered the lagoon while others scurried back and forth across the churning water. Scores of ships stood offshore lending fire support. Seeing this, a feeling of gloom began to seep into his soul. While he knew a soldier's duty was to die if needed in defense of the Empire and the emperor, Onuki had always believed he and his comrades would prevail because they were superior soldiers. Now, for the first time, he realized the strong likelihood that he'd never see Japan again.

"If we are to die," he told himself, "we will give a good account of ourselves."

Onuki had hoped to see American tanks rolling ashore. He longed to take one on, doing battle nobly man-to-man, tank-to-tank. But aside from the tracked landing vehicles which had mocked the island's natural defenses, there were no American tanks in view.

With no enemy armor to challenge him, Onuki quickly gave Shugo the command to open fire with the main gun. Shugo grabbed the wheel that turned the *Ha-Go's* hand-operated turret, bringing the 37mm weapon to bear on the incoming boats. Reaching below him, he hoisted up a round for the gun, fed it into the open breech, and sighted the piece. Then he fired.

At the airfield's easternmost taxiway, Kenji spotted a U-shaped mound of sand surrounding a well-camouflaged section of heavy mortars. The crews, sweaty and mostly bare-chested in the heat, were busy dropping 81mm rounds down the barrels, then ducking their heads until the tell-tale "thump" from the shell striking the weapon's firing pin told them the missile was on its way.

One man, probably the gun commander, lay atop the sand mound, binoculars focused ahead. He turned as Kenji entered the protective embrace of the emplacement and dropped to his knees. Kenji recognized the man as Warrant Officer Yoshiro Kiuchi, Third Company's weapons platoon leader. Kenji knew Kiuchi and so did Onuki. Maybe Kiuchi knew which direction the tank had traveled. Kiuchi's face, gritty from where fine particles of sand stuck to his sweaty skin, grinned when he saw Kenji.

"So, Fisherman," Kiuchi joked. "What brings you to this part of the world?"

Kiuchi, who had worked in a Yokohama department store before the war, always called Kenji "Fisherman." Kenji in turn referred to Kiuchi as "Shopkeeper."

"Not you, Shopkeeper," Kenji fired back with a grin. "I was sent by HQ to find Onuki. Have you seen him?"

"I have," Kiuchi replied. "He took that cast-iron coffin of his toward the cove. He told me he wanted to get into the fight. I told him he didn't have to look for the fight. It'll come to him if he waits." Kiuchi paused and his appearance took on a more serious look. "If you need to go up there looking for him, be extremely careful. The fighting ahead is very hot."

"I have my orders," Kenji said, saluted, and left.

Kenji recalled that Onuki had been billeted in the barracks area along with the Third Special Base Force so maybe his friend had gone there.

Kenji next made for the ruins of a small hut, its northern and western walls still standing. Behind this L-shaped barrier Kenji came across a medical corpsman tending a dozen wounded men. The *eisei-hei* was Tadamichi Yoshitomo, whom Kenji briefly served with while he was a member of Third Company before being transferred to First Company after the regiment departed from Japan.

"Kenji-san," Yoshitomo said as Kenji entered the protection of the shattered building. "It is good to see a friendly face."

Yoshitomo was always immensely polite even with blood now staining his clothes and smearing his arms as high as his elbows. He always referred to Kenji by adding the formal "san."

Yoshitomo had his hands full. The men lying before him had all been badly shot up and one was missing most of his left arm. Yoshitomo was assisted by one man, a Korean laborer wearing a used Japanese uniform without insignia. The man had evidently been pressed into service for which he had no training and did not seem happy about it. Kenji watched Yoshitomo attempting to bandage a hole in a man's gut large enough to insert a clenched fist. The soldier was semi-conscious and grunted in pain as the *eisei-hei* worked.

"My morphine is gone," Yoshitomo told Kenji by way of explaining the patient's discomfort. "He got the last of it, but only a partial dose."

Kenji glanced at Yoshitomo's open medical kit. Fully loaded it would contain peptic tablets for stomach problems, aspirin, morphine, tincture of iodine, an antiseptic called iodoform, zinc oxide, quinine sulphate or Atabrine for treatment of malaria, adhesive plasters, bandages, gauze, scissors, a thermometer, boric acid, Rivanol (a disinfectant), a syringe, sodium bicarbonate, cotton, a knife, and a small saw. But Yoshitomo's kit was more than half empty.

Kenji watched his friend work. Glancing to his right he noticed three partially bandaged dead men whose lives Yoshitomo had tried unsuccessfully to save.

He was no more successful now as his patient gave one last long, tortured exhale. Yoshitomo searched for a pulse. Finding none he turned to his assistant. The Korean, finding a job he was capable of, dragged the dead man away. Yoshitomo's work was not through, for even as one man died, two more arrived, one walking with his left hand supporting a right arm that hung crippled by a gaping shoulder wound, and a second man lugged on a stretcher by two Koreans.

"A field hospital is being set up at Admiral Shibazaki's headquarters,"

Kenji told the medic. "Your worst cases might get better treatment if you can get them there. The Americans could overrun this position."

Yoshitomo shook his head with profound sadness.

"The walking wounded, maybe," he said. "But some of these men cannot be moved." He looked at Kenji's concerned countenance. "But don't worry about them being dishonored." He walked a few feet away to some boxes covered with a canvas tarp. He pulled the tarp back and Kenji saw one box contained several hand grenades. "If I think we will be overrun, I will issue one of these for every man capable of arming them. They will close up tight to the more seriously wounded and set off the grenades."

Kenji nodded, bade his friend goodbye, and hurried on.

Moving slowly, he finally reached the taxiway, a deadly one-hundred-foot stretch of open ground. Steeling himself, Kenji sprinted out into the open, his eyes focused on a shattered maintenance building directly across from him. The high-pitched scream of an airplane engine told him he'd been spotted. Common sense told Kenji to dive into a shell hole to avoid the machine gun bullets certain to come his way, yet a survival instinct told him that stopping to dive into a hole would be fatal. His only hope was to run for all he was worth and pray that the Yankee flier's aim was off. As he ran the aircraft engine's roar pounded ever louder in his ears. Kenji had covered about two-thirds of the distance when the first bullets began to seek him out. Large plumes of dust and sand sprang up all around him like decorative fountains. He was certain one of the bullets would pierce his body at any moment when suddenly the machine guns stopped and the airplane veered off. Miraculously, the American's guns had run dry, Kenji thought, or maybe they jammed. Either way, as he reached the safety of the gutted structure, he thanked the gods.

Unnerved by the close call, Kenji slowly began moving north among the ruined barracks buildings. He was close to the fighting front now and could plainly hear men shouting both in Japanese and in English. Small arms fire was intense and Kenji was forced to stoop low as he jogged forward. Then directly in front of Kenji a brisk fire fight broke out. A group of Japanese were defending a trench while less than ten yards to their front, just inland from the sea wall, American Marines occupied a captured trench. The two sides exchanged heavy fire, each trying unsuccessfully to dislodge the other. Between fusillades, the two sides hurled insults, with the Japanese telling their foes that Eleanor Roosevelt was a street harlot, and the Americans shouting back unintelligible words, of which Kenji only understood "Tojo," "Hirohito," and the repeated use of the word "shit." Kenji assumed the American comments were horribly disrespectful.

Something about the gesturing leader of the Japanese defenders looked familiar to Kenji. Then he saw. It was Warrant Officer Kiyoshi Ota of Kenji's own regiment. Kenji did not know Ota personally but knew that the veteran had served aboard the aircraft carrier *Hiryū* and had, in fact, been aboard her during the Pearl Harbor operation.

Kenji watched as men of both sides fired at each other. Grenades flew, only to be tossed back. Kenji heard Ota berate his own men in his loud, raspy voice, calling on them to follow him in a glorious attack to throw the enemy into the sea. Then, to the amazement of Kenji and just about everyone else regardless of uniform, Ota leaped out of the trench, whirling sword scything the air above his head, as he urged his men forward. He had gone just a short distance when he realized he was charging alone. His men, all of them, were still cowering in their trench and he was standing between the lines, a solitary figure. Amazingly, no one fired a weapon, not even the Americans, whom Kenji assumed gaped at Ota in stunned disbelief. Those few moments of mutual paralysis gave Ota a chance to dive back safely into his own trench. This incident might have been funny except that the Americans, recovering quickly, now launched a barrage of grenades into the Japanese position. As explosions erupted from the trench, the Americans charged forward to overrun it. What ensued was a wild melee of yelling men and flashing bayonets.

Thinking that this was a poor way for a valiant officer like Ota to meet death, Kenji turned and moved swiftly westward toward the cove. Then he spotted Onuki's tank. In a crouching run, Kenji raced to the tank and climbed on board. Onuki had drawn up to within thirty feet of the seawall and Kenji, keeping the *Ha-Go*'s steel turret between him and any hostile fire, was astounded to see the seemingly endless stream of incoming Americans struggling through the carnage. Some were wading past dead and wounded comrades, while others crawled forward.

About forty yards from the beach Kenji noticed one young Marine dragging a comrade toward shore, courageously risking his own life to save a friend. As Kenji watched this human drama, the American's eyes suddenly seemed to meet his own. For a few brief seconds the two men locked gazes. Instinctively, Kenji gave this brave soldier a modest salute.

What courage he has, Kenji thought.

Exposed to enemy fire atop the tank, Kenji had to quickly get Onuki's attention. As the tank's 37mm gun fired yet another round, Kenji removed his bayonet from its scabbard and used the hilt end to pound on the tank's steel skin.

"Tadao, it's me," he called loudly. "It's me, Kenji Sakai. I have orders for you."

He called it out several times, pounding on the tank all the while. Finally the hatch opened a crack and Onuki glanced carefully out, a pistol held at the ready. When he saw Kenji he relaxed and shoved open the hatch.

"What in the name of heaven are you doing here?" an amazed Onuki asked.

Kenji explained that radio communications were down and that his tank was required back at headquarters. Onuki nodded and signaled Mitsuru to return to the headquarters bunker.

"Get in here," he said, and squeezed to one side of the cramped compartment.

Kenji rose up in order to step over the rim of the hatch, feeling rather than hearing enemy bullets whiz by his head as American Marines took advantage of this target. Even as Kenji settled into the turret, he heard bullets clang off the tank's armor. Onuki yanked the hatch close behind his friend. Cramped enough with its three-man crew, with four inside it, the tank now seemed about to burst at the seams.

As the *Ha-Go* turned east, Kenji saw Onuki's grease- and smoke-stained face break out in a grin.

"You should have seen the enemy dropping into the sea like raindrops from the sky," he shouted above the engine and battle racket. "I think we dampened their spirits." His face grew somber. "But the power they possess, Kenji. I fired until the barrel of my main gun was red-hot, but they keep coming as if they have unlimited numbers. As for us, we've seen our magazines and food dumps go up in flames and our men fall. We grow weaker and they grow stronger." Onuki's face took on an anguished expression. "I am afraid they will overpower us."

This doom-and-gloom defeatist talk coming from his usually happy-go-lucky friend left Kenji deeply disturbed.

"They may be materially stronger," Kenji said, trying to put confidence in his voice, "but they cannot defeat us if our spirit remains strong and firm."

"I pray you're right," Onuki replied.

The conversation came to a sudden end when Mitsuru unknowingly steered the *Ha-Go* through an American defensive line. The young man had been driving pretty much the same route back that he had taken earlier, unaware that some Americans had advanced inland, cutting across his pathway. Now the tank's armored sides rang like the bells of a Shinto shrine as rounds bounced off it.

Then came the terrifying scuffle of boots as enemy soldiers climbed up on the tank's body and tried to force open hatches. Fearing grenades or a flamethrower, Onuki shouted, "Close the viewing slits! Get us out of here! Steer south!"

Hearing his commander, Mitsuru turned the tank, but the cantankerous Mitsubishi engine picked that moment to stall. Shugo got on the forward machine gun and opened fire, and Onuki indicated to Kenji that he should man the second gun, which poked through the turret at the five o'clock position. Kenji obeyed. Grabbing the gun and depressing the trigger, he fired wildly and almost blindly, swinging the gun to-and-fro in a sweeping motion. As Kenji and Shugo worked the machine guns, Onuki spun the wheel that turned the *Ha-Go*'s turret, hoping to use the main gun as a club to sweep the Marines from the tank's body. All the while Mitsuru fought with the tank's peevish ignition system. In seconds that felt like an eternity, the engine caught. Mitsuru threw the tank into gear, but the vehicle refused to move. Kenji was terrified. Why had he ever climbed into this death trap? Outside he heard Americans yelling and cursing as they pounded on the tank, trying everything they could to pry open the hatches.

Onuki squeezed down to the driver's side to help Mitsuru. Nothing seemed to make the *Ha-Go* budge. In desperation, Onuki frantically kicked the axle assembly near his feet and with a jolt, the tank leaped forward like a startled deer.

"Go! Go!" Onuki screamed to Mitsuru as the tank swept out from under the feet of the Marines on top.

Onuki, sweat pouring from his body, looked at Kenji who had plainly been scared to death, and a smile creased his lips. He watched as Kenji reached inside his shirt for his gold coin pendant. Withdrawing it, the young fisherman kissed the coin. Then, the tension of their near brush with death broken, the four men inside the cramped *Ha-Go* roared with laughter as the tank sped southward out of harm's way toward the command bunker.

CHAPTER 7

None of the Marine Corps training that Pete Talbot had endured during boot camp had prepared him for the carnage now surrounding him. His best friend was lying silent by his side. Scores of other dead men lay sprawled around him.

A wave of panic began to swell in Pete's breast. Should he remain where he was, cowering by the seawall, or was it his duty to find his company? He couldn't think. This feeling of bewilderment was unfamiliar to Pete. What the hell was he doing here? This was not his war. So why did Charlie enlist? He was not a fighter. Pete always protected him. Pete considered Charlie the smart one. He had a future, yet he had joined the most dangerous branch of the Navy. Now Charlie was dead.

Pete began to second-guess his own decision to enlist. Maybe jail would've been better. At least he'd have come out in two years and still be alive. But would he survive today?

"Get a grip, goddamn you," he swore to himself. "Move your ass."

Move he did. Mostly crawling on his knees, Pete fell flat every time machine gun slugs zipped by overhead. But perhaps even worse than the bullets were the many wounded who hugged the wall waiting for an overworked corpsman. Voices shouting "Corpsman" was the only word Pete could plainly hear. He tried to avoid tramping on these unfortunate men, but they lay so thickly that his foot often came down on a leg or arm.

"Oww!" A man would yell. "You goddamn clumsy bastard."

"Sorry," Pete automatically muttered for the tenth time, or was it the fiftieth?

As Pete edged carefully along the wall he was confronted with a jaw-dropping sight. Ahead a knot of two dozen Marines was crouched by the wall while atop it sat an officer, pipe planted firmly in his teeth, loudly berating them.

"You cowardly sons of bitches," the officer snarled. "Do you think you're in the goddamn Army? You're Marines, for Christ's sake. Get over this fucking wall and move inland."

He singled out a few for special mention.

"Private Baker," he snapped. "Your rifle is still a virgin. Get over the wall. Find a Jap and bust your piece's cherry. Melendez, you're a United States Marine, not some fuckin' wetback. Get over the wall and use that Thompson. Sgt. Massy, get over that wall or you'll lose those precious stripes. Be an example to your men."

His insults spurred a few, including the harried sergeant, to brave the wall, but not enough to make the captain happy. Pete was astounded by this act of bravery no matter how foolhardy he found it. He lightly smacked a Marine on the arm and, pointing to the captain, said, "Who the hell is that crazy son-of-a-bitch?"

"Capt. Wentzel," the Marine replied. "Capt. George Wentzel. And you're right. He's got more balls than brains."

Pete shook his head in disbelief and continued around the stalled Marines. He had moved a short distance when he heard an anguished wail behind him. Turning, he saw Wentzel, pipe still in his mouth, lying on his back, one leg and one arm dangling over the edge of the wall. The Japanese had gotten his range. The captain's death spurred his men who began pouring over the wall to take their revenge.

The roar of a diesel engine caught Pete's attention and he spotted an LVT grinding toward the beach ahead of him. As the alligator neared the sea wall to unload its human cargo, three Japanese materialized from an unseen trench. The trio raced forward, screaming their outrage. While one fired his rifle at the LVT, the other two pulled grenades from their belts.

Yanking the pins, they activated the grenades. One hurled his at the alligator only to see it bounce off the steel hull and explode harmlessly in the water. Moments later he was almost cut in half by the boat's heavy machine gun. The man firing the rifle also collapsed, a victim of the same machine gun.

The third Japanese leaped from the seawall onto the LVT's forward deck and, still clutching his live grenade, threw himself into the boat's hold where Marines were jammed shoulder-to-shoulder. The grenade exploded with a roar. The Japanese attacker and most of the men in the craft died in the blast. Several of the injured began crawling out. Pete watched one wounded Marine try to lift himself over the LVT's gunwale. A Japanese machine gunner also saw him and the man's body was struck by a stream of lead. A second injured Marine was now struggling to get out. Angered beyond rational thought, Pete raced to the LVT. As bullets from the same Japanese machine gun clanged off the armored amtrac, Pete grabbed the wounded man by the shoulder straps of his knapsack, pulled him free, and dragged him to the seawall. The wounded man, a sergeant, looked up at Pete and weakly muttered, "Thanks, Mac."

Pete tried to see where the sergeant was hit, but there was too much blood. Unsure what to do next, Pete's dilemma was solved when a corpsman dropped beside him.

"I got him," the corpsman said.

Pete nodded and looked at the smoldering LVT. Being of no more use here he moved on.

A racket up ahead caught Pete's attention. Twenty Japanese soldiers burst over the seawall to engage the Marines in hand-to-hand combat. While some clubbed and hacked at the Marines with rifle butts and bayonets, a few ran out into the surf wildly firing their weapons. Moments later all of the Japanese lay dead in the surf.

By an abandoned LVT that got stuck mounting the seawall, Pete came across a stretch of beach being used as an aid station. In the meager shelter of the alligator, corpsmen had collected over a dozen wounded men. Pete was struck by the suffering as the Marines patiently awaited evacuation to a hospital ship if and when boats could be brought in safely to ferry them out.

About ten yards beyond the aid station Pete spotted a familiar form. It was Ray Colby, a trickle of blood flowing from an arm wound. Overjoyed to find a face he knew, Pete hurried to him.

"Colby!" he gushed. "Sweet Jesus, I was starting to think all of our guys were dead."

Colby did not respond but continued to sit where he was, knees pulled tightly to his chest and held there by clenched arms, a blank stare on his face.

"Colby!" Pete said again. "It's me. Hardball."

No response. It was as if Pete wasn't there.

Pete shook him by the shoulder.

"Dammit, Ray, it's me," he snarled. "Hardball. Snap out of it!"

This got a response, but the look in Radio Ray's eyes was not one of relief. Rather, the empty gaze was replaced by wide-eyed terror and it jolted Pete.

"Corpsman!" Pete hollered. "Corpsman!"

It took several cries, but soon a man from the nearby aid station was kneeling by Pete's side. But he was not a corpsman. The gold oak leaf on his collar noted the rank of major.

"You're a corpsman, sir?" Pete asked.

"No," he replied. "An MD. Dr. Blanding."

"He doesn't recognize me," Pete said, anguish lacing his words. "He's in my platoon but he doesn't know who I am."

Blanding put a hand on Colby's shoulder.

"Look at me, son," Blanding said.

Instead, Colby gave an animal-like cry, rose to his feet, and tried to flee. Pete reacted quickly. He spun and brought Colby down with a tackle that would've earned a grin of satisfaction from any Ivy League football coach.

"Hold him down," Blanding said. "I need to sedate him before he gets himself killed."

As the doctor jabbed Colby with a syringe, the boy emitted another bestial wail. Moments later he went limp. By now a corpsman had arrived. Blanding looked at Pete.

"He'll be manageable now," he told Pete. "You saved your friend's life. I can mend his body, but I can't mend his mind. Good luck, son."

Pete looked at the shell of a man who a few hours ago had been Raymond Paul Colby and wondered if the scrawny Oklahoman would be grateful.

Blanding and the corpsman dragged a semiconscious Radio Ray toward the aid station. As Pete watched them go, another thought occurred to him. Colby had been carrying the TBX set. Quickly, Pete looked around for the bulky radio, both along the shoreline and in the shallow water. It was nowhere to be seen. Giving up, Pete continued making his way toward the pier.

By now he had covered about half the distance from where he'd come ashore to where he figured his company had landed. It had been slow going, having consumed close to an hour.

"We need to knock out that damned pillbox," a voice ahead of him growled. Looking up, Pete saw a young lieutenant amid a flock of squatting Marines. The lieutenant pointed to a man carrying a flamethrower.

"Wickersham," he said. "You're on me. I need some volunteers."

Five men shuffled forward, their fears somewhat allayed by the confident-sounding young officer.

"Okay," the officer said, addressing the others. "The rest of you lay down suppressing fire." He noticed Pete kneeling in the surf observing the action. "You too, Marine."

"But I'm not in your squad, sir," Pete said, hoping to be on his way.

"You are now," the lieutenant said in clipped tones. "Pick a spot."

Reluctantly, Pete moved to the wall as ordered.

Gulping hard, the lieutenant said, "Follow me," and he led his volunteers over the wall.

"Suppressing fire," a sergeant ordered.

Pete saw that the pillbox, about twenty yards away, resembled a normal sand mound about four feet in height and ten feet in length. But that harmless-looking dune sported two Nambu machine guns, both spitting fire at the advancing Marines. The lieutenant and his men scurried toward a heap of shattered wood and corrugated iron that had once been a small structure. Three of the men never made it, including the courageous young officer. Pete saw him struck by machine gun slugs that jerked his body like a marionette operated by a drunken puppeteer.

Lying near the lieutenant was the man with the flamethrower. Two of the surviving Marines ran back to retrieve it. One was quickly shot down. The second Marine stripped the tanks off the dead man's back and began hurrying back. He almost made it. Then he, too, was shot down. One of the two remaining men crawled to the body, grabbed the dead man, and rolled him onto his side to prevent enemy bullets from striking the fuel tanks. Under covering fire from his comrades, the Marine removed the tanks from the dead man then scuttled forward a few feet to a downed coconut tree. Using its trunk for protection, he edged forward and into a bomb crater. He was now within five yards of the Japanese pillbox.

Three enemy soldiers materialized out of nowhere and charged the man with bayonet-mounted rifles. Covering fire from the seawall dropped the trio.

Meanwhile, the Japanese inside the bunker tried frantically to depress their machine gun barrels low enough to fire into the bomb crater, hoping to either kill the Marine or cremate him by striking the fuel tanks. The Marine rose and aimed the weapon's nozzle toward the pillbox. With a whoosh loud enough to be heard on the beach, the jet of liquid fire entered the pillbox. Amid this river of flame came unearthly screams as the crews inside were incinerated. The man with the flamethrower did not wait to admire his work, but dove for the ground as machine gun ammo began exploding inside the burning bunker.

Two men burst out of the rear of the pillbox, cursing the Marines who now turned their fire upon these new targets. One man quickly died under a hail of bullets. The second man fumbled with his rifle as he continued to scream obscenities. Pete, who had yet to fire a shot this day, sighted along the length of the Garand. Over his gun sight, Pete saw a young face with a look of unimaginable hatred in his eyes. Pete did not remember squeezing the trigger but still the Garand bucked gently and he saw a puff of dust rise from the man's uniform. The face under the steel helmet changed to surprise as he stumbled, then sank to his knees before toppling, slow-motion-like, onto his back. One tortured hand extended upward as if reaching for heaven. Then it dropped to the sand and lay still.

Pete stared at the silent figure for several seconds and wondered what kind of fate placed the young soldier in front of his rifle. Then Pete remembered Charlie entombed inside a submarine on the bottom of the Blackett Strait, and Ted lying in the surf, and the hundreds of other "Ted's" bobbing lifelessly in the lagoon.

Swallowing any remorse, he angrily muttered, "Fuck you."

The sergeant who took over for the dead lieutenant growled, "Let's go," and he and the rest of his men went over the wall. Pete held back, watching them go, but not without a sense of pride in seeing what a few determined Marines could accomplish.

He continued his journey.

About forty yards from the long pier Pete saw the first two men he knew aside from Ray Colby. Both were dead. The first was Cpl. Max Dugan of First Squad, a Guadalcanal veteran who had been wounded during the second battle on the Matanikau River thirteen months ago. The second was Bull Marino, Ted's Italian buddy and the BAR man. An Altoona, Pennsylvania, gas station attendant and mechanic, he once told Pete and Ted how he had hoped to return home and one day own a chain of service stations.

Three wounded men from First Squad sat by the seawall. The only one Pete knew was Andy Blascowicz. Like Ted he was from the Bensonhurst section of New York City and a die-hard Brooklyn Dodgers fan. Pete, Ted, and Blascowicz had been in the same boot camp training platoon.

"Hey, Hardball," Andy greeted. "Good to see you."

Pete knelt beside Blascowicz, glancing at his bandaged shoulder with macabre curiosity.

"How are you doin'?" he asked, then realized the stupidity of the question. Of course he was not doing well. The wound must hurt like hell.

"I'll survive," Blascowicz said.

He winced as a twinge of pain rippled through his shoulder. "You know, Hardball, this might just be a million-dollar wound," he continued. Then he laughed. "Hopefully, I'll be out of the hospital in time for next baseball season. Nuthin' wrong with me that watchin' Pee Wee Reese, Bobo Newsom, and the rest of those magnificent Bums won't cure."

"I'm a Chester boy, remember? I'll stick with the Phillies, even though most of their so-called sluggers couldn't hit an elephant in the ass with a bass fiddle," Pete smiled as they briefly rekindled their sports team rivalry.

"Maybe I'll visit Chester when I get home and say hi to that cute little Pollack babe whose picture you carry around inside your helmet," Blascowicz joked. "If she likes you, she'll positively swoon for an honest-to-God Polish boy."

"You go near her and I'll shoot you in the other shoulder," Pete replied. "Besides, she's half Irish so you don't have a prayer." He paused. "Where are the guys?"

Blascowicz jerked a thumb to indicate inland.

"We actually got a toehold on this goddamned island," he said. "I think some of us got as far as the taxiway by the airfield, although I'm not sure they can hold it without help. From what I seen, we lost a lot of guys."

"Who else got it?" Pete reluctantly asked.

"Don't know exactly," Blascowicz replied through a red haze of pain. "We got scattered coming in. Your buddies Aldrich, Marshall, and Harnish are okay. I haven't seen that Italian kid, Giovanni."

"He's dead," Pete told him.

"That's tough," Andy replied.

"How about Capt. Stacy?" Pete asked.

"He's okay last I saw him," Andy answered. "Stonewall's a lucky bastard. A lot of officers got hit. Lt. Pfeffer, the XO, didn't make it. He got about ten yards inland before he got stitched by a machine gun. He was hit about the same time I got this," he indicated his bloody shoulder, "but I managed to make my way back here. A corpsman came by a while ago and put a quick dressing on. He said he'd be back to do a better job, but I haven't seen him."

Pete steeled himself for what he had to do next: go over this damned wall and find his comrades.

"Be glad you're not coming in on Red 3," Andy said weakly, pointing to his right toward the long pier. "The Japs had a line of latrines just beyond the pier, little shacks built on walkways out over the water. Our guys coming in there not only had to wade through Jap machine gun fire, but floating Jap shit as well."

Despite his pain, Andy laughed at the thought.

Pete also chuckled at the image. It was a welcome relief.

"I'll see you around," Pete said, clapping Blascowicz on his good shoulder.

"Watch yourself, Hardball," he replied. "I overheard an officer talking on a TBX. He said our casualties are around eighty percent. Eighty! They're hittin' eight out of ten of us, for Christ's sake."

Pete nodded somberly, and with a deep breath, he hoisted himself up and over the seawall.

CHAPTER 8

It had taken Pete close to an hour from when he left the safety of the seawall to cover the 150 yards to the airfield's westernmost taxiway.

Close to half of the trees he passed had been denuded of their long, green fronds which lay carpet-like upon the sand. Torn trunks of fallen trees, victims of the battle, crisscrossed the terrain, much like the blanket of dead men sprawled among them. Adding to this devastation were blasted remnants of wooden structures, including sections of wooden plank walls and roofs once made of finely woven thatch. Among these ruins were spilled iron cots, some charred by fire, torn clothes, sandals, pieces of chairs and tables, and the twisted remains of bicycles. Lastly everything in sight, animate and inanimate, was dusted with a fine coating of pulverized coral as if nature was attempting to soften the horror.

Shortly after leaving the seawall Pete spotted a dead Marine directly in his path. It was his company executive officer, Lt. Ed Pfeffer. The XO lay on his back, his blue eyes staring skyward, a look of shock on his usually expressionless face. Pete had little time for people in authority, a trait he developed from growing up under the harsh rule of a domineering father. Yet as he gazed at the dead man, he felt an uncharacteristic pang of regret.

As he had done with Ted, Pete closed the dead eyes before they became fried by the sun.

That's when Pete noticed that Pfeffer's dead right hand still clutched his .45 automatic. Instinctively, he pried it loose.

"Sorry, sir," he told the corpse. "You don't need this anymore. I might."

He pulled back on the slide to make sure the weapon was loaded and armed, then setting the safety, tucked it into his web belt. Distasteful as he found it, Pete next rifled through the dead man's gear until he came up with two spare magazines for the pistol. He pocketed them.

Pete scampered to a clump of coconut trees that stood relatively unscathed. High overhead a dead sniper dangled on the end of the tether that had secured him to the treetop. His lifeless body gently swung from the tree like a macabre Christmas ornament.

Amid the embrace of this trio of palms, Pete took a breather, hunkered down in what shade their bullet-riddled fronds provided from the sun's relentless rays. To quell the sandpaper roughness he felt in his throat, he removed one of the two canteens from its canvas pouch, unscrewed the cap, and took a long pull. The tepid liquid felt sweet as it took the edge off his thirst. Pete fought off the urge for another slug, mindful of Nicholson's warning that water on the island would be scarce until a fresh supply could be brought in from the ships. God only knew when that might occur. Then Pete thought about Nicholson. Where was he? Was he still alive? *Of course he is,* Pete told himself. *You don't kill tough old leatherneck bastards like Earl Nicholson. Shooting his kind just pissed them off.*

Pete slipped off his helmet. The hot air felt cool as it brushed through his short-clipped auburn hair which lay plastered to his sweaty scalp. Reversing the steel pot, he peered at the photo tucked carefully above the webbing inside the hard, plastic shell. Though the picture was black-and-white, he could envision Aggie's fiery red hair and the blue-green eyes bequeathed to her by her Irish-born mother, a war bride brought home by her father-to-be, Aloysius, after what was then called The World War. This was the same father who bristled at the idea of his daughter's romantic feelings for the troubled son of an abusive, drunken ship worker from the Fishtown region of Chester.

Pete and Aggie had been friends since grade school. A sullen boy with a quick temper that got him into more than one schoolyard fight, Pete would usually sit alone at recess on one of the playground swings. He didn't mind the solitude. In fact, he preferred it. Then one day in third grade, during the school's lunch break, he found a red-haired girl clutching a brown paper bag standing by the swing gazing at him. He didn't know her name, only that she was in second grade, but that's all, except that, like him, she generally played alone.

"Hi, I'm Aggie," she said and planted herself on the next swing.

She mentioned that she had often seen him sitting there by himself.

"I don't have a lot of friends either," she said. "Maybe we can be friends."

With those amenities out of the way she began chatting gaily about her favorite game, hopscotch, and her jump rope skills. She seemed not to care that he seldom responded. Then noting he did not have a lunch bag, she reached into the paper bag and brought out an apple. She offered it to him. Pete was about to say no, but the apple looked delicious so he accepted. Aggie smiled.

From there the friendship blossomed.

Gazing at the well-worn photo Pete smiled as he thought about how happy Aggie made him. Now she was half a world away. Pete slowly replaced the helmet upon his head, making a mental note to ask Aggie to send him a new picture.

By now Pete had worked his way a meager fifty yards inland. Ahead lay another dead man he recognized, his own squad leader, Sgt. Toby Banks. Pete felt remorse at the loss of Banks. A Guadalcanal vet with combat experience, Banks had helped the squad ready themselves for battle with a no-holds-barred talk about what to expect. Now all of that valuable experience and talent lay in a crumpled heap on some goddamn island no one had ever heard of.

Pete cursed bitterly. Heaving a sigh of determination, he started forward again. Everywhere Pete came across one nightmarish scene after another. Added to this was the danger of being killed by friendly fire. Carrier planes roared overhead unleashing their machine guns at anyone who moved on the ground, friend and foe alike. Their dusty uniforms made them indistinguishable from the cockpit of a Hellcat screaming by at three hundred miles per hour. Twice Pete had to scramble for cover. Once he angrily fired two rounds from his Garand at a retreating fighter.

Around mid-afternoon the sky over Betio darkened malevolently.

Five traumatic hours after Pete had vaulted from the alligator and into the lagoon, he was crouched in a shell crater at the edge of the airfield's western taxiway. Fishing a rubberized bag from his knapsack, Pete drew out a new pack of Camels to replace the one ruined in the lagoon that morning. He lit one and deeply drew in the sweet smoke, remembering his first butt when he was fourteen. Creeping into the family living room one Friday night he'd stolen a partial pack from his father who was slumped in "his chair," a battered, high-backed wing chair of faded blue corduroy, dead drunk and snoring thunderously. He knew his old man would never miss it.

Now as Pete puffed he contemplated the danger in crossing this hundred-foot expanse of open ground where the only protection was a few jagged craters that pockmarked the crushed coral strip. Yet Pete had no alternative. The growling of the guns ahead told him that what passed for the frontline in this battle lay in that direction.

Reaching the taxiway Pete dropped inside a bomb crater, avoiding the brackish water that pooled at the bottom.

Then the sun was gone, or at least its brilliance was dulled.

Pete looked up expecting to see gathering storm clouds but there was no storm brewing. The dimming of the sun's rays was caused by greasy black clouds billowing skyward from burning fuel and ammo dumps mingled with smoke from artillery fire.

Pete spotted a lone Marine lumbering across the taxiway heading toward the rear. Draped across his shoulders was a wounded man. Looking closer, Pete spotted the B4 bag carried by Navy corpsmen and moments later recognized the figure as Pharmacist Mate First Class Ryan Magruder. Excited to spot someone who could help him find the company, Pete quickly moved to intercept Magruder.

"Doc!" Pete called. "Doc! Hold up."

Magruder, visibly tiring under the dead weight he was lugging in a fireman's carry, looked startled at first. Then his face relaxed. Reaching a small cluster of coconut trees Magruder sank to his knees and gently deposited the wounded man onto the sand. After a quick check on his patient, a corporal whose head was swathed in bandages, Magruder took a stiff pull from his canteen and waited for Pete to arrive.

"Christ, am I glad to see a familiar face," Pete said as he plopped down beside the corpsman.

"How're ya doin', Hardball?" Magruder said, fatigue plainly audible in his voice.

"Spent all fuckin' day dodging bullets and tryin' to find the company," Pete complained.

"Not much of it left," Magruder said grimly. "There's about sixty of them dug in up ahead."

"You're fuckin' kidding me," Pete was astounded. "Out of 140?"

Magruder nodded. He was tired and it showed.

"We're holed up with what's left of Fox Company and a bunch from First Battalion," Magruder said. "We got about two hundred guys in all."

He paused for another drink from his canteen, politely turning down a cigarette offered by Pete.

"It's been a helluva day, Hardball," Magruder suddenly blurted as his pent-up emotions poured out. "Third Platoon is down to eleven men and no officers. First Platoon is down to about nine or ten. In your platoon there's about fifteen guys, and your First Squad is completely gone. At least none have caught up to us. The Japs have been murdering us since we hit the lagoon. I've dragged so many wounded back to the aid station that I can't think straight anymore, guys like this poor bastard. I don't know why the hell he's still breathing."

"You're just bushed," Pete said. "Let me help you take this guy."

"We'll do a fore and aft carry," he replied. "I'll take his legs."

Grasping a leg with each hand Magruder began lifting his patient. Pete took the man under his arms and they hoisted him off the ground.

The field hospital was inside a bunker about twenty yards from the beach. Upon Pete and Magruder's arrival a medical orderly took a quick look at the wounded man and waved them inside.

"Head wound comin' in," he yelled through the doorway.

They hauled the Marine inside, ducking low under the five-foot-high doorway. In the gloom, two overworked doctors worked feverishly over prostrate men lying on stretchers supported by stacked crates of captured enemy supplies. The physicians, one of whom Pete recognized as the same Dr. Blanding who had helped him earlier that day with Ray Colby, worked in the dimness lit only by the faint glow of candles and flashlights held by orderlies.

"Put him over here," an aide told Magruder, pointing to an unoccupied stretcher-turned-operating table. Magruder and Pete laid the man gently on the bloodstained canvas.

"He has a deep wound from shrapnel above his right ear," Magruder said. "I managed to remove most of it, but I think there's still a piece or two in there. His pulse is thready and his breathing is shallow but steady."

"Morphine?" the orderly asked

"No," Magruder replied. "He's been unconscious since he was hit."

The orderly nodded and dismissed them with a curt, "All right."

As they left the bunker, Magruder said, "Wait for me here, Hardball. I gotta restock my kit, then I'll lead you back to the company."

Pete nodded. Left alone, he walked around to the front of the bunker. On the ground beneath the silent enemy strongpoint Pete saw at least two dozen injured men, some sitting propped up against the pillbox but most lying on stretchers. They were hovered over by a pair of harried corpsmen. The overworked doctors would get to these men based on the seriousness of their wounds.

Nearby several men sporting arm or leg wounds waited patiently while corpsmen bandaged their injuries and either sent them back to their units or, if unable to continue fighting, to a collection area on the beach to await evacuation.

Walking around to the rear of the bunker, Pete winced. On the ground were two long rows of dead men. Some lay on their backs, others on one side or the other. Each body was covered by a camouflage poncho with just legs visible. Pete stared at these men who just hours earlier had been alive on their troop ships, possibly sharing laughs with their buddies as they wolfed down their steak and eggs. Perhaps they had voiced their fears over the impending action, but more likely they boasted about doing great deeds, fighting through to victory, and perhaps even going home to march in victory parades and settle back into their lives. Instead they were butchered meat lying under a hot sheet of canvas while awaiting a crude grave on an obscure island.

Pete watched as a chaplain moved from man to man, praying over each corpse. *No one prayed over Ted*, Pete thought, *and sure as hell no one prayed over Charlie.*

Magruder arrived back after resupplying his B4 bag. He tapped Pete on the shoulder.

"How do you stand this?" Pete asked as he gazed at the suffering men.

"It's my job," Magruder said. "I didn't pick it. I joined the Navy because I wanted to see the ocean. I was seventeen and never saw the ocean. There's no ocean to see when you spend your life in Pocatello, Idaho. But after basic, me and a few other guys got volunteered to serve as medical corpsmen."

Both men were quiet for a few moments.

"Come on, Hardball," Magruder said. "Let's go home."

Wary of bypassed snipers, the two carefully maneuvered across the shattered landscape. They halted by a heavily camouflaged enemy machine gun position.

"The company took this bunker about two hours ago," Magruder said. "We lost five guys including two KIA doing it. If you wanna see what type of men we're fighting take a gander inside."

Carefully, Pete approached the low, gaping doorway at the rear of the bunker. The entranceway was doglegged to guard against grenades or flamethrowers. Once inside Pete saw three dead men on the ground. Two enlisted men sagged limply against the rear wall. Both still clutched their Arisaka rifles in their lifeless hands and both had one bare foot positioned by the trigger guard. Each had used his big toe to pull the trigger and shoot himself between the eyes. The officer, still holding his pistol, had placed the muzzle of the weapon into his mouth and fired. Pete reemerged from the bunker, grim-faced.

"We closed in on them," Magruder said. "They couldn't go any-where, so rather than surrender . . ."

He left the rest unsaid.

"I've heard stories about that from some of the old salts," Pete said in a stunned voice. "But I can't understand it."

"That's only part of it," Magruder said. "See that ruined hut over there?" He pointed across the taxiway to where two battered walls stood in an L-shape. "That was a Jap aid station. As the company closed in, the wounded killed themselves with grenades and then the corpsman shot himself. We took three prisoners, all Koreans. That's what we're up against." He paused to let his words soak in. "Let's get goin'."

Arriving at the edge of the taxiway, the two men hunched down to study the terrain. Then they were off. Once across the broad expanse they dropped into an abandoned enemy gun pit. Another short sprint brought them to a small clump of trees where they again halted. Ma-gruder pointed to what had been a sandbagged anti-aircraft gun position, its battered, twin-barreled 25mm gun still pointing skyward.

"That's the company CP," Magruder said.

"Our hold looks kinda shaky," Pete observed.

"You're tellin' me," Magruder said. "And it's not just us. I'm told by other corpsmen that we have a beachhead about two thousand feet wide and maybe a thousand feet deep. My dad's a construction engineer and he was teaching me to be a surveyor before the war, so I figure we con-trol less than a tenth of a square mile. That means we've lost a helluva lot of guys for damned little ground, and we're still a hundred feet shy of the airstrip we came here to capture."

"I gotta rejoin my squad," Pete told the corpsman. "Thanks for lead-ing me back, Doc."

He clasped the corpsman on the shoulder.

"Keep alert, Hardball," Magruder said. "I don't wanna have to lug you back to the aid station."

With a wink and a smile Pete was off.

Keeping low Pete swiftly ran to the sandbagged gun nest. Huddled inside he found Capt. Stacy, First Lt. Woody Long of First Platoon, and

Master Sgt. Thomas O'Leary. They all looked up from a map Stacy had been holding as Pete burst in.

"Private Talbot reporting, sir," Pete said, remembering not to salute in the presence of the enemy. "I got lost coming ashore. I'm sorry."

"Hardball," smiled O'Leary, an old 1930s China Marine like Nicholson who'd seen combat on Guadalcanal and New Georgia. "Glad you found us. We can use every man we can get."

"Were we hard to find?" Stacy inquired.

"Yeah," Pete replied testily, feeling as if Stacy was questioning his absence.

O'Leary smacked Pete on the back and said, "Rejoin your platoon, Hardball. They'll be on our left. And stay low. The Japs are dug in well and can see us even if we can't see them."

Pete nodded and scooted off.

He ran hunched over until he heard a rifle crack and his knapsack jerked from the impact of a bullet. Pete dropped instantly to the ground and lay flat. He cautiously reached around with his right arm to feel for a hole but found none. Then his fingers brushed against his entrenching tool strapped to the outside of the pack and he found that the slug had creased the wooden handle near where it met the steel blade.

"Idiot," he muttered to himself.

It was the fourth enemy round that day that had struck either his uniform or his personal gear but missed his flesh.

Cradling his weapon in his arms Pete slithered along the company's line on his belly. To his right, concealed in foxholes, shell craters, vacant Jap trenches, and behind fallen trees, he saw Marines hunkered down for cover while keeping a wary eye on the enemy to their front. Pete recognized the men as members of First Platoon, at least what was left of it. Continuing to snake forward, Pete spotted First Lt. Mike Cornwall. His platoon leader was sitting in a shell crater talking with Cpl. Ed Baker, team leader with the company's mortar section.

"If we get the go-ahead tomorrow to attack the airstrip," Cornwall was saying, "are you sure your guys can provide us with enough support?"

"We'll do what we can, Skipper, but I gotta tell ya, the ammo supply ain't good. We're tryin' to git more but the beach situation's all fucked up."

The lanky Tennessean continued, "On the bright side, we'll have fire support from Fox Company's mortars on our right and Charlie Company's stovepipes to our rear. We'll start dropping shit on the Nips half an hour before you jump off. We also have a few smokers we can use to help you get across that airstrip."

"That's something anyway," Cornwall said, obviously discouraged. "I just hope we have enough guys left by jump-off time to pull it off."

Baker nodded.

"This will help a little," Pete injected, removing the haversack Deaver had carried. "There are a few rounds in here. Deaver got hit in the shoulder coming ashore."

Baker accepted the bag with gratitude.

"Every little bit helps," he said. "Thanks, Hardball."

Then he left.

"Glad you made it," Cornwall told him. "Your squad is down that way." He pointed. "Cpl. McDougal is in charge. Banks didn't make it."

Pete nodded and was about to depart when Nicholson slid into the shell hole.

"Well, well," Nicholson said. "Look who decided to get back into the war." He clapped Pete on the shoulder. "Glad you're here, Talbot."

"Thanks, Gunny," he replied. "You have no idea how glad I am to be back."

"Last time I saw you, you were with Deaver and Feather Merchant," Nicholson said.

Pete nodded.

"Deaver took one through the shoulder," Pete said. "I've got the BAR ammo he was carrying."

Wordlessly, Pete fished into a pocket and withdrew Ted's identity disc. He handed it to Nicholson who glanced at it and handed it to Cornwall.

"Another letter for you to write, Skipper," Nicholson said glumly.

"Thanks, Gunny," the lieutenant replied sarcastically. "I thought I might run out of things to do."

"Have you seen anybody else from the platoon?" Nicholson asked. "We're missing a helluva lot of guys."

"Banks, Marino, Duggan," Pete said.

"I know about them," Nicholson said. "How about that feather merchant with the damned TBX?"

"I came across Colby on the beach," Pete said. "He didn't know me, Gunny. He'd gone fuckin' Asiatic. A doc took him away."

"The radio?" Cornwall asked.

"He didn't have it, sir," Pete answered. "I looked around but couldn't find it."

"Damn," Cornwall cursed.

Nicholson simply nodded and said, "Rejoin your squad, all eight of 'em. You'll find them holding our left flank. I'll be checkin' the line shortly."

Pete nodded. *Eight*, he thought. *Holy shit.* Then he was off, crawling along the platoon line like a sand crab.

Reaching the portion of the line defended by Second Squad, Pete discovered Pfc. Bernie "Rosie" Roseblum reclining by a shattered palm tree, cradling the BAR in his arms. By his side, and keeping watch on the enemy, was the squad's Texan, Private Sandobar "Sandy" Gutierrez, son of Mexican immigrants. Pete unslung the BAR ammo belt.

"Rosie," he said, gently tossing the belt toward the man. "Thought you might need this."

Roseblum snatched at the belt and said, "Thanks, Hardball. Good to see you."

Pete moved on, next reaching a short trench manned by McDougal, Honeybun, and Chuck "Bucket" Harnish. The latter happily clapped Pete on the back. Like Pete, the boy from St. Albans, Vermont, earned his nickname in boot camp. When the new inductees reported to Parris Island one of the first items they were issued was a metal bucket. For the first couple of weeks, the boots carried their buckets everywhere. Harnish forgot his bucket two days in a row. For the first infraction, their DI, "Bull Moose" Blakely, ordered Harnish to take his bucket and collect five hundred blades of grass, no easy task on the sun-parched plains of Parris Island.

"Not 499 and not 501," Blakely barked. "500. Exactly. They will be counted."

For the second infraction, Harnish had to place the bucket on his head and repeat "I am a shithead" over and over until Blakely told him to stop. If his voice faltered or he showed a lack of enthusiasm, Blakely and his assistant, Mike Collingwood, whacked the side of the bucket with MP night sticks. Harnish never forgot his bucket again, but he had earned his official nickname.

"Hey, Mac," Pete greeted McDougal.

"The lost lamb returns," McDougal said. "Find a foxhole and make yourself at home, Hardball. You'll find three guys in the next hole. Grab one and extend the line to the left about fifteen feet."

Nodding, Pete moved on. As McDougal had said, he came across a small, shallow Japanese rifle trench. Hunkered down inside he found Steve Aldrich, Miklos "Mickey Mouse" Kusaka, and Reb Marshall. Pete dropped into the trench and was greeted by his friends so enthusiastically that it embarrassed him.

"We'uns thought you was floatin' face down in the lagoon," Reb said, his helmet in his lap so the sun could dry his sweaty, straw-colored hair.

"Goddamned Japs tried," Pete replied.

He relayed some of his experiences of the day. His listeners were dismayed when he told them of Ted's death.

"He asked me to visit his mother when I get home," Pete said. "Then he died in my arms."

"He was a good little feller fer a Yankee," Reb intoned.

"Yeah," the Professor said with a sardonic chuckle. "It's so ironic. He was always boasting about how many Japs he was going to kill. Then he never even makes it to shore."

"Well, he got one Jap," Pete said. He held up his Garand. "This is Feather Merchant's weapon."

"You killed a Nip?" Mickey Mouse asked.

"Deader than shit," Pete replied. "But what's so funny is that with all the stuff I seen since landing, that was the only goddamn round I fired at the enemy all day."

"One bullet, one kill," said Nicholson as he slid into the trench behind Pete. "Sounds like you did the job the Corps trained you to do."

"It'll be dark in a couple of hours and it looks like we'll be here for the night," he continued, "so I want everyone to buddy up. There are Japs in the trenches out in front of us. We don't know how many or what they plan to do, so keep your eyes open. We expect a large Banzai attack sometime after dark. Maybe more than one, so I want fifty percent alert at all times. One hour on, one hour off." There was a sudden roar of engines off to the left.

"What the hell?" Nicholson spat as he saw two Japanese tanks clanking along on the airstrip's runway.

"Down!" Nicholson roared.

Pete and the others dove for the bottom of the trench as the two tanks pumped machine gun fire and 37mm shells into the American positions. All along the thin line Marines scrambled for cover.

"Fire on the sons of bitches!" Nicholson barked.

A smattering of gunfire broke out along the line followed by the pinging sound as their bullets glanced off the tanks' armor plating.

As he fired his Garand, Pete wondered if one of these tanks was the same one he saw on the beach when Ted was killed. Pete smiled to himself as one of the tanks seemed to stall out. Above the gunfire he could hear grinding as the driver frantically tried to restart the cantankerous engine. Meanwhile the vehicle's machine guns continued spewing rounds. Pete tried to imagine the men inside desperately attempting to kick over the tank's motor. Finally it coughed, sputtered, then roared to life and the two steel beasts rumbled off in the direction from which they had come, dinged by bullets, but otherwise unharmed.

Calling for a cease-fire, Nicholson said, more to himself than to his men, "If we had any fuckin' armor support they wouldn't be so damned gutsy."

Nicholson headed back for the CP.

Pete and Aldrich left the small trench and crawled to the east. The ground was heavily debris-strewn, mostly detritus from a shattered structure that had stood nearby. Splintered planks, part of a work bench, twisted sheet metal, tools, many still intact, and a blasted fuel drum indicated that the building might have been a repair shop, possibly for the aircraft. To reinforce that conjecture, a fighter plane, a red "meat ball" on its fuselage, lay just beyond, smashed as if stepped on by a giant.

Pete and Aldrich arrived at the edge of a shallow bomb crater. Crawling inside, both men unsheathed their entrenching tools and quickly deepened the hole. Finally "home," Pete eased off his pack for the first time that day then sank back, making himself as comfortable as possible.

"I need to grab some z's," he said. "Keep an eye out, will ya?"

Without waiting for a response, Pete dozed off.

CHAPTER 9

As Onuki's tank drew to a halt alongside the concrete command bunker, Kenji Sakai threw back the hatch and scrambled out like a man on fire. It had been a harrowing journey from the cove, even after escaping from the American position they'd blundered into. During the five-hundred-yard trip, the *Ha-Go* had been hit numerous times by enemy small arms fire and strafed twice by American planes. Most of the rounds bounced noisily off the tank, but one pierced the *Ha-Go*'s inch-thick armor skin at the rear of the turret. It ricocheted around the crowded interior before spending its fury and dropping to the floor. The gods of war favored the men inside the tank.

Dropping heavily from the tank to the sand, Kenji settled his nerves by taking a gulp of water from his canteen. Onuki jumped down beside him and put a hand on Kenji's shoulder.

"Do kashiteiru?" Onuki asked.

Kenji nodded, recapping his canteen.

"I'm fine," he replied. *"Dozo.* That was a little frightening."

Onuki threw back his head and guffawed.

"I'll make a tanker out of you yet," he joked.

Kenji was about to reply when he spotted Lt. Chuma hurrying his way.

"I see you managed to find the tank," he barked, slapping his cherished riding crop against his leg. "Now get up off your ass and report to the bunker. Because of the number of wounded, Admiral Shibazaki is allowing his bunker to be used as a hospital. The platoon is helping to carry stretchers and bring in as many of the wounded as possible."

"Hai," Kenji said, rising to his feet and bowing.

"Incidentally, Lt. Yuasa is dead," Chuma snapped. "Now get about your duties."

Without awaiting a reply Chuma turned abruptly and hurried off on his next errand.

"I think that man eats nails for breakfast," Onuki quipped after Chuma departed.

"Nails are too tender," Kenji replied and headed for the bunker.

The world inside the mammoth concrete structure was a nightmare of suffering. Even under the best of conditions the interior with its maze of corridors and large rooms was badly lit and overcrowded. Now it stank of blood, sweat, urine, and feces, and the walls rang with moans and shrieks of the wounded.

Picking his way through this charnel house, Kenji spotted his friend Tanaka. Kenji approached him. Once beside Tanaka, Kenji looked around in horror.

"This is far worse than I ever imagined," he said.

Tanaka, his tunic a bloody mess, nodded as he knelt beside a man. Suffering from a chest wound, the soldier could barely draw breath.

"Hai," he said as he checked the meager dressings that tried in vain to stem the bleeding. "I've been made a medic assistant. I've never done this kind of work."

Kenji nodded sadly.

"What happened to Lt. Yuasa?" he asked.

"We were helping carry a wounded man back from our bunker," Tanaka said. "A damned Yankee fighter attacked us. Bullets from the plane took Yuasa's head clean off. The wounded man was killed as well. Only I survived." He indicated his stained tunic. "Some of this is their blood."

Kenji stood silent, fixated on the carnage as the battle growled outside.

"Things aren't going well," he mused. "The Americans have suffered heavily, but so have we—and they have a beachhead."

"This bunker is heavily defended," Tanaka assured him. "I think we can hold it."

"And if we can't?" Kenji asked. "If the Americans break through, how do we move so many men inland to safety?"

"We don't," Tanaka replied. "The walking wounded are already being patched up and returned to the fighting. Grenades will be issued to those unable to return to duty. The rest are to be shot."

Absorbing the news, Kenji silently knelt beside another suffering man to see what comfort he could give. As he worked, the bunker was shaken by a loud rumble and concrete dust filtered down on the men as a bomb or large naval shell detonated against the bunker's steel-reinforced shell.

Amid the violence and clamor of the war going on around him, Kenji thought about his brother Ichiro. Unlike Kenji, Ichiro was never content with life in their tranquil fishing village.

Ichiro was blessed, or cursed, with a restless spirit. A life of toiling long hours fishing to reap whatever bounty provided by *Ryujin*, the great *kami* dragon of the sea, was not for him. So perhaps it was karma that rather than wait until he was conscripted, Ichiro volunteered for the army as soon as he came of age. He'd been assigned to the Twenty-Fifth Army under General Tomoyuki Yamashita during the invasion of Malaysia and was heavily engaged against the British at the battle for Singapore.

"I had the great honor of seeing the humiliation of the arrogant British officers as they walked into our lines carrying a white flag and suffering the disgrace of surrender," Ichiro wrote. "No honorable Japanese soldier would have endured such shame."

Kneeling over the desperately injured man, Kenji hoped Ichiro was safe.

As he worked a soldier burst into the room and shouted, "Attention! Attention! I have a message from the Imperial Palace. It is from our emperor." He stopped and bowed in the rough direction of Tokyo. "You have all fought gallantly," he read in a crisp, authoritative voice. "May you continue to fight to the death. Banzai."

Having performed his duty, the man raced from the room as quickly as he had appeared, disappearing down one of the dark passageways to deliver his news elsewhere.

Kenji's spirits plunged into gloom. *We have been written off,* he thought. *The Imperial Fleet will not be coming. We are dead men.*

————————

Petty Officer Toyojiro Hamada, who commanded the only other working tank assigned to protect the command bunker, hurried up to Onuki. He handed Onuki written orders from Admiral Shibazaki's second in command, Lt. Commander Wataru Esaka.

"We are to proceed to the airfield," he told Onuki. "The Admiral wants to know how far inland the enemy has advanced."

Alert for roving enemy fighters, Onuki led the two tanks to the airfield runway. They'd gone just over three hundred yards when small arms fire erupted to their right and bullets began to plunk off the vehicle's armored skin. Ordering a halt, Onuki slammed his hatch closed and cranked his turret in the direction of the fusillade. Spotting the source of the gunfire about a hundred feet north of the edge of the runway, he cut loose with his machine gun. Honing in on Onuki's tracers, Shugo pressed the trigger of his machine gun as well and together they raked the enemy line. An American .30 caliber machine gun began to stutter, its bullets clanging off the *Ha-Go*'s flanks. Onuki marked the gun's position from its red tracers. Loading a three-pound shell into the tank's 37mm gun, he pressed the trigger. The explosion from the round blossomed well in front of the enemy gun. Adjusting his elevation, Onuki fired another round which landed squarely on the pesky American weapon.

Then Onuki's expression of triumph turned to one of horror. While maneuvering the two seven-ton tanks into a better firing position, his unpredictable Mitsubishi engine failed again. Fearing that American planes would show up at any time, Onuki yelled to Mitsuru to get the motor started.

"I'm trying," his driver called back.

The ignition ground and ground as the eager Mitsuru strove to bring the engine back to life. Meanwhile Onuki and Shugo continued to pour fire at the Americans, as did Hamada's crew as his tank now pulled up close to Onuki's.

After several futile attempts, Onuki said, "We may have to abandon the tank. If we do, take cover behind Hamada."

"What about you?" Shugo asked between bursts from his machine gun.

"I will open valves and let gas flood into the turret," he said. "Then I will crawl out and drop a grenade inside to blow up our tank."

"You won't have enough time to escape," Mitsuru insisted.

"Then my spirit will see you both at Yasukuni Shrine," Onuki concluded.

He was about to give the order when Mitsuru's efforts finally paid off and the engine roared loudly. All three men beamed with delight.

"Now get us out of here!" Onuki yelled over the roar, gesturing with his hand for further emphasis.

Together, the two tanks retraced their path and retreated toward the command bunker, dented from enemy bullets but otherwise unscathed.

Safely back, Onuki left his two comrades by the tank as he dismounted and entered the command bunker in search of Esaka to report his findings. Knowing the command center was on the upper level of the three-story bunker, Onuki quickly moved through the airless, steamy passageways and through rooms echoing with the agonized moans of wounded men. Reaching a concrete staircase that led to the upper floors, Onuki bounded up the steps. At the top, he turned left and entered a large room. By an observation slit he spotted Admiral Shibazaki, binoculars to his eyes, scrutinizing the battle. Three aides stood anxiously by his side. Esaka was by a second observation slit when he spotted Onuki. He approached the tank commander. Onuki saluted, then related his experience, noting that he had run into enemy fire about three hundred yards west of the command bunker.

"How close are they to the airstrip?" Esaka asked.

"About a hundred feet," Onuki replied. "But it seems to be a narrow penetration. Also, from the volume of fire I'd say their line is thinly held."

Esaka nodded thoughtfully then turned to Shibazaki, who had ceased watching the battle and was listening to Onuki's report.

"If that's the case," the admiral mused, addressing Esaka, "then perhaps a determined counterattack after dark could break their line and possibly even cause their entire front to collapse. We could then drive the survivors into the sea."

Esaka agreed.

"It certainly coincides with reports we are getting from our units to the west." Shibazaki paused, then continued, "Commander Sugai says the Americans there are being held in check, and that their advance in the center is just a weak salient; a paper dagger easy to snap off."

The admiral and his deputy discussed their plan together, neglecting Onuki who remained at rigid attention.

"Since I am turning this bunker over to the medical staff, we shall move my headquarters to the south so that I have more control in the upcoming fight," Shibazaki said. "I want as many men as can be collected to launch a diversionary attack on the Americans while we relocate. I also want a platoon of men to escort us and provide cover in case we are attacked."

"I will alert Lt. Chuma's platoon," Esaka said.

"Very well," Shibazaki said. He consulted his watch. "We will move in about thirty minutes."

Esaka saluted then turned to Onuki.

"Return to your tank and make preparations," he said. "Also find Lt. Chuma and have him report to me."

Onuki saluted and left. As he hastened through the bunker toward his tank, he gave an involuntary shudder at the prospect of the desperate attack. For the first time since he arrived on Betio, he regretted giving up his previous assignment as a truck driver at the Sasebo naval station in hopes of seeing action.

Stepping outside the thick concrete bunker, Onuki drew in a deep breath of air that, while heavy with the scent of gunpowder and smoke, was still preferable to the hellish smell of death he had breathed inside the three-story house of misery. Glancing around, he hoped to see Kenji and fill him in on what he had heard firsthand from Admiral Shibazaki. Not spotting his young friend, Onuki returned to his tank to get his crew ready for battle.

CHAPTER 10

Kenji was unaware of any planned shift in Shibazaki's headquarters. Since arriving back after finding Onuki, he and the remnants of Second Squad had been helping the wounded. Relieved of that duty, the entire platoon now manned a trench forward of the command bunker. Two hundred yards ahead the squad could clearly see Americans struggling for every inch as they advanced. Yet they were told to hold their own fire unless the bunker itself came under attack.

"I feel useless sitting here while our comrades are fighting and dying right before our eyes," Seaman Third Class Masaichi Nagata muttered to Kenji. "Why can't we advance against the enemy's flank?"

"Because we're ordered to remain here as security for the admiral," Kenji replied. "But don't get too anxious. Before this all ends, you'll get your share of fighting." Then he smiled to his friend. "You are a long way from your father's tailor shop."

"Yes," the young man agreed. "The hills that embrace Nagasaki would look real good to me right now."

The men stopped chatting when they saw Chumo hurrying toward them as fast as his short, squat legs would carry him.

"My platoon, fall in," Chumo bellowed. "Form a line right here." For emphasis, he used his riding crop to draw an imaginary line on the sand ahead of him. The twenty-three men of Chuma's command, all that remained of First Platoon, obeyed instantly. Chuma then led them to where Shibazaki and his staff, having just emerged from the bunker, were huddled in discussion.

"We've been given the honor of providing an escort for Admiral Shibazaki," Chuma bellowed. "The admiral is shifting his headquarters, and we will be leaving soon under the cover of a diversionary attack led by Chief Petty Officer Onuki's tank. You may break ranks for now but stay close and be prepared to reassemble quickly."

The men obeyed and sat about talking among themselves. Some fired up cigarettes. Others took swigs of water from their canteens or munched on a rice ball. Kenji watched somberly as two soldiers emerged from the command bunker carrying stacks of documents. They advanced about ten feet from the bunker before setting the paper piles down side by side. Then one man lit a match and held it to the paper, which soon flared up as more and more sheets succumbed to the flames.

They're burning all our official documents, Kenji thought.

More papers were brought out and fed into the fire. Then Kenji gulped as the garrison's national colors were brought out and added to the conflagration. Shibazaki watched the burning of the colors with great solemnity, saluting smartly as the flames consumed the silk banner. His staff followed suit, saluting while the tears staining their cheeks glistened in the sunlight.

The pillar of white smoke from the flag's funeral pyre rising into the air made Kenji nervous.

"We should move from here," Kenji said to Takashima who was standing next to him. "The longer we stay in the open, the more chance of that smoke being spotted by an American plane or by a lookout on one of those destroyers in the lagoon."

Kenji kept his voice low. He did not want to be overheard doubting the commanding officer's actions.

"Be careful that Chumo doesn't hear you criticizing our officers or he may label you *gekokujo*. Shibazaki knows what he is doing," Takashima assured his friend. "We will move out soon."

Gekokujo? Kenji certainly didn't want his feelings of concern to be misinterpreted as insubordination. He shrugged and walked toward Onuki's tank about twenty-five yards away. Onuki was sitting on the sand behind the steel beast, poking through the tank's mechanical workings.

"Is your tank broken again?" Kenji asked half in jest.

"As a matter of fact it is," Onuki replied. "While Admiral Shibazaki and his staff move to a new location, I've been instructed to lead a diversionary attack. The trouble is, the cursed clutch is burned out and I'm not sure I can move this hulk."

"My detachment is escorting the admiral," Kenji said. Then he added sarcastically, "That is, if they decide to move out anytime soon." He paused a moment, regretting that he'd let his anger slip out. But Onuki, if he noticed, said nothing. "I must get back," Kenji said and left.

Onuki waved, then pounded on the tank's steel hull and yelled to his two crewmen inside the turret, "Get out here! I need some help."

Kenji saw Mitsuru emerge, followed by Shugo. Both men perched atop the tank while they spoke with Onuki who remained on the ground.

Kenji had covered about half the distance back to his platoon when a volley of 5-inch shells from a destroyer came crashing down. The first landed just beyond Onuki's tank, the blast hurling Onuki to the ground and sweeping away Mitsuru and Shugo. Two blinks of an eye later a second shell landed amid the waiting group of soldiers and a third squarely hit the bonfire by which the commanding officer and his staff were standing. A fourth shell plowed into the earth between the command and hospital bunkers, killing a dozen wounded men lying exposed along the bunker's southern wall.

The almost simultaneous explosions had a devastating effect, with men and parts of men pitching skyward. Kenji was bowled over as if viciously struck by an invisible fist. He writhed on the sand, a burning sensation in his left arm and the breath knocked completely from his body. Rolling and gasping like a fish in one of his father's nets, he fought to pull air into his lungs. On the verge of blacking out, convinced that death was just moments away, Kenji was finally able to draw a breath of smoky yet blessed oxygen into his tortured body.

Breathing deeply now, Kenji lay quietly on the sand for several minutes.

Slowly, he sat up, shaking his head to stop the loud ringing in his ears. His upper arm just below the shoulder felt warm and wet, and fingers that went probing the source came back bloody. A visual inspection confirmed that he had been grazed by shrapnel just below the left armpit.

Then he felt hands gently trying to lift him to his feet.

"Are you all right, Kenji-san?" a worried voice said. It was Onuki.

"I think so," Kenji replied.

"You're hit," Onuki said, spotting blood on Kenji's shirt. "Let's get you to the aid station."

Kenji nodded and allowed Onuki to guide him. Gazing ahead, Kenji's heart sank. Where moments ago his platoon had been assembling, he now saw nothing but carnage straight from a slaughterhouse. Not one man remained on his feet. Instead, bodies, some intact, others torn apart, lay scattered to all points of the compass on the scorched ground. Kenji shrugged off Onuki's helping hand and stumbled drunkenly toward the devastation. Shuffling among the dead, tears filled Kenji's eyes as he took it all in. Many men were unrecognizable, but not all. Lt. Chuma had been cut in two at the waist, the portions of his body lying perpendicular to one another forming a bloody T. Chuma's cherished riding crop remained clutched in his dead hand, its menacing slapping motion stilled at last.

Kenji discovered the head of Seaman Tadashi Araki, a factory worker from Kyoto, lying two feet from a headless torso, presumably his own. Kenji's friend, Tanaka, most recently serving as an unwilling medical assistant inside the command bunker, had both legs blown off. He had quickly bled out. A talented artist, he would never return home and take over his father's kimono shop. Kenji found remains he thought might belong to Seaman Yoshijiro Watari, the son of an Okinawan rice farmer, but he couldn't be certain. He could find no sign of either his friend, the pessimistic Harumi Takashima, Nagata, the tailor's son from Nagasaki, or of his squad leader, Kazunari Ihara. Maybe they survived or maybe they didn't. There were at least a dozen men whose bodies had been mauled beyond identification.

Kenji slowly walked toward the smoking crater that gaped malevolently near where Shibazaki and his staff had been standing. He stopped short, sickened by what lay before him. Rear Admiral Keiji Shibazaki; his number two man, Lt. Commander Wataru Esaka; his adjutant, Lt. Fujisawa Shigeo, and the rest had been blown out of existence.

Some walking wounded and medical orderlies from the field hospital now began to arrive and scour this place of death. Feeble moans were heard from the very few men who survived. Kenji's thoughts turned to Onuki and he rejoined his friend. As he did he nearly tripped over another body. It was Harumi Takashima, his fancy-stitched *senninbari* that Kenji had seen him wrap around his waist that very morning now saturated with blood. Ravaged by the explosion, Takashima's torso was brutally ripped open. As Kenji said a silent prayer for his dead friend he gaped in horror as he realized that this shattered man was still alive. As if awakened by Kenji's presence, Takashima opened his eyes and gazed up at his friend, hopelessness and agony radiating from his soft, round face. Takashima, a realist to the last, knew he was dying.

Unable to talk because his windpipe had been shredded, Takashima weakly lifted his right hand and, pointing his index finger at his own head, pantomimed shooting himself.

Kenji knew what his friend meant. Tears began to well from Kenji's eyes as Harumi renewed his silent plea, using the last of his strength to beg his friend to release him from his torment. Ignoring the pain of his own wound, Kenji unslung his rifle, chambered a round, and lowered the muzzle to just a few inches from Harumi's forehead. Closing his eyes, Kenji squeezed the trigger. Despite the rolling thunder of the surrounding battle, the single crack of the Arisaka rang out loudly. Without looking down at his dead friend, Kenji trudged off in Onuki's direction, weeping as he went.

"My friends are gone, too," Onuki said in a whispered tone as if speaking louder might offend the dead. "I looked for Mitsuru and Shugo but couldn't even find remains. Just a few traces of blood on the tank body."

Kenji nodded and allowed Onuki to guide him toward the hospital bunker.

Inside, Kenji had to await treatment while overworked *eisei-hei* tended those with more severe wounds. Onuki, who like many others had briefly helped tend the injured, examined Kenji's wound himself and found it contained no shrapnel. He sprinkled the cut with sulfa powder and wrapped it with a bandage from his own first aid kit.

"That should hold you for a while," he said. "You were very fortunate."

Kenji nodded and the two friends settled back in a corner of the bunker, leaning their backs against the wall. Outside the battle ebbed and flowed, sounding distant at some moments and just outside the doorway at others.

"We're a fine pair you and me, Kenji-san," Onuki said with a sardonic chuckle. "You're an assistant squad leader who's lost his squad, and I'm a tank commander who lost his tank."

"It sounds like the Americans are gaining a foothold," Kenji mused.

"They have, but it is a weak one," Onuki said and related to Kenji the details of his patrol. "I heard Admiral Shibazaki say he was going to order strong counterattacks tonight that he believed would collapse the thin American line and push the Yankees back into the lagoon."

"But the admiral is dead," Kenji pointed out. "So is Commander Esaka. There is no one left to order the attacks."

Both men knew what that meant. The island was lost and so were they.

Just then a disheveled man, his uniform torn and bloodstained from minor wounds, raced into the bunker. It was Nagao Shirasaki, one of Onuki's tank commanders. He was clutching a sword in his hand.

"Shirasaki," Onuki called to his comrade. "What is happening?"

"I just killed a dozen Americans," he loudly proclaimed. Then he spoke to every man within earshot. "Who among you will come with me and kill more of our cursed enemy?"

Ten of the walking wounded stood up and left the aid station, snatching up whatever weapons they could find. Both Onuki and Kenji knew it was a suicide mission.

"Fools," Onuki muttered. "Those men are going to just throw their lives away in some reckless charge rather than fight on."

Kenji did not reply. Rather, his mind drifted to his own plight. He did not necessarily want to die. He hadn't even wanted to fight. But isn't that what he'd been trained to do since childhood?

Like the other boys, Kenji wore his blue uniform to school. Each morning, toting toy rifles, the children would march outside to the schoolyard, forming straight columns before the school's *goshin'ei* shrine. Prominently displayed inside were photographs of Empress Kojun and of Hirohito, the 124th emperor of Japan, a direct descendent of Amaterasu, the goddess of the sun. The shrine also held a copy of the Imperial Rescript on Education from which the teacher would read, "Should any emergency arise, offer yourself courageously to the state and thus guard against and maintain the prosperity of Our Imperial Throne, coeval with heaven and earth." Then he would face the students and shout, "What is your dearest ambition?" "To die for the emperor," the children gleefully hollered back.

Student playtime included close order drill, judo, and kendo, as well as combat with long bamboo poles. As they grew older, the children took part in war games. The army supplied airplanes, and ammunition for the small-caliber rifles which the boys were issued. Kenji participated in these activities, even if his soul was not in them. His nature, unlike his brother Ichiro's, was not warlike. He would've been content to spend his life with his father aboard their fishing boat. But to show any sign of weakness, he knew, put one in jeopardy of ridicule, and he did not wish to be dubbed a *yowamushi*, or worm. After school was finished, Kenji did not go on to the university, so he was obliged to register for military service. Having done that, he returned to his father's boat until such time as he was called to active duty.

Inevitably the war caught up to him. A uniformed man and a contingent of elderly women arrived at his home one fall day in late 1942 to deliver the red postcard informing Kenji that he had "the honor to be conscripted into the service of His Majesty the emperor." He knew the day was coming but still, staring at the card in his hand and looking at the politely smiling face of the old man who had been dispatched to deliver it, he felt stunned. Kenji swallowed hard.

"You have been honored, sir," the man said, and bowed.

Kenji, as required, returned the bow and the man departed, carrying more red cards so honoring other young men.

As the date for his departure neared, family and friends gathered for a *sokokai*, or a marching party. Everyone bade him farewell, urging him to perform great acts of patriotism. There were no indications of sorrow, and no words of pity at his leaving, just heartfelt congratulations at the privilege of serving the emperor.

On the prescribed day, a military bus arrived to take him and other conscripts to meet a troop train at Kanazawa at the base of the Noto Peninsula. Before he mounted the steps to enter the bus, his mother, bowing deeply to her son, presented him with a *senninbari*, his thousand-stitch belt.

"Wear this, Kenji," his mother said, her impassive face masking the emotional turmoil that raged inside her. "And the gods will watch over you."

"Hai, Mother," he replied, bowing respectfully.

Then he stood stiffly and allowed her to wrap the belt a time and a half around his waist, before tying it securely. Goro Sakai next draped his war souvenir, the gold coin, over his son's neck.

"This Russian coin brought me strength and protection in battle, and it will do the same for you against the American devils," Goro said.

Caught up in emotion, Kenji bowed deeply and said, "*Domo*, Father. *Domo arigato.*"

A final embrace for his mother, and a deep, reverent bow to his father, and Kenji Sakai was off to join the war.

At the train station at Kanazawa, the new conscripts were met by members of the National Defense Women's Organization who passed out tea and rice cakes and wished them victory or a glorious death in battle.

Kenji's destination was Nagasaki Prefecture. Because he stood at five feet, eleven inches and was familiar with the sea, he had been assigned to the Navy's 7th Special Naval Landing Force based at Sasebo Naval Base. The SNLF was elite and had a proud tradition. Kenji recalled one instructor who drilled into the recruits the importance of the bayonet, linking it to the warrior spirit as the modern equivalent of the samurai sword. This *Seishin Kyoiku*, or spiritual training, was the very foundation of all their training and preparation.

"When you fix this bayonet, it's much more than merely attaching a steel blade to your rifle," the instructor informed the recruits. "It places iron into the soul of the soldier." He held the rifle aloft. "Your weapon is the symbol of our military spirit and the personal property of His Majesty, the emperor. You, too, are the emperor's property. Always remember that faith equals strength. Any misuse of this weapon is an act of irreverence and a corruption of the divinity of your soul. And also remember, you are more than just a soldier. You are the modern spirit of our samurai ancestors."

The modern spirit of our samurai ancestors. The words echoed in Kenji's brain as he listened to the fight outside. He was a fisherman, not a warrior. What was he doing here? He turned and looked at Onuki.

"What are you going to do, Tadao?" Kenji asked.

"My tank is here," Onuki said. "I will remain with my tank. The tank can't move but its machine guns still work. What about you?"

Kenji thought a moment then said, "After dark I will return to *shujin*. What's left of my company is still there. I will fight from the bunker."

"I was hoping you would remain here by my side so we can fight together," Onuki said. "We have both lost nearly all of our friends today. It would be nice to fight and die beside a familiar face."

Kenji smiled.

"I don't plan to throw my life away like others we have seen," Kenji said. "I will fall back and fight as long as I can."

"I have already heard men speak of wading from Betio to one of the other islands in the atoll and setting up new defensive positions," Onuki said. "Perhaps we can do that."

Kenji nodded.

"Maybe we can," he replied, and the pair lapsed into silence, both lost in contemplation of their bleak futures.

In the protection afforded by the hospital bunker, the two men huddled close together as outside the American attack seemed to stall. Kenji thought of the many friends who had died this day and marveled that he had survived. Then a new image came to his mind, that of a young American courageously dragging his injured comrade to shore, braving a wall of Japanese fire to save a friend. He wondered how the man fared, if he survived this first day or not. Oddly Kenji hoped he had.

As the silence of the night fell across the battlefield, they agreed that in the darkness they'd begin to make their way to Bairiki to fight again.

CHAPTER 11

The dream was always the same. It began with the startling crash like a sudden peal of thunder as depth charges burst in the water close by the submerged USS *Grampus*. The blasts jarred the boat and sent the men inside sprawling to the deck or grappling for handholds. In the cramped radio room just aft of the control room, Seaman First Class Charles Franklin Talbot was sitting on the steel floor pressed into a corner, knees drawn tightly to his chest, tears of terror flowing from his deep blue eyes.

Two more depth charges erupted, the concussion rocking the submarine to starboard.

Overhead could be heard the muffled thrashing of the propellers as two Japanese destroyers relentlessly rolled two-hundred-pound charges off their fantails.

Three more depth charges burst almost simultaneously outside the *Grampus*, ruthlessly slamming the boat around like a dog shaking a rabbit. Despite orders for silent running, men in the control room shouted, cursed, and prayed. Then came the sound of rushing water, a lot of water, pouring into the sub, flowing down the companionway like a river.

"Pete!" Charlie screamed as the water flooding into the radio room reached his chin. "Pete!"

"Charlie!" Pete cried aloud, sitting bolt upright.

"You okay, Hardball?" Aldrich asked, startled by the outburst.

Pete looked at his foxhole partner as he remembered where he was.

"Yeah," Pete replied, sweat rolling down his forehead. "I'm fine."

After a pause, Aldrich asked, "Who's Charlie?"

"Don't fuckin' worry about it," Pete replied. He had not told anyone about Charlie except for Ted Giovanni and only after being worn down by incessant badgering.

"Sorry," Aldrich said. "I didn't mean to pry. Jeez. No wonder they call you Hardball."

"I didn't mean to bite your head off, Professor," Pete said. "It's just a bad dream I keep having."

"Wanna talk about it?" Aldrich offered.

"No," Pete said curtly.

"Just trying to help," Aldrich said. "My major in college was psychology."

"Oh great," Pete moaned. "A foxhole shrink."

"Psychology, not psychiatry," Aldrich said. "Behavioral sciences. I like studying people."

"Then you're in the right place," Pete replied.

Pete sat back, rubbing his eyes with the back of a sleeve. The dream had begun shortly after he had departed from San Diego for the three-week zigzag voyage to New Zealand. And it was always the same, with Charlie dying a slow and terrifying death and shouting for his brother. What pissed Pete off was he had no idea how Charlie died. Maybe it was gradual like in the dream, or maybe the damned pig boat just exploded. Who knew? He certainly didn't. All he knew for sure was that his brother was forever entombed in the wreckage of the USS *Grampus* on the bottom of Blackett Strait in the Solomon Islands.

So why was the dream so detailed? Was Charlie reaching out from beyond the grave to blame Pete for failing to protect him, not from the Japs, but from their own father?

Pete's thoughts were interrupted by an ungodly racket from the gathering darkness.

"What the hell . . .?" Pete moaned as he tried to focus his eyes.

"Better get ready," the Professor said. "It sounds like the Japs are whipping themselves up. They might be getting ready to attack."

As Pete and Aldrich steeled themselves, they listened to the jabbering voices.

The platoon line was about forty yards from the edge of the runway. About seventy feet in front of Pete's foxhole was a major Japanese defensive position consisting of a long trench flanking a coconut-log pillbox.

"They're not good at noise discipline, are they?" Pete quipped.

"It's to pump up their nerves and scare the crap out of us," the Professor answered.

Suddenly Cpl. McDougal was lying prone in the sand behind the foxhole.

"They'll be coming," he told the two privates. "When they do, don't fire 'til ordered, then give 'em hell. Whatever you do, stay put. We're holding this line."

"Right, Mac," both men said, and he was gone.

The evening shadows had deepened and Pete gazed to the west where the sun seemed balanced on the edge of the Central Pacific, its color as red as the blood spilled on this gruesome island.

What a waste of a gorgeous sunset, Pete thought.

Suddenly out in front came a cry of "*Totsugeki.*" A hundred Japanese soldiers seemed to spew from the earth led by a pistol-wielding officer who again shouted "*Totsugeki.*" Charging as ordered, the attackers did not fire their rifles but carried them waist-high, gleaming bayonets thrust forward. Covering the ground quickly they were soon sixty feet away from the Americans' line. Then fifty feet. Then forty.

Someone yelled "fire" and the Marines opened up. The crack of rifles, the chatter of Thompsons, and the bark of Rosie's BAR rippled along the perimeter. The first rank of attackers, including the officer, fell as if they'd hit a trip wire. Another fusillade from the Marines and more Japanese dropped.

Pete and the Professor fired into the charging mass as rapidly as they could work the triggers. To his right, Pete saw a few of the enemy cracking the Marine line, overrunning the remnants of First Platoon. The two sides grappled hand-to-hand with bayonets and Ka-Bars. Above the clamor Pete heard shouts and cries of anger and pain as steel bit into flesh. Then the intruders were all dead.

The attack quickly spent its fury as the battered remnants of the assault slipped back into their trench. The rest were sprawled across the landscape. Most lay quietly but a few twitched and whimpered and cried weakly for "mizu."

"What the hell is mizu?" Pete asked. "They callin' for a medic?"

"No," Aldrich replied. "Mizu is water." Pete glanced at the Professor who shrugged. "I know a few Japanese words. I also like studying languages."

Despite the obvious suffering of these wounded men, no one was foolish enough to risk going out to help. To do so guaranteed that the Good Samaritan would catch a Japanese bullet, either from the enemy line or from the wounded man himself. Those unable to crawl back to their trench would remain where they were either until the Americans took that patch of no-man's-land or until they were dead.

Surveying the carnage, Pete muttered, "What fuckin' madness."

Aldrich nodded, then he was silent for a while. The two men went for nearly an hour without exchanging a word until Aldrich gave a soft yawn.

"I need to grab some sack time, Hardball," he said. "Can you keep an eye out?"

"No problem," Pete replied, but the Professor was already asleep.

By 2000 hours the sun had dropped below the horizon and darkness fell like a curtain. A refreshingly cool breeze kicked up, carrying away the heated air and blowing out to sea the all-pervading stench of death. For the first time since landing, Pete could draw in a breath of air without almost retching. The tide had begun to ebb again, carrying the bodies that had been left floating in the lagoon out beyond the reef. Pete hoped Ted had been recovered by now or at the very least that the tide had not carried him away.

Keeping his eyes focused on the dark ground ahead, Pete recalled his first meeting with Feather Merchant aboard the train that would carry them to Parris Island, South Carolina.

——————

Stepping into the dull-brown, Pullman Pete looked around for a suitable place to plant himself. He spotted one group of four seats, two facing front, two facing rearward, occupied solely by one olive-skinned young man with deep-set brown eyes, a broad nose, and thick, curly black hair. He was seated by the window facing forward.

"This taken?" Pete asked, pointing to the opposite window seat.

"No, no," the young man said eagerly. "Help yourself."

Pete tossed his well-worn high school gym bag in the overhead rack and dropped onto the upholstered seat. As he settled in the young man across from him stuck out a hand.

"Giovanni," he said, brightly, his eyes alight with eagerness to make a new acquaintance. "Ted Giovanni."

"Pete Talbot," he replied, giving the man's hand an obligatory shake.

His traveling partner then launched into a lengthy dialogue about being from the Bensonhurst section of Brooklyn, Sixty-Eighth Street near Twenty-First Avenue to be exact. To Pete's dismay, the young man explained his eagerness to join the Marines, especially after seeing his favorite actor, Robert Taylor, in a new movie entitled *Bataan*.

"I saw it and thought what a bunch of gritty fellows those Marines must be," Giovanni burbled. "And they have those snazzy blue uniforms, so I enlisted. I'm gonna get one of those suits just as soon as we get to Parris Island. You from Philly?"

"Almost," Pete replied vaguely.

"I never been to Philly," Giovanni said. "I never been much of anywhere beyond Brooklyn. What made you join the Marines?"

"The blue uniforms," Pete lied, then rested his head back against the seat, wondering where all of this was going to end. Undaunted by his companion's silence, the young man rambled on.

This is going to be a long, fucking train ride, Pete thought, and closed his eyes, trying to shut out the chatter. He hoped that when they reached Parris Island he and this annoying little twerp would be separated. But God, Pete soon learned, had a sense of humor. Not only were he and Ted assigned to the same drill platoon, but they ended up sharing a two-man tent. So little by little, day by day, week by week, Pete found himself being ground down by Giovanni's enthusiasm. Before he knew it he began to actually care about the guy.

———————

Now like Charlie, Ted was gone.

You fuckin' idiot, Pete scolded himself. *This is why you don't make friends. Guys like the Professor, Reb, Mickey Mouse, and the rest were good to fight beside. But you have to keep your distance.*

Did that go for Aggie as well?

Pete's reflections were interrupted when he thought he heard a faint scuffing sound coming from the blackness out in front. Since darkness fell, all had been quiet. *Too quiet*, he thought. A few gunshots echoed up and down the line. Maybe guys were shooting at Jap infiltrators, or maybe they were just nervously popping off at shadows. Either way, there had been no indication of the much-anticipated Banzai charge.

Yet.

"Wake up," Pete whispered, shaking Aldrich. "I thought I heard something."

"Like what?" came the groggy reply.

"I'm not sure," Pete answered.

Then came the noise again, a faint, shushing sound like something being dragged across the sand. Fingering the trigger of his rifle, Pete strained his eyes in hopes of penetrating the dark.

Nothing.

Maybe it was just a sand crab, he thought.

Then with heart-stopping suddenness a shadowy form rose up from just in front of the foxhole. The figure screamed as he charged forward, his rifle pointed at the Americans. Even though the moon had yet to rise, Pete could see the malevolent shape of a bayonet attached to the weapon's muzzle.

Instinctively Pete rolled left. As he did so his Garand barked twice. There was no need to aim. Both bullets tore into the charging man's chest. Still on his feet, the attacker's momentum carried him into the foxhole before he thudded to the ground. Terrified, Aldrich drew out his Ka-Bar and drove it into the man's body.

Pete was stunned, unable to speak or even move. He simply sagged against the side of the foxhole and stared at the huddled form lying on the sand. Aldrich, too, was speechless after the abruptness with which the one-man attack had burst upon them.

"Holy shit, where did he come from?" Aldrich blurted out, finally finding his voice.

"Out there," Pete puffed. "Bastard was probably playing possum waitin' for dark."

"How many more of them are pretending?" Aldrich wondered.

Still shaken, Pete couldn't answer.

"You fellas okay over there?" a voice from the next hole said in a loud whisper.

"Yeah," Aldrich responded as loudly as he dared. "We're fine, Mickey Mouse."

Pete removed one of his two canteens and took a long swig of the tepid water. Then he shook the canteen to see how much was left. Even conserving it as he did, under the day's blazing sun Pete had already gone through one canteen and the second was nearly half empty. He hoped more would come up soon.

About half an hour later the taunting began.

"Marine, you die tonight!" an unseen Japanese soldier yelled.

"We drink Marine blood!" another intoned.

As the shouts continued, a dark form appeared. It was Reb. He stopped at the rim of the foxhole.

"I'm passin' the word along from Nicholson," he whispered. "Japs may be fixin' to attack around midnight. Keep sharp. Hunnerd percent alert." He eyed the dead Japanese soldier. "Nice shootin' fer a coupla Yankees."

Out in front of them an unseen voice called, "Roosevelt eats shit!"

A bemused smile crossed Reb's face.

"Hope Ah don't have to shoot tha' boy," he said. "Ah think he's a fella Republican."

Reb returned to his foxhole.

"You know," the Professor said. "When the sun comes up in the morning this guy's gonna start drawing flies. We'd better move him now while it's dark."

Pete rose to his feet and grabbed the dead man by the collar. He dragged the corpse rearward. Ridding himself of his grisly burden, the release of tension caused his bowels to rumble. Spotting a fallen tree, he walked over to it, hiked down his dungarees and skivvies and squatted by the trunk. He craved a cigarette but dared not light one. Cleaning up with pieces torn from a palm leaf, Pete returned to his foxhole.

"You were gone long enough," the Professor chided. "Where'd you drag that Nip? Hoboken?"

"Nope," Pete said. "If I'd taken him there I wouldn't have come back."

Aldrich laughed and the two men resumed their vigil.

As the night deepened Pete remembered his last sunset aboard the USS *Zeilin*. Standing on the ship's stern, he recalled watching a pair of dolphins knife through the water beside the ship. He had even spotted the distant spray of water from a whale breaching the surface.

Sitting now in a dark foxhole almost within spitting distance of the enemy, Pete savored the memory of the setting sun as it painted the sky in shades of orange, crimson, and blue-gray. He would recall those blissful moments for the rest of his life, he thought, although he could not help but wonder how long that life would be.

"Charlie," Pete prayed to the stars overhead. "Wherever you are, watch over me."

PART II

SUNDAY, NOVEMBER 21, 1943

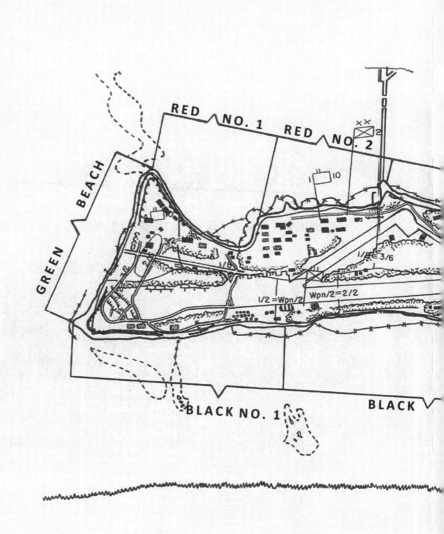

RED NO. 1　RED NO. 2

GREEN BEACH

BLACK NO. 1　BLACK

INTELLIGENCE MAP BITITU (BETIO) IS
TAWARA ATOLL, GILBERT ISLANDS

SITUATION 1800 D+3

500 400 300 200 100 0　　　IC

MAP 9

TAKEN FROM 20 M
SPECIAL ACTION R

POSITION AT SUNSET

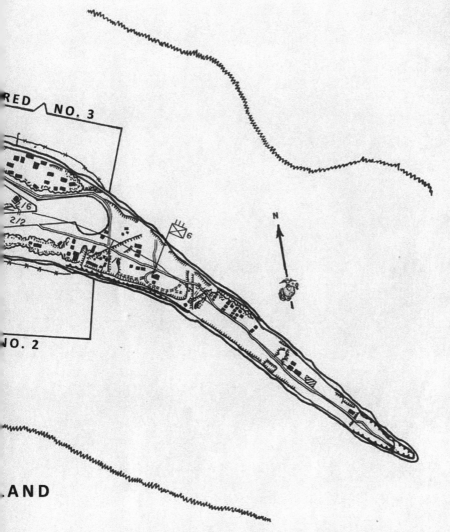

RED NO. 3

16
2/2

6

N

NO. 2

AND

NOTE: LINES ARE GENERAL INDICATION ONLY.
GAPS WERE COVERED BY SMALL GROUPS.
AND BY FIRE, SECONDARY LINES WERE
ESTABLISHED WHERE POSSIBLE BEHIND
FRONT LINES.

O YDS

R DIV
PORT

CHAPTER 12

Pete's first night on Betio had been unexpectedly quiet. The silence was profound, broken only on occasion by the sharp crack of a rifle as some Marine fired at an enemy infiltrator, or possibly some hapless crab scuttling by to nibble on the flesh of the dead.

A pale nearly full moon appeared in the east, climbing slowly above the rim of the Pacific. A gibbous moon the Professor called it, and through its pallid light, Pete checked his watch. It was about 0100.

Pete glanced at Aldrich who had nodded off again out of sheer exhaustion. By rights it was his turn to get some shuteye, but Pete wasn't the least bit tired so why not let Aldrich catch a few extra z's?

———————

Listening to the Professor's soft breathing, Pete thought about the platoon's last day aboard the troopship. Second Squad was sitting in a group soaking up some sun. Pete was seated Indian-style on the cover of the ship's aft hold using a whetstone to put a razor-sharp edge on the seven-inch blade of his Ka-Bar.

"What time is it?" Private Lance Tuthill asked.

"About 0930, Gabby," Pete replied.

Tuthill, a tall, slender boy from Oklahoma, was a man of few words, earning him the nickname Gabby.

"Not here," Tuthill said. "I mean back home."

"Who cares," Reb answered.

"I care less about the time than I do the date," Harnish said.

After a silence, Pete said, "Jesus, Bucket. You going to tell us why or do we have to kiss your ass?"

"I'm getting there, Hardball. Jesus Christ," Bucket fired back. "It's because we're supposed to invade this island tomorrow, November 20. Well, November 20 is also my mom's birthday and, well, I don't wanna get killed on her birthday. She'd be awfully upset."

"I can hear her now," Pete said. "'Goddamn it if Chuck didn't go and get himself killed on my birthday. He always did just think of himself, the selfish prick.'"

"Go to hell, Hardball," the lean Vermont farm boy whined while his squad mates chuckled. "That's not what I meant."

"If it's any solace for you, Bucket," Aldrich cut in, "tomorrow is not your mother's birthday."

"You may've gone to college, Professor," Bucket blurted out. "But damn it, I know when my mom's birthday is."

"What I mean is," Aldrich continued while loading loose .30-caliber rounds into clips for his Garand. "We're west of the International Dateline. So back home tomorrow is today, November 19."

"Problem solved, numbnuts," Pete taunted, smacking Harnish on the back of the head. "Now you can get killed tomorrow with a clear conscience."

"You can be such an asshole, Hardball," Harnish scolded.

"Here, here," Honeybun agreed.

"Hey Rosie," Reb Marshall called to Private Bernie Roseblum. "Y'all a Jew, ain't ya?"

"What gave me away?" the dark, curly-haired boy from Poughkeepsie, New York, asked. "Was it my last name or the fact that I don't eat bacon or ham at breakfast?"

"What about the Spam we had today?" Cpl. McDougal asked. "I saw you eat that."

"I don't know what Spam is," Roseblum replied. "I'm not even sure it's real meat."

"I hear it comes from unicorns," Lance Cpl. Bob Willoughby injected.

"Yes, Reb, I'm Jewish," Roseblum affirmed.

"Then yore circumcised, right?" Reb asked.

"Why," Pete said. "You hidin' something from us, Cornpone? Are you a Nancy-boy?"

"What Ah'm sayin' is, Ah wasn't circumcised when Ah enlisted, but the gawdamned Marine Corps wouldn't take me until Ah was," Reb complained. "And it wasn't jest me. Six other boys from my town also had to have the tips of their dicks whacked off before they could join up."

"Ouch," Aldrich said.

"Damned right," Reb replied. "Some of my pals paid a hunnerd bucks for the privilege of gettin' snipped. Luckily, Ah found me a little ole country saw bones who done it for sixty."

"Why the lower price?" McDougal asked. "No anesthesia?"

"Hey corporal," BAR-man Bull Marino asked. "Where's our valiant squad leader?"

"Sgt. Banks is in sick bay with about a hundred other veterans, Bull," McDougal replied. "So's Stuyvesant. It seems the farther we sail into the tropics the more malaria flare-ups there are among the old salts. I've been lucky so far. Mine hasn't come back yet."

"You got malaria, Mac?" "Pots" Potter asked.

"Hell yeah," the assistant squad leader replied. "Most of us old-timers do."

"What's it like?" Honeybun asked.

"First you get hot all over, like your body's gonna burst into flame and you sweat like a racehorse," McDougal said. "Then comes the chills and you think you're gonna break every bone in your body from shivering. You get nausea and the skids, which is especially rough when you're on the line and you're shittin' your brains out. When that happens you sometimes just have to crap in your foxhole 'cause there ain't nowhere else to go without getting your ticket punched by a sniper. Some guys would shit into an empty K-ration can and then throw the can at the

Japs yellin' things like 'Merry Christmas' or 'Have lunch on me.' Hell, one day on the 'Canal I crapped twenty-three times, mostly all blood."

"Damn," Reb swore. "If mah recruitin' sergeant had told me about that, Ah'd still be home in Georgia with mah dick in one piece."

———————

Pete remembered that exchange with a tinge of sorrow. A day and a half later, Gabby, Ted, Marino, and Banks were dead, and if he was still alive, Pots was on a hospital ship while Cpl. Willoughby and Pfc. Mark "Sty" Stuyvesant were missing. Of the original sixteen men of the oversized squad who left the *Zeilin* yesterday morning, only nine remained. And they were still the largest squad in the platoon.

Pete glanced at Aldrich again. Pete bitterly admitted to himself that he liked the Professor. Maybe that was because the guy reminded him of Charlie even though the Professor's long, narrow face bore no resemblance to Charlie's pleasantly round countenance. Aside from that, similarities were easy to find. Not once since Pete had met Aldrich had he heard the man utter any curse word stronger than "shit." Similarly, Pete could count on one hand the number of times Charlie cursed. Aldrich was smart and had attended college just like Charlie would've done if not for the war. He'd never heard either one say a bad word about anybody, and Charlie would not raise a hand even in his own defense. Pete admired those qualities in his brother while their father thought his younger son was just weak.

Pete thought about his father. Benjamin "Benny" Talbot was a hard drinker with an evil temper. A welder with a shipbuilding company, Benny made a handsome salary of just under $1,700 a year. That changed in 1932 when the company laid off most of its workforce, including Benny Talbot. Like the rest of America, Chester, a blue-collar city of factories and dockyards, was pummeled by the financial collapse. Jobs dried up, leaving Benny and a legion of other idled men looking for work that did not exist. For the next several years he did any crap work he could find. It took a war to get Benny Talbot back to a decent-paying job.

During that time Benny's self-pity fueled his anger, which he directed more and more at his two sons as if they were to blame. Backhanded slaps often delivered for no reason became punches. Sometimes Benny hit too hard. When Pete was fourteen he was hurried to Chester Hospital by his parents. X-rays revealed two broken ribs resulting from, his father claimed, a "bicycle accident." A year later Charlie suffered a broken arm from, his dad reported, "a tumble down the stairs."

The memories came flooding back to Pete as he remembered that terrible Saturday night in May of 1942 when the family shit truly hit the fan.

Benny had been drinking most of the day and was ramping up for what promised to be another hellish night. Pete and Aggie had planned on taking in a movie and then going out for ice cream, but Benny's increasingly dark mood gave Pete second thoughts. Charlie insisted that his brother and Aggie should go and have fun, promising to stay out of their father's way. Pete reluctantly agreed.

That night after dropping Aggie at home, Pete headed for his house on West Mary Street. Parking the family's Essex by the curb, he mounted the porch feeling good about the time he and Aggie had shared. But the moment he passed through the screen door he sensed that something was terribly wrong. In the living room his father sat slumped in his overstuffed armchair drunk and mumbling curses to himself. Pat Talbot, looking frayed and worried, hurried over to her son. She told him that Benny and Charlie had a terrible argument and that he'd better look after Charlie. Their father had been hard on him.

Hurrying upstairs he found Charlie sitting on his bed, his clothes badly rumpled and his hair disheveled. He had been sobbing. Pete noticed streaks of blood staining the back of Charlie's white T-shirt from where the belt had bitten too hard.

Charlie told Pete that their dad had accused him of smoking his last cigarettes.

"He knows I don't smoke," Charlie sobbed. "Then he accused me of taking money from his wallet and other stuff I'd never do in a million years."

In the heat of anger Charlie told his father that he wouldn't have him to beat around much longer, that after graduation he'd be "out of here" and that his dad could go to hell. At that point Benny removed his belt and began lashing his son until Charlie retreated to his bedroom and locked the door.

Pete cursed and threatened to call the police but Charlie stopped him.

"No, Pete, no!" Charlie implored. "I can take it a little longer."

"You shouldn't have to take it," Pete said. "Neither of us should."

Then a thought jolted Pete.

"Wait a minute," he said. "What do you mean you'll be out of here?"

Charlie hesitated, then told his brother he had joined the Navy last month right after his eighteenth birthday.

"And you didn't tell me?" Pete said, his mind reeling.

"You just would've tried to talk me out of it," Charlie said.

"You're damn right I would've," Pete replied. "There's a war goin' on, or haven't you heard? People are shootin' at each other. What about college? You're the brainy one. You want to be a schoolteacher. Hell, someone in this family oughta make something of his life and you're the only one with half a chance. God knows it's too late for our father and I'll probably spend my whole life as a deckhand sailing across the Delaware on that stinkin' ferry."

"Yeah, I want to go to college, but I'll wait until after the war, I guess," Charlie said. "It just takes too long, Pete, and I don't have the money. College is expensive."

"Christ, Charlie, I've been saving from my pay for your college," Pete said. "I got almost five hundred bucks squirreled away. That'll get you started. And I'll be saving more for you. Hell, I don't need much to live on."

"It's not just the money," Charlie explained. "I gotta apply to a college, then I have to wait to see if I get accepted. The earliest I could start is September. That's just too long."

Pete lit a Camel and puffed on it while he thought.

"So when do you leave?" he finally asked.

"Graduation is June 2 and I board a train the next day," Charlie said.

Pete nodded, cigarette smoke drifting around his face before dissipating into the room. He rose. He got his brother to his feet and headed him for the door.

"Let's go into the bathroom and get you cleaned up," Pete said.

The dazzling light of a flare brought Pete back to Betio. He watched its fiery arc as it streaked into the night sky, then blazed brilliantly over the western tip of the island. The crisp crackle of gunfire now reached Pete's ears, rolling across Betio's spectral moonscape.

"Is this it?" Aldrich muttered sleepily. "Are the Japs coming?"

"It's nuthin'," Pete told his friend. "Don't worry about it."

The Professor didn't and soon drifted off to sleep again.

The volume of small arms fire laced with the harsh ripping cough of machine guns rose the longer the light burned and then, like the flare, flickered out.

Once again, an uneasy quiet descended on the island.

As promised, the day after his graduation Charlie left for basic training at the naval training center at Great Lakes, Illinois. Pete and a tearful Pat Talbot saw him off.

"Why the hell did you do it?" Pete erupted as they stood on the train platform. "This isn't our war. Why do you think I didn't run out and enlist after Pearl Harbor like so many of the suckers in town did? It was always just us. You and me. No one ever gave us a break. We don't owe nuthin' to nobody."

Charlie reached out a hand and clasped Pete's shoulder.

"You're wrong, Pete," Charlie said. "Our country was attacked and I just can't sit at home. I've given this a lot of thought."

Pete stared at his brother, then glanced at their mother who stood helplessly by. An NCO in a dark-blue naval jacket yelled, "Great Lakes contingent, let's get aboard." Dolefully, Charlie picked up his bag which he had placed on a bench. First he hugged his mother tightly.

"Please take care of yourself, son," she half whispered.

Charlie nodded and kissed her cheek.

Then the brothers embraced, clutching each other tightly. Charlie fell in with a bunch of other nervous young men also clutching small suitcases. He boarded the Pullman and, taking one last rearward glance, was gone.

Charlie's letters home began within a week of his departure. He wrote about the drills and endless physical training. It was initially harder than expected, he admitted, but as the letters went on Pete could see in Charlie's writings that he was changing.

Following his basic training, Charlie wrote that he decided to become a radioman and was being transferred to the communications school at New London, Connecticut. He included a photograph of himself in uniform, taken after the graduation at Great Lakes. No longer looking like a kid, Charlie stood tall and erect, shoulders back, chest thrust forward, eyes gazing with determination at the camera. This was not the same nervous boy he had embraced on the train platform.

Hard on the heels of the letter about his becoming a radioman came Charlie's decision to volunteer for submarines, New London also being a major sub base.

"Submariners are a cocky bunch of fellows," Charlie penned. "They are gutsy, rugged, and seem to share a bond between them that is stronger than the men of the surface fleet. Going underwater in a sub is scary I'm certain, but if I have to serve, I think these are the type of guys I'd like to go to war with."

Pete shuddered at the thought of submarines yet he admired his brother's courage. Still, he tried to talk Charlie into seeking some safer duty.

"I know you feel subs are probably the most dangerous way for a sailor to go to war," Charlie wrote, "but risky or not, this is something I really want to do."

Pete was harshly brought back to the present when a dark figure pounced on top of him. A hand roughly lifted Pete's head and a raspy voice whispered into his ear, "You're dead, Talbot. And because you were doping off, Sleeping Beauty next to you also just got his throat cut."

Pete, usually defiant when so gruffly confronted, uncharacteristically sagged under the withering stare of Gunny Nicholson.

"Sorry, Gunny," he stammered. "It's the quiet of the night. I guess I let my mind wander to . . ."

"I don't care what your mind wandered to," Nicholson snapped. "Keep your goddamn focus on the job at hand. Think of nothing but those damned Japs out there and how much they'd like to stick a knife in your guts."

Pete nodded sullenly.

"One hundred percent alert for the rest of the night," Nicholson said. He nudged Aldrich with his boondocker. "Wake up, Sweetheart. You ain't bein' paid to sleep."

Aldrich sat bolt upright trying to focus his eyes.

Nicholson turned to Pete and said, "Keep your head out of your ass and stay sharp. The password is Lucky Lucy. We're getting reinforcements tomorrow. The 1/8 is coming ashore so maybe we can finally make some headway against the Nips."

He turned to leave when he suddenly froze and stuck up a hand to indicate silence. Startled, Pete thought the Japs might be attacking. Then he heard a low thrumming in the overhead blackness from somewhere out over the lagoon. Navy searchlights began to stab the darkness, their powerful beams slicing across the inky heavens. Next came the growling of anti-aircraft guns followed by bursts of light in the starry sky.

"Sonofabitch, Jap planes," Nicholson cursed. Turning to the two men with him he snapped, "Flat on your bellies. Cradle your head in your arms."

Pete and the Professor did as ordered as the rumble of aircraft engines grew louder. The ship batteries ceased fire to avoid peppering the Marines ashore with shrapnel as the enemy planes, Mitsubishi "Betty" bombers probably from the Jap base at Rabaul in New Britain, soared over the island. Now the Marines heard a new and more terrifying sound, a swooshing rattle that grew louder and louder as bombs plunged toward the earth.

The first explosions erupted near the landing beaches. Then came the asshole-puckering realization that the bursting bombs were "walking" inland. One detonated a short distance to the rear. Men cringed as the ground heaved.

The bombs continued marching inland, now carpeting the Japanese lines out in front.

"They don't know where the front is," Gunny Nicholson muttered. "They're just droppin' their loads anywhere."

"I didn't realize we had a front," Aldrich said.

"We don't, but they don't know that," Nicholson replied with as close as his face could come to a smile. "Remember, eyes and ears open."

Nicholson faded back into the night.

All along the Marines' line men waited nervously as that first night crept by. About an hour before dawn the taunting began. Yells and insults hurled at everyone the enemy could think of including Betty Grable.

A few Marines barked back with "Tojo fucks sheep" and "Emperor Whore House Hito eats shit" until their officers stepped in.

"Shut your yaps," Stonewall ordered the Marines of Dog Company as he moved quietly along his thin company line. "They're just trying to pinpoint your positions."

Capt. Thomas Jackson Stacy, called "Stonewall" by his men, was a tall, square-jawed, ruggedly handsome Virginian with unruly blond hair, icy blue eyes, and a slightly bent nose that had been broken at some point in the past and improperly set. A reserve officer in the pre-war Marines, he had the firm, solid type of persona that oozed leadership and men knew that when he was around things were under control, even here, where nothing seemed to be under control.

"When they come, fire on my command," he added.

But they didn't come. Not then, not later, and as the first hints of dawn began to streak the eastern sky, overpowering the feeble light of the one lone star that hung low to the west, men began to hope that the soul-wrenching attack they dreaded would not be launched at all.

Everyone began to breathe easier.

CHAPTER 13

With the rising of the morning sun, the first smattering of gunfire rippled across the island.

Pete fired up the day's first cigarette. Gazing at a magnificent sunrise, he drew in that initial puff. In twenty years of living in Chester, he'd never seen the sky look so beautiful. Yet he'd rather be in Chester than here.

Inexplicably, the image of the young Japanese soldier he had seen yesterday mounting the tank on the beach popped into Pete's head. He wondered who the man was and if he was still alive. Maybe, Pete thought, he was one of the dead men lying out there on the sand. Then his thoughts again returned to Charlie and Ted and he muttered angrily to himself, "Fuck him." Yet the man's image remained.

———————

Less than two hundred yards from Pete's foxhole Kenji Sakai also saw the sun rise, but his thoughts were not on the brave young American he saw dragging a comrade to shore. Kenji was wondering about the fate of Tadao Onuki. Together they had remained in the hospital bunker behind the command center until around midnight on that first day of battle. Outside the conflict still raged, only closer. Tadao leaned against his friend.

"Perhaps now is the time to go," he whispered. "If the Americans get too close we might not have another opportunity."

Kenji nodded. They had agreed to flee to Bairiki, and then possibly to one of the other islands in the Tarawa chain. There they hoped to link up with other refugees, men like themselves blown free from their home units. Once that was done and embracing the national spirit of *gisei, giri, meiyo, hokori, sekinin*—sacrifice, duty, honor, pride, responsibility—they would die gloriously for the emperor.

Getting to the next island would not be difficult since at high tide, the water separating the islands was no more than chest-deep. When the tide was out, one could walk across with dry feet. No, the hard part was not getting to Bairiki, but getting off Betio.

To the background of artillery and mortar fire, the two slipped from a rear entrance in the bunker and struck off into the darkness. Moving slowly and cautiously to avoid being shot by nervous countrymen, Onuki led the way. As the first wisps of dawn streaked the eastern sky, American ships resumed shelling the island as 5-inch and 8-inch rounds from destroyers in the lagoon and cruisers farther out to sea burst all around.

"Take cover!" Tadao yelled to his comrade as he heard the scream of the incoming shells.

Onuki dove to his left into a shell crater. Kenji lunged to the right into an abandoned trench, occupied only by a dozen or so dead *rikusentai* whose corpses blanketed the floor of the trench. As explosions rippled the earth around him, Kenji huddled into the earth works as deeply as he could, then lay there as the ground around him heaved and convulsed under the brutal punishment.

Kenji did not know how long the bombardment lasted but it seemed eternal. Finally the firing ceased and Kenji lifted his head, relieved that he was still unhurt.

"Tadao," he said. There was no answer so he tried again only louder. "Tadao."

Panic was Kenji's first emotion when he realized Tadao was not there. Unsure how close the Americans were, Kenji dared not call out too loudly, so after looking over the dead to make sure his friend was not among them, he cautiously struck out into the smoky predawn gloom in the direction he thought his friend might have gone.

———————

The dawn of a new day of killing also made Aldrich reflective.

"What makes them do it?" he mused aloud as he surveyed the dead. "What makes them throw their lives away like that?"

"They're Japs," Pete replied. "They're fuckin' nuts."

"That's not it," Aldrich said.

"You think too much, Professor," Pete replied. "You remind me of my brother."

Mentioning Charlie brought back to Pete's mind the last time he saw Charlie. It had been a bittersweet reunion.

———————

Freshly graduated from submarine school and en route to the West Coast and overseas, Charlie had obtained a leave to visit home. With Pete at the wheel, the brothers drove to a dilapidated pier along the Delaware River. As boys they had spent many happy hours here fishing and watching warships slice through the water on their way to and from the nearby Philadelphia Navy Yard. Parking the car, they walked to the small dock whose ragged, aging boards creaked and sagged under their feet.

"We sure lost our share of hooks and sinkers in this water," Charlie said.

"That feels like a million years ago," Pete observed. "It was here that you first told me you wanted to be a teacher."

"I still do," Charlie replied. "After the war. There are rumors that the government might help servicemen get jobs and training, and maybe give guys money to go back to school."

"I wouldn't get my hopes up," Pete sneered.

Pete stooped and picked up a flat stone, then looked at his brother who smiled and did the same.

Cocking an arm, Pete said, "Ready?"

Charlie nodded.

"Now," Charlie said and they threw the stones, skipping them off the water's surface. Pete's skipped three times, Charlie's four.

"I won," Charlie exulted, thrilled to relive one of their childhood games.

————————

Pete shook the memory from his head.

"What are you doing here, Professor?" Pete asked, taking one last drag and flicking the butt away. "You're smart. You've been to college. You didn't have to sign up for all of this." He waved his hand toward the corpses.

"I have two brothers in the Navy," Aldrich explained. "Todd is on a destroyer escort hunting U-boats and Simon is at a supply depot at Pearl." He paused and then continued. "For me, I just had to get in and pull my weight. If I'd stayed at Towson two more years, the war might've been over before I graduated."

"Yeah, but with college, you coulda been an officer instead of just another mud crusher like me," Pete said.

"I didn't want to be an officer," Aldrich insisted.

"You're a chump," Pete snapped.

Aldrich chuckled.

"What about you?" he asked. "What brought you to this happy fraternity?"

Pete was silent for a moment.

"I got into a fight," he reluctantly confessed. "Beat a guy up pretty badly and got arrested. The judge gave me a choice: the military or jail. Since I didn't want to live in a cell for two years, I enlisted." He paused before adding, "Guess that makes me a chump, too, huh?"

"Was the fight just some pointless brawl or was it a matter of principle for you?" Steve asked.

"Principle, definitely," Pete replied emphatically.

"If you had it to do over would you do the same thing?" Aldrich inquired. Pete nodded. "Then no, Hardball, you aren't a chump."

Keeping one eye on the ground ahead, Aldrich fished a K-ration breakfast box out of his knapsack, opened it, and removed the tin of chopped ham and eggs and a small packet of crackers. He held up the dried fruit bar.

"I hate this thing," he announced. "Want it?"

"Sure," Pete replied and caught the bar as Aldrich tossed it over.

They ate in silence as they listened to the crescendo of battle steadily rise, especially at the western end of the island.

"Sounds like someone's catching hell," Pete mused.

Aldrich munched thoughtfully on his crackers and said, "I had a professor during my last semester at Towson who went on and on about humans evolving from a primitive beast-like creature into today's modern man: well-dressed, well-educated, and civilized—far superior to that cave-dwelling ape," Aldrich laughed ruefully. "I believed him. Until yesterday. What I saw men doing to each other, the savagery and barbarity. I became convinced that we've not evolved at all."

Cpl. McDougal slid into their crater. He held a canteen in his hand.

"Gimme your cups," McDougal beamed. "I got hot joe."

"Damn, Mac, if you were a dame I'd marry you," Pete said as he quickly separated the tin cup from its canteen and held it out. Aldrich did likewise and both grinned ear to ear as McDougal filled the cups halfway with the steaming black liquid.

McDougal sat back and drained the last of the coffee from the canteen into his own cup. Taking a sip he smiled and said, "I feel almost civilized now." Taking another swig of the piping hot brew he said, "Did you boys ever hear the story about how Betty Grable once blew me a kiss?"

The two men snickered.

"I'm not shittin' ya," Mac told them. "It was May, a year ago just before we shipped out for New Zealand. We were still at Camp Elliott. Banks and me got liberty so we hitchhiked from San Diego to Hollywood and hit the Palladium where all the Big Bands play. Glenn Miller, the Dorseys, Goodman, Ted Lewis, they all played there. That night Grable was at the joint and as she strutted her stuff around the hall I yelled, 'I love ya, Betty,' and she looked right at me, smiled, and blew a kiss. I damn near pissed myself." He got pensive and added, "Now Banks is dead and Betty's married to Harry James. Life stinks."

As the men sipped their coffee in silence the roar of guns exploded from the direction of the lagoon. "The 1/8's coming in," McDougal observed. "Stay loose in case we suddenly have to move." Then he was gone.

Silently the two Marines sipped their coffee and listened to the pitch of the battle increase by the minute. Even with more than four thousand Marines already onshore, the 1/8 was still catching hell from the Japs. Gunfire erupted to the northeast, adding to the cacophony as the day's battle song swelled. The two-hundred-odd men holding the thin line near the airstrip braced themselves amid the amphitheater of violence that was expanding all around them.

"Why don't they hit us?" Pete asked.

"Don't rush it, Hardball," Aldrich replied. "We have a nice quiet spot here."

The two men lapsed back into silence.

"How'd you get the name Hardball?" Aldrich asked. "Did you play a lot of baseball in civilian life?"

Pete snorted.

"Baseball?" he said. "Hell no."

"Then how?" Aldrich insisted.

Pete did not answer for nearly half a minute before he sighed and said, "It was given to me by my DI. I hate being bossed around, always have."

"No kidding?" Aldrich deadpanned.

"I didn't get along too well with my DIs." Pete chuckled. "What a pair of bastards. They rode my ass all the time. Second day in camp Blakely gets into my face and says, 'You wanna play hardball, tough guy? That's fine because Red Mike and me, we love playin' hardball with tough guys.' They kept their promise. The name Hardball just stuck."

Pete grinned suddenly.

"Do you know what those sonsabitches did the day we graduated from the island?" he went on. "They took us to the slope chute and bought us rounds of brewskis until we were three-quarters pissed. Then Blakely took me aside and told me that I got a chip on my shoulder the size of a battleship, but that if I got rid of it I'd make a good Marine."

"Not quite," a gruff voice behind them said. It was Gunny Nicholson who had dropped into the shell crater. "He said you'd make a 'damned fine Marine.'"

Pete, mouth agape, was astounded.

"How the hell did you know?" he asked.

"I'm a fuckin' gunny sergeant," he said. "I know everything." He paused, then continued. "Truth is, Blakely and me go back years—boot camp, China, the Philippines, Guam. Then he shipped over to become a DI. He keeps track of his boys when he can and if any come my way, he writes me and gives me the lowdown. You made an impression on him, Talbot. He still smiles over that toilet-water gimmick."

"That's why I joined the Corps," Pete sneered. "To make that prick happy."

"Toilet-water gimmick?" Aldrich asked.

"Some other time," Pete replied.

Nicholson guffawed. Then his face sobered.

"At ten hundred we're gonna attack the Japs," he said. "We need to secure that airfield."

"Meaning no disrespect, Gunny," Aldrich said, "but the Nips tried to take our line yesterday and now most of them are ripening in the sun."

"Unlike them we'll have mortar support," Nicholson told the pair. "The stovepipes will drop fire on the Japs' heads before we rush 'em."

"Any chance of us gettin' reinforcements?" Pete inquired.

"Nope," Nicholson said. "The Japs have retaken the ground between us and the beach. That taxiway we crossed yesterday? The Japs set up machine guns and can sweep the entire place. Crossing it is suicide."

"We're cut off," Aldrich said somberly.

"This keeps gettin' better," Pete snarled.

"What about the 1/8?" Aldrich asked, pointing toward the roar of gunfire coming from the north.

"They're getting chewed to pieces," Nicholson said. "From the reports

Capt. Stacy is getting from Fox Company's radio, it's just like yesterday. Maybe even worse because some Japs waded out into the lagoon
overnight and set up machine guns in knocked-out amtracs, so they're
taking incoming Marines from the rear. It's a fuckin' slaughterhouse."

A terrible thought struck Pete.

"Gunny," he said nervously. "Could we lose this damned battle?"

"No," Nicholson shot back emphatically. "We're going to take our
objective. The three of us may get killed, but the Marines will not lose
this fight."

Nicholson left as quickly as he appeared.

"Jesus," Pete sighed, "he's full of good news, isn't he?"

The two returned to their vigil. Pete studied the enemy position with
keen interest. The centerpiece of the line was a bunker. About three feet
of it protruded above the ground and it appeared to consist of coconut
logs blanketed by sand. Its main feature was a wide slash across most of
the emplacement's ten-foot length. Two nasty-looking Type 11 Nambu
machine guns protruded menacingly from the slit, one at each end.

A long trench for infantry support flanked the bunker and passed
behind it.

"You know, if we could somehow get into that trench, maybe somehow flank them, we could root the Japs out and maybe get a shot at
that pillbox," Pete said, more to himself than Aldrich. "But the bitch is
getting in there."

"Maybe you ought to be the officer," Aldrich observed. "You just
indulged in some clinical thinking."

Pete was about to blow him off until he realized his friend was serious.

The seconds seemed to creep by as the Marines awaited the order
to cross this deadly space. Facing such danger, each man was lost in his
own thoughts. Pete removed a rubberized pouch from his haversack.
Opening it, he removed a well-thumbed letter from Aggie.

He could hear her gentle voice saying, *"Dearest Pete. I hope you are
well and pray this letter finds you safe. It is so terribly lonely here. I am so
grateful for my job in the supply office at the Navy Yard because it makes*

*me feel as if I'm helping you and the rest of our boys overseas and takes my
mind off of how much I miss you and how sad I am about Charlie. Ever
since we were kids I have had a special place in my heart for the Talbot
boys, but I'm sure you already know that."*

He had read and reread this letter many times and it gave him
comfort.

"I was happy to read about your friend Ted," her letter continued.
*"I know it's hard for you to let people get close and how your dad terror-
ized you and Charlie. That's horrible, but you have to believe in yourself,
so maybe having a friend like Ted is a good beginning."*

Aggie's words stayed with Pete. He could not see his life without
Aggie in it. Still, nowhere in this letter, or in any of her letters, did Aggie
mention the word "love." Pete knew full well that Aggie loved him but it
was unspoken, not because she wanted it that way, but because he did.
To Pete, the years of being physically and emotionally slapped down by
Benny Talbot had fucked up his life to the point where he wanted no
one, especially Aggie, to grow too close. He could not allow her to share
the same hellish life his mother and brother had endured. Pete loved
Aggie. He knew that, yet the scared and battered boy inside his hardened façade worked diligently to keep those feelings at bay.

McDougal slipped into the shell crater. He'd been making his way along
the line of his squad with last-minute instructions.

"What's that?" the corporal grinned, gesturing toward the letter Pete
still held in his hand. "A sugar report?"

"No," Pete snapped then amended, "well, sort of."

McDougal chuckled.

"So, Hardball has a soft side," he chortled. "Who'da guessed?"

Then he grew serious.

"The stovepipes will be opening up in ten minutes," he said. "Our
platoon's objective will be that pillbox." He pointed toward the enemy
line. "Knock that out and we can break this end of the Jap line. We

have to cross that ground quickly. We don't want to get bogged down out there." He paused. "Okay. Wait for the command and good luck."

McDougal headed back for his foxhole.

Pete and the Professor looked at each other, their faces ashen. Pete tucked Aggie's letter away and returned the pouch to his haversack. Envisioning her smile, he longed to hold her again.

Ten minutes later he heard the thunk of mortars launching their shells.

CHAPTER 14

The falling mortar rounds blossomed along the enemy's earthworks. Risking the jagged shrapnel whirring overhead, Pete glanced over the lip of his bomb crater to see what effect the shellacking was having on the Japanese. One large 81mm shell "with eyes" crashed with a roar directly inside the trench on the enemy's extreme right flank, throwing up dirt and severed limbs.

Over the drumbeat of the bombardment, a new sound reached Pete's ears, the whine of aircraft engines. The Professor pointed and exclaimed, "We got air support!"

A quartette of sleek, two-toned blue Navy Hellcats soared just a few hundred feet overhead. Pete watched three of the planes wing over to begin a swooping dive. The lead aircraft's machine guns blazed. The other pair followed, raking the enemy line and the runway. After one quick pass three of the Hellcats zoomed off in search of new targets. Satisfied grins crossed the faces of the Marines but quickly evaporated when they saw that the fourth Hellcat, hurrying to follow his comrades, banked his plane too soon.

"Down! Down!" Pete heard Nicholson bellow over the whine of the approaching fighter.

Pete and the Professor burrowed into the sand, instinctively curling up into tight balls. Then came the muffled thuds as the heavy rounds chewed up the earth around them.

Then the aircraft was gone. On the ground the cry "corpsman" rose up along the line.

Pete sat on the sand shaking, not sure if it was from fear or anger. As the mortar bombardment resumed, McDougal crawled into Pete and Aldrich's crater.

"Everyone okay here?" he asked.

"Everything's fine except for my temper, Mac," Pete snarled. "It's bad enough gettin' shot at by the Japs, but by our own fuckin' Navy? Jesus H. Christ, whose side are they on?"

"Easy, Hardball," McDougal cautioned. "Gettin' strafed by our own planes is a pisser but it happens, especially when we're eyeball-to-eyeball with the Nips."

Aldrich took a swig of water to steady his rattled nerves then asked, "Were we hurt bad, Mac?"

"We got off lucky," McDougal said. "Eddie Coogan in Third Platoon got nicked, but that was it. The regiment had six other guys wounded, one seriously. But the 1/2 had a coupla guys killed." He smacked Pete on the back. "Save that anger for the Japs. We're gonna advance soon."

Still jittery, Pete began checking his empty ammo pouches on his bandolier where he kept his cigarettes. He was down to two packs. If he wasn't careful, he'd end up having to smoke the Chesterfields in his K-ration boxes.

"Many more close calls like that and I may take up smoking myself," Aldrich said. Pete offered him a coffin nail. "No thanks, Hardball. I'm just cracking wise. No offense but I think smoking is a ridiculous habit."

"It is," Pete agreed. "Every time I go to the slop chute to buy a carton, I tell myself there are better ways to spend that half buck."

The cry of "Move out!" rippled along the line. Exchanging glances, the two men rose and jogged forward. Their attack had covered about a third of the ground when the Japanese unleashed a devastating volley. In an instant, fifteen Marines went down while the rest charged on. Five more quickly fell before the rattled survivors instinctively sought cover behind anything that might stop a bullet. Even the heat-swollen corpses of dead *rikusentai* served as protection.

Pete and the Professor dropped behind the trunk of a fallen tree and returned fire. A few yards out in front of his position Pete saw a wounded Marine writhing on the sand, clawing at his clothes in a frantic effort to feel how badly he'd been hit.

"Stop moving! Stop moving!" Pete heard other Marines call to the man. Pete recognized him as Pvt. Willie Brockman of Third Squad. He and Brockman had been squad mates at Parris Island. Brockman, a South Carolinian whose home was less than twenty miles from PI's front gate, had even tried to set Pete up with his sister during their first post-boot camp liberty.

"You'll really like Annabelle," Brockman had told him. "She's easy on the eyes and a helluva cook."

"I don't know," Pete replied, trying to change the subject.

"She's pretty good-looking," Brockman insisted. "We're twins."

"That's not a selling point," Pete replied, half in earnest.

The date never happened.

Now half a world away from home and crazed by pain and fear, Brockman continued pawing at his shirt.

"Dammit Brockman," Pete cried. "Lay still until a corpsman can get to you!"

Either Brockman didn't hear the warnings or he was too panic-stricken to understand. Either way, his thrashing attracted the attention of a Japanese gunner who turned his Nambu on the hapless Marine. Brockman's body jerked spasmodically as rounds from the machine gun slammed into him. All signs of life quickly vanished, yet the Japanese gunner continued to pour rounds into the corpse. White-hot anger flashed through Pete's brain as he watched this senseless mutilation. In sheer rage he emptied a clip at the machine gun position hoping against hope that he hit someone. Anyone.

About half an hour after the attack bogged down, Pete saw McDougal crawling toward them, bullets kicking up sand around him.

Reaching Pete, the corporal grinned and said, "Bastards almost punched my ticket that time." The grin vanished as he continued, "In fifteen minutes the mortars will begin plastering the Nips again. After they soften them up, we're gonna make another attack. We gotta crack that line."

Something inside Pete made him speak up.

"I got another idea," he said, surprising everyone, even himself. "The Jap line is open on their right flank. One of our 81s nailed that section of the trench and they haven't reinforced it. I think if we can get a few guys onto their flank, put some grenades on them, we can maybe rattle the Nips, force them back and get a shot at that pillbox."

Both men stared at Pete, McDougal with curiosity and Aldrich with a combination of concern and horror. He knew who the "few guys" would be.

"Come with me," McDougal said.

Pete soon found himself in his platoon CP where he repeated his idea. Lt. Cornwall then took him to the company bunker where Pete explained his plan for a third time in front of Capt. Stacy and a bemused Gunny Nicholson.

"It might work," Nicholson observed.

"Probably better than charging headlong into their machine guns," Stacy said. He glanced at Cornwall. "What do you think, Mike?"

"Okay, Hardball, take the Professor and your buddies Reb and Honeybun and see if you can get on the Jap flank," Lt. Cornwall said. "I'll have Rosie cover you with the BAR."

"To keep the Nips occupied, we'll have Pogey Bait drop mortars on them as well," Stacy said.

Pete was pleased that Capt. Stacy liked his idea. In fact, he surprised himself with how the plan came together in his mind. But he balked at being the guy to lead it.

"I shouldn't be in charge, sir, I'm just a private," Pete said. "I take orders, not give them."

"I can fix that," Cornwall said. "Effective right now you're McDougal's new assistant squad leader."

Pete opened his mouth to object but McDougal beat him to it.

"What do you want, Hardball? Egg in your beer?" McDougal replied. "You got your orders, Marine. Get on it."

As he turned to leave, Stacy said, "Wait a minute, Talbot." He retreated to the back of the CP bunker and returned carrying a Thompson and an ammo belt containing several twenty-round stick clips. "You'll need more punch than four rifles. Leave your weapon and bandoliers here and take this."

Reverently, Pete laid Ted Giovanni's rifle down and took the Thompson.

Cautiously he picked his way back the way he had come. Plopping down on the sand he filled in Aldrich.

"So what are your orders, Skipper?" Aldrich asked with a smile.

Pete fought off a reply. Instead, he yanked the cocking lever on the Thompson to chamber a round. Suddenly the danger of what he had proposed struck him, danger not only to himself but to his three best friends. Was he leading them into certain death?

Carefully Pete lifted his head to scan the terrain then rapidly dropped down as bullets from one of the Nambus hummed by.

"Damn," he cursed. "I need to know that bastard's field of fire."

In basic training they'd been taught that the best way to take a pill-box was to flank it until you were beyond the gunner's range of vision.

"Reb! Honeybun!" Pete called. "Get your asses over here." To the Professor he said, "When they get here give them a heads-up and then come one at a time when I signal."

Using the thick tree trunk for cover, Pete slinked to his left a dozen feet then popped his head up and down. He did it quickly but not so fast that the enemy gunner failed to see him. Another flurry of bullets sailed his way. Pete crawled on. Three more times he stuck his head up and twice he ducked just in time to avoid having it shot off. The third time no bullets greeted him. Certain he couldn't be seen he moved on. The trunk, about eighty-five feet in length, narrowed as Pete moved along it, increasing the danger that he might be spotted. Halting, Pete signaled Aldrich and watched as the Professor, Reb, and Honeybun began their crawls.

As he waited, Pete pondered the next leg of their advance. This move would require him to cross over the protective tree trunk and creep or roll a short distance to the bloated corpse of a Japanese infantryman. Anticipating the stench, he focused on the body and got the eerie sensation that the dead man was moving. He wrote it off to imagination sparked by a healthy dose of fear.

When the others reached him, Pete said, "Hold here until I signal, then follow me."

"Hope y'all know whut yore doin', Yank," Reb whispered.

"So do I, Hillbilly," Pete replied. "So do I."

As the first of Pogey Bait's mortar rounds dropped on the Jap trench, Pete crept over the trunk and swiftly snaked his way toward the corpse.

Reaching it, the putrid stench of rotting flesh made Pete's eyes water. Up close, he saw thousands of maggots coating both the man and his blood-soaked uniform. It was their wriggling that he mistook for body movement. Horrified, Pete stifled a cry of disgust. Instead, he quickly eyed his next objective, a profusion of splintered wood and sandbags that had been a gun position. Reaching it, however, would involve the most dangerous aspect of this entire move since it required crossing fifteen feet of wide-open ground. The move would bring him to just a few yards from where the mortar shell had struck the enemy trench.

With the Thompson snuggly tucked in the crook of his folded arms, Pete set out. As he crept, Pete kept a wary eye on the blasted section of the enemy trench for any sign of life. Perspiration flowed down Pete's forehead, stinging his eyes. His mouth felt as dry as the sun-parched sand.

Lt. Cornwall ordered the covering mortar fire to be lifted as Pete's men drew close to the enemy works. Now Rosie's BAR began its distinctive bark, kicking up sand geysers all around the Japanese forcing them to duck low. *Bless you, Rosie*, Pete thought. He heaved a heavy sigh of relief when he reached cover.

Pete found himself amid the ruins of a pentagonal-shaped artillery revetment. A large-caliber shell had landed here with devastating effect. Two of the position's five walls were collapsed, wooden timbers were shredded, and heavy sandbags cast about like bean bags. The silent barrel of a 75mm gun aimed uselessly toward the beach while around it lay the smashed remains of eight men. Flies buzzed so thickly over the corpses that they created a shadow.

Ignoring the gory mass, Pete signaled his team and watched as they made their respective moves. At the rotting corpse, each man recoiled briefly before heading on to the artillery position. As he had done for Pete, Rosie covered their moves with his BAR.

"Whut's next, Ginral?" Reb asked.

"I'm thinking," Pete replied.

Dear God, can I do this? he thought. But the time for second-guessing was over. Committed, there was no going back.

Cautiously, Pete eyeballed the enemy trench. The mortar-blasted section ahead yawned empty, manned only by the dead. Beyond that he could clearly see the enemy's main line. The trench was about four feet in depth and maybe five feet in width and stretched westward thirty yards. Its walls were shored up with sandbags. Armed infantry, thirty or more of them, lined the trench's northern parapet. Pete could see a few bodies on the trench floor, evidence that at least some of the Marines' fire had struck home. Beyond sat the pillbox, its guns chattering away. None of the enemy were looking his way.

"We've done it," Pete muttered. "We flanked the bastards."

"Grenades?" Aldrich suggested.

Pete nodded. It was a hefty throw, but they had been drilled over and over on tossing grenades at Parris Island.

"We'll start with five grenades which you will throw a distance of twenty yards," Pete recalled his instructor saying. "By the time we're through, you will be able to throw one of these pineapples thirty-five yards so accurately that you'll be able to land one into a Jap's hip pocket."

Pete wasn't sure about the hip pocket part, but he had been able to toss his grenades almost forty yards, the best distance of any other man in Training Platoon 621.

"Yeah," Pete told Aldrich. Then he unhooked one of his last two grenades from his webbing. "We each toss one into the Jap position. We gotta get them into the trench and take out as many Nips as we can. Professor, you throw into the near end. Reb, you and Honeybun aim for farther up, and I'll go long. We charge on my command. Take the trench. I'll make for the bunker and try to get a grenade in the gun slit. Honeybun, you're on me. Reb. Professor. You fellas cover the rear doorway. Shoot anyone who comes out." He paused, then said, "Fix bayonets."

Grimly each man slipped his bayonet from his scabbard, looped the ring over the muzzle, and seated the weapon firmly on the lug under the barrel. Each next pulled a grenade loose from his belt, wrapping his hand around the projectile, thumb firmly securing the safety lever. With a nod from Pete, they rose to a kneeling position and with a twist and pull, yanked the pins while still holding down the spoons.

"Now," he said and each man hurled his pineapple, letting it roll off his fingertips, textbook style, so that it would spin in flight like a football. After the throw all four men flattened. Seconds later explosions rocked the earth.

"Let's go!" Pete cried as he rose up and charged the enemy line.

Inside the trench some twenty enemy soldiers lay in bloody disarray. Some were killed outright by the blasts while others writhed in agony from jagged wounds. A few men thrown to the ground, either with minor wounds or simply shaken up, were struggling to their feet. The charging Marines, rifles blazing, quickly cut these men down. With Honeybun and Pete firing down from the parapet, Reb and the Professor jumped into the trench and turned their Garands on the remaining wounded Japanese until all were dead. Farther along the trench enemy soldiers startled by this sudden flank attack returned a feeble fire, then bolted.

Reb let out a yelp as one of these wayward rounds fired by a stocky, unshaven *rikusentai*, creased his left cheek, nicking his ear lobe. The Professor, spotting the wooly-chinned Jap, fired at the man but missed. He charged and drove his bayonet into the man, the blade biting up and under the rib cage to pierce the heart. The Professor felt the man's final breath blow directly into his face. He tried to back off, but his bayonet stuck as the man's guts contracted. Pinching his eyes shut in disgust the Professor fired off a round and the bayonet jarred loose.

Pete unleashed a few quick bursts of fire into the trench as he dashed for the pillbox. Honeybun quickly followed. Reaching the east wall of the bunker, Pete knelt and paused for breath, Honeybun right beside him. The two inched along toward the front. Pete slipped his last grenade off his webbing and held it in his hand. Before tossing it he looked back at

Aldrich and Reb in position by the bunker's rear entrance. Pete leaned in close to the front of the pillbox. Around the corner the two Nambus chattered away, their gunners unaware that they'd been flanked. Pete yanked the pin of the grenade then let the spoon fly. Counting to three he leaned around the corner and lobbed the grenade through the gun slit. Ducking back, he felt as much as heard the dull thud as the pineapple detonated in the confines of the bunker. Smoke and debris still sifted from the gun slit as Pete and Honeybun swiftly stepped out in front of the bunker. The two Marines stuck the muzzles of their weapons into the slit and emptied them while traversing left and right.

"That's for Willie Brockman," Pete said aloud after emptying his magazine.

Seconds after the explosion a Japanese soldier burst out of the rear door and was cut down by an angry Reb, blood still flowing down his face. Two more Japanese emerged only to be bowled over in a hail of fire from both Reb and the Professor.

Seeing the pillbox silenced, Capt. Stacy rose to his feet, waved his M1 carbine over his head, and yelled for the 2/2 to charge. To the battalion's right, the 1/2 followed. As the howling wave of Marines surged forward, the Japanese scrambled from the trench and began fleeing across the airstrip's exposed two-hundred-foot-wide runway. Some made the run successfully but others did not, their bodies dotting the sunbaked airstrip. The Marines took possession of the trench.

Pete and Honeybun joined their two comrades behind the now silent bunker.

"You okay?" Pete asked Reb, who'd pulled some gauze from his first aid kit and was dabbing his bloody cheek.

"Yeah, but Ah'm afraid it'll leave a scar," he drawled.

"Don't worry," Honeybun replied. "It can't make you any uglier."

The men smiled, less from the joke than from the release of tension. Sobering, the Professor pointed to the dark opening to the bunker.

"Think any more are in there?" he asked.

"Only one way to find out," Pete replied.

Setting aside his empty Thompson, Pete slipped the late Lt. Pfeffer's

.45 out of his waistband. Pausing at the doorway he said, "God I hate this."

"Want me to go?" the Professor asked.

"I got it," Pete replied. "But you can go along and hold my hand."

Creeping cautiously into the opening, Pete and the Professor found a sandbag buffer inside that doglegged to the right. Beyond this was a large, gloomy room that had served as sleeping quarters. The plank-lined roof was supported by several coconut logs, and there were half a dozen sandbag revetments each capable of protecting two to four men against blasts. The room reeked of sweat and urine, mingled with the smoky scent of spent gunpowder. Diagonal across the room was another doorway leading to the machine gun position. Stooped over to avoid whacking his head on the low ceiling, Pete crossed the room and poked his head cautiously through the opening. Seven men lay sprawled on the floor. Most were torn by the grenades. One had been shot through the head. The seventh man lay on his back glaring at Pete.

Stepping through the doorway and pointing his .45 at the man Pete ordered, "Get up."

He knew the man couldn't understand him so he made corresponding gestures with his handgun.

"Get up," he barked again.

"Watch him," the Professor said nervously from the doorway. "They're tricky."

His .45 trained at the man, Pete watched him slowly struggle to his feet. Glaring at Pete, his brown eyes burned with hatred. Pete noticed that the man's right hand was tucked under his tunic clutching his bloody left shoulder. Carefully Pete gestured for the man to follow him out.

"Come," Pete said. "Come. This way."

The wounded man took a few careful steps in Pete's direction. Pete ventured a quick peek at the Professor. The glance only took a moment but in that moment the prisoner yanked his arm from his wounded shoulder. Clutched in the hand Pete saw the ominous shape of a grenade. The man emitted a guttural cry, raised a hand to yank the pin and activate the weapon. Because of his wounded shoulder he was a hair's breadth too slow. Startled, Pete squeezed off a round from the .45 that struck the man in the chest. The impact threw the *rikusentai* backward against the wall of the pillbox. Pete fired three more times. The soldier slipped to the floor, the grenade rolling harmlessly from his dead hand.

Pete stood frozen, the smoking pistol hanging limply in his hand. Suddenly outraged he shouted at the corpse, "Why didn't you surrender!? What the hell's the matter with you people!?"

Pete looked at the Professor who gave him a reassuring grin. The Professor retrieved the Type 97 grenade and handed it to Pete, who'd used up his own supply.

Back outside Reb asked, "I heard shootin' in theah. Whut happened?"

The Professor explained while a corpsman bandaged the Georgian's bloody cheek and ear.

"Them Japs are crazier than you Blue Bellies at Fredericksburg," Reb replied.

The squad saw Nicholson and McDougal approach.

"That was good work you boys did," Nicholson said. "Capt. Stacy is real proud and so am I."

"I can't believe they ran away so quickly once we hit 'em," Pete said.

"That's because you caught them by surprise," Nicholson told him. "The Jap soldier is not trained to think for himself. The unexpected throws them off their game."

Suddenly very tired, Pete just nodded and said, "So now what?"

"We dig in and await orders," Nicholson replied. "You didn't hear this from me, but I'm certain that our next move is across the runway. Our D-Day objective was to seize the south beach and cut the island in two. I don't know that those orders have been changed. Get some rest. You're gonna need it."

Nicholson departed.

"Gawd damn," Reb moaned to McDougal. "The Japs just crossed that thar airstrip and lookee how many guys they left behind. Now we gotta cross it? Them Japs'll just love that. Ah kin see 'em lickin' their lips now. Christ on a crutch, our ginrals must be Yankees."

"Take it easy, Reb," McDougal said.

"I'm not a general, Mac," Pete said, slipping a new clip into the Thompson. "But in order to cut the island in two, don't we need to have support behind us? If we do reach the southern beach, we're gonna be left there with our balls hanging out."

"Sooner or later the rest will catch up," Mac answered grimly. "Meanwhile somebody's gotta lead the way."

"What a fitting epitaph," Aldrich said.

CHAPTER 15

Crouched in a trench on the northern lip of the runway, the 187 Marines remaining from the First and Second Battalions awaited orders that would send them across the airstrip.

A few Marines ambled among the dead Japanese that littered the trench grimly searching through pockets and knapsacks for souvenirs. Cpl. Edward Hainley, a New Georgia veteran with Third Platoon, leaned over each body and forced open the dead men's mouths in search of gold teeth. When he found any, he pried them out with the tip of his Ka-Bar. Probing deep into one man's mouth, Hainley noticed Pete watching him.

"I'm from Canon City, Colorado, Hardball," he snarled. "I left home when I was eighteen to pan for gold along Cripple Creek near Leadville and came up with barely enough to live on." He held up a cloth drawstring bag and shook it. The contents rattled. "This is a damn sight easier than panning. I ain't goin' home broke."

Hainley returned to his grisly gold rush, leaving Pete to ponder the depths to which war plunges some men's sense of morality.

Plopping down on the sandy floor of the trench, Pete removed his helmet. A smile creased his dirt-caked face and a feeling of calmness swept over him as he gazed at Aggie's full round face and soft features. Her deep-set, blue-green eyes seemed to twinkle despite the battered state of the photo.

Pete recalled the date he and Aggie were on the night Benny Talbot had beaten his youngest son.

———————

They'd gone to see the movie *Journey into Fear*. It had everything Pete liked: action, spies, a sultry love interest, and diabolical Nazis. Exiting the theater afterward hand in hand, Aggie rubbed her cheek on Pete's shoulder as she told him she liked the movie. Pete suspected she was humoring him. Still, it had been his turn to choose since last time Aggie had selected a comedy called *To Be or Not to Be* with Carole Lombard and Jack Benny. Pete never told Aggie that he was no Benny fan.

The two drove along MacDade Boulevard, Aggie snuggled tightly against Pete, his right arm draped across her shoulders. At their favorite ice cream shop they shared a picnic table bench while Aggie enjoyed her traditional double malt. Sipping from a frosted mug of root beer, Pete jibbed Aggie about his outlay of forty-two cents for gas, eighty cents for the movie tickets, a nickel for popcorn, and now an expensive seventeen-cent dessert.

"You're not a cheap date, are you?" he kidded, giving her a peck on the cheek.

Aggie playfully stuck her tongue out at him and said, "I'm not letting you off easy."

As she dipped a long-handled spoon into her shake to break up a small clot of ice cream that had clogged her straw, Aggie stared at Pete across the red Formica tabletop.

"You seemed distant all evening," Aggie told Pete. "More trouble at home?"

"Ahhh," he soured. "The old man's got a bee up his butt. Nuthin' new there, huh?" He lapsed into a brief silence then added, "I'll tell you, Aggie. Sometimes I wish the SOB would just drop dead."

"I know your dad can be hard to live with," Aggie replied. "How's Charlie been taking things?"

"Like me, he tries to avoid Dad," Pete replied. "Charlie's quite fond of you." He paused, then added, "So am I."

Aggie smiled.

"The feeling's mutual," she said.

"Too bad your dad doesn't feel that way," Pete replied. "He doesn't appreciate you hanging around me. He never has."

"Don't worry about Daddy," she answered. "I learned a long time ago how to handle him."

"I don't doubt it," Pete said. "Sometimes I'm afraid you'll learn how to handle me."

Aggie leaned close and gave Pete a gentle kiss.

"What makes you think I haven't?" she asked.

———————

Pete grinned to himself. He wished he could speak to her right now.

Pete replaced the helmet, stood, and resumed scanning the terrain beyond the airstrip. His attention was diverted by a small sand crab scuttling past him headed for the runway and the bodies roasting under the hot sun.

"Oh man," Pete said to Aldrich who was also watching the crab. "What I wouldn't give to be home enjoying a batch of steamed crabs. Ever eat them?"

Aldrich laughed.

"Are you serious, Hardball? I'm from Rock Hall, Maryland, remember? It's right on the Chesapeake's eastern shore. Almost everyone in town is either a waterman or someone who buys the catch from the watermen or works in one of the town's seafood shops filleting fish or picking crabmeat. I had summer jobs on work boats since I was fourteen, mostly with a crusty old skipper named Captain Jack." A smile creased Aldrich's lips. "The guy was like a character straight out of a Herman Melville story."

"Who?" Reb Marshall, sitting at Pete's right, injected.

"He wrote *Moby Dick*, you ignorant Hayseed," Honeybun quipped.

"Moby who?" Reb asked.

"Ignore him," Pete told Aldrich. "Go on."

"Captain Jack had a short, grizzled white beard that was always stained with tobacco juice—he chewed Red Man like a kid eats candy—and every fourth word coming out his mouth was a cuss word," the Professor recalled fondly. "Unless he was mad. Then it was every word."

"He sounds like a Marine DI," Pete said. "What did you do on his boat?"

"Mostly we did crabbing," Aldrich recalled. "He had about forty of these big chicken-wire crab pots scattered in the bay from just north of Swan Point, south past Eastern Neck Island almost to Love Point. Every morning at dawn we'd board his boat, a forty-footer he called *Jacks or Better*, and we'd shove off. We passed through the breakwater at the harbor mouth and chugged off to check the pots. Each was marked by a yellow-and-red buoy and as we reached one, I'd hook the buoy and haul up the crab pot, open it, and dump the crabs into a large basket. Then Captain Jack would throw some bait fish into the wire pocket on the trap and toss it back into the water and we'd turn the boat toward the next one and repeat the process. It took us until late afternoon, when we'd head back to harbor to sell the day's catch. First we'd grade the crabs one, two, or three depending on size and put them in separate bushel baskets. Sometimes he held back a bushel and had them steamed and we'd sit on the wharf and have a feast." The Professor blushed. "Once in a while he shared his beer with me even though I was underage. I didn't have the heart to tell him I don't like beer."

"Sounds like a great life," Pete observed.

"Oh, it was," Aldrich replied. "As I got older he'd let me take the wheel when we brought *Jacks or Better* into the harbor. And what I earned working for him helped pay a sizeable chunk of my college tuition—that and an academic scholarship I'd earned."

"Scholarship?" Pete said astounded. "And yet here you are sittin' in a foxhole with a high school dropout whose job included swabbing toilets on the Chester Ferry."

Just then Pfc. Kusaka tapped Pete on the shoulder. Mickey Mouse held out a folded white square of cloth with red markings that he had picked up while scavenging.

"Here you go, Hardball," Mickey Mouse said.

"What's that?" Pete asked.

Kusaka unfolded the item to reveal a rising sun flag brimming with Japanese characters scribbled in ink. Reddish-brown spots on the white fabric marked dried blood. There were also a few red splotches of fresh blood.

"That Jap who tried to kill you in the bunker had it on him," Kusaka said. "I don't know what this Nip writing on it says."

"It's most likely a unit flag," the Professor injected. "Those are probably the names of his buddies. His must be on there."

"Yeah," Kusaka said, refolding the flag. "Anyway, since he tried to blow you up, I figured he owes you." Pete took the flag, clutching it tightly. Then Kusaka held out a brown billfold. "Maybe you want this too."

Pete took the battered leather billfold. Opening it he was confronted by a creased photo of an elderly couple seated amid three young men, all in uniform, standing upright, one with a samurai sword perched tip-down before him. Pete recognized the young man on the far left as the one he'd shot in the bunker. For a few moments he gazed at the man's family. He knew he wouldn't want some Jap to take his photos off his dead body to keep as trophies. He snapped the billfold closed.

"What the hell do I want that for?" he groused. "Put it back where you got it."

Kusaka took the billfold and Pete sank back into a sullen silence, stuffing the flag into his knapsack.

"Mah, mah, mah," Reb intoned as he stared across the cratered expanse of the runway. "That don't look none too good. Do y'all remember the day we wuz gettin' ready to leave the ship and we wuz told about some officer who said we Marines would land, polish off whatever Japs wuz left alive after the Navy got done shellin' 'em, and then be back on board the ships in time for evenin' chow? Well, Ah wish Ah had that sumbitch here right now to charge 'cross this here airstrip alongside me."

"And I'd be right behind him with my bayonet up his ass," Honeybun added.

"I think I heard that it was some admiral who made that prediction," Aldrich said.

"In the next war I'm coming back as an admiral," Honeybun quipped.

"You can't," Pete replied. "To be an officer you gotta be stupid and the more stupid you are, the higher your rank."

The men sank back into silent brooding on the task ahead. The open runway looked flat as a griddle and just as hot. Waiting for them on the other side was a malevolent tangle of underbrush and a small forest of battered palm trees. For its part, the runway was sprinkled with shell and bomb craters. About halfway across a wrecked Japanese single-seat fighter plane lay on its belly, its fuselage twisted into scrap.

Then it was time.

It began with the dull thunk as the mortar tubes launched their rounds. The shells burst along the tree line on the far side of the runway. More thunks were followed by still more explosions.

Then a cry up the line bawled, "Let's go! Let's go! Keep your intervals! Go! Go!"

The men of the two battalions scrambled forward. Two hundred feet away the enemy line erupted in gunfire. Bullets snapped and hummed all around but the Marines kept running. Ahead Pete saw several Japanese using the battered carcass of the fighter plane for cover.

Calling to Roseblum, Pete said, "Rosie! Spray that airplane!"

Roseblum paused, leveled the BAR, and peppered the plane. A spotter with the mortar platoon also noticed the airplane-turned-pillbox and called in the 60s. The first two shots fell short but the next pair blew the airplane and its defenders apart. Gasoline still in the wing tanks erupted in a ball of fire, emitting a smoke screen that drifted over the charging Marines, helping to conceal them during the final yards of their attack.

The sprint across the airstrip lasted just a few minutes. Suppressing fire from the mortars helped keep Marine losses lighter than anyone dared hope.

One of those wounded was Cpl. McDougal, who took two shots to the body and collapsed face down on the crushed coral. Pete, seeing McDougal was still alive, raised him to a sitting position.

"Reb! Help me!" he shouted above the battle racket. The Georgian skidded to a halt.

"Two-man carry," Pete barked as the pair scooped up the injured vet and lugged him forward as enemy rounds skipped off the runway.

Reaching the edge of the airstrip they crashed through the tangled underbrush and over the twisted bodies of three slain Japanese soldiers. They finally set McDougal down in the shelter of a small triangle of fat palm trees. As Reb shouted for a corpsman, Pete tore open the corporal's bloody shirt. The wounds, two jagged holes surrounded by torn tissue, looked fierce at first. From his training, he knew McDougal would not be allowed to drink with a belly wound, so Pete removed one of the corporal's canteens from his web belt and poured water on the wounds to wash away the blood. Having done that he saw that one wound appeared to be just a grazing injury. The second, square in the gut, was more serious.

He ripped Mac's first aid kit off his web belt and opened it.

"When you're treating a wounded buddy, always use his first aid kit instead of yours," one of the instructors at Parris Island had remarked to the new men. "Someone may need to use yours to treat you."

Taking out some gauze, he tore open the packaging and applied pressure to the most serious of the injuries to stem the flow of blood.

"Don't die on me, you ugly sonofabitch," Pete told the wounded man. "Stay with me."

Moments later Ryan Magruder arrived and instantly took charge.

"I got him, Hardball," the corpsman said. "I got him."

Fearing that McDougal was going into shock, Magruder told Reb, "Drag that dead Jap over here. We need to raise Mac's feet."

As bullets clipped the foliage around them, Reb pulled one of the dead enemy soldiers close by the wounded corporal. Pete helped the corpsman raise McDougal's feet and propped them up on the corpse.

"It's okay, Hardball," Magruder said. "Go. Both of you."

Pete absently wiped his bloody hands on his pant leg.

The two made their way forward to where the squad was digging in. Pete rolled into a small gully beside Aldrich. The Professor glanced at his friend and asked, "McDougal get it?"

"Belly wound," Pete replied tersely. "Doc has him."

"Guess that makes you squad leader," Aldrich said.

After a brief silence, Pete replied, "I guess so. What of it?"

Aldrich smiled wryly, "Congratulations."

Under heavy fire, the Marines advanced inch by inch toward Betio's southern shore, codenamed Black Beach. A bullet fired from above clipped Honeybun's knapsack. The North Carolinian dropped and rolled onto his back. Glancing upward he sent four rounds into the fronds of the nearest palm tree. A rifle plunged to the ground. The body that fell next was jerked up short by a stout vine looped around the sniper's waist.

Inching their way from tree to tree, shell hole to shell hole, the Marines slowly gained ground. Dead ahead of Second Platoon stood a bunker thirty feet long at its base, and tapering upward to a height of about ten feet above ground level. The main armament, a 75mm gun, was aimed uselessly at the ocean awaiting an American landing that would never come. However, the bunker's two heavy machine guns, supported by an unknown number of infantrymen, were entrenched in stout positions to the rear of the pillbox to face the approaching Marines.

The fight became a test of strength between twenty-five well-dug-in Japanese, determined to hold their ground or die, and the forty-one survivors of Dog Company, equally determined to reach Helen's southern shore alive. For the next nerve-shattering hour, Dog Company advanced barely ten feet. Second Battalion was effectively bogged down.

So was First Battalion on the right flank where Marines faced another stout bunker plus enemy troops fighting from aircraft revetments.

Pete was startled to feel someone yanking on his foot. It was Gunny Nicholson.

"Fox Company is sending us a flamethrower," he hollered above the din of small arms fire. "But we gotta get him close enough to use it."

Pete nodded.

At Pete's signal the squad fixed bayonets for the second time that day. The squad began edging forward using whatever cover they could find. When they had gotten to within twenty paces of the bunker's entranceway, Pete realized they could go no further without fully exposing themselves to the well-dug-in defenders. At this range even lifting their heads to return fire was risky.

But the fighting had taken its toll on the Japanese as well. Defensive fire had diminished. A few stubborn *rikusentai* remained. The rest were either dead or had escaped the bunker from the seaward side. For the most part, it was the deadly bursts of the two heavy machine guns that were keeping the Americans at bay. Then one gunner near the bunker's entrance got careless. To expand his field of fire he revealed his otherwise well-hidden position by moving a protective piece of corrugated iron sheeting. Roseblum spotted him and loosed a burst from his BAR. Two of the slugs struck the man square in the forehead. The gunner's terrified assistant fled rearward.

Lt. Cornwall saw the gunner's death as a window of opportunity as the Japanese fire momentarily slackened.

"Second Platoon let's go!" he called and rushed forward.

Eighteen men followed, running hard to close the open ground between them and the bunker. The men sprayed fire into any opening they saw. A feeble fire came back at them but the Americans stormed through it and began ascending the sloping bunker. Their goal was two T-shaped ventilation pipes protruding from the roof created to allow fresh air into the dank, stale interior.

Half a dozen Japanese defenders inside the bunker slithered out through the main gun aperture facing seaward and began climbing the forward slope to meet their tormentors. With bayoneted rifles they reached the top and charged with a soul-curdling wail. Three were shot down. One determined *rikusentai* ran his bayonet into the chest of a young man from Third Squad whom Pete only knew by his last name, Lingle, before he, too, was struck by numerous rounds from angered Marines. Lingle and the Japanese soldier fell dead together. A fifth attacking Japanese soldier made for Sandy Gutierrez, hollering unintelligibly. Sandy fired his rifle and sent a bullet into the man's open mouth. The man collapsed like a rag doll at Sandy's feet. The last of the six men charged Nicholson. The gunny squeezed the trigger of his Garand only to hear a heart-stopping click as the weapon misfired, its mechanism fouled by sand. The Japanese soldier thrust his bayonet-tipped Arisaka forward. Dropping his own weapon, Nicholson deftly sidestepped the thrust, then grabbed the rifle by the barrel and wrenched it from the hands of the startled soldier. Reversing the piece, Nicholson drove the butt end of the Arisaka into the man's horrified face, knocking him to the ground. Then he reversed the weapon a second time and impaled the prostrate man, pinning him to the sand with his own bayonet.

For a few moments all was quiet atop the bunker until Rosie, pointing, yelled, "Japs in the open!"

Ten Japanese soldiers had squeezed out of the forward gun aperture and were dashing eastward toward the island's long narrow tail and their own lines. The men of Second Platoon sent a hail of bullets after them, dropping six before the rest made their escape by weaving among the palm trees and scattered mounds of debris.

"Grenades," Nicholson barked, pointing to the two air vents. "In there. Quick."

Several men plucked grenades off their web belts, yanked the pins, and dropped them down the air shafts. Pete added his captured Jap grenade to the lot, returning it to its owners. With a muffled thump the grenades burst inside the pillbox. A Marine with a flamethrower strapped to his back appeared at the base of the pillbox near the doorway. Lt. Cornwall signaled the platoon to follow and led his men off the bunker. Once they were clear, Cornwall yelled "Burn it." The Marine with the flamethrower aimed the nozzle toward the door and unleashed a plume of orange fire into the opening. Almost instantly horrific cries of agony emanated from the bowels of the bunker. A Japanese soldier, his body enveloped in orange-and-blue flame, burst through the door, possibly in hopes that he'd be mercifully shot by the Americans.

"Let 'im burn," someone barked, so no relief-giving bullet was fired. The screaming man ran a few agonizing steps before collapsing into a fiery heap.

Knowing that bunkers are compartmentalized, the flamethrower moved around to the seaward side of the bunker where he sent a second stream of fire in through the main gun port. Again unearthly screams were heard from inside what had now become a crematorium.

Stop it, Pete's rattled brain silently shouted. *Just stop it.*

But there was no stopping until the howling finally subsided, replaced only by the crackle of flame and the deadly black smoke. The fight was over.

Slowly walking to the top of the smoldering bunker, Pete gazed at Black Beach 2, the southern coast of Helen where the Japanese commander had assumed the Americans would land. To his right he saw three Marines race forward heading toward the water's edge, each wanting to be the first American to officially cut the island in two, even if that severance was merely symbolic. Unsupported from the rear, all the Marines had done was to create an isolated pocket that even now the Japanese were probably starting to close around.

A flash of light and a loud, sharp crack startled Pete as he saw the second of the three running Marines cartwheel through the air. He landed on the wet sand and rolled two or three times before stopping, blood from the ragged stumps where his legs had been staining the gentle waves red as they lapped around him. His two comrades froze to immobility, stared briefly at the legless dead man, then gingerly picked their way back to the tree line, careful to step in their own sandy footprints. The word quickly came down to stay off the beach. It's mined.

"Second Platoon on me!" Lt. Cornwall hollered, waving his rifle over his head.

He led the seventeen remaining men a short distance east of the bunker where Nicholson, Lt. Long, and Capt. Stacy stood waiting.

"Dig in here," Stacy commanded, using his arm to trace an imaginary line south to north. "Five pace intervals. Third Squad on the right keeping clear of the beach. Second Squad next. Lt. Long's First Platoon will tie in there."

Stacy removed his helmet and ran a hand through his sweat-caked hair.

"I needn't tell you we're spread pretty damned thin," he said in his firm voice that oozed with a confidence his men found reassuring. "We've cut their damned island in half, taken everything they've thrown at us. They're going to be pissed off and they will try to take this ground back. They won't succeed because we are holding here. HQ is trying to push reinforcements to us and we'll be here when they arrive. I'm proud of you men. You've been through a lot since yesterday, but I still need more from you. Now dig in and get ready."

He turned and left.

"I think I'd follow that man anywhere," the Professor said.

"Who wouldn't?" Reb chimed in. "He's a Virginian like Bobby Lee."

He grinned as he slung his rifle and unsheathed his entrenching tool.

As the men of Second Platoon spaced themselves and began digging in, Nicholson sauntered over to Pete.

"I guess you know that Second Squad is yours now, Talbot," he said.

Pete's face fell visibly. This was a responsibility he hadn't wanted.

"Look, kid," Nicholson said, taking a more hard-line approach. "Ever since you joined the platoon you've worked hard to be a loner. But there are no loners in the Corps. We're a team and there comes a time when every man has to step up and do his part, and your time is now. You've made a point of trying to show me how tough you are. Now prove it. You're a good Marine. You just have to convince yourself. By the way," he added as an afterthought, "corporal stripes go with the job."

Pete sat quietly for a few moments as he sorted out the praise from the criticism.

Changing the subject he asked, "How's Mac?"

"Haven't had a chance to check yet," Nicholson replied. "But you know as well as I do he ain't comin' back on the line. Anyway, I'll approve whoever you pick as your assistant."

"Aldrich," Pete said with no hesitation.

"He would've been my choice," Nicholson said. "All right. Get 'em ready, Corporal. Time to earn that ten-dollar-a-month raise you just got. The Nips will hit back at us and it won't take long."

Nicholson turned and headed off. Pete watched "his men" preparing for the expected enemy attacks. Thirty hours ago the squad had sixteen men. Now it was just him and six others.

He glanced up at the bright afternoon sun and wondered how many would be left this time tomorrow.

———————

Kenji Sakai searched the wrecked landscape in vain for his friend for as long as he could. But as the sun rose in the sky, any movement on the ground became risky as American carrier planes circling overhead seemed eager to dive on any stirrings they saw that did not appear friendly. Three times he had to leap into a shell hole or the remains of a blasted bunker to escape death at their hands.

By the time the sun was directly overhead, Kenji had pretty much given up on finding Tadao. As far as he knew, his comrade had reached the coast and made good his escape. Perhaps he was even then on Bairiki waiting for Kenji to show up. He decided to wait until dark and then try again.

CHAPTER 16

Even as the Americans had wrested this thin slice of ground known as Black Beach from the enemy, the unseen foe was gathering strength to annihilate this isolated pocket. With their backs to the sea, the ground the Marines held was roughly two hundred yards long where it paralleled the airstrip, and about eighty yards wide at each end.

Pete liked their position. About forty yards out in front stood a heavily pummeled grove of palm trees. Standing on average twelve to fifteen feet apart, these trees would provide the approaching Japs with modest cover, but once they left the tree line they would encounter open ground.

Ever aware of snipers, Pete moved toward Aldrich's foxhole where he found the Professor reclining inside. He held a small dark can in his hand from which he was scooping out some sort of meat.

"What are you chowing down on?" Pete asked.

"Jap ration, some type of tinned fish," he said and tossed a can to Pete. "Took it from a rucksack whose former owner had no further use for it. Try it. It's pretty tasty. And have a couple of these." He indicated a small packet of biscuits. "The Japs call them kanpan."

Pete pried open the can lid with his Ka-Bar.

"How do you know so damned much?" he asked.

"I told you," the Professor replied, "I read a lot." He paused to down another chunk of the fish. "Saw you in conference with the gunny. What's up?"

"Ah shit," Pete snarled. "He made me a corporal. Probably out of spite, the bastard."

The Professor grinned.

"Don't laugh," Pete shot back. "You're my assistant. It should be your promotion anyway. You're a damned sight smarter than me. You even know what Jap hardtack is called."

"Book smart, yes," Aldrich said, swallowing his last forkful of fish and tossing the can out of the foxhole. "I could spout psychological mumbo-jumbo until your ears bleed. I could lecture you about my personal favorite, Alfred Adler, whose theory is that everyone is born with a sense of inferiority which they try to overcome by attempting to be superior. Adler believed this is the driving force behind all human behavior. True or not, that doesn't do us any good here." He waved his fork in the direction of the distant gunfire. "What we're doing here is all about survival, and you my friend, are a survivor. That's what the squad needs at its head if we're gonna get through this."

Pete had no response, something that didn't happen very often. Except for Charlie and possibly Aggie, no one had ever expressed such trust and confidence in him. He fidgeted uncomfortably.

"Tell you what, Professor," Pete said, putting a hand on his friend's shoulder. "If we survive this war and you ever become a shrink and hang out your shingle, I'll be your first customer."

"They're called clients," the Professor replied as he bit into a kanpan.

Pete pried open the can and stared at the dark slivers of whatever sea life it contained.

"You're sure about this shit?" he asked.

"Yeah. Try it."

Pete dug a fork out of his mess gear, scooped up a small portion, and tasted it tentatively. Aldrich was right. It had a mild, fish flavor mixed with a sweet sauce. He devoured the rest, licked his fork clean, and replaced it in his kit.

Taking advantage of the lull, Pete settled back. He opened his haversack and rummaged around inside until he located his much-cherished weatherproof bag. From it he delicately withdrew a well-cared-for, black-and-white photograph. Charlie Talbot's impish smile beamed from the photo.

"Is that your brother?" the Professor asked.

Pete glanced at Aldrich and just nodded.

"Looks like a great kid," Aldrich added.

"Yeah," Pete said.

Aldrich did not need psychology to see the emotion welling up inside Pete, but he knew his friend too well to push this discussion too far. Still, one question needed to be asked.

"Charlie's dead, isn't he?" he asked.

Pete flinched and quickly replaced the photo. Aldrich reached out and placed a comforting hand on Pete's shoulder.

"You're a good man, Hardball, but you've got to learn to trust people, especially your buddies," the Professor said firmly. "You can't bottle things up until you explode. That's not good for you and it's not good for the squad."

Pete was mulling over what Aldrich said when the jabbering of many Japanese voices from beyond the palm grove told him the anticipated counterattack was on its way.

———

As the sun slid higher into the morning sky, Kenji was still looking for a location where he could safely await his next opportunity to catch up to Tadao while not being exposed to enemy planes. Spotting a seemingly abandoned trench and a battered bunker, he hurried to it and jumped in. When he got to the bunker itself, he discovered that he'd stumbled upon a small command center containing about seventy men under a Lt. Hikoki Umeza.

"Your name and rank," Umeza barked authoritatively.

"Leading Seaman Kenji Sakai," he responded crisply.

"Where is your unit?" Umeza asked.

"As far as I know they are all dead or scattered like me," he replied.

Umeza nodded, then said, "You will join me as one of my squad leaders. We've just received orders to join other units at the eastern end of the airfield. I am told there are some burned-out trucks there by the turning circle. Our forces are rallying just beyond them and are preparing to attack the enemy as they advance. We will drive the round-eyed devils into the sea or meet glorious death trying."

"I lost my rifle," Kenji said.

Umeza pointed toward a concrete bunker.

"There are dead men in there," he said. "Take what you need."

Sakai saluted. He thought of Tadao and said a soft, "Goodbye my friend."

CHAPTER 17

The first assault was hardly an attack at all.

Under the mid-afternoon sun, fifty Japanese soldiers surged forward through the small forest of beat-up palm trees. Nerves strained to the tautness of steel cables, the Marines opened up on the *rikusentai* as soon as they were visible. Braving this storm of lead, the Japanese raced out of the palm grove and into the open. Screaming "Banzai," they pressed the attack even as their comrades dropped like grain sacks all around them. By the time the attackers had closed to within twenty yards of the Americans, their number had been cut nearly in half. The survivors suddenly pulled up, then began to rapidly retreat, finally disappearing the way they had come. Two or three of the fallen that littered the field moaned and squirmed. The rest lay silent.

"Whut the hell?" Reb whined. "That wuz as easy as shootin' coons back home on Jack's Knob."

Pete turned as Gunny Nicholson approached from behind.

"Everything jake here?" the gunny asked.

"So far," Pete confirmed. "What the hell was that?"

"They were gauging our strength," Nicholson replied, "sacrificing themselves so their officers could count our numbers and pinpoint our positions and types of weapons. Next time there'll be more of 'em."

"Say Gunny," the Professor said. "What's the score on Mac?"

"Doc says he'll pull through," Nicholson told them. "By the way, Talbot, Magruder said you did a good job helping Mac before he got there. He asked if you wanna be a corpsman."

"I'd sooner pull permanent KP and finish my tour as a bubble dancer," Pete said. "But as far as Mac goes, I just did what it said in the Blue Book. Shit, I was barely off the train at PI when they shoved the manual at me and took a buck out of my first pay. So you damned well better believe that since I hadda buy the book, I read it."

Nicholson grinned.

"Still," he said, "Mac's pissed off at you."

"What the hell's his gripe?"

"His last instructions to you were to keep moving yet you stopped yourself and this Georgia peach here," he gestured toward Reb, "to drag him off the runway."

"Well fuck him," Pete said, a hint of a smile creasing his sweaty, dirt-streaked face. "Next time I won't save his ass."

"Sure you won't," Nicholson said. Then he added, "Okay. Get ready but pass the word, wait to fire until you hear the command."

Nicholson disappeared and Pete had just pulled out another Camel and was about to light it when the assault that Gunny predicted burst upon them.

"Better postpone that smoke," Aldrich said tersely. "Here they come."

Pete tucked his unlit Camel behind his right ear.

As his men aimed their weapons, a wave of enemy soldiers emerged from the trees heading straight for Dog Company's line. They were led by a sword-wielding officer screaming "*Totsugeki!*"

When the human tide was about halfway across the open expanse, Capt. Stacy hollered "Commence firing!" The Dog Company line opened up, chopping down the first rank of charging *rikusentai*, all except for the officer. Hit several times, he tottered for a moment, then kept coming. The presence of his sword made him a not-to-be-neglected target. After three or four steps his body was pummeled by rifle fire from Marines aching to bag an officer. The impact sent him staggering backward against the trunk of a heavily battle-scarred tree. He collapsed to the ground, leaving a bloody smear on the bark.

Gunfire rippled along the American line. In the enemy ranks men fell, particularly in front of Roseblum's position where the deep-throated cough of his BAR chopped a wide swath through the attackers. Despite their losses the Japanese came on screaming "Fuck Babe Ruth" and "Death to Marines." "Go to hell you bastards," came the hoarse reply as Marines desperately emptied their weapons, reloaded, and emptied them again.

The Japanese attack broke in blood and the survivors poured rearward. About sixty more enemy dead were added to the butcher's bill, their contorted bodies scattered across the outraged landscape. In front of Rosie's BAR the dead lay stacked three deep. Quickly the curly-haired kid scurried out of his gun pit and, assisted by Sandy Gutierrez, dragged the corpses aside to clear his field of fire for the next charge.

It wasn't only Japs who fell in the attack. Less than twenty minutes earlier, Dog Company had contained thirty-nine men. As Stonewall took a head count now, that total had dropped by five, including two dead.

The next assault wasn't long in coming, this time striking the Marine perimeter from the north across the runway. The attack nearly swamped a part of the line held by Easy and Fox Companies and what was left of First Battalion. Pete and the others, reduced to anxious spectators, could only watch the rising battle smoke and listen nervously to the angry shouts and curses.

"Hold the bastards, fellers," Pete heard Reb murmur. "Hold 'em."

"They'll hold 'em," Bucket said in a worshipful tone, half in faith and half in prayer. "They're Marines. They'll hold 'em."

They did hold them and the cacophony of battle eventually grew dimmer and dimmer until it flickered out entirely.

A lull settled over the battleground. Pete removed the battered and slightly bent cigarette from behind his ear and set it alight with his Zippo. Checking the pouches on his ammo bandolier he found it contained just two twenty-round clips. With two spare clips for the automatic, six left in his Thompson, and three in his pistol, he had just sixty-five rounds to fire if, or rather when, the Japs returned.

"Better see how the guys are fixed for ammo, Hardball," the Professor suggested.

Pete nodded. Cautiously he kept low as he hurried to the squad's far right where Kusaka was lying behind a small barricade of wood and corrugated iron roofing. Kusaka was the squad's best marksman. He had shot expert in boot camp and, toting an '03 Springfield he called "Beelzebub" that mounted an 8-power scope, he was a qualified sniper.

"Stay alert, Mickey Mouse," he said, "The Japs'll be back. How's your ammo?"

"Low," Kusaka said. "I got two clips plus four rounds in Beelzebub."

Pete moved on to Bucket Harnish.

"I sure wish I was back in St. Albans tapping maple syrup out of my pop's trees," Bucket said dreamily. "A guy could get hurt out here."

"No shit?" Pete said. "Ammo check."

Bucket had three clips left.

It was the same all along the line, with the worst off being Reb who had fewer than two clips including the one in his Garand. Pete's sole good news came from Roseblum who still had ten magazines ready for use, largely thanks to his squad mates who had each lugged a spare clip ashore to feed the hungry Browning.

"I'm in good shape," Rosie beamed.

Pete slapped Rosie on the shoulder and said, "I'm gonna try to get us some more ammo, so hang tight."

Pete hurried rearward to find Lt. Cornwall or Gunny Nicholson. He located both near the Jap bunker that still emitted wisps of smoke from its openings. Close by corpsmen were tending a dozen wounded men including McDougal, a few with bottles of plasma hanging above them attached to upturned rifles. Hurrying up to his CO, Pete reported his ammo situation.

"We know all about it, Hardball," Cornwall said. "Everyone is running low."

"So what are we supposed to do, sir?" Pete asked. "Another attack like the last one and we'll be throwing coconuts at the bastards."

"Colonel Jordan just made it up here," Cornwall said. "He's the acting regimental CO. They're bringing ammo and other supplies in some amtracs. After they drop the stuff off, the amtracs will take our wounded back. They'll be here as soon as possible."

Pete nodded and looked to Nicholson.

"Get back to your squad and hold the line with what we got until the cavalry arrives," the gunny said.

"Aye, aye," Pete said and headed back to the squad.

Hunched over, Pete moved along the squad's line, informing them of the promise of ammo and supplies. As he moved along, his brain harbored the fear that he was not up to the task of looking out for the welfare of these men. *Why the hell didn't they pick someone else?*

Pete slid into the hole occupied by Bucket Harnish. He paused silently for a few moments. Then Bucket, familiar with Pete's moods since boot camp, noted the concern on Pete's face.

"What's troublin' you, Hardball?" he asked.

"I was just remembering boot camp," Pete said, "and how Blakely and Collingwood tried to kick me into shape. They seemed to delight in busting my ass and telling me how I needed to join the team and about how Corps spirit and teamwork could save guys' lives. I was remembering how much their lectures pissed me off. But ya know what? Those two motherless bastards were right."

"Blakely and Collingwood," Bucket snorted. "I wonder what they'd say if they saw us right now."

"That's easy," Pete smiled, grateful for even a brief break in the tension that was twisting his gut. "'Quit skylarking, shitheads! Straighten up and act like Marines you sad, sorry hunks of dog crap.'"

Both men laughed.

The laughter was cut short as the sound of Japanese voices and shuffling of hundreds of feet rose up from out in front.

"Here they come," Pete said, clapping Bucket on the shoulder. "Get ready."

Pete scuttled to his left to take up a position just behind the middle of his squad's line behind a small ripple in the landscape. Then he saw them, a tide of gray-green uniforms, gold-colored anchors gleaming on their helmets, surging forward. Pete's heart sank. Their right flank extended well beyond the Marines' left. This mammoth attack would hit Dog Company's entire front and wrap around the left flank and hit Easy Company and God alone knew who else.

At Stonewall's command, gunfire and bursting mortar shells ripped gaping holes in the enemy line. *Rikusentai* dropped like rag dolls. The rest surged forward relentlessly, ignoring their losses and screaming their oaths. Bayonet-tipped rifles were held at the ready as the charging mass, undeterred by the idea of death, swept forward, ready to die.

With terrifying certainty, Pete realized that Dog Company was about to be swamped. He stopped firing. His attention became focused on his squad as the Japs closed on them. Everything and everyone seemed to be moving in slow motion. Pete watched Mickey Mouse and Bucket fire desperately into the oncoming mass, their mouths open and screaming oaths Pete could not hear. Six of the enemy staggered and fell dead causing half a dozen more to falter and drop back. He saw Reb cut down three Japs in quick succession and thought that perhaps the hillbilly actually did hone his skill by shooting coons on Jack's Knob, wherever the hell that was.

Two Japanese drew close to the Professor's foxhole. Both died there as the college boy from a small Maryland fishing village shot each man so quickly that the two rounds sounded like one discharge.

Then Pete saw something that snapped him out of his stupor. A phalanx of nine *rikusentai* were closing on Rosie's BAR, intent on taking out this hated weapon even at the cost of all their lives. By the time the clump of men got to within ten paces of Rosie, the sustained fire from his BAR had hacked down four of them. He got one more with what proved to be his last round. Quickly Rosie ejected the spent magazine and fished for a fresh one. Sandy Gutierrez on Rosie's right had been focused on the enemy to his front, but now he spotted the threat to his comrade. He swung his Garand left and fired, dropping two of the four final attackers. Instinctively Pete snapped off a short three-round burst that hit another man who screamed sharply as he spun and fell. The last attacker by a heroic effort reached Rosie's position, kicked the BAR aside, and lunged with his bayonet-tipped Arisaka. Knocked to the ground and helpless, Rosie saw the fifteen-inch blade coming. With a short, terrified scream, he twisted his body to the left. The result was that instead of his chest, the long-bladed bayonet plunged through his right shoulder. Rosie wailed in agony as the Japanese soldier drew the bloody weapon out and prepared to make the killing thrust. Honeybun, on Rosie's left, deftly fired a round into the attacker's head. The impact sent the man's helmet flying, accompanied by a red plume of blood and brain. Dead on his feet, the man toppled backward out of Rosie's foxhole.

Gutierrez was the first to reach Rosie. With his hands he applied pressure to the mangled shoulder as Pete cried, "Corpsman! Corpsman!" all the while firing at the onrushing *rikusentai*.

Pete, Honeybun, and the Professor provided what covering fire they could as Gutierrez held fast to Rosie's wound, feverishly trying to stem the blood that oozed from between his fingers. A corpsman, Third Platoon's Calvin Ettinger, responded to the call and dropped into the foxhole beside Gutierrez and the two worked together on Rosie.

The Japanese wave overwhelmed the embattled American line. Gunfire was punctuated by the thud of bodies colliding and the animal-like grunts of hand-to-hand combat. Above it all, voices in Japanese shouted "Banzai!" and "Die, Maline!" while American voices screamed back, "Come and get it you sonsabitches" and "Fuck you!" One Marine yelled "Bastards!" over and over as he fired his rifle.

Two *rikusentai* approached Reb's foxhole. One jumped in on top of the Georgia boy who responded by yanking his Ka-Bar out of its leather scabbard. They rolled about in a tangle but somehow Reb managed to drive his knife into his intruder's neck. Twisting the blade, he severed the carotid artery. The second Japanese leaped over the foxhole then turned with the intent of finishing Reb off. Pete, his Thompson empty, drew the .45 out of his waistband and squeezed off a round. The heavy slug hit the man high in the back. He turned toward Pete and was greeted by two more blasts to the chest. He fell backward into the hole, landing on top of Reb, who was still trying to free himself from the bloody corpse of the man he'd killed. Pete extended a hand and helped Reb up.

The fight grew increasingly vicious as men stabbed each other with knives, bashed in faces with rifle butts, and crushed skulls with any heavy object that came within reach. The snap of breaking bones, the sickening thump of steel penetrating flesh, and the hiss of a man's dying breath blowing into the face of the man who'd killed him was all-consuming. Then, almost as suddenly as it had it started, the attack was spent. The bloodied Japanese filtered back the way they'd come while the Marines, fatigued to the limits of human endurance, sagged to the ground, gasping for breath, and wondering how they had survived.

Pete crawled over several dead Japanese to reach Rosie's foxhole where Gutierrez and Ettinger were still at work. Blood was everywhere.

"How's Rosie?" he asked.

"He'll make it," Ettinger replied as he worked. "But it was close. A couple of inches to the left and that bastard would've killed him."

Pete looked to Honeybun.

"See if you can rustle up a stretcher at the aid station," he said. "When those damned amtracs get here with the promised ammo, I want Rosie on one of those things and headed back for the beach."

"Gotcha," Honeybun said and was off.

With the shooting over for now, Pete cautiously rose to his feet for a look around.

The slide bolt of Pete's .45 yawned open, so he replaced the spent magazine then chambered a new round. He also fed his last clip into the Thompson. Scanning the battlefield, Pete felt as if he could've walked the length of the battalion's line from beach to runway, stepping only on Japanese corpses.

In some places, Americans and Japanese lay side by side. To Honeybun's left along First Platoon's line, Pete gazed at a horrific encounter between one *rikusentai* and a kid named Bobby Toliver. As Pete read the scene, the Jap had jumped into Toliver's foxhole at the same time Toliver raised his rifle to defend himself. The Jap shot Toliver square between the eyes while possibly at the same time Toliver's bayonet plunged into the Jap's chest. Toliver's body lay sprawled across the dead Jap's legs.

Pete turned away.

Checking in with his own squad, Pete was relieved to find that Rosie was the only casualty. Within twenty minutes Honeybun was back with a stretcher and he and Ettinger carried the wounded man to the aid station. Pete picked up the bloody BAR. He wiped the weapon off on the shirt of the dead Japanese soldier and carried it along with Rosie's ammo belt to Reb's foxhole.

"You should be damned near out of ammo, Butternut," Pete told Reb. "As I recall, you handled one of these pretty good at PI. You're our new BAR man."

"Gee, thanks," Reb snarled as he grasped the sixteen-pound weapon. "I don't mind shootin' the damned thang, but carryin' it's a pisser."

"Bitch, bitch, bitch," Pete said with a smile and walked away.

Aldrich strolled up beside him.

"I'm so glad Rosie's gonna make it," Pete said to his friend. "He was our only casualty. We were lucky."

"You handled things really well, Hardball," Aldrich said.

Pete glanced at the Professor, an unfamiliar feeling of accomplishment washing over him.

"Thanks," he returned, pleased by his friend's reassurance. "Get me an ammo count."

"Aye aye, Skipper," Aldrich said with meaning. Pete smiled to himself.

After getting the ammo count and finding that the next attack would have to be fended off with spitballs, Pete left to again check on the resupply effort. He located Capt. Stacy, Lts. Cornwall and Long, and Gunny Nicholson in conference about thirty yards behind First Platoon.

"How's your squad holding up?" Nicholson asked when he saw Pete.

"I got six guys left and about twenty rounds per man," he replied. "Where in the hell is that ammo?"

Nicholson grinned and pointed. Off to the north, just starting to cross the runway, Pete saw three amtracs churning in their direction.

"Thank God," he muttered and waited for the tracked vehicles to arrive.

As the amtracs reached them, Marines manning the line jubilantly slapped the backs and shoulders of the amtrac crews, then lent a willing hand to unload the crates of ammunition. As this was going on, a call went out to bring up the wounded for transport. Pete hurried to the bunker where he located Rosie, who had been placed beside a stretcher holding Cpl. McDougal. The corporal, a large, bloodstained bandage wrapped around his abdomen, smiled weakly when he saw Pete. As a stretcher team picked him up, he snatched Pete's wrist.

"Thanks for draggin' my ass off that airstrip, Hardball," he croaked, throat dry from the heat.

"Yeah, well I only do that once," Pete replied, then smiled.

He watched as Mac was carried out of the war. Rosie's stretcher was next.

"Can I get a hand here?" A corpsman asked Pete.

"Sure thing," Pete replied.

Together they picked up Rosie's stretcher and toted it toward an amtrac. As the stretcher was laid on the steel deck, Pete knelt beside Rosie.

"You made it, buddy," he said. "You're goin' back. Maybe even to the States."

Rosie, weakened by loss of blood, grinned through the pain.

"Thanks, Hardball," he said in a frail voice. "I'm sorry about leavin' the squad. Tell the fellas to take care. I don't wanna see them carried back like me. I'll be back if they let me."

Pete nodded and turned away. Before returning to his squad, he stopped by a stack of ammo crates that had been piled near the bunker. First he claimed a partially filled crate of grenades, then he began to feverously snatch up bandoliers loaded with .30-caliber clips to disperse among the squad. He also took several .45-caliber sticks for himself when Capt. Stacy approached.

"Hardball," he said in a voice that sounded unusually cordial. "I didn't have an opportunity to mention it before, but you and your squad did a helluva job earlier today in taking out that pillbox. You guys jarred the Nips' whole damned line loose and that's a lot of the reason we're where we are right now."

"I was just obeying orders, sir," Pete replied.

"Yeah," Stonewall agreed. "But it was well executed and you guys pressed the Japs hard. Anyway, I'm putting you in for a Silver Star. And

I'm putting Hullihen, Aldrich, and that Rebel in for Bronze Stars. Nothing may come of it since making those final decisions belongs to men way above my pay grade, but either way the recommendation will look good on your two-oh-one form."

"Thank you, Skipper," Pete said with a smirk, "I admit that my service record could use the help."

"So I hear," Stonewall said with a smile and turned away.

Pete shouldered the ammo bandoliers, hoisted up the box of grenades and Tommy gun clips, and headed back toward his boys.

CHAPTER 18

Laden with bandoliers, each holding eight ammo pouches, Pete arrived back with the squad. There he found his comrades busily dragging "monkey meat," their bitter label for enemy dead, away from their positions. This grisly task was meant to clear their fields of fire while also putting distance between themselves and the bodies already putrefying. Dead Marines were spared this fate. A short distance to the rear there appeared a row of nearly two dozen earthen mounds, each marked with an upturned rifle topped by an empty helmet.

Dropping first into Aldrich's foxhole, Pete handed over an ammo bandolier.

"Thanks," the Professor said, taking it without lifting his eyes from the object he held in his lap. It was a bloodstained white sash about six inches wide and four feet long with small red knots tied in neat rows along almost the entire length.

"Where in the hell did you get that rag?" Pete inquired.

"Off one of those guys," the Professor replied, absently waving in the direction of a half dozen bodies lying twenty feet away. "I don't know the Japanese name but I think it's a thousand-stitch belt. Each stitch is a prayer for the wearer."

Pete looked at the white sash with its ugly, darkening splotches of crimson.

"The guy should get his money back," Pete said. Then he noted, "You've read a lot about the Japs."

Aldrich carefully fingered the sash.

"My mother is German although she grew up in Belgium," he said. "During the First World War her family were refugees having fled across the Belgian border into France. My dad's outfit found the family hiding in an old farmhouse. My dad took pity on the family and swiped food from the mess area to give to them. He was enchanted by the family's teenage daughter and after the war, with the family having moved back to the small village of Gouvy, he proposed to her by mail. She accepted and Dad brought her over. I naturally became interested in her German background, so I am well-versed on Teutonic culture. I just wish I'd read more about Japan."

Pete looked ahead thoughtfully.

"All I wanna know about Japs is what's out there," he finally said. "And it scares the shit out of me." The words were scarcely out of his mouth when a sniper's round kicked up sand a foot to his left. "See?" he said, sliding deeper into the hole to present a less tempting target.

Handing a pair of grenades to Aldrich and hooking two on his own belt, Pete scooped up the bandoliers and the grenade box and left to distribute the ammo.

His last stop was with Harnish. The normally happy-go-lucky boy looked pensive.

"Problem, Bucket?" Pete inquired.

"I was raised as a God-fearing Baptist," he said quietly.

"And I was raised as a Democrat," Pete said. "What of it?"

"My folks raised me and my brothers and sisters in the faith," Bucket continued. "They dragged us to church every Sunday unless we were at death's door. My mom taught Sunday school for over twenty years, and Dad's been a deacon at our church for as long as I can remember." He licked his parched lips then took a long drag from his canteen. "We kids had to memorize the Ten Commandments and recite them in order. My dad even had pop quizzes. It was like boot camp where Blakely would make us recite the General Orders. 'Chuck,' Pop'd suddenly say,

'What's the fourth commandment?'" He stopped and was silent for a few moments. "So if I live through all of this, how can I go home and tell him what I did here?"

Pete was unsure what to say. Bucket continued.

"Do you know how many men I killed today?" he asked. "Six that I know of. And that was just today. There were at least three yesterday and God knows how many during the Jap attacks when all of us were just shooting into a mass of Nips. And tomorrow it'll start all over again. And maybe even the next day and the next. And then what? When the fighting here is over, those of us left alive will be pulled out, retrained, re-equipped, and sent to another island for the whole thing to begin again. There's no end to it."

What do I tell the guy? Pete wondered.

"Look Chuck," he said, using Bucket's given name for the first time since boot camp. "I don't know what God's take on the war is. I'm not a church-going person. I haven't cracked open a Bible since I was ten, but I know this. You don't have to explain anything to anybody, not your dad, your mom, or anyone. You're not fightin' for them. Christ knows I'm not fightin' for my folks. I'm not even sure I'm fightin' for our country or the American way of life or mom's apple pie or any of that crap. I'm out here fightin' for the Corps and my buddies and to stay alive."

Any further words choked in Pete's throat. He left Bucket's position and walked back to his foxhole. As he gazed at the blood-red sun perched on the edge of the horizon, he pondered what he had just said to Bucket.

He thought back to a conversation between himself and Charlie on the train platform the day his brother left for basic training. "Our country was attacked and we all gotta do our part," he could still hear Charlie say. At the time, Pete blew it off. From the day he'd heard the news about Pearl Harbor, getting involved in a shooting war was not in his plans and he classified those who rushed to enlistment offices as fools. It wasn't that he was afraid to fight, Pete told himself. Or was he? If he was really out to avenge Charlie, why didn't he join up the day after that telegram arrived from the War Department? Why did it take more than three months and a judge's decree to force him into taking action?

Something's happening to me, he thought. He was no longer that tough punk from Fishtown. Tough? Really? He remembered the gut-wrenching fear he had felt as the amtrac approached the beach. He recalled the hopelessness he felt as he wept over Ted's body in the bloody surf on D-Day. Then suddenly all of those feelings had evaporated, replaced by determination and purpose. He realized that he was coming of age as a man and a Marine. For that's what he now was. A United States Marine, hardened in battle and thrust into a situation where he was responsible for the lives of five other men. The all-too-familiar anger coupled with the self-doubt he had lived with for most of his life was now replaced by pride and sense of purpose. Now he understood the ideals his drill instructors tried to instill in him in boot camp.

"I'm fightin' for the Corps," he had told Bucket Harnish.

"Damned right," he muttered.

The sun was halfway below the horizon by the time Pete's mind returned to dusk-shrouded Betio. He rose and walked back to the squad, dropping into Aldrich's foxhole. He remained silent.

"You okay?" the Professor asked.

"Sure I am. Why?"

"I don't know. You seem unusually subdued, and I heard what you told Bucket. That was totally out of character for the solitary Hardball. You had an epiphany."

"If that means I'm starting to see things differently, then you're right," Pete said. "If it means that I finally realized that I'm not fighting this war alone, that the Japs did not bomb Pearl Harbor just to piss me off, you're right again."

"Your talk with Bucket was well-delivered, Hardball, but you left someone out," Aldrich said.

"And who might that be?"

"That girl back in the States," Aldrich said. "Don't you think she's worth fighting for as well?"

Pete was silent as Aldrich's question seeped into his mind. He thought back to shortly after his trial on assault charges and the judge's enlist-or-jail ultimatum.

———————

"So what happens next?" Aggie asked.

He told her he had to report to 30th Street Station Thursday morning.

"A bunch of us new recruits are heading to South Carolina to a place called Parris Island," he said. "The Marines have a recruit station there and we'll undergo something they call boot camp. That's where they'll teach us to do shit like marching and standing at attention. I don't expect that'll be too bad. They'll also train us in marksmanship. That's what I'm most interested in. Let me get my hands on a goddamn gun and I'll kill every Jap I see."

Aggie gently touched Pete's forearm.

"Please, Pete," she said softly but firmly. "Don't be so eaten up with anger that you take foolish chances."

Pete smiled.

"You're thinking that I'm being too rash," he said, "that I need to stop and think before I act."

"You're right," she said. "Look, I know you feel betrayed by your parents. But think of your mom. You know she's not a strong woman. What would she do if something happened to you?"

Aggie stopped and weighed her next words carefully.

"And what would I do?"

Pete looked into Aggie's concerned face.

"I wanted to talk to you about that," he said. "Charlie left me his life insurance money. With what I saved for his college I have a little over ten thousand bucks in a savings account. I'm going to add your name to that account."

"Me?" she asked. "Why me?"

"You're the most important person in my life," Pete replied. "You have been since we were kids, even if I don't always show it. So when I ship out for wherever they send me, I'm going to take out a policy of my own, naming you as beneficiary. If anything happens to me, you'll be well taken care of. And if I come home safely," he added, squeezing her hand to bolster his own courage, "it'll make a nice start on our future."

Aggie smiled. This was the first time Pete had discussed a future that included her.

The sun was nearly gone and gloom began settling over the island. Dipping into his backpack, Pete dug out a K-ration marked "Dinner" and slit open the waxed box.

The can he pulled out was stenciled "pork loaf." Using the attached key, he opened the can, jabbed his fork into the exposed glop, and absently began to eat, not really tasting the food. He nibbled at the biscuits and studied the small pack of cigarettes, four Chesterfields in a small box. He chuckled as he added them to his dwindling supply of Camels and thought about Robert Sherrod. *Wherever he is on the island, he must be very happy with his K-rations*, Pete thought.

As he ate Pete noticed a large body of men double-timing across the airstrip. Since none of the defenders were shooting at them, he assumed them to be Marines. Reinforcements maybe. He put it out of his mind and resumed his meal. Sometime later Gunny Nicholson approached and knelt on the sand beside Pete.

"Makin' the rounds," he said. "All okay here?"

Pete nodded, then said, "We get reinforcements?"

"Sort of," Nicholson replied. "C Company finally made it across the airfield. Bad news is there's only about fifty guys left, so their arrival does little more that make up for our losses today."

"Gunny," he said, "You fought the Japs since the 'Canal. Were they so fuckin' crazy there?"

"Almost," he replied. "I first saw them in action in China. After boot camp, me and Blakely were assigned as guards on battleships, first aboard the *Arizona* and later on the *California*. The Corps calls us sea-going bellhops. In '32 we were both sent to the Philippines and Dug-Out Doug McArthur, God's right-hand man. When the Japs invaded China in the summer of '37 a bunch of us were sent there to safeguard American property and civilians, although I don't know what the handful of us would've done against the Jap army." As he listened, Pete offered gunny a biscuit. He accepted and munched on it.

"Blakely, me, and a few others were posted in Nanking at the American embassy along Shanghai Road. As the Japs approached the city, the Westerners—American, British, Danish, and even a couple of Krauts—created the Nanking Safety Zone. It was about a three-mile area that the Japs were supposed to ignore. The Japs never officially bought into it, yet it seemed to work, maybe because the committee that formed it was led by a Kraut. Yeah, the Zone got bombed a few times and the Japs killed several hundred Chinese refugees by raiding some of the nearly two dozen refugee camps inside the Zone. But overall, if you were in the Zone you did okay. It did manage to save thousands of Chinese lives."

Absently, Nicholson made like he was going to light up a cigarette, then remembered that the sunlight was almost gone and with it the opportunity to smoke.

"Outside the Zone it was another matter," Nicholson continued. "The Japs bombed the shit out of Nanking, and when their troops moved in, they went on one helluva killing spree. They tied men's hands behind their backs and used them for bayonet practice. Women were raped until they were dead. Kids were slaughtered. I saw one big ugly Jap NCO grab a baby by the ankles and kill it by swinging it against a stone wall. They had head-chopping contests and two officers made a wager on which one could kill one hundred people with just a sword in the shortest time. Their men laid bets as if it was a fuckin' horse race. I don't know how many people the Japs killed but it had to be tens of thousands. You could hear the screams outside the Zone. Hell, I still hear them. Nip bastards!"

Nicholson stopped, took a swig from his canteen, and said, "I've gabbed too much. Make sure your squad is buttoned up. You might want to double them up. It'll thin your line but that way one guy can grab some fart sack time while the other keeps alert for infiltrators. Password is lollipop."

Pete nodded.

"Think they'll hit us after dark?" Pete inquired.

"Anyone's guess," Nicholson answered. "I told you back on the ship, don't second-guess them. But we hurt them pretty badly today. If I were their CO, I'd have my men crawl back into their holes and let us try to root them out. They want to kill more of us than we do of them, and that way's as good as any. But I'm not their CO so stay alert."

After a brief silence, Nicholson lowered his tone and added, "By the way, scuttlebutt says we might be getting reinforcements tomorrow from the Marines driving in from the west, and maybe even some armor. If that happens, we will probably start pushing east. The Japs still control the eastern third of this island and it's high time we end this thing." Nicholson winked. "But you didn't hear any of that from me."

With that Nicholson was off.

Pete doubled up his men for the night, having Mickey Mouse and Bucket share a hole, Honeybun moving in with Sandy, and Reb setting up the BAR with the Professor. Before moving Mickey Mouse, Pete warned Eddie Coogan on Third Platoon's left that the gap between their squads was being widened by ten feet.

"I'm gonna keep moving along the line so I'll try to watch out for any Japs who try to come through in the night," Pete told Coogan.

"Don't worry about it, Hardball," he said. "I got eyes like a fuckin' cat."

"Okay," Pete said. "How's the arm?"

Coogan had gotten nicked when the line had been strafed by a Navy Hellcat that morning.

"Just a scratch," Coogan said. "What pisses me off is no Purple Heart for being hit by our own guys."

"I'll try to get that changed next time I write to Eleanor Roosevelt," Pete said and headed back for his own squad.

As he did, he stopped with Bucket and Mickey Mouse.

"Congratulations Bucket," Pete said. "I think you said on the boat that yesterday was your mom's birthday. You made it. You didn't get killed."

"Well, the Japs sure tried," Bucket replied.

"So do you think your dad took her out somewhere nice or that maybe she had a party?" Pete asked.

Bucket shook his head and said, "She probably did what she always does since the war began, listen to the news and wonder about her kids."

"How many are there?" Mickey Mouse asked.

"There are seven kids in our family," Bucket replied.

His friends guffawed.

"That's not a family," Pete said, "that's a herd. Maple syrup farming must give your dad a lot of spare time."

"There are four boys and three girls," Bucket said. "Two of my brothers are in the service, one with the Army Air Force in England repairing B-17s, and one in the Navy in Norfolk."

He could see a look of sadness on his friend's face.

"Don't worry about it," Pete said, clapping Bucket on the back. "You'll see 'em again."

He knew it was trite, but he didn't know what else to say to ease his friend's mind.

Arriving at the foxhole shared by Reb and the Professor, he joined them.

"Everyone tucked in for nighty-night, Pa?" Reb drawled.

"Up your ass, Johnny Reb," Pete replied, and Reb howled in laughter.

"Nicholson have any words of cheer?" the Professor asked.

"Ahh, the usual," Pete said. He didn't elaborate. "Look, I'm planning a long night for myself, so I'm gonna grab some z's now. Wake me in two hours."

As darkness settled over the tormented island, Pete curled up on the sand. Using his knapsack as a pillow, he absently listened as a Marine somewhere off in the blackness quietly began singing what had become a Second Marine Division favorite since 1941. Put to the tune of "As the Caissons Go Rolling Along," the Marine sang:

> "Over sea, over foam,
> Wish to Christ that we were home,
> But the transports go sailing along.

In and out, near and far,
Wonder where the hell we are.
As the transports go sailing along."

As the unknown Marine quieted down, Pete fell asleep. Sometime later, the dream returned. He heard the drumbeat bursting of the depth charges, felt the submarine tossed side to side as men shrieked in terror. Then came the swoosh of water rushing into the boat and from the radio room he heard Charlie cry out, "Pete!"

He sat bolt upright. As always, the dream caused the sweat to course down his face.

Pete noticed that both Reb and the Professor were staring at him.

"Y'all okay?" Reb asked.

"Yeah. Someone else grab some z's. I gotta check the rest of the guys."

"What's with Hardball?" Reb asked Aldrich after Pete left the foxhole.

"Bad dreams," the Professor replied. "He'll tell us when he's ready."

Pete hastily moved to his left toward Honeybun and Gutierrez. He laid flat on the lip of the foxhole. Honeybun was asleep. Gutierrez, who had been staring pensively ahead, glanced up at Pete.

"Everything okay here?" Pete inquired.

Sandy nodded, then said, "I've just been staring at all them dead hombres out there." He paused, then said, "You know Hardball, I don't think I'm gonna make it through this battle. So much death. So many guys killed already. I just got a feeling my number is coming up."

Pete was taken aback. Sandy was usually upbeat, never one to feel dispirited.

Automatically Pete replied, "You gotta shake those feelings, Sandy." It just seemed like the right thing to say.

Sandy smiled sadly.

"What are our chances?" he said. "We left the ship yesterday with a hundred and forty-five guys in the company. Now First and Second Battalions together only have about that many. We had sixteen guys in the squad, now we have seven."

"That's all true," Pete acknowledged, "but most of our losses were yesterday during the landing. Of the nine guys we lost in the squad, only two of them were hit today, Mac and Rosie, and they're both gonna be fine. Right now they're offshore on a hospital ship, probably goosing nurses. The odds are in your favor."

"Maybe," Sandy replied, sounding not at all reassured.

"Then think about your family," Pete said. "They're where? Texas?"

Sandy nodded.

"They have a small cantina in Presidio," he said. "My brother and two sisters work there too."

"Sounds nice," Pete said.

"Not for me," Sandy replied. "I got tired of seeing cactus and parched ground and barren hills. I wanted out so I worked my way east. I harvested wheat in Oklahoma at two bits an hour, worked on the docks in Saint Louis, and picked corn in Indiana. When Pearl Harbor happened, I was working in a hardware store in Dayton, Ohio, at thirty-one bucks a week. Good pay. I felt like a millionaire."

"Where were you heading?" Pete asked.

"Nowhere in particular," Sandy answered.

"Well," Pete said. "Keep your mind on your job and you might make it there someday."

After checking on Bucket and Mickey Mouse, Pete retreated once again to his makeshift foxhole behind the center of the squad line, settled in, and began reflecting on events. He recalled their second day out of Wellington's picturesque Hawkes Bay en route to Tarawa. The men had no idea where they were going, but somebody knew they were on their way because the sultry radio voice of Tokyo Rose cooed, "A hundred ships are sailing away from New Zealand, and our gallant Japanese submarines have a torpedo waiting for every one of them."

Not to be outdone, one veteran leatherneck bunked near Pete bellowed back, "I got a torpedo waitin' for you too, baby. Hubba Hubba."

The men catcalled and whistled in delight.

That night he had the dream, a vision of Charlie trapped inside the USS *Grampus* as it was being blasted by depth charges from two Jap destroyers. The vision was terrifyingly real and ended, as it always would, with Charlie crying out Pete's name. Pete jolted awake, knocking his head against Ted Giovanni who occupied the upper berth.

"Goddammit," Pete muttered.

"Shut the hell up over there," a drowsy Marine in another rack cursed.

"Go fuck yourself, Mac," Pete snarled into the darkness.

With sweat pouring off his face far in excess of what the sultry heat of the night might squeeze from a man, Pete swung his legs over the side of the rack and dropped to the deck. Ted leaned over the side of his bunk and glanced down at his friend.

"You okay, Pete?" he inquired.

"Yeah, I'm fine, Feather Merchant," Pete curtly responded.

Ted was the only man in the platoon who called him Pete. "I'm going topside for some air."

"Want me to come along?" Ted inquired.

"You wanna hold my hand?" Pete growled. "Go back to sleep."

"I'm just a concerned buddy," Ted grumbled. "No need to bite my head off."

"Ah," Pete said. "I'm just bitchy. I'll be back in a little bit."

———————

Pete smiled sadly to himself as he recalled that night. He had been hard on Ted, far harder than the kid deserved, and now he regretted it.

He wondered if they'd recovered Ted's body yet.

———————

As Lt. Umeza and his men prepared to move out as ordered and take part in attacks on the Americans, Kenji wondered what fate had befallen his friend Tadao Onuki. He had no way of knowing that Onuki had spent much of the day hiding in a trench with several other men. In the confusion after he and Kenji had been separated, Onuki had inadvertently wandered, not farther from, but closer to the battle line. Huddled there with these strangers, he tried to get his bearings when with a sudden "Whoop!" American Marines seemed to materialize from nowhere, firing their weapons at the easy targets in the trench. Panic ensued as men tried to escape this deadly fusillade. Tadao was literally buried under a wave of terrified men. Then came a deep whooshing sound and an incredible wave of heat enveloped him. All about, men screamed in agony as the flames of hell seemed to overtake them. These agonized voices were the last sounds Tadao heard before blackness overtook him.

It was evening when Tadao Onuki opened his eyes. A pungent smell of kerosene and burned meat permeated the air around him and filled his nostrils. Now Onuki found he could not move his hands and he felt like his body was being pressed by some object. To his horror he realized he was beneath a pile of charred bodies. Frantically he began clawing his way free. As he worked, something hot and sticky oozed through his fingers. Eyes open in terror he saw it was the scorched flesh of the man above him which slid off the bones as Onuki struggled to free himself. Onuki realized he was surrounded by men horribly burned to death by a flamethrower. Only because he'd been covered by the others did he alone survive. Being shielded by their bodies saved him.

Finally freeing himself from his former comrades, Tadao Onuki headed for the Betio coastline.

PART III

MONDAY, NOVEMBER 22, 1943

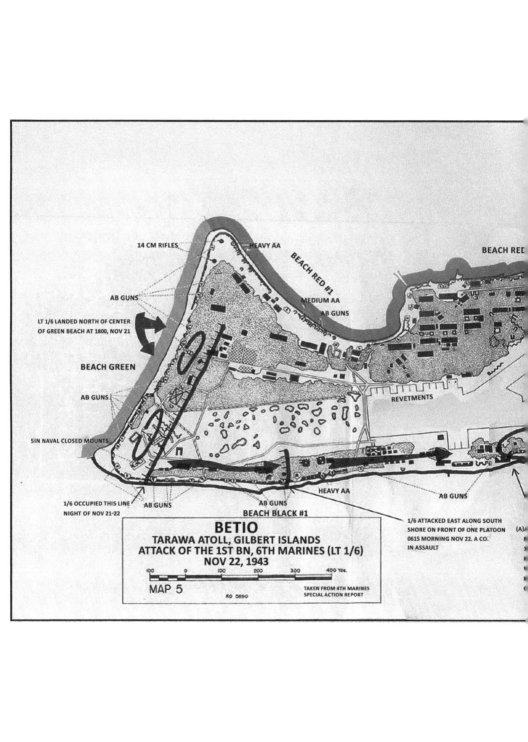

14 CM RIFLES

HEAVY AA

BEACH RED #1

BEACH RED

AB GUNS

MEDIUM AA

AB GUNS

LT 1/6 LANDED NORTH OF CENTER
OF GREEN BEACH AT 1800, NOV 21

BEACH GREEN

AB GUNS

REVETMENTS

5IN NAVAL CLOSED MOUNTS

1/6 OCCUPIED THIS LINE
NIGHT OF NOV 21-22

AB GUNS

AB GUNS

HEAVY AA

AB GUNS

BEACH BLACK #1

1/6 ATTACKED EAST ALONG SOUTH
SHORE ON FRONT OF ONE PLATOON
0615 MORNING NOV 22. A CO.
IN ASSAULT

BETIO
TARAWA ATOLL, GILBERT ISLANDS
ATTACK OF THE 1ST BN, 6TH MARINES (LT 1/6)
NOV 22, 1943

100   0   100   200   300   400 Yds.

MAP 5

RO 5890

TAKEN FROM 4TH MARINES
SPECIAL ACTION REPORT

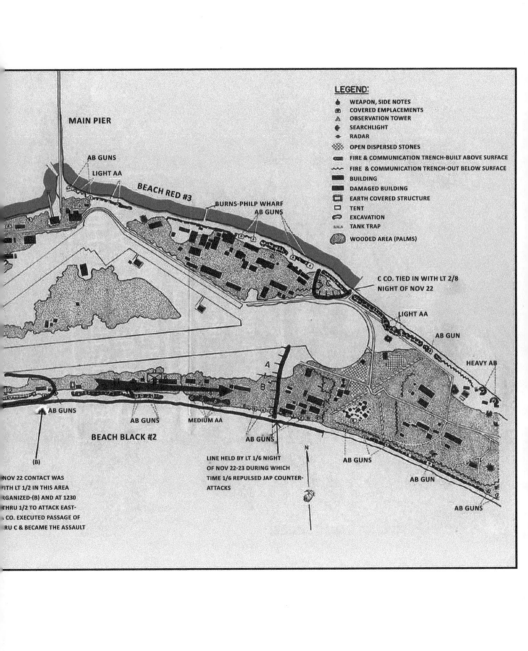

LEGEND:
- **WEAPON, SIDE NOTES**
- **COVERED EMPLACEMENTS**
- **OBSERVATION TOWER**
- **SEARCHLIGHT**
- **RADAR**
- **OPEN DISPERSED STONES**
- **FIRE & COMMUNICATION TRENCH-BUILT ABOVE SURFACE**
- **FIRE & COMMUNICATION TRENCH-OUT BELOW SURFACE**
- **BUILDING**
- **DAMAGED BUILDING**
- **EARTH COVERED STRUCTURE**
- **TENT**
- **EXCAVATION**
- **TANK TRAP**
- **WOODED AREA (PALMS)**

MAIN PIER

AB GUNS

LIGHT AA

BEACH RED #3

BURNS-PHILP WHARF
AB GUNS

C CO. TIED IN WITH LT 2/8
NIGHT OF NOV 22

LIGHT AA

AB GUN

HEAVY AB

A

B

AB GUNS

AB GUNS

MEDIUM AA

BEACH BLACK #2

AB GUNS

AB GUNS

AB GUNS

AB GUN

N

AB GUNS

(B)

NOV 22 CONTACT WAS
WITH LT 1/2 IN THIS AREA
RGANIZED-(B) AND AT 1230
HRU 1/2 TO ATTACK EAST-
CO. EXECUTED PASSAGE OF
RU C & BECAME THE ASSAULT

LINE HELD BY LT 1/6 NIGHT
OF NOV 22-23 DURING WHICH
TIME 1/6 REPULSED JAP COUNTER-
ATTACKS

CHAPTER 19

Alone in his foxhole in the spectral light of a nearly full moon, Pete found his thoughts drifting toward Aggie. In his loneliness he reflected on her friendship and affection.

———————

It was early September. Boot camp graduation had come and gone and many of the new recruits had been shipped to Quantico, Virginia, for additional training. After a few weeks of advanced infantry instruction, orders came for Pete, Ted, the Professor, and the other recruits to report to the Fleet Marine Force in San Diego. Before shipping out, the men were granted a week's furlough to allow for final visits with family. Pete's first stop was Boston to see his Uncle Dick.

Richard Swift, Pat Talbot's older brother, had been heartbroken by the way his sister's family had been torn apart by Benny. Uncle Dick had never warmed to his brother-in-law and had earned Benny's wrath when he stood by Pete through the hearing that followed the violent argument between father and son. Still, he urged Pete to at least see his mother before he shipped. Pete lied and said he'd think about it.

Arriving in Chester on a Friday with just the weekend left on his furlough, Pete checked into a hotel and called Aggie on the phone.

Since he had enlisted, Aggie had taken a job in the secretarial pool at the Philadelphia Navy Yard. Along with two other girls from her office, Aggie moved into an apartment closer to her work. To enable her to get around, Pete had urged her to withdraw enough money from their joint savings account to purchase a used Plymouth.

Aggie met Pete at the hotel where they clung to one another in a long embrace. Together they spent the day at Crozer Park, walking and talking about his time in boot camp, her new job, and her roommates. She also questioned Pete's green Class A uniform.

"I thought you Marines all wore that fancy blue uniform," she teased.

"You gotta buy them piece by piece," he said. "Jacket and slacks alone cost nearly thirty bucks, and the cap another four. I'm a lowly private. I only make fifty bucks a month."

There was a brief silence.

"Have you called your mother?" she asked.

"Nope," Pete said. "And I don't plan to." He hesitated. "I want to spend what time I have here with you."

Aggie's eyes closed as she leaned against Pete, feeling comfort in the coarse wool of his jacket against her cheek.

Later that day they had dinner and took in a movie. Afterward, with Pete at the wheel, they drove in silence through the streets of Chester. Aggie sat as close to Pete as she could get, and now she laid her head on his shoulder. A warmth flowed through Pete and he reached down from the wheel to pat her hand, misjudged, and ended up touching the cotton skirt covering her thigh. Aggie didn't seem to mind.

Arriving back at the hotel they got out of the car.

"It's late," Aggie said. "I should be getting home. The girls will worry about me."

"No," Pete said. "It is late. Too late for you to drive alone. Your friends will be fine. Stay here tonight."

Aggie looked at Pete, her lips trembling, her eyes soft and questioning.

"I'll crash on the couch," Pete added.

"I have no pajamas," she said. "No change of clothes."

"I'll loan you something and tomorrow we'll go shopping and I'll buy you a new dress. How's that sound?"

Aggie could just nod and they entered the hotel.

That evening it began to rain and they sat together on a well-worn sofa listening to the splash of raindrops against the window. Aggie sat dreamily as Pete described the men he had met so far, particularly Ted Giovanni. He mentioned his irritation about Ted's unwelcomed interest in him.

"He's just trying to be friendly," she said.

"I'm not there to make friends," Pete replied.

"Don't be such a hard ass," Aggie said.

Startled, Pete looked at her.

"What?" She asked innocently, a mischievous smile creasing her lips. "I learned the phrase from you."

Pete laughed loudly and threw an arm around Aggie. She snuggled close, her head on Pete's shoulder. They sat quietly for a time. Then Aggie tilted her head up and gazed at Pete. He looked down at her.

"I'm frightened for you," she told him in a soft voice.

Pete brushed a strand of red hair from Aggie's face. Then he lowered his head and kissed her. Pete could feel Aggie's lips tremble.

Before turning in, both now wearing Marine Corps-issued T-shirts and skivvies, they curled up together on the bed talking and laughing until well past midnight when, by the hardest of efforts, they took to their respective beds. Although neither knew it, both had trouble falling asleep.

———————

Thinking of her, Pete recalled Aggie's soft cheeks and pug nose, her deep-set blue-green eyes and flowing red hair. His pulse raced as he recalled the delicate smell of the rose-scented soap she always used.

When he was with her, he was truly happy. So why was it so hard to tell her he loved her?

Charlie had often told Pete that he and Aggie were meant for each other and that his older brother would realize that fact if he could just rid himself of the fear of his father. Benny Talbot seemed to delight in tramping on the hopes and dreams of both his sons. Charlie's answer was to leave home for the Navy while Pete just simply numbed his emotions and stopped trying to feel.

"You have to move on from Dad," Charlie said on his final visit home. "I've done it and so can you. You need to start thinking of Aggie."

He knew his little brother was right, but Pete still lacked the courage.

———————

But now, on this terrible island where life had become precious, Pete began to realize he was not the same brash punk who waded ashore nearly two days ago. No matter how uncomfortable it made him and no matter how it happened, Pete realized that everything he believed about himself had changed. His mind flew back a few hours to his conversation with Bucket about why he, and they, were fighting this war. He remembered how the Professor had pointed out that Aggie was worth fighting for as well. Pete now understood that his friend had shot a bull's-eye.

Pete had indeed undergone what the Professor called an epiphany. He also came to the realization that, just as Charlie had insisted, he was hopelessly in love with Aggie.

"You were right about me again, you sly little bastard," Pete whispered to his brother.

Pete was brought back to the here and now by a loud rattle of gunfire that rippled across the dimly lit landscape. It was coming from the north, near the landing beaches some seven hundred yards away. Amid the clamor Pete heard faint shouts. The battle sounds were persistent. The crack of rifles and the staccato rattle of machine guns mixed with the crump of distant grenades and squat 75mm pack howitzers.

"*Jap counterattack?*" Pete wondered.

He glanced at his watch. It was about 0130. Pete decided to check on the squad again and discovered that the distant battle had wakened nearly everyone.

"Will someone turn off that goddamned radio?" Mickey Mouse complained as he rolled over and tried to get back to sleep.

The only man not bothered by either the firing or the flares was Honeybun. This surprised no one. While en route to Tarawa Atoll, the *Zeilin* was alerted to the possibility of a Jap submarine stalking the invasion convoy. The Marines, forced to wear Mae West life vests during the entire voyage, were herded below deck and the crew piped to General Quarters. Klaxons sounded, steel hatches slammed shut and were noisily dogged, and the escorting destroyers rolled a few random depth charges off their fantails. It turned out to be a false sighting and the all-clear was sounded, hatches undogged and opened. Honeybun slept soundly through the entire incident.

Pete returned to his foxhole. He listened as the battle off to the north reached a climax, then slowly faded away.

As the night resumed its stillness, Pete's thoughts again drifted homeward and for a few moments he envisioned his mother. As a youth he had been close to her, but her turning a blind eye toward Benny Talbot's abuse had strained their relationship, particularly after that awful night when Charlie had suffered so cruelly under his father's leather belt.

After tending to Charlie's injuries, Pete had left his brother in his room and angrily stomped downstairs to the kitchen to remove a cold bottle of beer from the ice box. Popping the cap on a wall-mounted opener advertising the Chester Brewery, he entered the living room. Pat Talbot appeared more frail and tired than Pete had ever seen her. She sat slowly rocking back and forth on her late father's wooden rocker. Pete approached her.

"Where is the son-of-a-bitch?" he said harshly.

"If you mean your father," she replied dully, "I finally got him to bed."

Pete took a long pull from the beer bottle.

"Why don't you let me kick the bastard out?" he said.

"I can't," she moaned.

"When Charlie and I were kids, I'd have bought that," her son retorted. "But I'm almost twenty. I'm working and so are you. We can pay the bills and live just fine. We don't need him."

"He's my husband," Pat replied. "I can't just leave him."

"For Christ's sake, Mom, you got me," Pete urged.

"For how long?" she asked. "What happens when you go out on your own? And what if you get drafted and go off to war? Then what? If I were you, I'd want to get out of here."

Pete took another swig of beer while he thought.

"I just can't imagine he's the same man you married. Granddad always told me how you were such a happy young girl. Bubbly, he called you. I can't picture that girl marrying a guy like Dad."

Pete drained the beer.

"Did Charlie tell you he joined the Navy?" Pete asked.

From the startled jerk of her head it was obvious he hadn't. Pete nodded.

"He can't," Pat gasped. "He's just a boy."

"He enlisted right after his eighteenth birthday," Pete said, placing the empty bottle on an end table. "He leaves the day after graduation."

Pat sank further into the rocking chair.

"So," Pete said harshly. "You've got one son who can't wait to get away from home and another ready to toss his old man into the gutter. Welcome to our happy family."

———————

Pete heard a noise to his left and turned to see Capt. Stacy making his way along the line. He stopped by Pete's foxhole.

"Everything okay here, Hardball?" Stonewall asked.

"Yeah, Skipper," he answered. "It's all quiet. Can't say the same for the guys on the beach."

Stonewall nodded, then said, "I just got the word. The 1/6 is pushing in from Green Beach and expects to link up with us by noon. They may push through us and continue east with us in support. Or maybe we'll be up front helping to lead the charge. I don't know which yet. They're also supposed to bring up armor although I'm not gonna cheer until I see it for myself. Either way, have your guys rested. It's gonna to be a busy day."

He paused a moment, then lowered his voice and said, "I want you to take care of yourself. We hit the landing boats on D-Day with a hundred forty-five men. Now I have thirty-two fit for duty, including two lieutenants, three sergeants, and five corporals, three of whom, like yourself, were battlefield promotions. So when this bullshit is over, I've got an entire company to rebuild. Some of our wounded will come back, but most of the guys coming in will be boots straight off the boat and I'm gonna need NCOs, hard-asses like yourself, to kick them into shape."

"I don't plan on getting shot, Skipper," Pete replied.

Stacy gave a brief smile and a wink and was off.

"*I've finally got something to live for,*" he silently told himself.

CHAPTER 20

The captain's parting words to Pete left him uneasy. But he also felt a sense of pride. He reflected on the grass-green recruit who arrived at Parris Island just over three months ago, an angry young man who detested authority.

Pete had been asleep when the train rolled into the depot at the drab little South Carolina town of Yemassee. Almost before the wheels stopped rolling, the raw recruits were ordered off the cars by red-faced, screaming men with stripes on their arms. Passing through the main gate, Pete noticed a sign tacked to a post that read, "Let's be damned sure that no man's ghost will ever say, 'If your training program had only done its job.'"

To Pete that sounded far more reassuring than the taunts coming from other Marines who sat watching the new men arrive. As the motley column shuffled by trying to keep in step, old salts regaled them with, "You'll be sorrreeee . . ." Shaken and angered by the treatment he'd received so far, Pete worried that they may be right.

The recruit depot at Parris Island was situated on a low, sandy, almost treeless island cut off from the mainland by a narrow creek which connected the Beaufort River to the north and Broad River to the south.

Pancake flat, the base always seemed to be swept by winds blowing in from the sea. The summer sun made the place hot as a skillet, making it a perfect spot to breed determined swarms of mosquitoes. Equally annoying was the fine sand that swirled in the wind and coated everything.

Pete grinned as he recalled being herded into the mess hall and fed. Then it was off to the post sick bay where they were ordered to strip naked and pass through a gauntlet of doctors and Navy corpsmen armed with what many men later swore were syringes affixed to square needles. Each man was then subjected to a battery of inoculations simultaneously being jabbed in both arms and their ass checks with assembly line precision. Blood was drawn, sight and hearing were tested, and a full medical profile was worked up for each man. Next came the shearing of the new recruits' hair. Pete was especially incensed by this but yielded to it despite the rage welling up inside as he watched his hair, auburn like his mother's, fall to the floor in clumps. He held his tongue but almost exploded when a corporal broke the news.

"Those haircuts will cost you twenty-five cents and it'll come off your first pay," he said.

Pete found trouble on day one. The uneasy boots stood on the parade field for fifteen minutes in the hot sun as Staff Sgt. Edward "Bull Moose" Blakely and his assistant, Sgt. Michael "Red Mike" Collingwood, nonchalantly paced the line.

"Platoon, ten-hut!" Blakely snapped and the recruits straightened up into what each assumed was attention. It wasn't.

"No, no, no!" Collingwood screamed. "Put your heels together, feet at a forty-five-degree angle. Keep your goddamn knees straight, hips level and drawn back slightly. You there," he pointed to one young man. "Where the hell are your knees? Get 'em straight but don't lock 'em. Let your arms hang natural, palms out, thumb along the seam of your dungarees. Get your heads up. Up, goddammit. No, not that far! You ain't spottin' for aircraft. Chins down! Jesus Christ. Eyes dead ahead. Balance your weight on the balls of your feet. Can't you assholes get anything right?"

Once some semblance of "attention" was achieved, the DIs approached the row of nervous men. With a coldness that sent chills down the spines of the hapless recruits, the two NCOs walked along the line, glancing at each man with well-rehearsed disdain and commenting on each as they passed him by.

"Feather merchant. Feather merchant. Lard ass. Redneck. Jerk off," they observed. Every so often the pair stopped in front of an unfortunate boot and one of the NCOs would say, "I don't know what the fuck you are."

Finishing their inspection, the sergeants returned to stand in front of the men.

"I'll be a sorry sonofabitch," Blakely said, his eyes scanning the platoon. "What a bunch of sad-assed bastards." He turned to Collingwood. "Where the fuck does the Corps find this many assholes to send us? And we're supposed to turn them into Marines?"

"I don't know, Bull," Red Collingwood replied. "I've flushed better material down the crapper."

Blakely turned to address the men.

"Listen up you sad-assed bastards," he bellowed. "We are your drill instructors. If you wish to speak to us, you will call us 'Sergeant' or 'Drill Instructor' and ask permission. Call either of us 'Sarge' and it will be the sorriest day of your miserable life." His gaze swept the line. "You have no past. You have no rights. You have no privileges. You have nuthin'. You are not men and you sure as hell are not Marines. You are shitheads, the lowest, slimiest, stupidest form of animal scum on the planet.

"You shitheads are now Training Platoon 621. Remember that. I ain't one for repeatin' things. Me and Sgt. Collingwood have been directed to knock you into shape, but frankly we feel it's a lost cause. Still, those are our orders and they will be obeyed. We are bastards and we will work you like you've never been worked before, and then when you feel about to crap out, when your ass is draggin' lower than a snake's dick in a wagon rut, we will work you some more. Unless told otherwise, you will move everywhere at the double-quick, even if you're just goin' to the head to take a dump. You will salute every man above the rank of boot. Remember. You may've given your heart and soul to Jesus Christ . . ." Blakely stopped. When he resumed, men swore he had a gleam in his eye. "But the Marine Corps gave us your ass."

Blakely continued his rant for another twenty minutes, seldom re-peating a curse word twice. During this screed Pete made the mistake of glancing in Blakely's direction instead of remaining at "eyes front."

Blakely, who seemed to possess some type of infraction radar, stormed in Pete's direction. Getting up close so their noses nearly touched, he sneered, "Why are you eyeballing me, shithead? Do I fascinate you, shithead? Do you want to butt fuck me, shithead? Are you a homo?"

"No!" Pete snapped crisply.

"No what?" Blakely continued, loudly.

"No, Drill Instructor. I am not a homo!" Pete replied.

"I can't hear you, shithead," Blakely taunted.

"No, Drill Instructor. I am not a homo!" Pete shouted loudly, wish-ing the earth would open up and swallow him.

"Are you saying you don't love your DI, shithead?" Blakely pushed.

Pete thought, *What the hell do I say now?* He knew that if he said yes, the DI would again accuse him of being homosexual. And if he said no, God knows where the dressing down would go. Instead, he fell back on his short time in Sunday school and the lessons of respecting one's elders.

"I respect you, Drill Instructor!" Pete barked.

Blakely stared at him. Pete could almost hear the DI's brain work-ing. Pete fought back an urge to smile, a fatal response to be sure, as he realized that Blakely didn't have a reply for what was intended to be a no-win question.

Finally, Blakely snarled, "Fall out and grab your bucket. You're gonna police the parade ground. And I want it clean. You pick up every piece of paper, every cigarette butt, every scrap of gum, every dog turd, cat turd, bird turd, and any other piece of shit that God didn't personally put here."

For Pete, that punishment was just the start of a succession of re-dresses. He fucked up again the next day by speaking to Collingwood without asking permission and had to collect three hundred cigarette butts, which proved a monumental problem on the well-policed grounds of Parris Island. Pete had to beg Marines to light up just so he could collect their butts. Finally, he stashed his bucket outside the slop chute, then went inside and emptied ashtrays into his pockets.

Collingwood and Blakely continued to ride Pete hard. After screwing up close-order drill his fifth day in camp, he was forced to take two buckets, his and Ted's, and double-time to the Beaufort River, fill them to the brim with water, then carry them back.

His rebelliousness became a thorn in the sides of his DIs. In his first two weeks at PI they had Pete police the parade ground six times, run countless laps—sometimes along the beach, not on the sand but in the surf which proved to be sheer hell—and do push-ups until every muscle in his body screamed.

The act that finally brought Pete into line, the one that Nicholson had referred to as "the toilet water gimmick," occurred when he was assigned to latrine duty with Giovanni and a boot named Crosley. Pete bristled. He had not joined the Marines to scrub piss pots so he sat on his upturned bucket while the other two men did the work. Stopping in to check on the progress, Blakely found Pete lounging on the bucket and smoking while Giovanni and Crosley busily cleaned the urinals. Fixing Pete with a blood-chilling stare, Blakely angrily dismissed Ted and Crosley and ordered Pete to clean all of the toilets.

"And they better sparkle," Blakely growled. "I want them clean enough to drink from."

Pete scrubbed the commodes well and was glad he did, for when Blakely returned he got down on his knees and inspected them as if he was Sherlock Holmes looking for clues. Then he fished a collapsible metal cup from a pocket, dipped it into one of the toilets, and handed it to Pete.

"Bottoms up," he said, and Pete drank.

———

Sitting in his foxhole in the predawn darkness, Pete smiled to himself. That was the last time Blakely and Collingwood had problems with him.

It had been a long night's vigil, but eventually the pink and purple clouds to the east told of the approaching sun. As expected, dawn rejuvenated the battle whose clamor rose along with the brightness of the new day. Based on Stonewall's information, Pete knew that the men of the 1/6 had begun today's push which would, everyone hoped, lead to their breakthrough to this isolated pocket on Black Beach. As he watched the sun lunge from the sea, bringing with it the promise of a resumption of bloodshed, he recalled his favorite line from a Civil War story he had read in high school. Penned by Lt. Frank A. Haskell, a Union officer, and called *The Battle of Gettysburg*, Haskell wrote of being roused from his sleep by the rattle of musketry on the third day of that battle fought eighty years ago. "Come day of battle!" Haskell had written. "Up Rebel hosts, and thunder with your arms! We are all ready to do and to die for the Republic!"

See, Professor, Pete thought. *I read too.*

Studying the scene of yesterday's carnage, Pete remembered his grandmother's death from cancer when he was nine years old. He recalled the funeral. How could the silent woman in that wooden box be the same happy lady who had played on the front porch with him and Charlie and would take them to DeShong Park to enjoy the playground and wading pool?

The last two days, however, he had seen so much death that he wondered if he was becoming immune to it. Then his mind brought up the image of the young Japanese soldier he had seen as he came ashore. Their eyes had met. They had made a connection; one young soldier fighting for his country against another doing the same thing and neither knowing why. Was he one of the bloated corpses lying out there? Oddly, Pete hoped not.

Aldrich, who had awakened by now, noticed Pete's pensive mood.

"You look deep in thought," he said. "Thinking about your brother?"

"Actually no," Pete replied. "I was thinking about a Jap. A particular Jap."

"Hirohito?" Aldrich quipped.

Pete snickered.

"Not that lofty," he said. "I was thinking about a young enlisted man I saw as I was coming ashore." He related the story to his friend. "We were two guys just doing what we'd been trained to do. He saluted me and I feel maybe he was telling me that he admired what I was doing for my comrade."

"Maybe he was," Aldrich said. "Japs have a strong warrior code and they appreciate acts of bravery and devotion to cause."

Pete shrugged.

"Maybe that's it," he acknowledged. "But I see his face so clearly. Then I ask myself why I should care about the guy. I should hope he is one of those bodies out there. Screw 'em all."

Pete sank back into silence.

His reverie took him once again to that last day aboard the *Zeilin*. The ship's loudspeaker kept barking out how religious services, including last-minute baptisms, were being conducted in this hold or that hold. At the announcement for a Roman Catholic Mass, Ted rose to his feet.

"I gotta get to confession," he told his friends.

"Christ, Wop," Pete said. "You've never even gotten laid. What the hell do you have to confess? Did you call the Pope a prick? What? Tell me."

"You've just got the red ass because God wouldn't touch you with a ten-foot pole," Ted replied. "I'll catch you guys after Mass."

Pete smiled sadly at the memory. Ted had fallen and Pete cried over him. But now, after forty-eight hours of killing, he wasn't sure he had any tears left. At least not now. Maybe later.

With the sun now fully clear of the horizon, Japanese snipers snapped into action. Pete flinched as two bullets twittered past him. He gave these sharpshooters some respect by hunching over as low as he could get as he began making the rounds of his line.

Honeybun was brushing sand from his rifle, a seemingly endless job, while Mickey Mouse breakfasted on a can of chopped ham and eggs.

"Sounds like we got noisy neighbors," Honeybun quipped, pointing toward the gunfire to the west.

"That's the 1/6 movin' up," Pete replied. "They should be here before long, provided their officers put a little fire up their asses."

"They gonna relieve us?" Mickey Mouse asked.

"More likely we're gonna reinforce them," Pete responded. "They're gonna keep pushing east."

Further along, he found the Professor keeping a wary eye on the enemy position while Reb scribbled on a slip of paper with a stubby pencil.

"What are you doin', Hillbilly?" Pete asked as he sat down beside his friend.

"Ahm writin' a letter, if ya must know," Reb answered.

"Wow," Pete said. "It's amazing what they can teach you in just four years of schooling."

Reb ignored the jab.

"Ah wrote mah momma, but Ahm enclosin' a note to mah brother Bucky, remindin' him to keep his hands off mah car."

"You have a car?" Pete asked.

"Yup," Reb said proudly. "It's a '32 Model 18. Ah bought it three years ago for jest fifty bucks. 'Course, it had hit a tree or two along the way so it's dinged up, but Ahm fixin' it." He looked up at Pete. "It has a flathead V8 engine," he continued proudly. "221 cubic inches. They wuz new to Fords that year. Up until then, Ford only put V8s in Lincolns, but then in '32 Lincoln went to the V12 so they stuck the flathead V8 in the Model 18 after they stopped makin' the Model A."

"I'm not really a Ford guy," Pete said. "It's the only car I hate worse than my old man's Essex. How does it run for you?"

A pained look crossed Reb's face.

"Well, it ain't really runnin' at all raht now," he admitted. "The engine got beat around some, but Ah was rebuildin' it til the damned war came along and made parts scarcer than nuns in a cathouse. Plus it needs a coupla tires which are impossible to get with rationin'. So it's never really gotten out of my folks' shed yet, which is why Ahm tellin' Bucky to keep his damned hands off it. He thinks he's some sorta handyman but the dumb bastard's all thumbs. He'd fuck up pluggin' in an electric fan."

"Well," Pete said, "don't be too hard on him. He's your brother and you're lucky to have him."

He went back to writing and Pete moved on.

"Lucky to have him? Bucky? Whut the hell wuz that all about?" Reb asked the Professor.

"Just write your letter," Aldrich said.

Pete dropped into his foxhole just as a sniper's bullet kicked up sand a few yards to the rear. Fatigued beyond measure, Pete ignored the near miss. Folding his arms across his knees, he rested his head on them and fell into an exhausted sleep.

CHAPTER 21

As the 1/6 advanced eastward they flushed Japanese soldiers like quails from a thicket. *Rikusentai* who chose not to die at their posts or end their lives by their own hand could now be glimpsed beyond the airstrip as they retreated. A few eager Second Battalion Marines inside the pocket took pot shots at the scurrying figures, but at that range and with the nimbleness of their targets, a hit was highly unlikely. Still, it was considered good sport.

Not all the enemy was withdrawing. At around 0900 shouts of "Banzai" erupted and a wave of Japanese came storming from the tree line in front of Second Battalion.

Almost as one, the Marine line loosed a savage volley that took down a number of the attackers. The battalion's mortars dropped a flurry of shells that exploded upon the Japanese.

As he emptied his Thompson and inserted the fresh magazine, Pete found himself immersed in the spectacle taking place before him. Waves of Japanese soldiers pathetically charged to certain death as bullets tore them apart. Running men stumbled over slain comrades then rose back up only to be felled by Marine gunfire.

The actions of one man in particular left Pete spellbound. Struck by bullets in the abdomen and left shoulder and obviously unable to advance or retreat, the *rikusentai* screamed curses at the Marines. As he ranted, he reached into his blood-soaked tunic and pulled out a grenade. Continuing his defiant harangue, Pete watched the man activate the grenade. Still bellowing, he clutched the grenade against his chest with both hands. The blast nearly tore the man in half, blowing open his chest, shredding his lungs and heart, and leaving bloody stumps where his hands had been.

Pete sank down into his foxhole, stunned by what he'd witnessed. *What is going on here?* he thought. *What the hell is happening?*

Pete's brain became a swirl of images. He saw the faces of his dead comrades, the courageous but doomed young lieutenant who led his men against a Jap pillbox, and Capt. Wentzel, pipe clenched in his mouth, defiantly sitting atop the seawall shaming his men into advancing until he was killed. He recalled the Jap who had hurled himself into a loaded amtrac filled with Marines while clutching a grenade, a man set afire as he was thrown from an exploding bunker after it had been lit up by a flamethrower. He saw Ted lying in the surf and Radio Ray Colby huddled on the beach, reduced to idiocy by the carnage, the first man he had shot upon landing, and the enemy soldier with the boyish face who had saluted him amid the wreckage of the landing beaches. Lastly, he saw Charlie.

My God, he thought. *Bucket was right. It never ends.*

Then he became aware that he was being shaken. It was the Professor. "Hardball. Hardball," he called as if from a distance. "Are you all right?"

Pete looked at him stupidly at first then shook his head to clear his brain.

"Yeah, yeah," he replied. "I'm fine." He looked around. The fight was over. "Anybody hurt?"

"No. Squad's fine." The Professor paused, unsure of his next words. "You're okay, right? For a few seconds I was afraid you were going battle happy."

"I'm good," Pete growled. "Don't worry."

"Want to talk about it?"

"No," Pete snapped.

Aldrich wasn't about to accept that answer.

"Talk to me, you stubborn bastard," he said forcefully.

Pete was astonished. The Professor never swore. So Pete told him about the Japanese soldier he'd seen killing himself with a grenade.

"He blew himself up," Pete said, still not believing what he'd seen. "Just . . . blew himself up."

Aldrich thought for a moment, then said, "There's a poem I saw in a book while I was studying about the Japanese that struck me, and I memorized it. It goes:

> 'Corpses drifting swollen in the sea depth
> Corpses rotting in the mountain grass.
> We shall die.
> By the side of the Emperor we shall die.
> We shall not look back.'

"I thought it poignant."

"I get that they don't want to be POWs, that it's somehow shameful," Pete said. "Still, and I know this is stupid, when I saw that guy blow himself all to hell, I thought about his family back home. I wondered, *did he give them any thought as he did it?*"

Aldrich removed his helmet and brushed a hand through his sweaty brown hair.

"They don't think like us, Hardball," he said. "When they go off to war the soldier doesn't expect to come back."

"I don't know about any of that," Pete said. "I just know that if that guy had been my brother, I'd rather have him come home disgraced than splattered all over the landscape."

"Now I understand," Aldrich said. "This isn't about that Nip and his family. You're thinking about Charlie. This has been eating at you since we left New Zealand. Maybe longer." He paused and replaced the helmet. "Tell me about him."

Pete turned and stared at the Professor.

"No you don't," he said. "After the war you can get me on a couch and I'll pay ya five bucks an hour to root around in my head. But not now."

Aldrich smiled ruefully.

"After the war, you'll be lucky to get away for ten bucks an hour," he said. "Luckily, today I'm free. Talk to me."

Pete stared silently at his friend. He realized Aldrich was not about to be put off any longer.

"He was a helluva kid," Pete finally said. "Movie star handsome, fair-haired, and with the bluest eyes you ever saw." He dug the cherished photograph out of his haversack and handed it to Aldrich. "He was the only one in the family with blue eyes. Don't know where the hell that came from, although I used to joke with my mother because our mailman also had blue eyes. It pissed her off. Charlie was smart like you. Much smarter than me. I quit school the end of my junior year but he coulda gone to college. In fact, I wanted him to. I even saved a few hundred bucks to help him pay for it, but he was too eager to get out of the house, so he joined the Navy instead."

"Why the Navy?" the Professor inquired, handing the photo back.

"Well, you know I'm from Chester, Pennsylvania," Pete continued while replacing the picture, "a section called Fishtown, just a few blocks from the Delaware River. We'd watch carriers and battleships and everything else sail in and out from the Navy Yard at Philly. We loved the water. Hell, I think I told you that I took a job as a deckhand on the Chester Ferry, going back and forth between Chester and Bridgeport, New Jersey. It was only a six-minute run each way, but I did it over and over every goddamned day. Sounds boring but I sorta enjoyed it."

Pete paused to stub out a cigarette, then fished a fresh one from a battered pack in his shirt pocket, lit it, and drew in a deep breath. He blew out the lungful of smoke slowly, lost in thought, and watched the smoke float away on the breeze.

"Your brother's eagerness to get away from home," Aldrich asked. "Was it because of your dad?"

"Our father is a worthless drunk with a nasty temper who liked to beat on his kids as a way of proving he was a man," Pete spat. "Not your warm, homey *Saturday Evening Post* cover."

The two men sat together in an awkward silence broken only by the battle sounds rolling across the flat landscape from the north and west.

"Tell me about the dream," Aldrich said.

"No," Pete barked testily.

"You gotta get this out, Hardball, it's tearing you up," Aldrich implored. "And it's not just for your sake but for the squad's. You're in command. You freeze up again during an attack and you might not only get yourself killed, but the rest of us as well."

Pete sat silently for what seemed like hours. Opening up his soul to anyone, even to this man who had become his closest friend, was against all of his instincts. Then, like a flooded dam, it burst out.

"It begins with the boom of exploding depth charges," Pete said. "The sub, Charlie's boat was the USS *Grampus*, is submerged and the explosions jar the boat, tossing the crew around."

So Pete unloaded, telling Aldrich the whole morbid story from the depth charges to the flooding sub to the water slowly creeping up to drown his brother as he screamed Pete's name.

"'Pete! Pete!' Charlie screams as the water rises," Pete told Aldrich. "But I'm not there. I'm not able to save him. I keep wondering what his last thoughts were."

Pete realized that tears were flowing down his cheeks. The Professor pretended not to notice.

"But it's just a dream," he said. "You don't know what really happened."

Pete shook his head.

"I tell myself that all the time," he said. "Maybe it was quick and he didn't suffer. But the dream's painful detail haunts me." He swiped a shirtsleeve across his face to dry his eyes. "I wasn't home when the telegram arrived, but when I walked into the house and heard my mother bawling, I knew something terrible had happened. She was sitting on the living room sofa, unable to talk. All she could do was point to the sheet of paper lying on the coffee table. I'll never forget the words. 'The Secretary of the Navy regrets to inform you that your son, Seaman Charles Franklin Talbot, is listed as missing in action on March 5, 1943, in the Solomon Islands. Additional information will be forwarded to you as it is received.' I felt as if I'd been punched in the gut. I knew what the phrase 'missing in action' meant, especially when it came to submarines."

Pete sat quietly for the longest time.

"I can certainly see why you're so angry and why you joined the Marines so you could fight the Japs," Aldrich said.

"It's not just the Japs," Pete snapped. "Yeah, they dropped the depth charges. But it's as much my old man's fault. He's the one who drove Charlie out of the house. I hate him and I wish to hell I'd killed the sonofabitch when I had the chance."

"How did your father react to the telegram?" Aldrich asked.

After giving the question a little thought he replied, "He just got drunker than usual. That night I thought I heard him bawling in his bedroom but I can't be certain."

Pete snatched a canteen from his web belt and took a swig. After capping it, he shook it, listening to the splash of the little bit of water he had left. He turned back to the Professor.

"Let's get back to work," he said. "Go find Nicholson and see when we can expect to get some fresh water. At this rate we'll be drinking our own piss by noon."

Aldrich knew to back off.

"I gotta go check on the squad," Pete said.

Shortly after 1100 hours, the advancing point men of the 1/6 made contact with the Marines of the 1/2 lining the western edge of the Black Beach perimeter. Before long the newly arrived Marines were having their backs slapped and hands shaken by the men who'd been holding this corner of hell for the past eighteen hours.

Hard on the heels of the 1/6, another round of cheers went up as six Stuart tanks lumbered into view, their Cadillac engines growling as they clanked along the coral runway. The Stuarts were followed by a heavier, more lethal Sherman with "China Gal" painted on its armored skin and packing a formidable 75mm gun. A second Sherman was close behind. One of the Stuarts swerved out of column and rolled into Second Battalion's perimeter. The tank's turret was adorned with a painting of a shapely brunette in tight red shorts and a checkered men's shirt tied off at the midriff. Accompanying the painted image was the name "Li'l Lil." The vehicle drew to a halt near Gunny Nicholson. The tank commander, a sergeant, threw back the top hatch, popped out of the tank and, reaching down, pumped

Nicholson's hand vigorously. They talked for several minutes after which the tanker climbed back into his Stuart and hurried forward to rejoin the others. Nicholson continued on to where Pete and the Professor were standing.

"What was he looking for?" Aldrich asked. "Directions to the nearest USO?"

"Nah," Nicholson replied. "We went through boot camp together, then I stayed with the infantry and he went into armor. Our unit supported his tanks on the 'Canal along the Matanikau and at Point Cruz."

"So who's Li'l Lil?" Pete asked.

"Certainly not his wife," Nicholson replied. "I've met her."

Aldrich gazed after the tanks as they formed a front, spacing themselves about fifteen yards apart on a line nearly one hundred yards in length.

"Sometimes I wonder if a tank isn't the best way to go into battle," he mused. "All that metal around you."

"It has its advantages," Nicholson answered, "until an armor-piercing shell cuts through that two-and-a-half inches of steel and explodes inside the crew cabin and turns you into hamburger. Or a Jap clutching a mine to his chest throws himself under your treads." Pete glanced at Nicholson questioningly. "It happens. I saw a crew get broiled alive that way on the 'Canal. I'll take a nice safe foxhole over an iron coffin every time."

Nicholson plopped down on a nearby palm log.

"You guys asked about fresh water a while ago," Nicholson said. "Some just arrived in Lyster bags back by the pillbox. Have your men fill up."

Turning toward his squad line he called to Gutierrez and Bucket and ordered them to fill the squad's canteens.

As this was being done Pete asked, "So what's the word? With the 1/6 here, are we being pulled off the line?"

"No such luck," the gunny replied. "At 1300 hours the 1/6 will advance eastward on a one-hundred-yard front with the tanks in the lead. For now we're gonna remain here but be ready to move up in case the 1/6 needs support."

There was a brief silence among the men. The only sound was the distant growl of battle to the west coming from a four-acre area near the cove called "The Pocket." Then Nicholson was off.

Noting Pete's silence, Aldrich asked, "Still thinking about your brother?"

Pete nodded.

"It's funny how the house where Charlie and I used to play as kids suddenly became so terribly lonely after he died," Pete said. "I'd sit alone in Charlie's room. He loved cowboy movies, and his walls were filled with pictures of his favorite stars: Roy Rogers, Gene Autry, Red Ryder, and Little Beaver. He loved them all." Pete sighed deeply, then continued. "But what made me saddest was a photograph Charlie kept on his dresser. The picture was taken about nine years earlier, not long after cancer killed our Grandma Florence. Our family never had the money to take any fancy vacations, but on my tenth birthday our granddad—his name was Charles, Charlie was named for him—took us and our mom to the Philadelphia Zoo. Dad wasn't along, which made it a great day. Mom had saved up four bucks to buy me a Brownie camera so I took a lot of pictures. The one Charlie kept on his dresser was of all of us, arms around each other standing in front of a cage containing three Bengal tigers. Grandpa had asked some stranger to take the picture so we could all be in it."

For the second time that day tears welled in Pete's eyes as he recalled the happiness reflected in all their faces.

"Two years later our granddad died of a heart attack," Pete concluded.

He shrugged.

"Charlie had so many dreams and so much ambition," Pete told Aldrich. "And now," sorrow was heavy in his voice, "now he's just dead. Nothing. No future. Not even a gravestone to lay flowers at."

Pete looked into Aldrich's eyes.

"I'm okay, Professor," he said. "I mean it."

CHAPTER 22

It was shortly before 1300 when the men of the 1/6 rose wearily to their feet, hoisted their LMO packs onto their backs, and began to reform for their eastward push. Breaking into platoons they gathered around the tanks. The armored beasts began to lumber forward. Engines roared, spewing plumes of exhaust that engulfed the Marines walking behind them. In advancing, several of the Stuarts, *Li'l Lil* and a pair of unnamed M3s, were forced to churn their way across the blood-soaked landscape. Inevitably their treads took on the semblance of meat grinder blades as enemy corpses were crushed beneath them.

"I wish my great-uncle Walt could see this," Honeybun said as he squatted on the sand near Pete. "Tanks named for his beloved commanding officer charging into battle like modern-day cavalry." He stopped and turned to Pete and the Professor. "Did I ever tell you that my Uncle Walt was with General Stuart the day he was shot?"

"No," Kusaka said, feigning weariness. "But I'm sure you will."

Not one to be put off by jabs, the North Carolinian continued, "It happened on May 12, 1864, at Yellow Tavern, Virginia. Stuart was always randy for a fight, so he got right up on the firing line, shooting that LeMat pistol he loved, ya know, the one with nine rounds in the cylinder and a short shotgun barrel under the main barrel? Well, he was up on the line when he got hit. It lifted him right out of his saddle, and dropped him back down again." He raised himself up slightly then plopped down to demonstrate. "My uncle and two other fellas eased the general off his horse and onto the ground and he looked up at my uncle and said, 'Honeybun, how do I look in the face?' Uncle Walt lied and told him, 'You are looking all right, General. I think you will be fine.'" Honeybun paused. "I don't think Stuart believed him because he told Uncle Walt, 'Well, I don't know how this will turn out but if it is God's will that I die, I am ready.' So Uncle Walt helped load the general on a wagon and he was taken to Richmond to his sister's home." He paused again. "The general's wife, her name was Flora, and their two kids were sent for, but they didn't get there in time. At about seven o'clock that evening Uncle Walt heard the general say, 'I am going fast now. I am resigned. God's will be done.'" There was another pause. "He was just thirty-one. My uncle may've told me that story a thousand times, and I never got tired of hearing it. Until he was too old and weak to walk, every May 12, Uncle Walt would take my cousins and me to Richmond so he could lay a wreath on Stuart's grave in Hollywood Cemetery."

"That's a heck of a story," Aldrich said.

The tanks and men of the 1/6 advanced seventy-five yards to their jump-off position, then halted to await a softening-up attack by the Navy. Minutes seemed like hours to the men tensed up for their forward thrust. Then came the waves of low-flying carrier planes, Hellcats, Corsairs, and some of the new dive bombers, the Helldiver SB2C that its pilots dubbed "Son-of-a-Bitch Second Class." The planes swooped in at treetop level, their machine guns chewing up the ground. Five-hundred-pound bombs dropped from wing racks. The eruptions sent lethal blossoms of smoke spiraling into the sky. After unleashing his firestorm, each pilot nosed his plane back up into the azure sky before gracefully looping over for another pass.

The advance began as soon as the aircraft departed. They'd covered less than seventy yards when the Marines drew small arms fire. Twenty yards more and the forward move stalled completely as enemy fire intensified, the clatter now mingled with the cough of knee mortars. Rounds burst among the Marines who scrambled for cover, flattening their bodies as much as possible to avoid flying steel. The Japanese mortars were soon answered by rounds launched from Marine 60mm "stovepipes" and a platoon of heavier 81mm mortars that had come up with the 1/6.

A trickle of wounded men began dribbling rearward. Many hobbled along on their own, some with an arm slung over the shoulders of a buddy or a corpsman. Still others were carried back on a stretcher or in some Marine's arms. From between pain-clenched lips came their personal impressions, some accurate, a few wildly inflated by fear, on the action up front. Some said the Japs were heavily entrenched while others claimed the enemy had landed thousands of reinforcements. True or not, the fight seemed to be nothing more than a repetition of what the Marines had been experiencing since landing fifty-two hours earlier, a slugfest where progress was measured in inches gained and blood spilt.

Like every other Marine in the battalion, the men of Second Squad listened somberly to the fight raging just beyond the grove of palm trees to their front. Sandy Gutierrez was thoughtfully chowing down on a can of potatoes and hash.

"Those poor hombres," Sandy said, waving his spoon toward the embattled 1/6. "They pushed halfway across this island and now they have to push across the other half."

"Well, I wouldn't get too worked up about them," Pete said. "If they get bogged down, guess who their reinforcements will be. So enjoy your chow while you can."

Sandy guffawed.

"Enjoy this?" he said, indicating the hash. "My momma makes the best enchiladas you ever sank your teeth into and here I am eating dog food."

"That's right," Pete replied. "You started tellin' me your folks had an eatery somewhere in Texas, right?"

"A town called Presidio," Sandy said, "My parents settled there just before I was born. They had a small farm across the border in Mexico, a few miles south of Ciudad Camargo. It was hard going so they came to America for a better life for them and us kids. At first they worked as farmhands, but my mother loves to cook, so they pulled together all the money they had, borrowed some from relatives, and opened a little cantina, Neuva Esperanza, which means New Hope, which is exactly what it was for them."

"Did it work out?" Aldrich asked.

"It's been difficult, but yeah," Sandy answered. "Some of my mother's dishes are hard to resist, especially her albondigas, meatballs to you gringos, and her *pollo motuleño*, which is chicken, orange juice, and plantains. They're like bananas only with more starch and less sugar."

"But the cantina wasn't your cup of tea, huh?" Pete asked.

"Texas wasn't my cup of tea," Sandy answered. "Texans hate us Mexicans. To them we're all wetbacks and should be deported. We all live together in a section of town called Little Mexico and hardly ever enter the white section. The only job a Mexican can get is working in the fields at fifteen cents an hour. Owning a small business is very hard for my parents. Mexicans have little money and gringos seldom came into our cantina." Sandy finished his stew and tossed the can away. His face hardened. "I left because I got tired of being spit on and called a 'filthy spic.' If I live through this and when my enlistment is up, I may just ship over. I feel more at home in the Corps than I ever did in Texas."

Pete stared at Sandy as if he was just seeing the man for the first time. He had never realized that Sandy was a lot like him. Angry, disillusioned, alone. He also now came to understand how little he knew about any of the men in the squad—the Professor, Mickey Mouse, Reb, Honeybun. Even Ted Giovanni, his best friend, died almost a stranger.

"*You stupid sonofabitch*," Pete swore to himself.

The sound of gunfire ahead seemed to be a little more distant as the enemy was beaten back inch by agonizing inch. As the frontline crept eastward, the scavenger hunters, wary of stray bullets from the battle ahead, now descended on the dead Japanese like vultures, rifling through knapsacks, uniform pockets, and the mouths of the enemy. Pete hurried to the Professor's foxhole.

"Professor," Pete said. "You have a kid brother. How'd he like a samurai sword?"

Remembering the Jap officer who'd been killed in an attack the previous day, Aldrich smiled.

"The 1/6 cleared out any snipers, so let's go get it before Hainley adds it to his collection of gold teeth," Pete said and the two hurried off.

They easily found the officer's bloodied corpse. The sword was still grasped in the dead hand. With an effort the Professor pried it from the stiffened fingers. The scabbard was attached to an over-the-shoulder brown leather strap by two "D" rings, each on the end of a green canvas hanger. Pete drew his Ka-Bar to slit the hangers and free the scabbard. Taking the prize, they hurried back to their lines but not before Hainley, kneeling over a mangled *rikusentai*, offered Aldrich half a dozen gold teeth in exchange for the sword.

Back in the Professor's foxhole Pete watched as Aldrich admired the forty-inch-long, gracefully curved wooden scabbard, its highly polished black lacquered finish gleaming in the sun. Aldrich almost reverently slid the twenty-nine-inch blade in and out of the scabbard, holding it by its hardwood handle delicately wrapped by a thin brown cotton cord that ended in a large knot by the hand guard.

"Such exquisite craftsmanship," Aldrich said, awe in his voice. "You know, they've been making these things for centuries. It's the true sign of a warrior."

"Well, I don't know about its previous owner, but you've certainly earned it," Pete said. "Hope your little brother likes it. What's his name, anyway?"

"Oh, Ah know," Reb injected. "Hen-RREEEE! Henry Aldrich!"

"Coming, Mother," Honeybun replied in a falsetto voice, delivering the line so familiar to radio listeners.

The squad guffawed at the joke but Aldrich looked deadpan and rolled his eyes.

"Oh, come on, Professor," Reb whined. "Tell me y'all don' enjoy *The Aldrich Family.*"

"I hate it, Reb," Aldrich said. "And I wish I had a buck for every time some clown made that same joke. I could pay the last two years of my college tuition and have enough left over for a nice car." He paused.

"Unfortunately, my mother loves that show. She's glued to our Philco every Thursday night."

The Professor turned to Pete.

"Actually, my brother's name is Mike," Aldrich said. "He's itching to graduate in June and get into the war like his three older brothers." He shot a cold glare on Reb. "None of whom are named Henry." He turned back to Pete. "I didn't have a real problem with his wanting to enlist until I landed here. I don't want my baby brother, or anybody's baby brother, to go through something like this." He stopped when he saw hurt in Pete's eyes. "Sorry, Hardball. I forgot for a moment."

"It's okay, Professor," Pete said. "You didn't kill him. It was the Japs. And my bastard old man."

Aldrich was about to ask a potentially touchy question when they were interrupted by Gunny Nicholson.

Nicholson slapped Pete on the back. "Come with me. Skipper wants a meeting of all officers and NCOs."

The surviving leaders of Dog Company now collected around the CP.

"Take a knee," Stacy said. "Have a smoke. Whatever."

All but two of the men knelt and several fired up coffin nails. Stacy remained standing.

"Here's the word," he began. "The 1/6 has moved beyond the end of the runway to the area of the turning circle, and right now that looks like about as far as they'll be able to go before digging in for the night. They've taken losses and they have gaps in their line. We're gonna be plugging those gaps, mostly between the 1/6 on the right and 3/8 on the left. We'll start moving around 1700 hours. Tomorrow morning at 0700 the Navy is gonna open up with everything it has: planes, bombs, naval gunfire, plus Marine artillery. The idea is to pulverize the tail of this island, which is where the Japs are still holding out. It'll be a helluva show, but you are all as aware as I am that despite the shellacking, when we move forward there'll still be plenty of those little yellow bastards waiting for us." He stopped to see if there were questions. Hearing none, he continued, "But before all that fun starts, we have to get through tonight. We pressed the Japs back pretty far today and are squeezing them tighter and tighter. They're not idiots. They see the writing on the wall. They know how this fight will end, so we expect heavy counterattacks tonight. Go easy on your men. Have them catch some z's while it's still light. We go on full alert at dusk. Caution your men against moving around in the dark. They could get shot. Password is Lola's thighs. If there are no questions, make sure all your guys have water and ammo. Dismissed."

CHAPTER 23

As the gathering broke up, Pete turned to Nicholson who had seated himself on the trunk of a felled palm tree.

"How many of the bastards do you think are still waitin' out there, Gunny?" Pete asked.

"If there's one left, it's too damned many for my liking," the gunny replied.

Pete smiled.

"How long you been in the Corps?" Pete continued.

Nicholson turned to Pete, a bemused expression on his whisker-stubbled face.

"What's this?" he said. "Hardball taking an interest in someone besides himself?" He paused. "I enlisted in '30. My mother signed the papers the day after my seventeenth birthday, and just in time. The Depression was starting to really be felt, even in tiny Lithopolis, which is where I'm from."

"Where the hell is Lithopolis?" Pete asked.

"Ohio. It's on the Fairfield-Franklin County line," Nicholson said. "It's tiny, only a few hundred people live there. It's not far from Lancaster, which is where General Sherman was born."

Pete guffawed.

"Does Honeybun know that?" he asked.

"Nope," Nicholson answered. "Reb doesn't either. No need for them

to. Anyway, jobs were scarce, especially in Lithopolis, which has no factories or anything. Ohio as a whole wasn't much better off. Soup kitchens
were drawing longer and longer lines, so I joined the Corps. It provided
me with clothes, a roof over my head, and three squares a day. I could live
cheap and I sent part of my pay home to help my mother and younger
brother and sister."

"Your dad?" Pete asked.

"You are changing, aren't you?" Gunny said. "Pop was a Marine as
well, in the first war. He got gassed in the Argonne. It ruined his lungs and
left him partly blind. He spent two years in the hospital. I was four years
old when he shipped out for Europe in 1917, six when he came home
from the hospital, and ten when he died." Nicholson stopped to fire up
a Lucky Strike. "He couldn't work anymore so the family was in hock. I
quit school at fifteen to find odd jobs wherever I could until I enlisted."

"You must've liked it," Pete observed.

"Mostly," Gunny answered. "After a year assigned to the fleet, I did
duty in Hawaii, Guam, the Philippines, China, then back to the Philippines. I really loved the Philippines and hated leaving, but in February of
'41 when the Corps activated the Second Division they needed experienced NCOs and reassigned me. As things turned out, it kept me from
dyin' or being locked up behind Jap barbed wire like a lot of my buddies."

Pete was quiet. Then said, "Sandy said he was thinkin' of shipping
over when his tour runs out. I'm thinking that, too."

"You could do a lot worse," Gunny told him. "You've become a lot
less of a pain in everyone's ass. But what about that girl?"

"I haven't worked that part out yet," Pete said thoughtfully.

"Well you better," Gunny said. "There are married Marines, Capt.
Stacy, for instance. He has a young wife and two kids. Even crusty Master
Sgt. O'Leary has a wife, if you can believe some broad would actually
have the old bastard. But it's a tough life for a woman. There are long
periods of separation, and you never know when you're getting called
or where you might end up." Gunny stopped. "We've shot the breeze
long enough. You'd better get back to your squad and get 'em ready. We
could get the word to move at any time."

Pete shuffled back to the squad. Passing the row of stovepipes, he saw mortar team leader Cpl. Ed Baker. His men were ripping open crates of ammo for dispersal among the tubes as Baker sat brewing coffee in a steel helmet over a small Sterno stove. The smell caught Pete's senses.

"How's 'bout a cup of joe, Pogey Bait?" Pete asked.

Baker had been dubbed Pogey Bait by the men of the company because he always seemed to have hard candy somewhere about his person.

"Gimme your cup, Hardball," he said, reaching out a hand.

Pete freed a cup from one of his two canteens and passed it over. A loving look flooded over his face as he watched Baker tip some of the steaming brew into it. The coffee looked rich and was black as a witch's heart. Pete seated himself on a sandbag and carefully sipped some of the hot fluid.

"Ahhh," he sighed. "Damn but you mortarmen make good java."

Baker smiled at the compliment.

"Have you heard any news about Deaver?" Pete asked.

"No," Baker replied. "Most likely he's sitting on a hospital ship. Might even be headin' back for Hawaii right now."

They were interrupted by one of Baker's men who shouted, "Hey! I got one."

He hurried over to Baker, a yellow card in his hand. He flashed it in Pogey Bait's face.

"You lucky bastard," the corporal said. "That's the third one you found."

"What'd he find?" Pete asked.

"It's a love note from home on a range card," Pogey Bait said and handed it to him.

The printed card contained columns of figures denoting azimuth, deflection angles, types of terrain, elevation, and other information mortarmen used to effectively drop their rounds. But it also had something else. On a blank section of the card was a set of big, luscious lip prints made using bright red lipstick and the words, printed with the same red lipstick, "Come back safe. Love you, Margie."

Pete looked at Pogey Bait.

"It's from the broads who work in the ammo factories back in the

States," the veteran said. "After they pack the rounds, every so often they'll kiss the cards and write some sort of lovey-dovey message. It does wonders for morale."

"I'll bet," Pete chuckled and handed the card back to the lucky man who had found it.

"There ya go," Pogey Bait told the man. "Now quit pattin' yourself on the back and get those rounds dispersed to the other tubes, especially those illumination rounds. We may need 'em tonight."

The Marine scurried away.

"That fuckin' does it," Pete said, standing up. "Next battle I'm comin' back as a mortarman. Great coffee and love letters from home."

He headed back for the squad.

The word to move came just after 1700 hours. With the sun dangling low over the sea to remind all of the approaching darkness, the men of the 2/2 and 1/2 started eastward. All around them were the scars of battle, from shattered airplane carcasses to burned-out bunkers still smoldering from the kiss of the flamethrower, to mangled bodies, Japanese and American, their thickly coagulating blood turning black under the relentless sun.

One revetment had been converted into a defensive position and the torn corpse of a Jap tank sat amid blasted coconut logs and sandbags. The tank's dead commander still sat in the hatch staring straight ahead as if he were watching the victorious Americans hike by. Pete hoped it was the same tank that killed Ted but he had no way of knowing.

Meeting no resistance, Second Battalion quickly reached its assigned position and the men were ordered to dig in. Just fifty yards ahead Pete could see a narrow service road that skirted the turning circle. On it sat the bomb-twisted hulks of five wrecked Japanese trucks, ideal for sniper positions. *What kind of asshole officer decided not to move the line another few yards forward to take in this obvious defensive line?* he wondered.

The squad settled in, each man steeling himself for whatever the night might bring. Pete scraped out a shallow hole midway along his squad's line. As Pete worked, the Professor came over from his foxhole and knelt beside him.

"Some things you said to me the last day or two have been bothering me," he said. "You told me that you joined the Marines because the alternative was jail, and that you beat someone up pretty badly. Not long after that you mentioned your father and said, and I'm quoting here, 'I should've killed the sonofabitch when I had the chance.'" He paused. "The guy you beat up. Was that your dad?"

Pete looked up at his friend and a sardonic grin creased his lips.

"Damn. You are good, Professor," Pete said.

So he told his friend about the blow-up that tore the fragile Talbot family apart.

On June 21, 1943, the Navy removed the USS *Grampus* from its Naval Vessel Register, closing the book on Charlie and his shipmates. Hot on the heels of that announcement a letter arrived for Pete from the Veterans Administration in Washington, DC. It was a check made out to him under the National Service Life Insurance Act of 1940 in the amount of $10,000.

"I knew the old man would explode if he found out that Charlie left the dough to me instead of him and Mom, so I secretly deposited it into my own savings account," he told Aldrich. "But I fucked up. I left a copy of the insurance form lying on my bedside table where my mom found it. She made things worse when she told Dad, so he was madder than a wet hornet when I got home from work that evening. He demanded to know where the money was, so I told him. I added that Charlie left it to me rather than have him piss it away on beer."

———

"That $10,000 is more than that little fucker was ever worth," Benny cursed, his words slurred by the beer. "So you get your ass to the bank first thing tomorrow and get that money out."

"Benny, don't," a terrified Pat pleaded. "Pete. Please."

"You bastard," Pete swore, ignoring his mother. "You're the reason Charlie is dead. You killed him just as certain as the Japs did."

"You're as worthless as he was," Benny roared, his face beet red.

"Why don't you go off to war and get yourself killed, then I can be rid of both my useless brats."

"You should know all about being worthless, you sad, sorry lump of shit," Pete snarled.

Benny slipped off his leather belt.

"Don't you dare," Pete warned.

Benny swung the leather belt. The strap lashed Pete painfully on the left shoulder. Benny pulled it back for another strike but his actions were slowed by the alcohol. Pete grabbed the end and yanked the belt from his father's surprised grip. Clutching the buckle end in his right hand he waved the belt menacingly.

"You've hit me for the last time, old man," Pete growled.

He swung the belt hard against Benny's torso not once, but several times. The leather snapped like a whip as it struck flesh. Benny yelped in pain and crouched defensively. Pete brought the belt down across Benny's back and shoulders hard enough to make his father again cry out. Benny fell to the carpet and rolled up in a protective ball but Pete, in a blind rage, began whipping his father until Pat Talbot grabbed his arm and pulled him back.

"Stop it, stop it," she pleaded tearfully. "Stop it, Pete, please."

Pete lowered his upraised arm. As the pounding in his head subsided and the red mist before his eyes cleared, he looked down almost in surprise at his father who lay whimpering at his feet. Pete dropped the belt and sank dejectedly into a chair as Pat tended her injured husband.

"Look what you've done, Pete," she wailed through her tears. "Look what you've done."

"Meanwhile," Pete continued as Aldrich sat mesmerized by the story, "the neighbors who'd heard the God-awful ruckus called the cops. Two of them came into the house and saw my pop lying on the floor and one called an ambulance. The other one just kinda stared at me."

"Does someone want to tell me about it?" the officer asked.

On the floor Benny gazed up at his wife and she down at him. Then Pat turned to the police officer and as if in a trance mumbled, "My son and his father got into an argument . . ."

"My son attacked me," Benny injected from the floor.

Pete's jaw dropped.

"Was there anything to provoke the attack?" the cop inquired. "Did you threaten your son?"

"No," Benny said.

Pete could not believe his ears. He looked to his mother but her eyes could not meet his.

"Tell him the truth, Mom!" he pleaded with her, rising out of the chair. "Tell him of the years of beatings. Of the bruised bodies and broken bones Charlie and I suffered. Tell him how he drove Charlie to join the service where he got himself killed. Tell him how Dad came at me with his belt!" He turned to the cop. "How do you think I managed to hit him with his own goddamned belt?"

The cop did not answer but jotted down notes. The ambulance crew arrived and Benny became the center of attention.

"He beat me. He beat me," Benny muttered over and over. "I want him arrested."

The officer turned to Pete.

"You're going to have to come with me, son," he said.

Pete meekly rose. As the officer handcuffed him, he looked despairingly at his parents.

"Well," he said sadly, addressing both his father and mother. "You both got what you wanted."

———————

"I spent three days in a cell waiting for my hearing," Pete said. "I lost my job with the ferry company and my only visitors were my lawyer and Aggie. The hearing was short but sweet. I was charged with aggravated assault and my old man lied through his teeth saying it was all my doing. Through it all, Mom couldn't say a damned word. She just cried half the time. When asked questions by the lawyer she just said she couldn't remember. Lucky for me the judge was fair. He listened as my lawyer told him about my dad's heavy drinking and the beatings. He was sympathetic, saying he didn't think I was bad, just misused. Still, he sentenced me to two years." Pete paused as the memory filled his head. "But then the judge told me that rather than sit in jail my 'energies' should be directed at our country's enemies, and he gave me two weeks to enlist in the service of my choice."

Pete, his throat dry as sandpaper from talking, took a slug of water from his canteen.

"That was a Friday," Pete told his friend. "On Monday I joined the Marines. So there you have it. Now let's get ready. It's getting dark and the boogie man is at our door."

CHAPTER 24

Having spilled his guts, Pete withdrew into a sullen silence. Steve Aldrich still knelt on the sand beside him.

"I understand why you hate your father so much," Aldrich said. "I'd probably feel the same way. But your mom's not supporting you must've really hurt. Moms are supposed to support their kids. My guess is she was afraid of your dad. Did you ever think about that?"

"Aggie told me the same thing," Pete said.

"Smart girl," Aldrich said.

Pete grinned and shook his head.

"You know, at first it pissed me off when you tried to get inside my head. But I'm sorta glad, so thanks. Now quit skylarkin' and get back to your position."

Aldrich grinned and headed for his foxhole.

Yeah, Pete thought. *Moms are supposed to support their kids.*

———

The last time he saw his mother was that final day he and Aggie had shared before he was due back at Quantico. They had gone shopping that morning for the new dress he'd promised her. Now he was reclining on the bed in his room at the hotel, smoking and watching her model the new outfit in front of the bureau mirror. A knock on the door got him to his feet.

"Well, speak of the devil," he said as he saw his mother standing in the corridor.

"May I come in?" Pat Talbot asked quietly.

Pete stepped back and let her pass.

"So what do you want?" Pete replied as he closed the door.

Spotting Aggie, Pat gave a slight smile and said, "Hello, Agatha."

Pat turned to face her son.

"I had to call around to six hotels before I found you," she said. "Why didn't you call me when you got home? I had to find out from my brother who called long distance to ask if we've mended our fences."

"Well, let me see," Pete said, stubbing out his cigarette. "The last time I saw you we were in a courtroom where my old man was trying to send me to prison while you didn't say a word to stop him. That doesn't make for a happy family reunion. As for mending fences, there are no fences to mend," Pete said. "You and Pop burned them to the ground."

Pat's face fell.

"I'm sorry, Pete," she said tearfully. "I was hoping we could talk about . . ."

Pete cut her off.

"No, we can't."

"You have no idea what it's like to be afraid of the man you married, of being afraid to go home." She paused to choke back tears. "Throw him out, you tell me. That's easy for you to say but you don't know what it's like for a divorced woman to make her way. You can't get a good-paying job. You're looked down on. Other women whisper behind your back."

Pete didn't reply. He turned and walked to the apartment window overlooking the street and said no more. Pat Talbot knew the discussion was over. She turned and sadly retreated to the door. Aggie caught up to her, touching her on the arm.

"Mrs. Talbot," Aggie said in a low voice, "don't give up on him. Just give him some time."

Pat looked sadly at the young woman and touched her gently on the cheek.

"Dear Agatha," she said. "I've known you since you were just a little girl, and now you are a beautiful and caring young woman. You've carried a torch for my son for a long time. He knows that, yet he squeezes you out as well. How do you cope?"

"The same way you do, Mrs. Talbot," Aggie replied. "We both love him."

Pat Talbot gently kissed Aggie on the cheek and left. By the window, Pete continued his vigil. Moments later he spotted his mother exiting the building and shuffling away. It struck him how frail and alone she looked.

Aggie walked over to Pete and touched his shoulder.

"What did she think coming here would accomplish?" Pete said.

"You don't know a frightened woman when you see one, do you?"

Pete turned toward her.

"She's terrified, Pete," Aggie continued. "Her world is collapsing. Don't you see it? Or is your pity only reserved for yourself? Another thing. That money you have in the bank. Be mad at your dad if you want, I understand. But you need to help your mother. I can't believe you'd totally turn your back on her. That's just not you."

Pete stared silently out the window.

"Okay, I understand what you're saying," Pete conceded. "And I know what she's saying. Dad's been hard on her as well. I didn't always think about that. We'll forgive each other eventually, but right now I feel so betrayed that I can't. I just can't."

––––––––––

Pete had been hard on his mother. He knew it at the time the argument had occurred in that dingy hotel room and he knew it now as he sat in his foxhole half a world away.

Pete longed for a cigarette but the darkness was all-encompassing now and a lighted scrag would invite a sniper or, worse, a mortar round. So he fought the urge and settled back to await whatever the night might bring.

It was not long in coming. Around seven in the evening the by-now-familiar cries of "Banzai" and "Marines you die" began to ring out louder and louder. With his gaze fixed dead ahead, Pete did not know Nicholson was coming up on his rear until a voice said, "Have your men fix bayonets and stay in their holes. There's no pulling back."

Pete nodded then crept along the line passing the word to his squad.

The assault began around 1930 hours. Hordes of Japanese emerged from rifle pits and bunkers about five hundred yards to the east and surged forward. Officers waved swords and men brandished their rifles, some firing from the hip. Before they'd covered the first hundred yards, Marine artillery rounds began bursting around them. Initially the fire came from a battery of 75mm pack howitzers to the rear of the Marine line. Soon these were joined by the deep-throated detonations of larger 105mm shells, some coming from guns emplaced on Bairiki, the next island in the Tarawa Atoll lying across the three thousand yards of water that separated it from its tormented sister.

On a battlefield now being lit up by star shells launched from mortars, the 105s proved exceptionally lethal, creating a wall of smoke and jagged steel. The Japanese leading the attack ran headlong into this hellish barrier and men were torn to shreds.

From their foxholes Marines watched the carnage. Surely the Japanese would be so badly chewed up that the attack would fall back in panic and disarray. But as the smoke of that initial volley cleared, the men stared in disbelief as succeeding waves of Japanese surged over the remains of their slaughtered comrades. Marine artillery shells "walked" in lockstep with the Japanese as they advanced under the greenish-white light of the flares.

The machine guns on *Li'l Lil*, parked behind Pete's squad, began to stutter as did other machine guns along the line. The air was sliced by glowing tracer rounds as more Japanese toppled. Still the survivors came grimly on. Crossing the deadly ground, they plunged headlong into the Marines. Up and down the embattled line, bayonets flashed and rifles barked as men fought off the attackers. Voices in Japanese and English shouted curses, oaths, and insults as they lunged with bayonet-tipped rifles or bashed faces in with rifle butts.

Two Japanese ran straight for Honeybun's position. The North Carolinian dropped one with a shot to the heart. The second one fired his Arisaka and missed. Honeybun thrust his rifle upward as the Jap plunged into the foxhole, impaling himself on the bayonet. Both men went down under the impact of the collision. Honeybun quickly regained his feet, then drove his bayonet into the dying man's chest.

One Japanese soldier jumped into Mickey Mouse Kusaka's foxhole and tried to run him through. Kusaka parried the jab with his own rifle, batting the man's weapon aside. Then he drove the Springfield's butt into the man's startled face. The *rikusentai* fell and Kusaka, in a towering rage, brought the heavy butt down again and again until the soldier's face was an unrecognizable goo.

Sandy Gutierrez shot one attacker through the chest but the man, dead on his feet and driven by momentum alone, fell into the foxhole on top of Sandy. Sandy threw the corpse off, half in panic and half in disgust, then bayoneted him for good measure. Pete dropped two attackers with a short four-round burst, both falling less than six feet from his foxhole.

Then the fight was over. Gunfire slackened all along the besieged line before fading altogether. The bedraggled Marines heaved a sigh. All of the attacking Japanese lay dead.

The next thirty minutes passed in relative silence. Then Pete thought, *Did something move out in front of me? Is someone there?*

Aloud he said, "Password."

No "Lola's thighs" came back. Nothing. Just an ominous hush.

A dull thunk from behind him told Pete that a mortar had been discharged. The fiery trail of a star shell arced through the India ink sky and erupted overhead, casting the landscape in a ghostly greenish-white glow. Almost immediately a figure rose up in front of Pete not six feet away. It was one of the two men he had fired at earlier and thought he had killed. Now suddenly this "dead" man was thrusting a rifle tipped by an ugly bayonet straight at him. With no time to raise his own weapon, Pete instinctively dropped it and reached for the oncoming Arisaka. His hands seized the weapon's barrel six inches beyond the muzzle but not before he felt the razor-sharp blade slice along the underside of his left forearm. With his hands locked around the enemy's rifle barrel, Pete yanked, pulling its owner into the foxhole where they crashed to the ground together. Both men lost their grip on the rifle but Pete, in the dying glow of the flare, saw the man yank a knife out of his belt. Pete scrambled out of his foxhole and reached into his waistband for Lt. Pfeffer's pistol. It was gone. It must have fallen out when he and the Jap fell. Nervously Pete pulled his Ka-Bar from its leather sheath. The *rikusentai* followed him out of the foxhole and the two men, knives firmly in hand, sized one another up, each looking for an opening from which to strike.

The star shell winked out but not before dulling both men's eyesight as the lit sky returned to blackness. As their eyes readjusted, the enemy soldier jabbed at Pete who parried the blade aside with a sweeping motion. The blades clanged off each other, sounding like church bells in the gloom. Pete's return thrust was also knocked aside. They continued circling, occasionally making jabs or thrusts with each attack being foiled by a countermove. Quick as a flash, the *rikusentai* reached down, scooped up a handful of sand, and tossed it at Pete's face. Pete saw it coming and twisted to his right just enough to avoid a faceful of grit. The infiltrator lunged at the same time he tossed the sand but Pete's sudden pivot threw off his aim, and Pete heard his shirt tear as the knife blade slashed through the fabric close to his abdomen. Pete jabbed back on a textbook thrust, up under the center of the rib cage. He felt warm blood flow over his hand as he looked directly into the man's startled brown eyes and watched his sweat-streaked face contort in pain. Locked together for a moment, Pete and his opponent went down onto the ground. Pete gave the knife an extra twist before withdrawing the blade. He wiped his hand and the gory knife on the dead man's tunic, then returned to his foxhole.

Retrieving his Thompson and locating his missing pistol, Pete collapsed in nervous exhaustion, breathing deeply to regain his composure. Now he became aware of the warm, wet feel of blood on his left arm. Removing his personal first aid kit from his belt, he pried open the small tin box. With one hand he fumbled in the dark for the field dressing, opened it, and wrapped it as tightly as he could around the wound. He'd have Doc look at it in the daylight.

As he contemplated the man he'd killed, Pete heard another quiet shuffling noise. It brought him bolt upright.

"Password," Pete said.

"Lola's thighs," came the response. It was Ryan Magruder, the corpsman. "I heard sounds of a scuffle somewhere around here so I'm making rounds to see how everyone is." He spotted the dead Jap. "Looks like you had company. Are you okay?"

"He nicked me with his bayonet but it's not too bad," Pete replied. Magruder slipped into the hole.

"Lemme be the judge," he said.

Pete surrendered his left arm. Magruder took out his flashlight and whipped his rain poncho over his head. Removing Pete's dressing he examined the wound. From under the poncho Magruder said, "Make a fist, then release it." Pete did as told. "That's good. No nerves damaged." The corpsman reemerged. "Nothing vital's been cut but it's still pretty deep and could use some stitches. Let's go back to the aid station."

"No," Pete said. "I can't leave the line. There'd be a gap if the Japs come back. Just bandage it up again."

Magruder thought for a moment then said, "I have a suture kit I swiped from the field hospital. I can stitch it."

"Then do," Pete said.

"But I don't have anything to numb the arm," Magruder said. "And I need a couple of guys to hold ponchos and someone to hold a flashlight."

"Reb! Sandy!" Pete called as loud as he dared. "I need you both. Professor. On the double."

The three men materialized from the dark. Magruder handed his poncho to Reb while Pete handed his to Sandy. Magruder instructed them to hold the ponchos high. This would block the beam of the flashlight from enemy eyes. He threaded the needle and gripped Pete's arm.

"It's going to hurt like a sonofabitch," Magruder warned.

"Just get at it, Doc," Pete said and braced himself.

Magruder wasn't exaggerating. Pete had to fight hard not to yank his arm back as the needle passed through his flesh. To Pete it felt as if Magruder was using a red-hot poker rather than a needle to mend the skin. Pete wanted to cry out but dared not, enduring the ordeal as tears of pain streaked down his cheeks.

Finishing, Magruder rewrapped the injury. Gunny Nicholson materialized out of the gloom. He watched Magruder put the finishing touches on Pete's arm.

"Congratulations, Hardball," Magruder said. "Those six stitches just earned a Purple Heart."

"Now I got something to tell my grandkids," Pete snarled, his arm throbbing.

Magruder chuckled and disappeared into the night.

"You okay?" Nicholson asked.

"Yeah," Pete replied.

Pete sent his men back to their foxholes then scrutinized his bandaged arm in silence for a few moments.

"Think the Japs'll be back again?" he asked Nicholson.

"Oh yeah," Nicholson answered. "They'll be back. They know that their only choices are surrender or dying gloriously for the emperor, so these won't be the standard Banzai attacks we've seen so far. They'll be suicide charges by men hoping to take as many of us as possible along to hell with them."

There was a long silence, then Nicholson said, "Something bothering you?"

"No," Pete replied. "Well, yeah. "I'm wonderin' how far I can push my luck. When we came ashore a Jap bullet smashed my Garand. It never touched me. Shrapnel grazed my helmet, sliced a gash in the camo lining. My LMO pack was hit once by a machine gun slug, and I have two holes in my uniform where bullets passed through and missed hitting me. Then this bastard's knife cut my arm and sliced through my shirt near my gut. When Feather Merchant got hit, he was in front of me. And I mean directly in front of me. If he'd been a step or two to the right or left, those two rounds would've hit me and he'd be sittin' here whining to you and I'd be the one lying on the beach with my big feet sticking out from under a blanket." He paused. "How much luck is a guy entitled to?"

Nicholson thought for a moment, then said, "I was never one to believe in good luck or bad luck or saying a guy's number is up. It's

bullshit. I knew a sergeant named Ricketts swore by his lucky moustache. Wouldn't have shaved it off under threat of court martial. Got
his head, moustache and all, blown off on New Georgia. To me, living
or dying in combat is about one-third experience and two-thirds being
in the wrong place at the wrong time. On the 'Canal me and two other
gyrenes manned a captured Jap rifle pit during the Second Battle of the
Matanika. Guy on my left was named Brenner and the Marine on my
right was a fellow we called Digger. I don't recall his real name. Anyway,
I was between the two when the Japs attacked, coming at us in waves.
Bullets flew past so thick a mosquito couldn't have avoided being hit. Yet
I wasn't touched. Benner and Digger were both killed. On New Georgia, we were being drowned in a downpour of rain and slogging around
in calf-deep mud that sucked your boondockers off. I was checkin' foxholes, moving along our line, giving the guys a little pep talk. I'd just
stopped in with an old salt named Seabags, a guy I'd known for three
years, then moved on. I barely got to the next hole when a round from
a Jap 75mm mountain gun dropped right into Seabags' lap. What we
found of him you coulda put into an ammo can. My point is, even with
my years of experience, if I'd stayed there a few seconds longer I'd have
been blown to hamburger as well. It wasn't good luck. Just me not bein'
in the wrong place at the wrong time."

Pete nodded his understanding.

Nicholson slapped Pete on the knee and said, "Check on your boys.
They're probably tired. Make sure they don't nod off."

He left.

Another star shell popped and sizzled overhead and Pete checked
his watch. It was just after 2300. He was preparing to do as Nicholson
had suggested and check his men when cries of "Banzai" and "Marines!
We come to drink your blood" split the gloom.

Unlike the first attack which struck the remnants of 2/2 and A
Company of 1/6, this one was launched farther to the south, along the
coast against the 1/6's B Company. The entire assault lasted just twenty
minutes, followed by another ominous silence.

Pete now moved along his line, checking in with the men.

"Stay alert," he told them. "They'll be back."

Returning to his own foxhole, Pete waited. Although Pete didn't know it, their worst night since landing on the shores of Betio was just getting started.

It was close to midnight when Lt. Umeza and his seventy men arrived at the place where they would be folded into a larger force and do battle with the Americans. Kenji Sakai, at the head of his squad of fifteen *rikusentai*, noticed in the gloom to his right a line of burned-out trucks sitting on a roadway near the airfield turning circle. Their orders had been to look for the trucks and then move to the command center located to the east.

"Lieutenant," Kenji called quietly and pointed to the trucks. Umeza nodded that he understood, and the column turned east. Arriving finally at the command bunker, Umeza reported to a colonel who appeared to be in charge.

"You will take your men to the truck line where you will be assigned a jump-off position," the colonel said. "We will be attacking again soon."

Saluting, Umeza led his men toward the row of trucks. As they neared the position, Kenji heard the sound of intense firing off to the north. The gunfire continued for about ten minutes before subsiding. Kenji knew he would be part of the next assault.

PART IV

TUESDAY, NOVEMBER 23, 1943

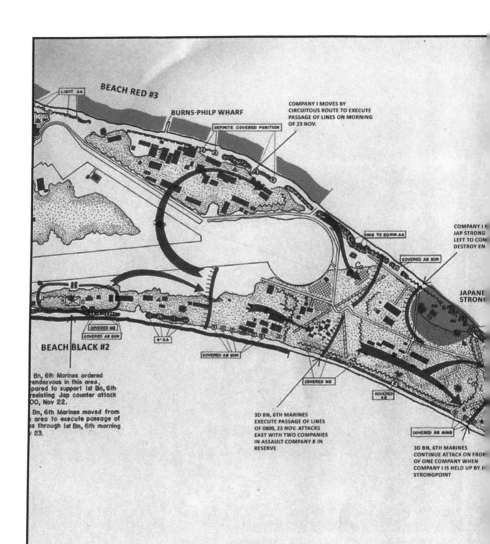

BEACH RED #3

LIGHT AA

BURNS-PHILP WHARF

DEFINITE COVERED POSITION

COMPANY I MOVES BY
CIRCUITOUS ROUTE TO EXECUTE
PASSAGE OF LINES ON MORNING
OF 23 NOV.

MG TO 20mm AA

COVERED AA GUN

COMPANY I
JAP STRONG
LEFT TO CON
DESTROY EN

JAPANE
STRONG

COVERED MG

COVERED AA GUN

BEACH BLACK #2

4" AA

COVERED AA GUN

COVERED MG

COVERED
AA

Bn, 6th Marines ordered
rendezvous in this area,
pared to support 1st Bn, 6th
resisting Jap counter attack
00, Nov 22.

Bn, 6th Marines moved from
area to execute passage of
s through 1st Bn, 6th morning
23.

3D BN, 6TH MARINES
EXECUTE PASSAGE OF LINES
OF 0800, 23 NOV. ATTACKS
EAST WITH TWO COMPANIES
IN ASSAULT COMPANY K IN
RESERVE

COVERED AA GUNS

3D BN, 6TH MARINES
CONTINUE ATTACK ON FRON
OF ONE COMPANY WHEN
COMPANY I IS HELD UP BY J
STRONGPOINT

BETIO
TARAWA ATOLL, GILBERT ISLANDS
ATTACK OF THE 3RD BN, 6TH MARINES
NOV 23, 1943

100   0   100   200   300   400 Yds.

MAP 7

RD 5890

TAKEN FROM 4TH MARINES
SPECIAL ACTION REPORT

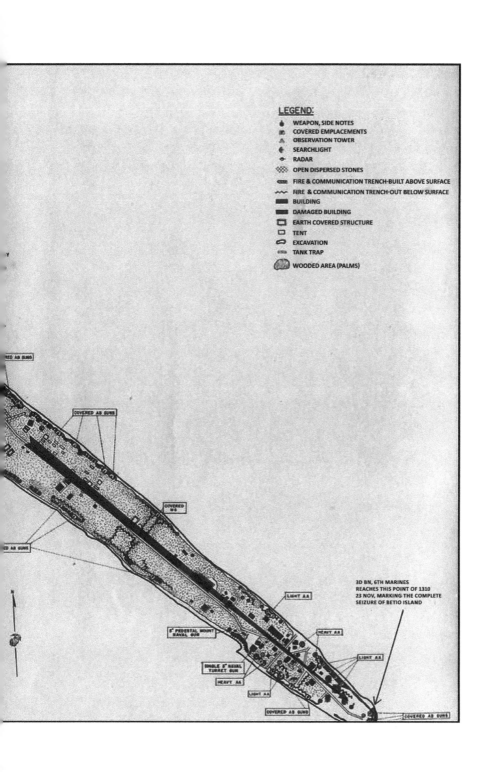

LEGEND:

- ● WEAPON, SIDE NOTES
- ▓ COVERED EMPLACEMENTS
- ▲ OBSERVATION TOWER
- ⚡ SEARCHLIGHT
- ◆ RADAR
- ▒ OPEN DISPERSED STONES
- ▬ FIRE & COMMUNICATION TRENCH-BUILT ABOVE SURFACE
- ∿ FIRE & COMMUNICATION TRENCH-OUT BELOW SURFACE
- ▬ BUILDING
- ▬ DAMAGED BUILDING
- ▭ EARTH COVERED STRUCTURE
- ▢ TENT
- ⬭ EXCAVATION
- ▬ TANK TRAP
- ◉ WOODED AREA (PALMS)

RED AB GUNS

COVERED AB GUNS

COVERED U-6

RED AB GUNS

LIGHT AA

3D BN, 6TH MARINES
REACHES THIS POINT OF 1310
23 NOV, MARKING THE COMPLETE
SEIZURE OF BETIO ISLAND

5" PEDESTAL MOUNT
NAVAL GUN

HEAVY AA

LIGHT AA

SINGLE 5" NAVAL
TURRET GUN

HEAVY AA

LIGHT AA

COVERED AB GUNS

COVERED AB GUNS

· CHAPTER 25

The fourth day of battle wasn't twenty minutes old when another Japanese attack burst upon the dug-in Marines. This one struck the 2/2's left along the 3/8's line. The darkness crackled with the staccato bursts of machine guns and the rapid crack of rifles punctuated by mortars and grenades. Pete and his comrades were relegated to the role of anxious spectators, listening to the battle racket while keeping their own tense vigil in case the attacking wave engulfed them as well.

The violent encounter lit by distant flares lasted just ten minutes before the heavy curtain of silence descended again. Everyone breathed a little easier.

Another star shell lit the night over the beaches to the north. In its glimmer, Pete spotted the Professor in his foxhole and gave him the "okay" sign. Aldrich returned the gesture.

Pete had not known Aldrich in boot camp since they were members of different platoons, but he had heard about this brainy recruit with a passion for playing shrink. Shortly after their graduation from PI in early September and before shipping out for the coast, weeklong furloughs were made available. Pete and Ted headed north together. The convivial Giovanni had chatted up Aldrich at the bus depot outside the camp's gate. Learning that they were all boarding the same train, Ted invited him to tag along. Pete's initial peevishness at this intrusion soon turned to delight when he discovered that Aldrich did not drink even though he was twenty-one and could legally purchase spirits. During a long layover in Washington, DC, Pete talked his traveling companions into accompanying him to a nearby tavern. Seated at a table, he cajoled Aldrich to buy shots of whiskey for himself and his two traveling companions. Aldrich was hesitant but finally caved. Pete quickly disposed of his own and then finished off Aldrich's untouched Jack Daniel's as well.

It was during this drinking session that Aldrich mentioned he had attended college. Pete thought about Charlie and yearned to ask Aldrich more about himself, but given his own aversion to people poking their noses into his life, he dared not ask. That didn't stop Giovanni.

"So you've been to college," Ted said. "Wow. Did you graduate?"

"No," Aldrich replied. "I completed two years, although I plan to go back after the war."

Ted was impressed.

"Did your folks go to college, too?" he asked.

He shook his head.

"They married right after high school," Aldrich said. "After that, we kids started coming, so Mom was busy raising us. Dad was a woodworker and took a job in a boatyard."

That struck Pete.

"My old man worked for a shipbuilding company in Chester until the Depression," he said. "He was called back to the company when the war started."

"There my dad was lucky," Aldrich said. "Depression or not, people have to eat and fishermen need boats, so pop was always busy. He's the best boat builder in town."

As the train chugged into Baltimore, Aldrich rose and grabbed his sea bag off the overhead rack.

"Here's where I get off," he said. "I'll see you fellows back at camp."

"How are you getting home from here?" Pete asked him. "You told me that Rock Hall's across the bay."

"Are you kidding?" Aldrich replied. "I know a hundred watermen. I'll just make my way to the harbor and hop a ride across."

Pete admired the man's confidence and watched him walk off as the train began chugging away from the platform.

"He's an interesting fellow, isn't he?" Ted asked his traveling companion.

Pete didn't reply, but Aldrich intrigued him and he hoped they'd be assigned to the same unit once they arrived wherever the hell they were going.

Giovanni and Pete continued on to Philadelphia. There they caught a train to New York because Pete planned to visit his uncle in Boston before returning to Chester. At Penn Station, Ted tried to coax Pete into visiting Brooklyn to meet his family.

"On your way back from Boston, why not stop in and meet my folks and spend a day or two with us?" Ted asked as the two stepped from the Pullman. "I'm sure your mom and dad wouldn't mind."

Wouldn't mind, Pete thought. *They wouldn't mind if I never came back.* He politely declined.

"See you back at camp," he told Ted.

Following the furlough, the men found themselves boarding a San Diego-bound troop train. By the last week of September, they lined the rail of a converted cruise ship watching their homeland disappear as the vessel sailed out of the harbor, passing the Naval Air Station on the tip of Coronado Peninsula.

The trip to New Zealand took three weeks, thanks to the zigzag course meant to throw off enemy submarines. Outside of rough seas that turned many a stomach when they hit the Roaring Forties two days out of New Zealand, the voyage was uneventful except for the day the ship stopped dead on the equator so that all of the new men, Marines and sailors alike, could be initiated into the Court of King Neptune. Hauled before a swabby dressed to portray the monarch of the deep, the "Polliwogs," men heading south of the equator for the first time, were "sentenced" to endure a series of indignities foisted on them by the experienced "Shellbacks." These included running a gauntlet of pounding fists, being blasted by water from a fire hose, and culminated in having to lick a raw egg off the belly of the "Royal Baby," the hairiest, ugliest sailor on the ship.

For Pete, arriving in New Zealand was like traveling to another planet. Despite Charlie's descriptive letters home, Pete had never imagined that any place with such lush, green fields, picture-postcard villages, and clear blue water had even existed. He'd have loved to travel into the hinterlands but scuttlebutt said the division was preparing to move out, which meant he had little time for anything other than training, training, and more training. The most he ever saw of the New Zealand countryside was during forced marches along the roads leading to and from Camp Paekakariki.

For Pete, his only visit to Wellington, or "Windy Welly," as it was called to honor the westerly trade winds that caressed the city, was a bittersweet moment. Charlie had been to Wellington not once but twice. He had loved New Zealand, and his letters described the friendly people and his favorite night spot, the Allied Services Center. On a whim Pete headed for Manner Street.

Locating the Allied Services Club, he found himself in a large, crowded, smoke-filled room thickly studded with tables and chairs. All around uniformed men played cards or shot the breeze with the female volunteers who staffed the place. A large map of the United States hanging on one wall was heavily dotted with pins placed by men to indicate the location of their hometowns. He saw one pin about where Chester was located. Did Charlie place that one? In a larger, adjoining room, loud chatter punctuated by louder guffaws vied to be heard above the strains of an all-Marine band playing Harry James' "You Made Me Love You." A few brave couples, a smattering of Marines, sailors, and Kiwis each clutching a Donut Dolly, danced across the hardwood floor.

Pete hoped to reconnect with Charlie's spirit as he attempted to picture his quiet brother amid these boisterous gyrenes and swabbies, but couldn't. Instead, it made him sad and he left.

———

By the weak light of the Betio moon that had risen shortly before midnight, Pete put thoughts of Wellington aside and strained for a glimpse at his watch. It was just past 0200. Hoping to subdue the growing anxiety gnawing at him, Pete decided to shift his concern from himself to his men and check up on his squad. Moving quietly to the far right of his line, he found Bucket Harnish staring intently over his rifle barrel at the ground in front.

"Okay here, Bucket?" Pete inquired.

"Yeah," was the answer. Bucket nodded toward Pete's left arm. "What happened to you?"

"Cut myself shaving," Pete said. "Stay alert. They'll be back."

Bucket nodded grimly in the dullness of the night, still wondering how he could tell his folks about his war.

Pete moved left to the foxhole occupied by Miklos Kusaka who looked up as Pete drew up beside him.

"No password?" Mickey Mouse observed. "I coulda shot ya."

Pete smiled and said, "Not with your eyesight. You'd have seen it was me."

"Still," Kusaka said, "I'm tired as hell. I coulda made a mistake."

Kusaka was the only man in the squad, or what was left of it, that Pete had never gotten to know very well. Now he felt a need to rectify that.

"Where'd you learn to shoot anyway?" Pete asked.

"Back home," Kusaka replied. "I hunted rabbits and squirrels as a boy. You gotta be a good shot to hit a rabbit on the run."

"So where's 'back home,' Mickey Mouse?" Pete asked.

Kusaka perked up. "Wyoming County," he answered.

"You a cowboy or something?" Pete asked.

"Hell no," Kusaka guffawed. "Wyoming County, New York. A little town called Castile. My pop ran a tailoring and dry-cleaning store. He learned the trade as a boy in Greece." Kusaka stopped and smiled. "Pop's name is Gabriel, which is Greek for 'God's bravest man,' although the townsfolk called him 'The Peanut Guy.'"

Pete raised an eyebrow.

"Yeah," Mickey Mouse said, "he loves peanuts and about twenty years ago he bought a roaster. The damned thing's about as big as a kitchen stove. He sat it outside the shop and every day he roasted batches of peanuts. You could smell them all over town. Mmmmmm, man was that a great smell. We kids bagged them and Pop sold them. Sometimes he made more money in a week by selling peanuts than he did on tailoring jobs."

Pete shared the laugh with Kusaka, then said, "Well, stay alert and be ready and you'll soon be back eating those peanuts."

Pete moved on.

Bypassing Aldrich, Pete made his way to Sandy Gutierrez's foxhole. "All okay here?" he asked.

"Yeah," Sandy replied, his gaze still fixed ahead. "Those Japs are some *hombres muy locos*, aren't they?"

"Lucky for us," Pete said.

Sandy laughed as Pete moved on to the BAR position manned by Reb Marshall who asked, "How's the arm?"

"Hurts," he said. "Ammo holdin' up all right?"

"Hell," Reb snorted, "Ah'll run outta Japs before Ah run outta bullets." He paused, then said, "You know, Ah was jes' thinkin' about y'all and how Ah didn't like you very much in boot camp."

"Why should you?" Pete answered. "I made it loud and clear that I didn't give a shit about any of you guys."

"Ah was rememberin' that tussle you'n me got into one night behind the heads," he said. "Ah forget what the hell ya said, but we got into it."

"Oh yeah," Pete smiled in the darkness. "I think I said Georgia was one of the few places in the world where you were allowed to marry your sister."

"That's right," Reb recalled. "If Collingwood hadn't dragged us apart I'd a whooped your ass that night."

"In your dreams, Butternut," Pete said.

"Luckily, Ah changed mah mind," Reb said. "You're an okay feller."

"I'm getting outta here before you start blowin' me kisses," Pete said. "Keep alert."

The last foxhole in the squad line was manned by Honeybun. Pete found him asleep, rifle still pointing toward the enemy. Pete gently booted the sleeper in the ass.

"Come on, Honeybun, stay awake," Pete whispered urgently. "You'll end up with your throat cut."

Honeybun groggily came back to consciousness.

"I'm sorry, Hardball," he said. "Guess I was tireder than I thought."

"We all are, but you gotta keep alert."

"I'm good now," he said.

Pete clapped him on the shoulder and returned to his foxhole, where he found Gunny Nicholson waiting.

"All your cubs tucked in?" the gunny asked.

"Yeah," Pete replied, dropping into the foxhole. "Honeybun fell asleep for a bit but, hell, we're all dead tired."

"Better dead tired than just plain dead," Gunny said. "I'd have you spread your men into two-man foxholes if I could so guys could take turns catching some fart sack time, but we're stretched thin enough. Hell, we can't even spare men to take our wounded back to the field hospital. We have to drag 'em back beyond the mortars so the blister mechanics can tend to them."

"How long do you think this fight'll last, Gunny?" Pete asked.

"Until the last of those bastards are lying flat on their backs and staring up into the sun," he replied.

"I mean, do you think it'll end today?" Pete said.

Nicholson thought about the question, then said, "I think the Japs are gonna shoot their bolt tonight. They know the end's coming so they're gonna go down in a blaze of glory. There'll be some Japs left come daylight for sure, and they'll be entrenched to the eyes and we'll have to root them out. But I have a gut feeling we'll be able to mop up what's left before the sun goes down again."

"Then we can expect more attacks tonight?" Pete asked wearily.

"Count on it," Gunny said. "Keep your boys alert."

CHAPTER 26

Alone, Pete glumly listened to the distant drumbeat of mortars bursting to the north by the Japanese command center and in the west at The Pocket. Ahead in the direction of Betio's narrowing tail a brooding silence lay heavily across the dark terrain.

Leaving his foxhole, Pete crept cautiously toward Aldrich's position. In the weak moonlight the Professor saw him approach and whispered, "You sleepwalking?"

"Nah," Pete replied, sliding into Aldrich's foxhole. "I just missed your smiling face."

The Professor grinned. Pete took his helmet off and ran a hand through his sweat-plastered hair. Aldrich picked up Pete's helmet and gazed at Aggie's smiling face.

"She's pretty," he said. "Girl has to be a real Shirley Temple to fall for a Gloomy Gus like you."

"That's Aggie," Pete said. "I was never mean to her or anything, but I wasn't what you might call romantic, either. But she hangs on."

"How'd you feel about that?" Steve asked.

"Hanging out the old psychiatrist shingle again, huh?" Pete smiled. "I'm glad she hangs on. There was a time not that long ago that I thought, with Charlie gone, the only reason I wanted to survive and go home was to spit in my old man's face. But living life on the edge like we have for the past three days, my feelings have changed."

After a brief pause, Aldrich said, "Before you dropped by, I was sitting here thinking. You know what the day after tomorrow is?"

"Thursday, why?" Pete replied.

"It's Thanksgiving," Aldrich stated.

"So?" Pete said.

"It was always a big holiday at our place," he said. "All my grandparents would come to the house and it'd get hectic. To feed everyone, Mom made two turkeys, so we'd have leftovers until we couldn't face another drumstick." He paused. "What was your family's favorite holiday?"

"Every other Saturday when the Mose Watkins beer truck rolled up to drop off my old man's standard order, three cases of Ballantine," Pete replied.

Pete wanted to change the subject.

"You got a special girl back in Maryland?" Pete asked. "Any blonde, brainy, lanky librarian types who might've caught your eye?"

"Afraid not," Aldrich replied. "My classes kept me much too busy. My oldest brother, Todd, got engaged right after he graduated from college. He's a Navy officer, an ensign on a destroyer escort hunting U-boats in the North Atlantic. At first, he was aboard the cruiser *Indianapolis*. I wish he'd still be on her because the *Indianapolis* is sitting out there beyond the reef supporting our attack."

"Count your blessings that he's not on board her," Pete admonished. "If he was offshore and knew you were stuck in the middle of this stinkin' fight on this damned island, he'd worry himself to death."

"You have a point, Hardball," Aldrich confessed.

Pete headed back to his foxhole. His injured arm began throbbing again so he delicately massaged it as he waited in the darkness. The next move was up to the Japanese.

Two hundred yards from Pete's foxhole, Kenji Sakai and his comrades began crawling forward on their bellies. It was close to 0300. Lt. Umeza's small unit had been ordered to take part in an attack on a portion of the American line near the row of burned-out trucks. There would be hundreds of men involved, including walking wounded, some of whom were still heavily bandaged and carried clubs or knives as weapons, having no rifles. The hope was that their assault would crush the Americans' first lines and allow a large body of *rikusentai* to penetrate behind the Americans and destroy their supply dumps. That could maybe cripple the American forces.

As they moved into position, Kenji thought of Tadao Onuki, who was possibly waiting for him on Bairiki. Did he think Kenji might be dead? Would he ever see Tadao again? *Perhaps not in this life*, he concluded.

Then Kenji thought about the Marines lying in wait ahead. They were young men like himself, and soon they'd be in a life-and-death struggle against each other. As he wondered about them an image came back to his mind, the image of the young Marine dragging an injured comrade ashore through a thick hail of bullets and flying shrapnel. His training had not acknowledged the enemy's potential for courage. But the fortitude displayed by the Americans wading ashore in the face of death, and shown by this one young man, gave Kenji a sense of admiration for his foe. He especially admired this man's courage. Was he waiting right now beyond that row of trucks?

Kenji hoped not.

———————

Shortly after 0300 the stutter of machine guns broke the silence. The weapons, two light 6.5mm guns and what sounded like a heavier tripod-mounted 7.7mm Type 92, along with their crews, had taken up residence in the five burned-out trucks. With the wrecks a skimpy fifty yards away, it was like the Japanese were firing right down the Marines' throats.

In the feeble moonlight the enemy gunners weren't aiming the weapons so much as merely traversing them to-and-fro across the Marine positions. Pete burrowed himself deeply into his foxhole. Glancing skyward he caught glimpses of tracers zipping by so low he could've reached out and caught them.

Now another sound intruded upon the battle's clamor, the drone of an airplane skimming overhead. Pete strained his ears. The tone was not the throaty roar of a fighter, but the heavy, cumbersome hum of a multi-engine craft. It was a Japanese bomber looking for targets. Pete listened as the plane circled. He was more terrified of the aircraft a few hundred feet above him than he was of the machine guns fifty yards in front. He imagined the pilot frantically searching the shadowy ground for any sign of the enemy, all the while aware that American fighters scrambling from a carrier could suddenly descend on his head. Finally, in desperation, the bombardier blindly toggled his load and the bombs fell behind the Marines, further cratering the empty airstrip. The bomber hastily retreated.

The machine guns, now joined by about half a dozen snipers, chattered on.

The attack began with a fusillade of machine gun fire from crews concealed in the trucks whose rounds swept along the Marines' line. Kenji had no idea of the effect on the Americans that the machine guns had but the pitiful attempt by the bomber Kenji found embarrassing.

Then came the assault itself as the orders to charge filtered along the Japanese line.

"Forward!" Lt. Umeza shouted as he rose up. "We attack!"

With a cry of "Banzai" Kenji and his comrades charged forward. Beyond the shattered trucks the wave of attackers was met by a heavy volume of enemy fire. Men went down all around Kenji, some screaming in agony, others falling silently like sacks of flour.

The attackers picked up speed, closing the deadly gap between them and their enemies. Kenji saw three Americans manning a machine gun. Rounds from the gun cut down two of the men from his squad. Enraged, Kenji ran hard and fired his Arisaka. His first bullet killed the machine gunner and is next wounded one of the other men. He missed the third man entirely.

A gaggle of distant voices caught his attention. Braving the fire, Pete poked his head up over the lip of his foxhole. Beyond the defunct trucks, Japanese infantry, hundreds of them, came into view, emerging from their underground bunkers and burrows like a swarm of locusts. Led by sword-waving officers, many of the *rikusentai* carried rifles. However some came armed with only knives while others bore makeshift clubs or as many hand grenades as they could carry. While the majority of the enemy wore their uniforms, or the tattered remains of a uniform, about a quarter of them were bare-chested. A few were clad only in loincloths. Bloodstained bandages affixed to the arms, shoulders, and legs of innumerable attackers indicated wounds that, under normal conditions, should've sidelined them to aid stations.

This is it, Pete thought. *It's the end. The Japs are scraping the bottom.*

Star shells fired by mortars and American artillery lit the sky above the battlefield. Kenji ran forward through the harsh greenish-white glare when a line of artillery blasts tore into the charging men. A near burst from one shell knocked Kenji to the ground, his rifle tossed from his hands. He lay there writhing, the air knocked out of him. Catching his breath at last, he tried to stand but his legs felt rubbery and he collapsed again. Finally, he regained his feet. Now weaponless except for two grenades, he staggered forward as best he could.

Pack howitzers of the 1/10 commenced their grim business. Mortars, too, opened up in an effort to stem this rushing tide. High explosives ripped the oncoming ranks. Men disintegrated in a flash. Others were thrown into the air bodily or in pieces. Despite having to step on or over comrades who'd been blown apart, the attackers would not be stopped.

The Marines laid down a ruinous fire at point-blank range. Japanese soldiers fell heavily. Some lay silent. Others jerked like crazed marionettes as their bodies were peppered by steel-jacketed rounds.

Like his comrades, Pete frantically emptied his Thompson, reloaded it, squeezed off another stick magazine, reloaded, and fired again. As he shoved his third clip into the receiver, Pete knew this attack would not be halted and would sweep over the Marine line. Moments later the *rikusentai* were among the foxholes, firing their rifles, waving their knives, and tossing grenades.

On the left of Second Squad's line, Honeybun had just reloaded when three Japanese charged him. Snapping off two quick rounds, he dropped the lead pair of attackers. The third man, wearing a dirty, blood-stained bandage about his left thigh charged on, his bayonet-tipped rifle at the ready. His first jab missed and he did not get a second as Honeybun parried left with his Garand, knocking the Arisaka aside. He then rammed his own bayonet deep into the man's chest. Honeybun felt the man's muscles pucker tightly around the blade so he fired off a round to jar the bayonet free. The dead man slowly toppled backward. Ignoring him, Honeybun continued to fire at the charging horde.

Reb Marshall's BAR seemed to draw Japanese attackers but he had been able to fight them off. The BAR, a "hot-loaded" weapon, had the advantage because it was ready to fire the instant a new clip was fed into it, so Reb did not lose precious seconds fumbling with a cocking lever. What looked like an entire squad of nine or ten men charged straight for Reb. His BAR sang its deadly song, felling six of the oncoming men. The rest halted, then turned away, perhaps thinking that this wasn't the best time to die for the emperor.

Sandy Gutierrez saw a Japanese soldier, a heavily bandaged left arm dangling uselessly by his side, smack his grenade against his helmet with his still-good right hand. Then clutching the lethal weapon to his body, he ran directly for Sandy's foxhole in an obvious suicide charge. Sandy quickly fired two rounds into the man's chest, then dropped to the bottom of his foxhole. The *rikusentai*, still grasping the grenade, fell four feet shy of Sandy's position. The explosion jarred Sandy. His ears ringing and his nose bleeding from the concussion, Sandy rose up and peered at the dead man who'd been split open like a beef carcass. Sandy, who thought he had seen it all in the last sixty-six hours, puked.

The Professor had shot and killed a trio of enemy soldiers in rapid succession, dropping the last at the lip of his foxhole. Now two more Japanese were upon him. One jumped into the foxhole and the two men parried and thrust at each other as the second Japanese, still at the edge of the hole, anxiously watched for some opening so he could finish off this American dog without hitting his comrade. He waited too long. Aldrich knocked his attacker's rifle aside then quickly shot the second man. The first attacker still inside the foxhole yelled in outrage as he lunged at Aldrich. The Professor sidestepped him, then drove his rifle, butt-first, into the man's face. The *rikusentai* fell backward and had the chance to emit one last scream before the Garand's heavy butt smashed into him.

Mickey Mouse Kusaka had shot down at least two Japanese soldiers who, in their feverish attack, had run right past him without spotting his foxhole in the gloom. Now four more came at him, one an officer, and they knew exactly where he was. Kusaka quickly raised his rifle and squeezed the trigger, dropping one of the attackers. The Springfield cracked a second time and another fell to the ground, writhing in agony and babbling incoherently for a few moments before going silent. Quickly swinging his Springfield toward the third man he pulled the trigger. Nothing happened. His trusty "Beelzebub" had jammed. Frantically, Mickey Mouse thrust his bayonet-tipped weapon at the attacker. The man batted it aside and made a thrust of his own. He missed as well. The two rifles collided loudly and seemed to get entangled. Kusaka quickly pulled his own weapon back and thrust again, driving the blade into his opponent's throat. The dying man emitted a burbling sound as air escaped from his torn windpipe, blowing bloody bubbles, as he sank to the ground.

Kusaka turned back to face the enemy officer when he felt a blow that drove the wind out of him. Surprise was replaced by pain. Gazing downward he saw the blood-streaked tip of a sword protruding from his own body just below the right side of his rib cage. Then the tip disappeared as the officer drew his sword out of Kusaka's body. Slumping to his knees, Mickey Mouse had never felt such intense pain. Above him the enemy officer raised the sword high over his head, his eyes focused on the wounded American's neck where he planned to deliver a blow that would separate his enemy's head from his body. Instead it was his own head that was nearly taken off as a bullet struck him squarely between the eyes. Two more slugs tore into his chest and the man was dead before he crashed to the ground. Seconds later, Bucket, who had just dispatched two attackers himself before he saw Kusaka being overwhelmed, was in his comrade's foxhole.

———

The ground around Kenji was blanketed with dead men. Still others continued forward only to be chopped down by machine gun and automatic weapons fire. Seeing the futility of going any further Kenji stopped. Ahead was a line of enemy foxholes. Kenji saw Lt. Umeza lead four men in a charge aimed at a Marine fighting from his foxhole. The Marine had just shot two men who had run by him, and then shot down two of Lt. Umeza's charging men and bayoneted the third.

Lt. Umeza managed to drive his sword into the man. Umeza then lifted his sword to deliver the death blow to the wounded Marine. He never had the chance, because as Kenji watched, he saw Lt. Umeza's head seem to explode as one of the wounded Marine's comrades shot the brave officer dead.

"Useless," Kenji muttered to himself. "Useless."

———

"Easy, Mickey Mouse," Bucket said urgently. "Easy."

He began tearing open his first aid kit in search of gauze so he could apply pressure. Then realizing there were two bleeding wounds, one entry and one exit, he cried, "Help me, Professor! Mickey Mouse is hit. Help me!"

"Oh my God," Aldrich gasped as he responded to Bucket's cry.

"It was a sword," Bucket said. "He got run through."

The two men went to work on their injured squad mate.

Unaware of what was going on three foxholes away, Pete continued firing at the running figures overlapping the Marine line. He saw one Japanese soldier get shot and fall. Still alive, the man rose to his knees. His injuries prevented him from continuing forward so he squatted there, screaming unintelligible insults at the Americans until a comrade coming up behind the man leveled his rifle and shot him in the head. He then continued forward until Pete dropped him with a quick three-round burst.

This latest assault had gone on for over half an hour, but now it was quite clearly winding down. Pete could only see half a dozen Japs still on their feet. Yet these few came on, yelling insults and oaths at their foes while firing their rifles. One man fell heavily to the ground, tried to rise, then fell again and lay still. Then another dropped and another. Two quick rounds fired by Honeybun felled a fourth attacker while Sandy shot down a fifth. A concentration of bullets flew by as several of the dug-in Americans tore into the last attacker's chest and ended the charge.

———————

Like so many of the bloodied survivors of this latest charge, a thoroughly dispirited Kenji turned and headed back to his jump-off position.

"This is the end," he told himself. "Now there is only death."

———————

The attack was ended but the fight itself was far from over. The machine guns and snipers in the wrecked trucks continued hammering away at the Americans. Artillery and mortar shells soon found the range and their bursts smothered the twisted vehicles. This fire was lifted as a dozen stalwart Marine volunteers, braving the enemy guns, crawled to within grenade range of the trucks. Moments later their pineapples burst among the vehicles killing the remaining gunners.

Pete, already shaken by the violence of this last attack, was further jarred when a familiar voice called out in the night, "Corpsman! Corpsman!"

It was Bucket.

Pete was out of his foxhole like a shot, scuttling along his squad line. Arriving at Kusaka's position, Pete spotted the Professor and Bucket applying pressure to the man's wounds. He dropped down beside them as Bucket filled him in.

"Jesus Christ," Pete moaned. Then he knelt by the wounded man. "Mickey Mouse, can you hear me?"

Kusaka opened the eyes that had been pinched shut in pain. He tried to reply but only bloody foam came out.

Ryan Magruder arrived and shooed the others aside.

"I'll take over," he barked. "But don't leave. I may need help." Then to his patient, he said in a soothing voice, "Stay with me, Mickey Mouse. I'll take care of you."

Magruder began feverishly working to stop the flow of blood and stabilize Kusaka.

"Do you need anything, Doc?" Pete asked.

"Reach into my bag and get me a bottle of plasma," he said.

Pete did as told, handing the bottle to Magruder. Bucket jammed "Beelzebub" bayonet-first into the ground as Magruder attached the plasma to the upturned Springfield.

The Professor aided Magruder as a second pair of hands, so with nothing left to do Pete rose and looked around. Spotting the sword on the ground, he picked it up and fought off an urge to lop off the remainder of the dead officer's head.

Nicholson arrived. Taking in the scene he said, "How is he?"

"I don't know," Pete said in a voice numbed by fatigue. "He got run through with this." He held up the sword.

"He's lucky to be alive," Nicholson said.

Magruder, seeing Nicholson, rose to his feet.

"I gotta get him back," Magruder said to Nicholson urgently. "I know we haven't the numbers to spare, but I gotta get him back, Gunny. The blade may've nicked his lungs. I don't know."

Pete looked at Nicholson who mulled the request over.

"Send him back, Gunny," Pete pleaded. "We'll hold our line 'til my guys get back."

"We're stretched tighter than a belly dancer's G-string," Nicholson said. "Between us and the 1/6 we have about forty-five dead and 120 wounded." He thought some more. Then decided. "This last attack was heavy. An all-out effort. The Japs may be done. All right, go. But tell your men to get their asses back here pretty goddamned fast."

Pete smiled grimly, then barked, "Bucket. Grab a stretcher and you and Sandy carry him to the hospital. But get back here pronto."

Bucket smiled.

"Aye aye, corporal," he said.

Pete knelt by Mickey Mouse and held up the sword.

"I'll hang on to this for you," he told the wounded man. "I'll make sure it gets back to you. You sure as hell earned it."

Kusaka weakly smiled through a morphine haze.

Bucket soon returned with a stretcher. Kusaka was gently loaded onto it and was quickly whisked away, Pete hoped, back to Wyoming County, New York.

Pete watched him go.

"We're thin, and getting thinner," Gunny said. He turned to Pete. "Ed Hainley bought it."

Pete turned to stare at Nicholson.

"Holy shit," Pete said. It was always a shock when a veteran got hit. "What happened?"

"A Jap holding a grenade jumped into Ed's foxhole," Nicholson said. "Blew 'em both up. Blew up his sack of gold teeth as well."

Returning to his foxhole, Pete sat alone.

So much death, he thought.

His mind replayed something he had told Aggie their last night to-gether at the Edgemont Hotel.

They sat snuggled together on the sofa of Pete's hotel room. Aggie stared up at Pete and smiled.

"My mother always liked you," she said as her fingers softly caressed his cheek.

"That's more than you can say about your dad," Pete smiled back.

"Oh, his bark's worse than his bite," Aggie replied with a laugh.

Then she grew somber.

"I'm frightened for you," she said quietly.

Pete pulled her as close to him as he possibly could.

"Don't worry for me," he told her. "The war can't get both of the Talbot boys."

Aggie wrapped her arms tightly around Pete and held on as if she'd never let go.

Why had he made that stupid promise? With a shudder, Pete now felt Gunny Nicholson was correct, that life or death in combat was just a matter of being in the wrong place at the wrong time. How can a man defend against fate?

For the first time since he waded ashore, Pete Talbot felt he was not going to leave this island alive.

CHAPTER 27

Gunny Nicholson dropped down inside the foxhole beside Pete.

"It'll be getting light in about an hour. Capt. Stacy doesn't think the Japs will attack again," he said. "Double your men up and let them sleep in shifts. The fireworks start at 0700 and there won't be much sleep after that."

"Aye, aye," Pete said. "How many Nips are still out there ya think?"

Nicholson shook his head slowly.

"Could be a hundred, could be a thousand," he replied. "We won't know until we reach the tip of the island and count the dead. But you can bet they won't go down easy. HQ intercepted a Jap radio transmission that said their weapons had been destroyed and that they'll be launching a final charge. It ended with 'May Japan exist for ten thousand years.' Bastards."

Nicholson was quiet. Then said, "Too damned bad about the Greek. He's a good Marine. Hope he makes it."

"Yeah," Pete replied in a low voice. "Too bad."

He turned his head to see Nicholson eyeing him warily.

"Ignore it," Nicholson said.

Pete stared.

"Ignore what?" he asked.

"That voice inside your head telling you that you're not gonna make it," he said. "Don't listen to it."

"How'd you know?" Pete asked.

"I know the signs," Nicholson explained. "For the past three days you've been doing your job just like any other Marine, only maybe with a bit more of a kick-ass attitude, which is how you always operate," Nicholson said. "But when Mickey Mouse got tagged, I saw a change in you and I knew you were hearing that voice. Don't let it get to you. Hell, almost every Marine who's been in combat hears it one time or another, including an old salt like me."

"You've heard the voice?" Pete asked.

"Damned right," Nicholson replied. "It was ten months ago on the 'Canal. We were supporting the Army in trying to drive the Japs off a ridge called the Galloping Horse. Our platoon got too far out and we got pinned down, and I mean pinned down good. Japs had several machine guns and about a hundred infantry firing down our throats. We thought we had it and that voice was yelling in my brain. It took two days before we got relief. Half the platoon had been hit. Eight were killed, including our CO."

"You weren't under Lt. Cornwall?" Pete asked.

"He was XO," Nicholson said. "The CO was a fella named Ledbetter, Cyril Ledbetter. A nice enough guy but more of a paper shuffler than a line officer. A good line officer wouldn't have gotten us into that fix. As it was, Ledbetter stuck his head up to take a look at the Jap positions and took a bullet through the helmet. He was right beside me when it happened and I guess that's what really jolted me. But what I'm saying is, a lot of us hear that voice. Most of the time the voice is wrong."

"Funny," Pete said, "a couple of hours ago Sandy Gutierrez told me he was hearing the voice."

"What'd you tell him?" Nicholson asked.

"That most of our casualties were guys who'd been hit during the landing and that since then our losses have been light, so the odds were in his favor," Pete said.

Nicholson nodded. "That was a good answer," he said. "Now just follow your own advice." He slapped Pete on the back. "Give your guys some rest. They can each get about an hour before the show begins."

Pete watched Nicholson leave. After moving Honeybun in with

Reb and Sandy Gutierrez in with Bucket, Pete joined the Professor in his foxhole.

"Skipper wants the guys to get some rest," Pete told him.

"Go ahead," Aldrich said. "I'm still good."

Pete was about to argue but was too tired, so he laid back on the sand.

After a few moments of silence, he said, "Thanksgiving wasn't as special for us as it was for your family, but Charlie and I always looked forward to the weekend after. When I was nine and Charlie was seven, our Grandma Talbot died of cancer and Grandpa moved in with us, which was quite a change for us kids. Grandpa T was as good at being a fun guy as our father was at being an asshole. After Thanksgiving, he and my mother took us kids out to buy our Christmas tree. He'd tie it onto the roof of the Essex and he'd lead us in Christmas carols while Mom drove us home. Grandpa T made us a platform out of a large sheet of plywood and four wooden legs that he'd set up and cover with a white bed sheet to look like snow. We'd decorate the tree then put it into a stand in the center of the platform. We had this American Flyer electric train he'd bought us and we'd set the tracks up on the platform around the tree. Setting up the train was a magical time for us. The track was just a simple oval but to Charlie and me, it could take us anywhere we wanted to go."

Pete fell silent.

"That's a wonderful memory," the Professor said, but Pete didn't hear him. He was already asleep.

CHAPTER 28

By 0645 every Marine manning the line from the lagoon in the north to the ocean washing the southern beaches was alert for any signs of the Japanese. In fifteen minutes the curtain would rise on what each man hoped would be the final act of this grisly carnival. But before they could declare the battle over, the final two thousand yards separating them from the tip of this blood-soaked island had to be taken. That meant more hard fighting and more death.

The sun had clawed its way well into the eastern sky, its glow illuminating the preceding night's deadly work. More than six hundred enemy bodies blanketed the broad expanse in front of the Marines. Half of the dead, their corpses grotesquely stiffened, lay within 150 yards of the American line. Dead men lay in jumbled heaps three or four deep, a jutting tangle of legs and outstretched arms, fingers seemingly clutching as if they were trying to pull back their departing souls.

Gazing at the dead, Pete's mind returned to the young, round-faced Japanese soldier.

He's gotta be dead by now, Pete thought. *There can't be many of them left.*

Their numbers whittled down to about thirty men, the survivors of the late Lt. Umeza's battered command, plus two machine gun crews and about twenty other stragglers from the earlier attack, were jammed inside a concrete bunker awaiting the approach of the hated enemy.

And what if they come? Kenji thought. *What am I to fight them with?*

He now had just two grenades, but he vowed to expend them as best he could.

Pete looked at his watch. It was 0700. In the distance came the thrumming of aircraft engines out over the sea drawing nearer and nearer. Then they were visible; flights of fighters interspersed with dive-bombers. Moments later the aircraft were circling overhead like sharks in a feeding frenzy. With red identification panels laid out in front of their line, the Marines watched appreciatively as plane after plane, squadron after squadron, gracefully dipped their wings and swung into a sharp descent, their engines shrieking like banshees. Wing-mounted machine guns pounded like jackhammers. Midway into each plane's run, dark objects dropped ominously from its wings followed moments later by billowing clouds of smoke and debris as five-hundred-pound bombs slammed into the ground.

The Marines stayed low, many with fingers jammed into their ears and mouths open to protect their eardrums from the intense concussion.

By the time the flyboys departed a quarter hour later, black smoke billowed from Betio's tail, but the deadly pounding was just getting started. The aircraft had barely cleared the area when the 105mm and 75mm howitzers positioned behind the Marines and on neighboring Bairiki began their deep-throated song. The air overhead was torn by the whoosh of the "outgoing mail."

Another fifteen minutes and the artillery barrage ceased, giving way to the Navy. First came 5-inch salvos from the destroyers *Sigsbee* and *Schroeder* sitting offshore in the lagoon. Their fire was soon dwarfed by 8-inch and 16-inch shells blasted from a pair of cruisers and the battleship *Maryland* farther out to sea. For another quarter hour Betio shuddered.

On the fringe of the barrage Pete felt as if he was living inside a bass drum. He thought about the Japanese on the receiving end and wondered how much a man could stand before breaking.

"This has gotta be what hell is like," he heard Honeybun mutter as concussion waves rolled over them.

Huddled into a ball, Kenji endured the fiercest bombardment he had ever experienced. Around him men cried, moaned, and even yelled in anger and fear. Two men shit their pants. Kenji longed for one more look at the Noto Peninsula with its rolling hills and lush, green valleys, surrounded in many places by a coastline as rugged as it was picturesque. He visualized his fishing village a few miles from the town of Anamizu near a natural harbor in the midst of which rose the island of Notojima.

Amid these thoughts of home, he recalled the patriotic song "Umi Yukaba" that he sang as a new recruit.

> "If I go away to the sea,
> I shall be a corpse washed up.
> If I go away to the mountain,
> I shall be a corpse in the grass.
> But if I die for the Emperor,
> It will not be a regret."

His mother's delicate features appeared in Kenji's mind. As a tear streaked down his cheek, he found himself wishing that an American shell would find the bunker and bring him peace.

At 0800 the naval fire lifted. All up and down the line officers blew whistles and the cry sounded, "On your feet! Let's go!"

Exhausted after a sleepless night of staving off desperate assaults, the bedraggled Marines rose drunkenly and began plodding forward. Behind this ragged line, the engines of eight tanks growled to life. Pete glanced to his right as a Sherman, the name "Colorado" painted onto its steel skirting, passed him by, its treads rattling and groaning over the battle-churned terrain. Capt. Stacy and the twenty-four survivors of Dog Company gravitated toward *Colorado*, taking comfort behind its sixty-eight thousand pounds of Pittsburgh steel.

Following the tank called for hardened nerves as its path meant crossing a field of dead men. Corpses of the enemy slain in the previous night's attacks were chewed up by the mechanical beasts. The ground the Marines trod across became a bloody morass of crushed bodies and called for nimble maneuvering.

Fifty yards from their starting point Pete and his company passed the row of wrecked Japanese trucks burned out the night before. The hulks were studded with the charred remains of enemy dead.

Advancing deeper into "Indian country," the Professor was startled to see the low profile of a Japanese tank. It seemed to be buried in the sand and protected by a log wall with just its turret visible. He shot a hand into the air and shouted, "Jap tank!"

The cry caught the attention of Capt. Stacy who hurried forward.

"Where?" Stacy said. The Professor pointed. "Good eye, Aldrich," the captain said and hurried to the communication phone attached to the rear of *Colorado*.

"Nip tank," Stacy reported to the tank commander. "Eleven o'clock."

Slowly the turret traversed to the left and locked in on its target. The 75mm gun barked but the round fell short, bursting a few paces in front of the enemy. Oddly the Jap tank did not reply. Colorado's second shot was on target and flipped the turret off the hull while sending fragments of steel sailing into the air. Hurrying forward, the Marines reached the enemy position. The tank, an eighteen-ton Type 97, had been abandoned by its five-man crew who were all lying dead on the ground. Having expended their ammunition, the crewmen had crowded around their commander who activated a grenade. They died together just as they had served together.

Continuing on, Dog Company's second squad was walking to the left of *Colorado*, with Honeybun and Reb on Pete's left and Sandy, the Professor, and Bucket to his right. Pete glanced at Sandy and winked. Sandy smiled. Pete nodded. The voice of doom in his head had stopped.

———

The word spread quickly. The American Marines were advancing. Kenji could not resist the urge to take a peek, so he crept out of the bunker and into a shallow draw created by the undulating landscape. About seventy yards off he saw them, American Marines moving forward accompanied by a tank.

"Up! Up!" he heard the NCO who took over after Lt. Umeza's death. He shouted, "*Kuni no tame ni*—for the sake of our country—we attack!"

Two machine guns pointing toward the advancing Marines opened fire.

———

Machine gun fire crackled from dead ahead and Dog Company hit the ground. The guns, a pair of Nambus, poked menacingly from an aperture in a bunker cleverly hidden behind a cluster of vines and bushes. The Marines returned fire as *Colorado* rolled forward, bullets twanging off its armored skin. The Sherman rolled to within twenty yards where its gun pumped a round at the gun port. The shell missed. As *Colorado*'s gun crew reloaded, Pete and the others slinked forward, their weapons blazing away at the enemy. The second round exploded just outside the gun port. It silenced the two machine guns, but rifle fire began pouring out of well-hidden apertures. Half a dozen Japanese braved the Marines' bullets as they hurried from the rear of the bunker and took up positions on top of the sandy mound. They fired rapidly at the Marines until all the Japanese were killed as mortar rounds called in by Capt. Stacy rained down on them.

———

During Kenji's final peek outside he spotted the approaching tank. He huddled into a ball as an explosion outside the bunker shook everyone inside. A second blast struck the aperture and decimated the machine gun crews, their bodies strewn about the floor. Six men screamed in rage and ran outside, intent on getting on top of the bunker. Moments after they had gone, enemy mortar rounds began bursting all around the bunker. Kenji hunkered down.

With the Nambus silenced, Dog Company laid down covering fire. *Colorado* rolled closer. Its gun roared but the shell did not penetrate the pillbox's concrete and coconut-log construction. *Colorado* fired a second round at the exact same location with similar effect. Then the tank fired a third and a fourth, trying to punch a hole in the tough shell. A fifth round brought results, though not what was expected. Instead of finally silencing the obstinate bunker, it aroused the ire of the men inside beyond the breaking point.

The enemy tank fired several more times but even though the reinforced walls withstood the battering, the roar inside was almost beyond endurance. To his horror, Kenji realized the tank was blasting a hole into the bunker itself.

The NCO in command knew it was now or never.

"Outside!" He roared. "Attack! Attack! Banzai!"

At the command Kenji's comrades, many echoing the cry of "Banzai," flowed past him and into the open air. Running toward the Americans, the NCO out in front, they fired their weapons. In the crush of the attack Kenji had been bowled over. Regaining his feet, he staggered outside only to watch in wide-eyed terror as his comrades were mowed down by the Marines. The NCO was one of the first to die.

More than forty Japanese soldiers scrambled out of the rear doorway and charged at Dog Company, a pistol-wielding NCO in the lead. Those with rifles fired them wildly while screaming indecipherable oaths. Pete and the others raked the exposed enemy with small arms fire, dropping half before the rest turned and fled rearward, their leader dead. The survivors, numbering about twenty-five men, funneled into a narrow draw behind the bunker. *Colorado* had a clear shot and pumped a round in their direction. The shell passed clean through several men, cutting one neatly in two, before exploding in the midst of the closely packed gathering. When the dust and debris settled, every one of the *rikusentai* was lying dead in the gore-splattered confines of the draw.

Kenji watched in stunned disbelief as the survivors of the attack turned and fled into the draw where he had been earlier. Then came a terrific blast that almost vaporized his comrades and sent him reeling. When Kenji recovered, he stared at the carnage. He alone had survived.

Pete stared at the bloody aftermath.

"Jesus Christ," he heard Reb mutter in awe.

Pete was still frozen in place by what he'd witnessed when the company began to move forward. Sandy lightly nudged him on the right arm as he walked past.

"*Vámonos, muchacho*," he said. "We got these *bandidos* on the run."

What happened next seemed to take place in slow motion when, in fact, it was all over in seconds. Out of the smoldering bunker, a lone figure materialized from the smoke-shrouded sepulcher of his slain comrades. Armed with only a hand grenade, the man removed the safety pin, twisted the arming stem, and slammed it against his steel helmet to activate the four-second fuse. Next to Pete the Professor raised his rifle.

Kenji was stunned. There was no one left.

This is the end, Kenji thought. *Goodbye Mother. Goodbye Father.*

Preparing for his death, Kenji remembered the creed he had been taught since childhood: *Kamei ni kizu wo tsukeru bekarazu*—never bring dishonor to your family. He would soon join Onuki, Nagata, Takashima, Akiyama, and the others at Yasukuni Shrine.

Taking a deep breath, Kenji freed a grenade from his pocket and charged the Americans. As he ran toward them, he saw astonishment on their countenances. Then he noticed something else. Even as he activated the grenade, he spotted a face he knew. It was the Marine he had seen three days ago dragging a comrade toward the beach. In that brief moment he realized that the American recognized him as well. For a heartbeat their eyes locked just as they had on that first day. Then Kenji's resolve returned. He drew his arm back and prepared to throw.

Pete's eyes widened as he recognized the same smooth, young, rounded face with the broad, flat nose and deep-set eyes that had haunted his thoughts for the past seventy-four hours.

The *rikusentai* saw it as well and momentarily froze as he cocked his arm to throw. His face, which a moment earlier registered only despair, briefly flashed recognition mixed with surprise. But that lasted only for a moment as the man's sense of duty returned and the face once again reflected the grimness of the moment. He hurled his grenade at Second Squad.

For Kenji, that brief second of hesitation proved to be a life-and-death moment for both Pete and him. At the exact instant that he brought his arm forward to heave the grenade, he felt two hard blows to his chest as another American fired two rounds from his rifle. The impact caused Kenji to release the weapon a fraction of a second too soon and the missile sailed higher than intended. Sacrificing distance for height the grenade did not land among Second Squad but thudded onto the sand some ten paces in front.

———————

"Grenade! Down!" Sandy yelled.

He dove to his left, colliding with Pete who spiraled to his left under the impact. Pete landed hard, head and shoulders first, legs flailing in the air as the grenade detonated. With his blood pounding in his ears, Pete did not hear the explosion. His awareness of the bursting bomb came when he felt a heavy jolt that struck him hard on the right side. He involuntarily cried out as pain flashed through his body. The burning sensation was unremitting and he again yelped in agony and writhed on the ground, both arms thrashing. He soon became aware of calming hands on his shoulders and Reb's ragged Georgia drawl.

"Easy, Hardball," Reb said. "Yore buddies are heah." Then. "Corpsman! We need a gawdamned corpsman up heah."

Through pain-clenched eyes, Pete looked up and saw the Professor kneel by his side.

When he saw Pete's wound, Aldrich muttered, "Shit," which was the outer limit of the Professor's cussing.

"You'll be okay, Hardball," the Professor said unconvincingly. "Help's coming."

Through the waves of agony, Pete gasped, "Sandy. Check on Sandy. He might've been hit too."

Aldrich put a firm hand on Pete's chest.

"Don't worry about it right now," he said softly.

Ryan Magruder arrived and dropped by Pete's side. He glanced at Pete's bloodied leg, then checked his eyes.

"I'm here, Hardball, take it easy," he soothed. Then to the squad. "Someone elevate his good leg before he goes into shock."

"I got it," Bucket said, and Pete felt his left leg being lifted upward while Magruder began cutting away at the ragged right pant leg with a pair of scissors.

Pete moaned as another wave of pain swept over him. In his suffering he didn't see Magruder reach into his B4 bag and remove a morphine syrette, nor did he feel the needle's jab in his left thigh. All he knew was that the agony was suddenly diminished.

Pete grasped Aldrich's shirt with his right hand and pulled him down close. With his left hand he pointed toward the Japanese bunker.

"That Jap . . . the Jap who threw . . . threw the grenade," he gasped hoarsely. "He's the guy."

Aldrich looked befuddled.

"The guy?" he asked. "What guy?"

Pete, fighting to keep his mind clear as the morphine fog encroached, said, "On D-day, when I was dragging Ted to shore . . . the Jap who saluted me. He's the guy."

"Ahh, Hardball," said Honeybun who overheard Pete's words. "These fuckin' Nips all look alike."

"He's right," Aldrich said. "You only saw him for a second. And at a distance."

Pete gazed at his friend.

"I'll see that face in my mind as long as I live," he said, his words becoming slurred. "He's the guy. He knew it too. I saw it in his face. He froze. He remembered me."

"Okay, Hardball," the Professor said. "Okay."

Even in his pain-addled mind, Pete knew the others were placating him, but it wasn't important to him what they believed. It was only important to him. Pete took a last look at the silent body.

———————

Kenji lay on his back. He knew he was dying but he felt no pain. Slowly he turned his head toward the Americans. He saw several kneeling over the man he'd recognized. He saw a corpsman arrive and heard the men talking, although their words he did not know. Then he saw the man turn his head and gaze toward him. He spoke to a comrade while pointing in Kenji's direction. A slight smile crossed Kenji's lips and he raised his right hand a few inches up from the sand to acknowledge a fellow warrior. Then the hand fumbled inside his bloodied shirt and he drew out his father's Russian coin. Clutching it tightly in his fist he looked up at the blue sky and sun. Kenji Sakai gave a deep sigh and then he saw no more.

Pete stared at the enemy soldier as the man raised a feeble hand. Did he salute me again? He wondered. Then he turned back to Magruder.

"Doc," he asked. "How is it?"

Magruder didn't look up from his work, but replied, "The bad news is I doubt this will get you out of the war, but it will get you a few months in a hospital being pampered by some pretty nurses."

"If Ah thought that wuz true, Ah'd get myself shot," Reb said.

Gunny Nicholson hustled up, drawn by the call for a corpsman. "Goddammit," he muttered when he saw Pete lying on the ground.

Nicholson looked at Magruder who said, "We gotta get him back to the field hospital."

"Not a problem," Nicholson said. "His own buddies can lug him back once they rustle up a stretcher. We're gettin' pulled off the line and letting the 3/8 push on and win the battle." He looked down at Pete. "Congratulations, Talbot. You're probably the battalion's last casualty."

"Lucky me," Pete said. Then, "What about Sandy?"

Aldrich said, "Reb. Honeybun. Get a stretcher. I don't care if you have to get one at gunpoint."

They hurried off but Pete would not leave his question unanswered.

"Goddammit, Professor," he said forcefully. "What about Sandy?"

Aldrich gazed down at Pete.

"Sandy didn't make it, Hardball," he said gently. "He took a hunk of shrapnel in the heart. We didn't want to tell you right away."

Pete struggled to rise up on his elbows. He saw Sandy lying face down.

"Oh, fuck," Pete moaned and dropped back down on the sand.

By the time Magruder got Pete stabilized and his wounds bandaged, Honeybun and Reb were back with a stretcher. Before they loaded him onto it, Pete looked to Aldrich.

"Squad's yours now, Professor," he said. "All three of them."

"Only until you get back," Aldrich replied.

Thanks to the morphine, Pete suffered only slight discomfort as his ravaged leg was lifted onto the stretcher. Lying on the rough canvas, Pete gazed toward the Japanese bunker. The man who had saluted him seventy-four hours ago, and whose grenade had killed Sandy Gutierrez and tore into Pete's leg, lay silently upon his back, his tunic torn and bloodstained where Aldrich's bullets had struck. His head was turned toward Pete and Pete looked at the young face. Before the brief moment of recognition, Pete had seen fear on the man's countenance. Now that face was still, silent, and oddly peaceful, his right hand seemingly clutching some object.

Just before Honeybun and Doc Magruder toted him rearward, Pete feebly saluted the dead warrior.

CHAPTER 29

Wallowing in a morphine fog, Pete recalled very little of the stretcher trip across the island. At one point he did recall seeing bulldozers pushing tangled heaps of enemy dead into trenches and large shell craters and then covering them up. He also remembered seeing Marine dead being carried to assembly points where marked graves awaited them.

As the journey continued, Pete recalled being carried past a large, badly battered concrete structure that Magruder said had been the Japanese commander's HQ.

"Japs used it for a hospital until we overran it," Magruder said. "You should see the inside. Patients, medics, doctors, orderlies; everyone dead. Corpses are everywhere and all around the smell of blood, shit, and puke. It's worse than a Chicago slaughterhouse."

Pete listened glumly.

Yet amid the incredible destruction all around, Pete saw signs that the Marines were already making themselves at home. At one point he was carried past a PX that had been set up in a ruined Japanese hanger. Supply clerks were handing Marines free candy, cigarettes, razor blades, and soap. Men fresh off the line also were given coffee "blonde and sweet"—cream and sugar—if desired, as well as hot chocolate.

"Goddamn," Pete moaned. "What I wouldn't give for some of that joe."

"I'll get you a cup before I head back," Honeybun promised.

Beyond the PX Pete noticed a sign nailed to a palm tree and topped by a Jap skull that announced, "Tarawa Recruitin' Office." The wicked Marine sense of humor was returning.

The field hospital was located in a large wall tent about thirty yards inland from Red Beach 2. Medics and orderlies scurried around tending to wounded men who lay scattered around on stretchers or ponchos awaiting their turn to see one of the harried doctors.

An orderly met them and directed Magruder and Honeybun to set Pete by the coconut-log wall of a gun emplacement, its 75mm dual purpose gun facing a lagoon full of targets it would never shoot at.

While Honeybun took off to grab that promised cup of joe, a doctor tasked with sorting the incoming wounded based on degree of injury hurried up to them. Unwrapping the bandages from Pete's leg, he spread apart the ripped pant leg and gave Pete a cursory examination. Pete, who was sitting up, back against the log wall, reluctantly glanced at his right leg. He wished he hadn't. His split open thigh was red and black with both fresh and coagulated blood. He quickly turned his head away, thanking God that the morphine was working.

"That leg's pretty badly ripped up, son," the doctor said, "but I think you'll hold until we get you out to the hospital ship. Meanwhile, if the morphine wears off, just give a yell to one of the corpsmen." He sprinkled a little more sulfa powder and tightly re-bandaged the leg then patted Pete's shoulder and said, "You'll be fine."

He quickly left as stretcher-bearers carried in another Marine.

Magruder said, "We gotta get back too. Good luck Hardball."

Pete looked at Honeybun, who extended a hand and said, "You get back to us as soon as you can, okay?"

"Thanks, Honeybun," Pete said with deep feeling. "I will."

Honeybun handed Pete the coffee and departed.

Get back to us as soon as you can, Honeybun had said. Despite the throbbing in his leg, Pete smiled.

Sipping the coffee, Pete decided he needed a cigarette. Searching his ammo belt pockets he came up empty so he continued sipping the coffee.

Pete found himself between two injured men, one heavily bandaged around the gut and unconscious, the other shot through the shoulder. This second man kept telling Pete how he had been hit by a sniper while assisting a flamethrower team in torching a pillbox. Pete found the story interesting the first time, less interesting the second, and downright irritating the third, fourth, and fifth times the man told it. Pete became envious of the unconscious Marine.

As the injured man droned on, Pete's mind went back to the Japanese soldier. Even though the man's grenade had killed Sandy and ripped up his own leg, he could not feel hatred for his enemy. Oddly, he felt a kinship with the soldier, a young man just like himself, doing the job he'd been ordered to do. He thanked God it was the Professor's bullets that ended the soldier's life.

As Pete settled back against the log wall and tried to ignore the dull pain returning to his leg, he noticed the spare figure of Robert Sherrod picking his way among the injured men. As he drew nearer, Pete called out to him. Hearing his name, Sherrod glanced around, spotted Pete, and sauntered his way, a smile of recognition spreading across his sun-leathered face.

"Well, well," Sherrod said, kneeling beside Pete and extending a hand. "If it isn't Talbot from Chester. Glad you made it, son."

"You too, sir," Pete answered as they shook.

"When did they bring you here?" Sherrod asked.

"I got hit about an hour and a half ago," Pete answered. "Grenade shrapnel."

Sherrod eyed the bloody bandages wrapped around Pete's torn right leg.

"Hurt much?" he asked.

"Starting to," Pete replied. "They gave me morphine but I'm supposed to call a corpsman if I need more."

Sherrod nodded, then said, "Too bad you had to stop some steel now. The island has been declared secure. Colonel Shoup and the ground commanders are just waiting for the official word. The fight's over, at least here on Helen. They say about two hundred Japs are moving on foot up the chain of the atoll; you can wade between the islands when the tide is out, you know. The 2/6 is hot on their tail and once the Japs run out of islands, there's gonna be a fight unless they decide to surrender, and you know that isn't gonna happen."

"You got a smoke?" Pete asked. "I'm fresh out."

Sherrod reached into a pocket of his shirt.

"I'm afraid they're Chesterfields," he said with a smirk. "I remember how you feel about them."

"I don't give a fat rat's ass if they're Jap cigarettes," Pete replied. "I need one bad."

Sherrod handed a scrag over and Pete stuck it in his mouth as Sherrod lit it with his Ronson lighter.

"So what happened?" Sherrod asked, pointing to the leg.

Pete related the story.

"Now I guess they'll patch me up and land me on some other goddamn beach," Pete said. "What about you, sir?"

Sherrod thought for a moment then said, "Son, you and I have just survived seventy-six hours of the most brutal combat any man could endure. The viciousness we experienced I could never write about because the folks back home just wouldn't believe it. I know President Roosevelt personally and plan to meet with him when I get back, and I will tell him of my experience here and what I saw and about the valor of ordinary young men like yourself."

Two corpsmen strode up.

"You Talbot?" one asked. Pete nodded. "Okay, let's get you on a boat."

They helped Pete to his feet and he threw his arms across their shoulders. Just then cheers and whistles sounded and the din seemed to spread across the island. At sea, ship horns and klaxons sounded. According to Pete's watch it was 1305.

"What's that?" Pete asked.

"Island's been declared secured," one corpsman told him as they helped him hobble toward the beach where a Higgins boat waited, ramp down.

Pete asked the corpsmen to stop and he faced Sherrod.

"We came in on the same boat," Pete told the war correspondent. "I wish we were going out on the same boat."

"I'm not going the same way you are," Sherrod said. "But maybe we'll run into each other again."

"Yeah. Probably on another fuckin' Jap island," Pete answered.

Just then a loud engine roar drowned out all nearby conversation as a Marine Corsair, wheels down, touched onto the newly repaired airstrip.

"Now that," Sherrod said, pointing, "that's a sure sign of victory."

They shook hands again and Sherrod watched the corpsmen help Pete onto the boat. Moments later the ramp clanked closed and the boat's six-cylinder Gray Marine engine revved up as the craft backed away from the beach. Clear of the sand, the boat turned 180 degrees as the coxswain spun the wheel.

As the LCVP turned, Pete painfully hoisted himself erect and, propped up by the gunwale, watched Betio recede. His eyes scanned the island, then fixed on the spot by the cove where he had dragged Ted's body ashore. Pete thought of his squad mates now lying under the sand on Betio. Unconsciously he touched his haversack which Honeybun had thought to retrieve. Inside it was the waterproof envelope he had taken from Ted's body that contained his letters from home.

"When I get home, I'll see your mom," he silently reaffirmed to his friend's spirit.

When Pete first saw Betio, it was reeling under a heavy naval and aerial bombardment and seemed to be aflame from end to end. Now it lay ominously quiet under a cloudless azure sky. Only faint wisps of smoke still rose from the island whose surviving trees with their battered fronds stood tall and defiant.

Tarawa no longer burned.

CHAPTER 30

After nearly dying in the trench full of men burned to death, Onuki spent the next several days hiding from the Marines. At night he scavenged for food. Finally, as he and Kenji had planned in the hospital bunker, Onuki left Betio. He silently waded in the nighttime blackness across the three thousand yards of water to the next island in the chain, Bairiki. There he hoped to find other survivors. Instead, he met disappointment and despair when he discovered that the Americans had gotten there ahead of him. Again he hid during the day and fished for food at night. Over the next several days he lived on small fish and prawns while eluding American patrols. His anguish was somewhat relieved when he stumbled across six other survivors of the Betio garrison.

Certain that they'd be killed if captured, the men attempted to hang themselves but the rope they had procured was rotten and snapped under their weight.

Short of food and with almost no water, this pitiful existence went on for three weeks. Finally driven by thirst, Onuki ventured into open daylight to look for water when he was captured. Too weak to resist and with his spirit crushed, he put up no resistance. After his capture, Marines searched the rest of the island and discovered his six comrades. They too were taken alive.

Returning to Betio, Onuki found himself in a barbed wire compound near the long government pier with more than a dozen of his comrades, including Warrant Officer Kiyoshi Ota, the officer Kenji had seen launch a one-man charge on the American beachhead on D-Day after his men failed to follow him.

Onuki was saddened at the loss of so many of his comrades. He thought about his friend, Kenji. Certain that the Americans were going to kill him, Onuki was surprised when he was handed water and warm food.

Eventually Tadao Onuki was transported to Hawaii before shipment to the United States. As a POW he was interned in camps, first in New York and Wisconsin, then in Texas. In 1945 he was released and returned to Japan and resumed his job as a cab driver.

He was one of just seventeen Japanese to survive the fight on Tarawa.

Two days after the fighting on Betio ended, a Higgins boat churned across the lagoon and out to sea. Inside the boat more than twenty Japanese corpses were heaped in a bloody pile. Out of burial space on tiny Betio, these men were destined for a watery grave.

Standing over them were half a dozen Marines, angry men fed up with the shitty detail they'd been assigned. Stripped to the waist, their sweaty torsos were splattered with blood and the stench of decaying flesh. It was one thing to kill the Japs, they grumbled, but why were they also expected to dispose of their corpses?

A mile beyond the reef, the boat's coxswain stopped the craft and said, "Okay."

Immediately the six Marines, working in pairs, began the grim chore of heaving the bodies over the side.

As he reached for one corpse a Marine said, "Hey! Get a load of this."

Around the neck of the dead man was a chain and from it dangled a gold disc.

"What do ya make of this?" he wondered. "It's a necklace with some sorta coin on it."

The man knelt and scrutinized the project.

"Looks like Rooski writing," he said. "What would a Nip be doing with a Russian medal?"

"Prob'ly a good luck charm or something," his partner said. "Why don't ya keep it for a souvenir?"

"Why?" the man snorted, straightening up. "It didn't work for this poor bastard."

Together they lifted the corpse and heaved it over the side and into the sea.

Kenji Sakai's earthly remains hit the water, went under, then bobbed back to the surface. The body floated stubbornly for a few moments, then began to sink. As it did, a stray beam of sunlight caught the coin and it glittered brightly for an instant before disappearing forever.

The fisherman's son had returned to the sea.

EPILOGUE

FRIDAY, MARCH 10, 1944

The taxi rolled to a stop at the curb in front of the two-and-a-half-story frame house on Sixty-Eighth Street in the Bensonhurst section of Brooklyn. The rear passenger-side door swung open and a woman stepped out. Her lush red hair contrasted dramatically with the full-length gray wool coat she wore to fight off the March chill. Once out she turned back to the cab and removed a pair of wooden crutches. By this time the hack driver, a fiftyish man with thinning brown hair, had hurried around and was reaching into the cab. Together with the woman they helped a second man out of the cab, steadying him as he regained his equilibrium.

Once on his own two feet, Pete Talbot straightened up. Decked out in his newly purchased dress blue uniform, he placed his gleaming white-peaked cap squarely on his head. He straightened the midnight-blue jacket with its red piping and its golden globe-and-anchor pins that shone from both sides of the stand-up collar. Brand-new corporal chevrons were precisely centered between the shoulder and elbow of both arms of the jacket. Centered above the left breast pocket of the jacket were six ribbons laid out in two rows. These ribbons represented various service awards, with the top row consisting of the yellow-, red-, white-, and blue-striped Asiatic–Pacific Campaign Medal with one bronze battle star, the purple-and-white ribbon denoting the Purple Heart, and the red, white, and blue ribbon representing the Silver Star. Pinned on the left breast was a blue bar edged in gold, the Presidential Unit Citation awarded to the Second Marine Division for the Tarawa campaign.

"How do I look?" he asked Aggie.

She smiled. "Very handsome." She paused. "Are you sure you're up to this?"

Pete looked at her, "I promised him."

Aggie nodded her understanding.

The cabbie admired the crisp uniform and asked, "Where'd you get hit?"

"Tarawa," Pete answered.

The man's face registered his respect.

"This your home?" he questioned.

"A buddy's," was the answer. "He didn't make it."

"Look, Mac," he said. "Do what you gotta do. Don't fret the fare. It's on me. I was a Marine in the last war."

"Thanks," Pete said.

Aggie retrieved a musette bag from the cab and handed it to Pete. Inside was the rosary and packet of letters from home that Pete had removed from Ted's body. Slinging the bag over a shoulder he started slowly toward the house, putting some weight on the injured leg while still steadying himself with the crutches.

The three months since he had been hit had been a trying time for Pete.

After the Higgins boat ride from Betio, Pete had been moved to a transport ship serving as a temporary hospital vessel. His first surgery occurred shortly after his arrival. Several shards of steel from Kenji Sakai's grenade were removed from his thigh. One larger piece, more difficult to get at, remained inside him. The transport remained off the coast of Betio part of the next day, long enough for Pete to see the final victory in the fight for Tarawa.

"The flag's going up," someone announced, and Pete, with the help of two ambulatory patients, painfully struggled from his bed. He watched through a porthole as the American flag was hoisted up a defoliated palm tree. Faintly Pete could hear the bugle strains of "To the Colors" wafting over the water. He stood at attention as best he could while propped up by two other men but did not salute for fear of falling. This ceremony was followed by the raising of a Union Jack in recognition of the island's being part of the pre-war British Empire. Some of the wounded men around Pete shed tears. Pete caught hell from his medical orderly for getting out of bed.

"I fought for that moment and goddamn it, I want to see it," Pete snapped.

The orderly said no more.

The transport soon hoisted anchor and steamed seventy-five miles southeast to Apamama, the third of three atolls that, like Tarawa, comprise the Gilbert Islands. There the wounded were transferred to the former passenger liner SS *Iroquois*, now reconverted to a hospital ship and renamed the USN *Solace*, for a two-week cruise to the West Coast. Five days into the journey as the *Solace* sailed through gently rolling seas, Pete underwent the second of four surgeries to remove shrapnel and mend torn tissue and muscle. This time doctors removed the most damaging piece of Japanese steel. When Kenji Sakai's grenade had burst, the threaded spherical cap about the size of a half dollar with a sunburst design etched into it flew off intact and struck Pete's leg. Worse, the grenade cap still had about half an inch of its copper ignition tube protruding both top and bottom, which expanded the area of the wound and tore away at flesh and muscle.

After the *Solace* dropped hook at San Diego in early December, the wounded were transferred to the base naval hospital. Over the next several weeks Pete underwent more surgeries to repair the muscles and was set to begin his physical therapy to regain use of the leg. Then infection set in. He suffered a raging fever, his leg swelled, wounds oozed, and the skin darkened. Pete was shipped by rail to the naval hospital at Mare Island, twenty-five miles north of San Francisco. At first Pete hoped a new hospital would have some new remedy for his setback, but his hope turned to fear when he overheard a conversation between two nurses revealing that Mare Island was the West Coast's main center for amputations and prosthetic arms and legs.

His fear bubbled over during one examination with his assigned physician.

"You're not gonna take my leg, Doc, are you?" Pete implored. "Please tell me you're not gonna do that."

The doctor looked into the eyes of the frightened boy.

"That will be a last resort," he assured Pete. "We'll only do that if it becomes a threat to your life."

But Pete responded to treatment. He and the leg recovered from the infection thanks in large part, his doctor later told him, to an antibiotic just recently made available called penicillin.

It was mid-February when the Marine Corps, unintentionally, Pete was certain, did him a favor by scheduling his rehabilitation at the hospital at the Philadelphia Navy Yard. Pete was going home. On the three-day train trip east, made interminable because of frequent stops, Pete thought about his squad mates and the men of Dog Company who had departed Betio with the rest of the Second Division. Now they were bivouacked at Camp Tarawa, recently established on the "big island" of Hawaii. Then he thought about Sandy Gutierrez being a step or two in front of Pete when the grenade went off. Sandy had taken the brunt of the blast and had died instantly after he stepped out ahead during their advance. That seemingly inconsequential action resulted in Pete heading for home while Sandy's family would get a Western Union telegram.

Aggie was overjoyed that Pete was coming East and was at 30th Street Station when he and several other wounded Marines were carried off the train. Aggie threw her arms around Pete, nearly knocking him off the stretcher. Tears of happiness mingling with concern over his injuries flowed from her eyes. She visited him every day after work. Her support and Pete's desire to return to his comrades made Pete push himself hard during his rehabilitation. He quickly graduated from a wheelchair to crutches and by early March was able to put some weight on the leg, although not enough to walk unassisted.

Two weeks into his rehabilitation, Aggie showed up at his room as usual. She looked uncomfortable.

"I brought your mom along to visit," she said nervously. Pete didn't respond. "Look, she really wants to see you. She practically begged me to bring her." He still remained silent. "She made mistakes, Pete, but so did you. You can feel the way you want about your dad, that's up to you. But this is your mom and whether you realize it or not, she loves you. You both really need to work this out."

Pete turned it over in his mind then grudgingly agreed to see her.

Patricia Talbot entered looking older and sadder than Pete had ever seen her. She gasped when she saw her bandaged son sitting in a wheelchair, a pair of crutches close by. Stifling a sob, she sat heavily on a chair by the bed. Tears glistened on her cheeks.

"Pete," she said in a hushed voice. "I'm so sorry. How are you feeling?"

"I'm coming along, Mother," he replied impassively. "They get me up and walking every day."

"I feel responsible," she sobbed. "I failed to protect you and your brother. Maybe if I had, none of this . . ." She broke down and wept.

"The war would've happened regardless," Pete said. "Charlie and I probably would've been called up anyway."

Aggie placed a hand on each of Pat's heaving shoulders and shot a hard "say something nice" stare at Pete. Hesitantly, Pete wheeled his chair closer and took his mother by the hand.

"Look Mom," he said, pausing to collect his thoughts. "I got a hot temper and I don't always think before I act and I don't get over things easy. But the court thing, Mom. You staying silent as Dad lied to the judge. That's tough for me to get around."

Pat nodded somberly.

"I understand," she said and started to rise.

"No," Pete said and refused to let go of her hand. "I'm sorry I didn't see that you were as frightened of Dad as Charlie and I were. In a way I blamed you for what he was doing. That was unfair."

Pat gulped back tears, then leaned front and gave her son a gentle kiss on the cheek.

"It's going to take time, Mom," Pete told her. "I just need time."

Pat nodded then rose.

"That's all I ask," she said.

Turning to Aggie she hugged the girl tightly.

"Thank you, Agatha," Pat said. She added, "He needs you. You're good for him. You always have been."

After she left, Pete said thank you to Aggie, then added, "If she needs anything, Charlie's money is . . ." Aggie nodded. Pete continued, "Just don't let Dad find out."

As his rehabilitation went on, Pete's desire to fulfill his promise to Ted Giovanni became an obsession that led him to apply for a weekend pass to travel to Brooklyn. A ceremony at the hospital that was attended by two Marine Corps officers, Aggie, and Pete's mother, awarding Pete the Purple Heart and Silver Star, carried weight with the hospital's commanding officer. Also a holder of the nation's third-highest award for valor, he granted Pete's request for a seventy-two-hour leave.

The first day out of the hospital was spent at Aggie's shared apartment where, despite the discomfort and stiffness of his injured leg, Aggie's roommates fussed over Pete almost as much as Aggie, and graciously gave them privacy that allowed Pete and Aggie to spend a warm, passionate night in each other's arms. Because of Pete's close brushes with death and his awareness of life's frailty, he made love to Aggie with a hunger and intentness he had never experienced before. In the stillness of the night, the couple lay entwined.

"Oh, Pete," Aggie whispered. "You can't imagine how happy I am right now."

He squeezed her tightly. He had thought he'd never be happy again. *Dear God I love her*, he thought.

Now Pete slowly walked toward the four wooden porch steps at the Giovanni house, with Aggie keeping pace. Pete stopped.

"Ted died in my arms," Pete said, reliving the moment. "His blood flowed over my hands and into the water. The look on his face, the fear in his eyes. I'll never forget that as long as I live. And when he died, I bawled, Aggie." He felt her hands grip his arm tightly. "I bawled like a baby."

"You cried for your friend and you cried for your brother," she said soothingly. "You felt grief."

Pete glanced at Aggie, then at the house. Ahead the dark-brown wooden door loomed almost menacingly. In its window hung a rectangular banner, a gold star centered on a white field within a red border. Unlike the blue star which denoted a loved one in the service, the gold star spoke of tragedy.

Suddenly the somber contents of the musette bag seemed to weigh heavily.

"What do I tell her?" Pete wondered aloud. "How do I tell this woman that her son went to war and never saw the enemy, never got to fire a shot or even reach the goddamn shore, but laid there with the surf washing over him?"

"You don't tell her that," Aggie said. "You tell her that her son died a hero. That he didn't suffer and that he didn't die alone, that you were with him. That's what a mother needs to hear."

Pete nodded, then turned to face her.

"Aggie," the words suddenly blurted out, "I love you. I'm mad about you. I have been for practically my whole life but was too damned block-headed to admit it."

Pete's tongue flicked around his mouth to moisten his lips that were dry from the fear of his next words.

"Agatha Barnoffski," Pete stammered. "When this war is over, will you marry me?"

Pete's heart was in his throat, but it dropped precipitously when she replied, "No."

There was a brief moment of stunned silence. Then Aggie continued.

"But I will marry you *now*," she said. "Before you go away again."

"Really?" Pete said, amazed.

"Yes," she said. "I want to be your wife. I have since grade school. But I want to be your wife now, while you're home, while we have some time to be together. I can't count on later. I've done that for too long. Is that selfish of me?"

"You really wanna marry me now? With our future so uncertain?"

"I want to be yours now. Not later."

Pete gazed deeply into Aggie's eyes and nodded.

"Okay," he said, then lowered his head and they shared a long, sweet kiss.

"Do you want me to come along?" Aggie asked.

"No," he said. "I can do this. Wait in the cab for me."

As Aggie headed for the taxi, Pete, with some difficulty, mounted the steps and walked to the door. His knock was answered by a short, slightly plump woman who Pete easily recognized as Ted's mother. He had never seen her photo, but she had Ted's unmistakably sharp nose and wide, brown eyes, his olive complexion and dark hair. Ted also got his feather merchant stature from her.

"Mrs. Giovanni?" Pete said.

"Yes?" she replied, studying the man in the sharp blue uniform.

"I'm Peter Talbot," he told her. "I was Ted's buddy. I was with him on Tarawa. I'd like to talk to you about Ted."

Her dark eyes squinted, forcing out tears and she smiled, "He told us about you. Please come in."

Pete entered, closing the door behind him so firmly that the gold star banner bobbed as if acknowledging a promise kept.

ACKNOWLEDGMENT

My heartfelt thanks to my wife, Barbara, for her moral support during this project, and for lending me her expertise in editing and proofreading.